PATRIARCH'S HOPE

The Nicholas Seafort Series

MIDSHIPMAN'S HOPE
CHALLENGER'S HOPE
PRISONER'S HOPE
FISHERMAN'S HOPE
VOICES OF HOPE

Also by David Feintuch

THE STILL

All available from Warner Aspect

ONE MAN STANDS AGAINST THE TERRORS OF
THE ENDLESS NIGHT—
IN THE AWARD-WINNING,
BESTSELLING SEAFORT SAGA,
THE ACCLAIMED SERIES BY DAVID FEINTUCH

❖ ❖ ❖

"This series is probably the best military SF of the last
twenty years, and among the best SF of any kind."
—Science Fiction Chronicle

"Intelligently written . . . delightful."
—Washington Post Book World

"Excellent entertainment."
—Analog

"Plenty of exciting action."
—Locus

"Compelling . . . some of the best action scenes in the series."
—Booklist

"Impossible to put down."
—Philadelphia Weekly Press

"Slam-bang action-adventure. . . . Feintuch has a flair for
action that keeps you reading right along."
—Magazine of Fantasy & Science Fiction

more . . .

PATRIARCH'S HOPE

DAVID FEINTUCH

ASPECT®

WARNER BOOKS

A Time Warner Company

WARNER BOOKS EDITION

Cover design by Don Puckey
Cover illustration by Steve Youll
Hand lettering by Ron Zinn

Warner Books, Inc.
1271 Avenue of the Americas
New York, NY 10020

Visit our Web site at
www.twbookmark.com

 A Time Warner Company

Printed in the United States of America

Originally published in hardcover by Warner Books
First Paperback Printing: April 2000

10 9 8 7 6 5 4 3 2 1

To Emili Hernandez Rovira
My son and friend

PATRIARCH'S
HOPE

PART I

Jully, in the Year
of our Lord 2241

PART I

July, in the Year
of our Lord 2241

1

"... and so we gather to commission UNS *Galactic*, the greatest ship ever built, the pinnacle of human interstellar endeavor."

Surreptitiously, to avoid the attention of the pulsing holocams focused on the dais, I eased my aching leg, fixing a glazed stare at Admiral Dubrovik's broad back and the crowded London auditorium beyond. At my left Derek Carr smiled in sympathy.

Would old Dubrovik ever wind down? As SecGen and nominal Commander in Chief of all U.N. forces I could have blocked his posting to Lunapolis Command, but I'd interfered enough in U.N. Naval appointments over the years. These days, I tried to limit myself to where it would do the most good. Amid the dignitaries and officials patiently listening were a considerable number of officers I'd advanced because of competence rather than connections.

Yet also among the sober blue uniforms and starched dress whites were a few disgruntled Earth First sympathizers, disgusted that I wouldn't support retaking the few interstellar colonies that had achieved independence. There might even have been a few enviro fanatics, although zealots of that stripe were rare in the Navy. No doubt among the audience were quite a number who didn't give Christ's damn, as long as no one tampered with their pay billet.

". . . not since Earth's first convulsive leap into space two hundred fifty years ago have so many individuals, so many thousands of diverse corporations, participated in a public project."

And with good reason; their profits were enormous. *Galactic* was an error of judgment; I'd let myself be persuaded by Admiralty's unbounded enthusiasm and Senator Robbie Boland's deal with the Territorial Party, our opposition in the General Assembly, to give us a free hand on the Naval budget through the next Secretarial election—if we shared the lucrative construction contracts with their allies. What we needed were Alpha-class vessels like my first command, UNS *Hibernia*, not the vast and expensive behemoth we'd constructed.

I grimaced past my wife, Arlene, to my old friend Admiral Jeff Thorne, with whom I'd shared my misgivings.

Yes, *Galactic*, along with the nearly completed *Olympiad* and their two sister ships on the drawing boards, would help seed new colonies, but home system had been establishing colonies for nearly two centuries, and the existing colonies needed servicing too. I doubted it would prove efficient to send a huge vessel such as *Galactic* to supply Derek Carr's home colony of Hope Nation.

I glanced at the huge holoscreen, and the magnificent vessel that dominated its view. Lights blazing, she floated high above the planet, off Earthport Orbiting Station, at whose Naval wing she'd been built.

I shook my head. After the fiasco with UNS *Wellington* many years past, there was no thought of assembling a throng of dignitaries on ship for her dedication. We'd been lucky to escape with our lives that day, after the fish attacked. The aliens were gone now, victims of the caterwaul stations I'd devised. From time to time, in the dark nights when Lord God reproached me, I wondered whether to add genocide to the roll of my sins.

"Could even SecGen Seafort have imagined just twelve years ago, as he began his second administration, when the world was reeling from the Transpop Rebellion and not yet recovered from the attacks of the dread fish that he did so much to abate—"

My breath came in a hiss. Arlene's bony fingers squeezed my right elbow in warning.

I scowled at her. "The damned sycophant! Did you hear what—"

My wife leaned close, the ghost of a smile smoothing the wrinkles that caressed her still-bright blue eyes. "Cover your lips, Nick. They'll read you."

"By Lord God, let them. I—" Common sense finally intruded. I subsided, seething.

To my left, a cough that might have been a chuckle. I shot Derek Carr a steely gaze that would have withered him as a Naval midshipman, but unfortunately those days were decades past. My old friend had a laser glare of his own that had held him in good stead since he'd become First Stadholder of Hope Nation, and he was unimpressed by mine.

". . . with her vast cargo holds, a crew of eight hundred ninety, transporting over three thousand passengers, bristling with armaments, she'll carry U.N. prestige and authority to our far-flung colonies across the infinite reaches of . . ."

Derek leaned close. "He does go on."

I turned to Jeff Thorne, whispering. "Do you hear? Now the idiot's making policy. 'Carry U.N. authority' indeed. As if we need a warship these days to deal with our own dominions."

"With some of them, you might." He raised a hand to forestall my reply. "I think Dubrovik's wrapping it up."

". . . and so, to commission UNS *Galactic*, I have the honor to present His Excellency Nicholas Ewing Seafort,

Secretary-General of the United Nations." Turning, the Admiral flashed me a pleased smile, like a toddler expecting a parent's approval.

Welcoming applause rolled across the crowded hall, whose coolers labored to counteract the sweltering London summer.

I groped for my silver-headed cane, hoisted myself from my seat, and winked at Arlene, graying, gaunt, and lovely. "Shall I fire Dubrovik right now?" I was half-serious.

Her lips barely moved. "Of course, dear. The Territorials would love a martyr as a candidate, next election."

With a sigh, I limped to the waiting microphones.

"Voyager is landing," Mark Tilnitz, head of my security detail, muttered into his throat mike. Our heli set down precisely on the cross that marked the center of Devon Naval Academy's pad.

Tilnitz was an assignee of U.N. Investigations. General Donner was drawn from U.N.A.F., Karen Burns from Naval Intelligence, other security agents from New York Police Command. An odd system, but giving all services a hand in the SecGen's protection deterred the formation of a praetorian guard, with the resultant interservice jealousies.

I climbed out, under the sullen Devon afternoon sun. A security joey was waiting, to hover at my arm lest I slip. "Do I look feeble?" My voice was caustic. Perhaps I feared the answer. "Let me be. Here, Arlene." I extended a hand.

Ducking through the hatchway, she climbed slowly down the steps. "What's wrong, Nicky? You've been cross all day."

"Nothing." My knee ached. "I hate those public ceremonies." I forced a smile as Commandant Hazen hurried to greet us. Overhead, the helis and jets that constituted my unwieldy protection detail moved off.

Normally, security accompanied me everywhere, but from my first administration I'd drawn the line at Academy or the Naval wing at Earthport. Under no circumstances would I allow Tilnitz and his eclectic crew to pretend I needed guarding from the United Nations Naval Service, in which I'd served so memorably. I would wander the Academy grounds unprotected, except by the Commandant or his staff. It wasn't, after all, as if Academy were an open campus.

I looked about. A tall iron fence surrounded the compound, meeting itself at the guardhouse gate. As always, mulberry and juniper abounded, tended by Academy staff and cadets. Above, tall maples lent their shade. Devon Academy had once been far from town, but shops and pubs had sprung up to serve it. Still, our buildings were set well back from the fence, obscured by the extensive plantings, which allowed a modicum of privacy.

Arlene and I had just escaped the huge reception that followed my dedication of *Galactic*, and my cheeks were sore with the aftermath of my frozen smile. At least, standing about greeting dignitaries, I'd had time for a few amiable words with Derek Carr, before he went off to rejoin his Hope Nation trade legation. I'd be seeing him again in a day or so, at my retreat outside Washington.

"Welcome, Mr. SecGen." Hazen came to attention. Florid, the hint of a paunch lurking underneath his Naval blues, he still managed to look distinguished, a few touches of gray gracing his locks.

I returned his salute. "As you were." For a moment my heart eased. Devon was home to me. I frowned. *Had* been home, before my betrayal had forfeited all claim to it. Hastily, I turned my thoughts elsewhere. I'd made my peace with my transgressions years before, or thought I had. Either Lord God would forgive me, or He would not.

As we walked the unchanged footpath to the administration building I scrutinized the Commandant I'd met but once, at a Rotunda reception. Once, the Navy had been my entire life, and I wouldn't have dreamed of allowing the

Board of Admiralty to appoint a Commandant I didn't know well. But since the Transpop Rebellion, I'd been ever more preoccupied with civilian issues, and the nurture of our economy.

I cleared my throat. "You've met Ms. Seafort, I believe?" Arlene, knowing me well, smoothly took over the conversation while I brooded. A former officer herself, she knew Academy as well as I.

We strolled past the Commandant's quarters I'd once occupied, past dorms I'd inhabited as a cadet. Knowing my wishes—my aides had made them clear—Hazen hadn't interrupted Academy routine to put the cadets on show for me; his charges were at their usual classes. Nonetheless, the compound seemed almost deserted. Typically, a handful of cadets could be found scurrying about on special duty or, as punishment detail, set to manicuring the lawn with meticulous precision.

The Commandant seemed to read my thoughts. "I canceled outdoor activities, Mr. SecGen." He glanced upward, shading his eyes. "Sorry, I should have brought lined umbrellas."

I snorted my disdain. "I don't need shielding." Nonetheless, I hurried my pace.

"We've a radiation alert for the rest of the week, despite the seeding. If the gamma count gets much worse I'll send most of the joeys to Farside." Lunar Academy, whose warrens were on the far side of the moon, where cadets did advanced training.

"Over time, it's getting better."

He shrugged. "So they say, but were you ever kept indoors at Devon?"

"That was a half century ago." I made a face. "Things change." To my relief, we were nearing the Commandant's quarters. My knee throbbed, and besides, I wanted Arlene out of the newly menacing sun.

*   *   *

"How about Grierson?" I looked across the gleaming rosewood conference table.

Sergeant M'bovo replied; the boy was of his barracks. "Good attitude, willing worker, sir. Still waiting to see his Yall." Give your all, we cadets had been exhorted. Over the years the "Navy all" had become a catchword, shortened to the Yall.

"He's only fifteen." Arlene's tone was gentle. Where I was often harsh with green young middies, she tended to be more kind. Her parenting, even more than my own, had nourished our son, Philip. Of course, in his adolescence even P.T. had learned that Arlene's tolerance had limits. Lord God protect the youngster who overstepped them.

Not so many years ago, as Philip had reached manhood, Arlene and I had spoken seriously of having more children. But, with the cares of office . . . I sighed. Over my long career youngsters seemed to seek me out, as if expecting guidance or assurance only I could provide. In return, I'd gotten too many of them killed.

"Mr. SecGen?" Hazen held the file, waiting.

I snapped my attention back to our conference. "Very well, we'll see." I slid his folder into the "undecided" pile. Though a puter screen was inset into the table in front of each seat, the Navy cherished its traditions. One of them was using old-style paper folders for cadet candidate files.

The purpose of my Academy jaunt was twofold. First, Devon was one of the few places outside my own walled home in which I was free of the ubiquitous mediamen. The Academy grounds were closed, and woe betide the heli that overflew it.

My other motive was more complex. Once, as Academy Commandant, I'd selected a few cadets as special aides. It hadn't worked out; I'd gotten them massacred in one of my senseless follies. Yet my successors, blind to my misconduct, continued the tradition.

Years later, when I returned to public life as a Senator,

then as SecGen, I'd tired of the self-serving blather of my politically astute assistants, and sought out younger adjutants. I'd coopted midshipmen fresh out of Academy, and to my dismay, watched them grow into political creatures as unacceptable as those they replaced.

The solution I'd devised was to select them at Academy, before they became middies, then—with an occasional exception—send them to a year or two aboard ship. Thereafter, when they were offered a shoreside posting at the U.N. Rotunda, I had at least a hope they'd remember their traditions and the discipline of Naval life. Most of them did, as long as I didn't keep them too long. My current aide, Charlie Witrek, was a willing joey, one I'd come to like, but in a week he would be rotated back aloft, and we'd bring down some middy I'd chosen in previous years.

The system worked well, overall. Of course, none of the selectees must have any idea he'd been chosen to ripen in the fleet, else he wouldn't take his shipside duties seriously. For that I needed the cooperation of Academy's staff, and of course I had it. They too wanted their minions to mature as young midshipmen, and if that weren't enough, none cared to risk a SecGen's enmity.

Still, I found the selection process uncomfortably reminiscent of Final Cull, the miserable job of choosing who, among the myriad of applicants, was to attend Academy. One of my great pleasures as SecGen had been to return to the Navy the long-sought privilege of selecting its own officer candidates.

Today, for two hours, Hazen, Arlene, and I reviewed files with the staff sergeants, noting which youngsters showed promise.

Over the years Arlene and I had developed a fine working relationship. By my authority, she sat in on many of the conferences I was required to endure. Here, at Academy, her views were particularly valuable; we'd been cadets together and shared a knowledge and love of the Navy.

I opened another folder. "What about—"

The door flew open. "Commandant!" A sergeant, his breath coming hard. A red-haired midshipman was close behind.

Hazen reared up. "How dare you burst in like—"

"We couldn't reach you; your caller was set to 'don't disturb.' We've had an, uh, accident. Suit training, the pressure room. Five cadets . . ."

I grimaced, recalling cadet days. First, Sarge had taught us how to suit up. We'd endured his drills several days in a row, skylarking when his eye wasn't on us. Then, one day, after suiting, Sarge sent us one by one into a foggy room with an airlock at each end. About half of us, when we emerged, turned green. The other half had known how to seal their suits properly.

The five cadets who'd gotten a whiff of the gas would suffer no more than a day's sore stomach and the indignity of losing their lunch. A tough lesson, but far more gentle than that of unforgiving space.

"Take them to sickbay, Gregori." Hazen shot me an apologetic glance. "I'm sorry, Mr. SecGen."

"Sir, two are dead. The rest . . . the medics are working on them, but—"

"Oh, Lord God." My voice was strained.

The Commandant blinked. "Impossible! How? What . . ."

"I don't know!" Gregori sounded near tears.

I scrambled to my feet, lurched to the door.

"Nick, wait." Arlene.

I paid her no heed. Leaning heavily on my cane, I strode through the admin wing, outside to the late-afternoon sun, along the walkway toward the classrooms, the dorms, the suiting chamber halfway across the base.

By interfering, I was muscling in on Hazen's prerogatives, but anxiety drove me onward. Cadets didn't die in suiting practice. Not at Devon. Farside was another matter; there was no appeal from the laws of vacuum. If some of our charges were dead—I took a deep breath—Academy faced a scandal. Someone had been unforgivably negligent. And the Commandant would write letters this night, that would ravage families' lives.

By the time I neared the classroom area, all had caught up with me: the staff sergeants who'd joined our conference, the Commandant, Arlene, the agonized Sergeant Gregori, the middy who'd burst in with him.

Hazen panted to Gregori, "Full report!"

"Aye aye, sir. I took Krane Barracks to the suiting room at seventeen hundred hours. Later than usual, but we were keeping them out of the sun." The sergeant paused for breath. "Twenty-nine cadets; Cadet Robbins was confined to barracks. I had them help each other suit up. Same as always, sir."

"Get on with it!"

I opened my mouth for a rebuke, but held my peace. Hazen was in charge, not I.

"Then I sent them through. Midshipman Anselm, here, was helping. A canister of the emetic was already in place; Sergeant Booker used the chamber this morning. The first four cadets went through without incident."

Where in God's own Hell was the suiting chamber? I'd never remembered it as so distant.

Gregori slowed his pace, to match mine. "Cadet Santini doubled over as she came out the lock. I helped with her helmet and gave her a piece of my mind, but my eye was on the cadets going through the room." Abruptly he came to a halt, his gaze withdrawn to a private hell.

"I told you to report!" Hazen.

"Belay that!" My voice was a lash. Protocol be damned. I was Commander in Chief, and could do as I pleased. I limped to Gregori. "Are you all right, Sergeant?" He was responsible for the cadets' safety. Lord God knew what he must be feeling.

"Sir . . ." His eyes beseeched mine. "Other cadets were

falling ill. It's not their fault, they're young, they don't know to double-check the seals. I was trying to watch them all, and Santini had her helmet off. I knew she'd be all right. Except . . ." He shuddered. "When I looked down she was in convulsions. There was nothing I could do. Nothing!" His voice broke.

Awkwardly, I let my hand brush his shoulder.

He began to walk again, this time more slowly. "In the chamber, Ford pitched flat on his face. Then Eiken went down. I realized something was terribly wrong and yelled at Anselm to purge the room, but he didn't hear me, or didn't understand."

The middy stirred.

I raised a hand. "In a moment, Mr., ah, Anselm. Go on, Sarge."

"By the time I ran round to the other door and triggered the emergency oxygen flush, two more were down. I ordered Anselm to pull them out—he was suited, I wasn't—and ran back to Santini. She was staring at the sky." Gregori's mouth worked. "By the time we got the others out, three more were dying. I called sickbay, and rang for Lieutenant LeBow."

At last, the suiting chamber, a low, windowless, gunmetal gray building behind the nav training center. I recalled the suit room, with its rows of lockers where the cadets would enter. The airlock to the main chamber, the waiting lock at the far exit.

A covey of cadets milled about. I said, unbelieving, "You left your squad there?"

"Lieutenant LeBow told me to report to you, flank." And the sergeant would, of course. In the Navy, orders were obeyed.

My knee ached abominably. I bit back a foul imprecation as we neared the dazed cadets. Some were weeping. A few slumped on the grass. Among them were five motionless forms in gray. Three med techs worked over them, from scramble carts. A lieutenant watched, arms folded.

A cadet corporal saw us coming. "Attention!" His voice was ragged.

"As you were," I rasped. Then I had a glimpse of one of the casualties. "Oh, Lord." Blood had flowed, from her mouth and eyes. "You, there, any survivors?"

The med tech looked up, his eyes grim. He shook his head.

"What caused it?"

"I don't know." Wearily, he knelt on the grass. "We couldn't have been three minutes responding to the call. They were gone. We never had a chance."

I turned. "Sergeant M'bovo, escort the squad to barracks." The sooner the joeykids were removed from the sight, the better.

"Let me take them, sir. They're mine." Gregori.

"No, I want you here." If it was Gregori's blunder that had killed his cadets, he should be kept far from them. "Stay with them, Sergeant M'bovo. See that they're on light duty for three days."

"Aye aye, sir." There was little else he could say, to a direct order. Civilian I might be, and outside the chain of command, but I was SecGen. "You joeys, back to barracks. Double-time!"

When the cadets were out of earshot Hazen grated, "I'd have laid on extra drills, to keep them occupied."

So might I, in my younger days. "Let them grieve." I turned to the redheaded middy. "Let's hear your version." My wife flinched, and too late, I realized it sounded an accusation.

Anselm stammered out his story, but it corroborated the sergeant's in all details.

Arlene pulled me close, to whisper in my ear. "Nick, let Hazen handle it. You're stepping on his toes."

True, but I was beyond that. "Where's the emetic canister?"

"Still in the dispenser." Sergeant Gregori swung open the panel.

"Don't touch that!" I lowered my voice to a normal tone. "Commandant, have the gas analyzed. A party of three to take the canister to the lab. Send LeBow, there. And two sergeants who had nothing to do with the incident. Get these poor children's bodies to sickbay, we can't have them lying here. Well, what are you staring at? Get moving, flank!"

"Aye aye, sir." As if dazed, Hazen reached for his caller. Gregori said nothing, but his eyes bore mute reproach.

"And autopsies on the cadets. Tonight." I tried to think what else. "Seal the base." If rumors got out, we'd be besieged with mediamen, to the Navy's detriment. All mediamen were ghouls. "Gregori, Anselm, wait for us at the Commandant's office."

Hazen was busy on his caller.

"LeBow!"

The lieutenant jumped as if shot. "Yes, sir!"

"Suit up, and go into the chamber. Check out—"

"I won't need a suit, sir. It's been purged."

"Suit up." My tone was icy. "We'll take no chances."

"Aye aye, sir." At least he seemed abashed, as well he should, quarreling with a direct order. On the other hand, as a civilian I had no right to give him orders.

"Look around, report by radio anything that seems out of place." As he turned to the suiting-room door I added, "Careful with your seals!"

LeBow's expedition found nothing. By the time he emerged, the lifeless cadets had been carried to sickbay, and two staff sergeants had arrived to escort the canister to the lab. We all watched LeBow disconnect it from the intake. Ignoring common sense, I held my breath to inspect it gingerly. The customary factory label, the usual warnings. If the manufacturer had inadvertently sent us a contaminated canister, I'd see the culprit hanged. I hoped that was the case. The alternatives didn't bear thinking about.

There was work ahead, and I'd realized I didn't trust Hazen to do it alone. This was one of the moments I regretted refusing to carry a personal caller. An old habit, dating from my days as Commandant. As I'd learned on *Hibernia*, a commander who carried a caller had no peace.

"Would you give Branstead a call?" I gave Hazen my chief of staff's code. "Tell him to cancel my suborbital. I'll spend the night in Devon."

"Nick, we have to get home." Arlene looked apologetic. "Derek's coming, and tomorrow there's the delegation from Dutch Relief."

"Belay that, Commandant. Let me talk to him." I took the caller. "Jerence? Arlene's on the way home, I'll stay here." Arlene shot me a look of annoyance. "Lay on transport tomorrow, I'll let you know when. No, I'm fine. There's been an . . . incident. What? I don't care, reschedule him. Next week." I rang off, gave my wife an awkward hug. "Get ready for Derek, listen to the Hollanders for me. I'll see you soon."

Somewhat mollified, she rested her chin on my shoulder. "Nick, those cadets . . ."

"Yes, I know. Terrible."

"I mean the survivors."

"Death happens, Arlene. We've both seen it. They have to get used—"

"They're bewildered, and in pain."

"It's not my responsibility."

"You remember, don't you, Nick?" Her voice was soft.

I looked away. At last I said, "I'll do what I can."

In the gathering dusk Hazen and I walked slowly back to his office. "How well do you know Gregori, Commandant?"

"He's a good man. Even if he wasn't watching carefully,

how could he have caused their deaths? We've used the emetic for years."

My smile was grim. "Generations."

"It was surely an accident, Mr. SecGen. Contaminants."

"Do you believe that?" My own doubts were growing.

A long silence. "I want to."

Abruptly I liked him more. "I'm sorry. I know I've been taking over."

"That's your privilege, sir. You're SecGen."

I grinned, remembering an Admiral who'd commandeered my ship, long past. "That doesn't make it easier."

"No," he said. I admired his honesty. He added, "You don't remember me, do you?"

I cast about in my memory. "I was notified of your appointment. You had UNS *Churchill*, am I right?"

"I was in Valdez Barracks." He spoke as if he hadn't heard. "When you took command." He slowed his pace, so I'd have less difficulty keeping up. "Sergeant Ibarez."

"Ah." How could I make him change the subject? I loved Academy, truly I did. Yet . . .

"I was one of the few left here when you took the cadets to Farside. Else I'd have volunteered. I know I would." His face was red, and his gaze was carefully averted. "I'd fallen—we were skylarking in barracks. About a week before the fish attacked. I broke three ribs. Sarge said you were furious."

"It's a cool night," I said desperately. "After the sun goes—Commandant, I atone every night of my life for what I did to those wretched cadets. Be thankful you weren't among them." During the final alien attack I'd called for volunteers, knowing, but not telling them, I was sending them to their deaths. At least, with effort, I now could speak of it. For years I could not.

"Sir, do you know what it's like, to be class of '01, the last class Nicholas Seafort commanded? They say you called the cadets to Farside dining hall." His eyes were distant, as if reliving a memory he couldn't have known. "You said there'd be danger, and asked for cadets willing to go to the Fusers. Your voice ... hushed, urgent, almost desperately casual. Even as joeykids, they understood."

"Mr. Hazen ..." How could I divert him?

"For years, those who refused cast blame one on another, or you. Only Boland and Branstead could be proud. And Tenere." The pitifully few survivors, who'd sailed with me in the Mothership.

"And whenever it came up, I was hurt and defensive." His tone was conversational. "I would have gone, but how could I prove it? We fought, at times. I lost friends." He chopped off his words, cleared his throat. "When I was posted here, I couldn't fathom the honor. To walk where you walked, sit at your desk, command men you—"

"Stop it!" My cry echoed through the quadrangle.

He faced me, determined. "I wanted so to impress you. To make you see I had matters well in hand. You think I don't know what an idiot I sounded, shouting at Gregori? I could have bitten my tongue off."

"It's all right, Mr. Hazen. I've done the same."

"Not in front of your ..." He muttered something unintelligible.

"What?"

"Idol." His gaze was a challenge, as if daring me to object.

I muttered, "Lord God preserve us." We'd reached the steps. I took his arm, leaned my weight on it as we climbed. "I really ought to have this leg looked at."

"May I ask what it is, sir? I noticed you began to carry a cane a few years ago."

"Arthritis. The Helsinki crash aggravated it." Arthritis was curable, and had been for generations. But I deserved my infirmities.

He paused at the door to his office. "Will you see Gregori and Anselm now, or wait for the lab report?"

"Wait, I think."

"I could show you to the VIP suite."

"I know the way. Ring my quarters when you have the report." I limped to my apartment.

I peeled off my jacket, washed my face, combed my hair. I caught a glimpse of the aging visage in the glass, and paused. Wrinkles on my forehead, and my hairline was creeping upward. I hadn't let them give me cosmetic enzymes, though I'd had the primary anti-aging compounds. They were universally disseminated through drinking water.

Still, even past sixty, I wasn't all that old. The relentless extension of life was the main cause of Earth's overcrowding, and a terrible strain on our resources. I had another quarter century of active life, if I wanted it. Perhaps even more. These days, retirement benefits didn't start until eighty-five.

I passed a hand over the faint outline of the hideous scar that had once adorned my cheek. Many years ago I'd let them remove it, at the insistence of Admiralty. Joeykids had started to emulate my appearance, and that was intolerable.

Nearly fifty years, since Father had brought me to Academy's gates, guided me within, and strode off without a backward glance. The U.N. Navy had been then—and still was—the glamorous service youngsters dreamed of joining. The Army was a poor relative, and resented it.

Of course, the Navy had the advantage of starting its officers young. The discovery in 2046 that N-waves travel faster than light, and the accompanying revision of physics, led to the fusion drive, and superluminous travel. But the stars came at a cost: melanoma T, a vicious carcinoma triggered by long exposure to Fusion fields. It was an occupational hazard for spacefarers.

Fortunately, humans whose cells were exposed to N-waves within five years of puberty seemed almost immune. But the Navy couldn't put untrained children aboard its great starships. And so cadets were recruited barely into their teens, as I had been. After two years at Academy they were shipped off as green young middies to get their sea legs aboard a starship.

Gaunt eyes stared at me from the mirror.

As a middy, I'd been catapulted to Captain of UNS *Hibernia* on the death of her other officers. Later, on *Challenger,* I'd fought off relentless attacks by the alien fish. We'd survived to see home system, but not before I'd damned myself by breaking my sacred oath, to save my ship.

By then, to my infinite disgust, I was a media hero. Eventually, Admiralty appointed me Commandant of Naval Academy. And at Farside, when the fish attacked, I engaged in the greatest betrayal since Judas. I sent my cadets to their deaths with lies.

The caller chimed. "Yes?"

"Sir, the lab report." Hazen.

"So soon?" I glanced at my watch. I'd been staring into the mirror a full hour. "I'll be right there."

I smoothed my graying hair. Decades ago, Father Ryson had saved my sanity, in the hard peace of his neo-Benedictine monastery. Brother Nicholas would be at Lancaster yet, but for the desperate pleas of Eddie Boss, my transpop shipmate, whose tribe was under attack by the Territorial Administration. I couldn't refuse him. Leaving my haven, I'd used my notoriety to enter politics. As Senator from northern England, then as SecGen, I managed to have the relocations halted.

Despite my best intentions, my life had been political ever since. I'd left office in the Port of London scandal, and been glad. But the Transpop Rebellion of 2229 sucked me into its madness. I'd had no choice; my son Philip was caught up in it, and missing. His life was worth more than mine. I still thought so, despite what he'd become after.

When the rebellion was settled, given the attitude of the

Territorial Party toward our urban masses, I'd had no choice but to declare my candidacy once more.

I thrust on my jacket, limped to the Commandant's office.

"Nerve gas." Hazen jabbed a thick finger at the holo-screen. "Deadly toxin."

Stunned, I sank into my chair. I'd dreaded something of the sort, and the confirmation left me dazed. I grasped at straws. "Contaminating the emetic?" I peered at the screen.

"No, sir. Nerve gas in concentrated form. One canister, if opened in dining hall, could have killed the whole lot of us."

"Gregori said Booker had used the same canister earlier."

"His cadets are fine. I sent Anselm to check."

I asked, "Where is the emetic made?"

His face was grim. "I put in a call to the manufacturer. Chemgen Corporation specializes in hospital supply. They claim even if they'd made some sort of error, they produce nothing that could kill so fast."

"And the canister?"

"I already thought of that. They construct their own."

I let my eyes meet his. "Commandant, do you understand what you're saying?"

"Yes, sir. It was deliberate."

For a moment we were silent. Then I slammed the table. "That sergeant who used the suiting room this morning, Booker, was it? Send him and Gregori to P and D!"

"Sir, we can't."

"Cadets are dead."

"But there's no evidence. Nothing at all."

"They both used the canister."

Hazen took a deep breath. "That's not evidence of a crime, sir, and you know it!"

My jaw clenched. It had been a long while since anyone had spoken to me so. After a time, my fury abated.

He was right.

A defendant had no right to silence, not since the Truth in

Testimony Act of 2026. If there was other evidence against him, he could be sent for polygraph and drug interrogation. If the tests proved he had told the truth, charges were dismissed. If he admitted the charges, as sophisticated drugs forced him to do, his confession was of course introduced as evidence.

But to keep authorities from fishing in the recesses of a prisoner's mind, the law was quite clear. There had to be independent evidence of guilt before P and D could be ordered.

I sighed. "Sorry. Confine Booker to barracks until we sort this out. And call in the middy, would you?"

Together, we grilled the hapless Anselm until he was drenched with perspiration, and his lip beginning to tremble. At last, I relented. The boy was telling the truth: he'd seen nothing out of the ordinary before the cadets went down, and had no reason to suspect Gregori or anyone else.

"Pardon me, sir?" He addressed his Commandant.

"Yes?"

"Could you tell me what this is about?"

Hazen and I exchanged astonished glances. Middies, questioning their commanding officers? What was the Navy coming to? Reddening, the Commandant took breath, but I intervened. There was no reason the boy shouldn't know. "The cadets didn't die by accident. It was murder."

"Oh, no!" The boy's anguished cry was from the heart.

"Nerve gas."

"But, why?"

"We don't know." Abruptly I added, "Any ideas?"

"Lord God, it's impossible. Jimmy Ford? Santini? Who'd want to kill them?" His eyes were wet. "Yesterday was Ronny Eiken's birthday."

"You're to tell no one," I said. "It's quite important the news not get out." Not until we learned what had befallen us.

"Aye aye, sir."

I glanced at the Commandant. "Special duties?" The boy could be isolated from the other middies, to remove all temptation to gossip.

To his credit, Hazen shook his head. "Mr. Anselm is an officer, and his word is sufficient."

Coloring, I accepted the unstated rebuke, knowing it was warranted. A Naval officer's word was his bond. The entire Service was based on trust. Had I not been so distraught by the bloodstained children lying in the grass, I'd have remembered I was dealing with my cherished U.N.N.S., not a pack of amoral politicians.

Hazen took pity. "Dismissed, Mr. Anselm."

The boy fled.

I cleared my throat. "Question the sergeants."

"Gregori already told us his story."

"Then we'll hear it again." And so we did. During his recitation Sergeant Gregori eyed me with downright hostility. I could hardly blame him.

"As I said, sir, I have no idea what went wrong. The canister was in place, everything looked as it should."

"Did your cadets quarrel among themselves, or with other barracks?"

He balled his fists, checked himself. "Commandant, permission to speak freely?"

Hazen nodded.

"No one hated my cadets, in Krane or any other barracks. Even if he's SecGen, how do you stand such nonsense?"

"Sergeant!" The Commandant was scandalized.

"I've had enough! Court-martial me if you don't like it!" Gregori subsided, breathing heavily.

Hazen blinked. "I understand your feelings, but SecGen Seafort and I have to know—"

A knock on the door. A breathless middy saluted and came to attention. "Midshipman Andrew Payson reporting, sir. Sergeant Booker isn't at Valdez Barracks. His cadet corporal hasn't seen him since lunch."

I snarled to Hazen, "The gate!"

He punched the code into his caller. When he was through, he rose slowly from his seat. "Booker signed out early this afternoon. That God damned son of—"

I snapped, "Don't blaspheme!"

"—a bitch! The fucking whoreson! That—"

"All right!" I slapped the table hard enough so my hand stung. "Sarge, we owe you an apology."

"Bloody right you do!" Gregori looked ready to launch himself across the table. I had to admire his courage. Either the Commandant or I could break him.

The middy glanced between us as if we were all demented.

The caller chimed. Muttering an epithet, the Commandant answered. After a few words he handed it to me.

"Sir? Branstead here. Have you heard of an Eco Action League?"

"I'm busy, Jerence. Can this wait?" Even as I spoke, I knew better. My chief of staff wouldn't interrupt unless the matter was urgent.

"We've had a communiqué. They claim they've killed half a dozen Academy cadets."

My knuckles were white on the caller. "Go on."

"As long as you continue wasting funds on colossal boon-doggles like *Galactic*—their phrase—while tides continue to rise, they'll strike. It goes on for pages in the same vein."

"The sons of—" I marshaled my whirling thoughts. "Keep it quiet as long as you can. Get me out of here, before the media hear of my visit and make a circus of Academy."

"Sorry, sir. I got a copy of the communiqué from *Holoworld*. They want a comment, and verification that you're at Devon. The Action League says they struck during your visit to show that no one was safe from the wrath of the people. You have twenty-four hours to announce a change in policy, or they'll strike again, and disregard the cost in lives."

I cursed long and fluently.

When I wound down, Branstead said, "I'll send your heli."

"No, I'll see this through." I swallowed bile; my visit had caused the deaths of unwitting children. I cared not a fig for my reputation. By leaving I'd hoped only to spare Academy, and the Navy. If the news was out, my presence didn't matter.

"I'm sending in the heli; I want Tilnitz at your side. Security has nothing on an Eco Action League. Whoever they are, if they can strike at Academy, you're not safe."

"No. We've been through that."

For a moment I thought he would argue, but to my relief he didn't press the point. Instead, he said, "I rang up Winstead at the Enviro Council, and they're mystified as well."

"No doubt." My sarcasm was evident; the Council's hands were always clean, no matter what vileness their cohorts perpetrated. "Find the Eco League. Pull out all the stops."

"I'll notify Naval Intelligence, Academy's their bailiwick. By the way, I'll have to set up a news conference. As soon as you get back."

"Have Carlotti handle it." Let my portly press secretary appease the vultures of the media.

"Sorry, it's too big a story. They'll expect you."

I sighed. "Delay as long as you can." I rang off.

"Well, now." I glared at Gregori. "Are you an enviro, Sarge?"

"No." His gaze held contempt.

"I thought not."

The caller chimed again. I suppressed an urge to smash it. Hazen listened a moment, rang off. "That was sickbay. Autopsies confirm the lab report."

I grunted.

"Go home to your cadets, Sarge. Commandant, call up the

file on Booker, flank. Send a copy to Branstead. Midshipman, you're dismissed."

Sergeant Gregori favored me with a frosty glare as he stalked off. Well, I wasn't surprised, despite my apology. I'd as much as accused him of murder.

2

*T*he breeze was chill, but the sun bore down with bracing warmth. In T-shirt, faded work pants, and my usual scuffed boots, I loped steadily up the hill, my breath deep, my heart thumping, my whole body alive with the glory of a Welsh spring morning. It wasn't often Father let me spend the night at Jason's, and I ought not annoy him by returning late for chores.

I'd been running for a quarter hour, from Jason's home to ours. At last I rounded the rise of the knoll. There, below me, was our cottage, morning mist rising like a ghost from the stony farmyard. Beyond our fence lay the twisting Bridgend road to Cardiff.

I stopped for a few breaths, hands on my knees. The lee of the hillside was thick with thistles, but the eastern side was mostly grass, grazed short by our neighbor's sheep.

Father would have tea boiling. In a few moments he'd be glancing at the clock, lips pursed in disapproval.

I loped down the hill. Gravity and youth sped my steps. My lope became a trot, the trot a joyous gallop. My hair caressed the wind of my passage. My breath came easy. I was young, and happy in myself, and could do anything.

I cried out in delight, and woke myself.

I was in Devon, in the guest suite of Naval Academy.

Fifty irredeemable years separated me from the boy who raced down the hill.

I clutched my pillow like a life vest, washed by a wave of regret so sharp it threatened to carry me to a place of no return.

When finally it passed, I was drenched with sweat. I climbed out of bed, leaned heavily on my cane, hobbled to the bathroom. I stood a long while under the hot soothing shower, mourning the eager young joeykid I'd once been.

It was early afternoon, just past lunch. Sergeant Booker was nowhere to be found. Swarms of mediamen were camped outside Academy's gates.

I sipped at coffee, irritable from my interrupted sleep. "You had an enviro maniac on staff and didn't know?"

"It's not illegal to favor—"

I slammed the table, splattering coffee on Sergeant Booker's file. "Eleven years an enviro, and you didn't know?"

Hazen and LeBow exchanged glances. "He wasn't that outspoken, Mr. SecGen. In fact, other than a few pamphlets in his cabin there's no evidence he was—"

"Bah." I waved it away. "Screen these people out! It says Booker's sister suffered kidney failure after the Glastonbury spill. His mother died two years later, same cause. If that doesn't qualify him as an enviro fanatic . . ."

Hazen's tone was hot. "My brother is fighting melanoma, and we think it's from the California Daze." Incompetent techs had misread Los Angeles ozone depletion stats six days in a row, and thousands had unwittingly been exposed to high gamma counts. "Am I a terrorist? Do you want *my* resignation?"

"Of course not." I drummed the table, willing reason into my tone. "Sorry. I suppose we can't call every loonie enviro a security risk, but . . ." But they *were*, I knew. Even my own son had betrayed me. He— I bit off the thought.

LeBow took up his Commandant's defense. "Sir, they've become a potent force. Over thirty enviro supporters elected to the Assembly, and Lord God knows how many Supras or Territorials would vote enviro if they had a chance. Yes, a few are glitched, but on the whole, Winstead's crowd is respectable. There's no cause to suspect—"

"Don't lecture me," I growled. I'd been wading in the political sewer too long, and knew all its denizens.

"Still." Hazen sounded morose. "Even if Booker was unhinged by his family's loss, how could he kill his cadets?"

"Not his. Gregori's."

"It's the same." Drill sergeants would die to protect their charges. Over the years, many had.

On that sour note our meeting ended. The Commandant, three lieutenants, and a handful of middies accompanied me to the pad. I waited irritably for the heli blades to slow. Four grim-faced security joeys jumped out, weapons ready to guard me from peril. Mark Tilnitz himself headed today's detail. Of all the security agents I'd had to endure in years of political life, he was the most tolerable.

I adjusted my tie, oddly reluctant to board.

Hazen said, "We'll redouble base security, sir. There'll be no more incidents."

"You can't guard against everything."

"I can damn well try." The Commandant's language left me uneasy; in my middy days more than one officer had been beached for blasphemy. Of course, these days strict adherence to Church policy was on the wane, though I wished it weren't so.

Our state religion was an amalgam of Protestant and Catholic ritual, sprung from the Great Yahwehist Reunification. Religious union wouldn't have been possible, had not the Final War devastated Africa and Asia. But Christian resurgence in a revitalized Europe as well as America led

eventually to the miraculous conclave that established
Mother Church, guided by her holy Council of Patriarchs.
After the Armies of Lord God repressed the Pentecostal
heresy, the Church was adopted by and became the under-
pinning of our United Nations Government.

The Council of Patriarchs wielded less power today than
in days past, but they still represented the reunified
Church. I'd been summoned to meet with them two days
hence, in New York, and they hadn't disclosed our agenda.

Overhead, outside the gates, a heli droned daringly close
to Academy's no-fly zone. It bore the *Newsworld* insignia.

"You'd better go, sir. They probably have a lens on us."

"Yes." But my foot lingered on the step. "Those cadets
from Krane. Go easy on them."

"I will."

"They've been through . . ." I sighed, recalling my foolish promise to Arlene. I beckoned Tilnitz. "Wait here. I'll
be back shortly."

I refused to let the Commandant and his officers follow
me to barracks, but Hazen insisted on sending the middy
Anselm as an aide. It was easier to allow it than object.

Moments later, I stood outside Krane Barracks, breathing heavily from my hike. The dorm was as I remembered:
long, low, wooden, four steps above ground level. I'd spent
two years in—

"Oh, it's you." Glowering, Sergeant Gregori faced me at
the door. Clearly, I wasn't forgiven.

"May I come in?"

"If you must." With obvious reluctance he stood aside.

"What have you told them?"

"That we're investigating."

A young voice rang out. "Attention!" Twenty-five gray-
clad cadets dropped what they were doing, and hastily
formed a line.

Five of the bunks were stripped, the belongings piled
neatly on the mattresses. Sometime this day, each close

friend of the casualties would choose an item for remembrance. Then the remaining gear would be shipped home to grieving parents. It was the Navy way.

"As you were." I waited for the joeykids to relax. "I've come about yesterday's tragedy. You cadets have to understand . . ."

They would never understand. Death was something that happened to others. Not to their own kind. Through a haze of years I recalled the sense of immortality that had buoyed me, until the horrid day I lost my first and closest friend. Jason lay buried in Cardiff. Decades had passed, since last I'd visited.

"You, lad." I spoke to the cadet corporal. "What's your name?"

"Danil Bevin, sir." Why did the name sound familiar? I tried to concentrate, gave it up. He was no more than fourteen. Did he recognize me? No, cadets called everyone "sir." Anything that moved.

"I'm Secretary-General Seafort." His jaw dropped, with dawning recognition. "Did you know them well?" Of course he did, you idiot, they were bunkies. "I mean, particularly well?"

The boy's eyes glistened. "Jimmy—I mean, Cadet Ford, sir. He and I . . ."

"Who else?" I looked about.

"Santini tutored me in nav." A shy girl.

"Ronny Eiken came from my school."

Slowly, as if ashamed, the youngsters acknowledged their friendships.

I said, "There's nothing I can do, nothing the Navy can do, to make up your loss. I'm sorry." It sounded inadequate. "We failed to protect you. I apologize, on behalf of Academy."

Sarge gaped. My words approached heresy. Cadets were the lowest of the low. One never apologized to them.

"Sir?" It was the cadet corporal, daringly. Sarge frowned. Cadets spoke only when spoken to.

"Yes, Bevin?"

"What happened to them? Was it pollution?"

"We'll get to the bottom of this, I promise you. And when we do, we'll explain, as best we can." It seemed inadequate. No, more than inadequate: an outright lie. We knew what had been done. Heavily, I sank to the gray blanket of a perfectly made bunk. "Gather round, would you please?" I waited.

"Ford and Santini and the others were murdered. Enviros put nerve gas in the suit chamber. Your bunkies were selected as symbols, you see." It wasn't easy to face their inquisitive eyes, and I gave my frustration free rein. "Enviro fanatics used them to teach me a lesson. It's what comes of letting dissidents preach their poison."

"That's goofjuice!"

With one bound Gregori crossed the room, seized Bevin by the nape, cuffed him hard. "Respect your betters, you insolent young—"

"Let him speak." My tone was low, but it sliced like a knife.

Sarge thrust the cadet corporal toward me. The boy stumbled, caught himself by clutching my knees. I winced. "Well?"

Bevin took a deep breath, plunged ahead. "They're not enviros, they're terrorists. Can't you see the difference?"

"Are you enviro?"

"Yes! And so's my father. Are you making it illegal?"

"Bloody whale huggers," I muttered. "There's no talking to you."

"The Enviro Council elected representatives to the General Assembly. People are for them. We—"

"A few."

"—don't need bombs, or nerve gas!" Our eyes locked. The barracks was silent. Gray-clad boys and girls and their sergeant stood transfixed, watching a cadet beard the administrator of the world government.

I cleared my throat. "Five of you died. If it weren't for the enviros . . ."

"Terrorists, sir!"

"Don't you see, joey? It's the politicals who smooth the way for the killers, with their oily speeches, their bills submitted more for the approval of gullible masses than because they'd do any good." I knotted my fists, recalling the endless aggravations of the Senate, the clamoring hot-bloods in the General Assembly.

Repairing the ravages of the fish war took time as well as endless expense. We had obligations to our colonies as well as our own people. And there was nothing we could do to reverse centuries of environmental neglect; land and weather were in Lord God's hands. Enviros disrupted government, caused endless expense, divided families . . . Why couldn't they understand?

"Is that really what you think, sir?" The boy's face showed disapproval. More than that: betrayal.

My truculence collapsed. "I don't know what I think. I'm tired, and I've been SecGen too long." I leaned on my cane, hoisted myself to my feet. "I'm going home."

Bevin glanced at his sergeant, back to me. "Sir, I'm sorry if—"

"It's too late for that." I clumped to the door.

Outside, the middy came to attention. I noticed his eyes were red. "What are you bawling at?"

"Nothing, sir." Anselm's spine was ramrod straight, stomach sucked tight.

"Stand easy," I growled. The cadet corporal's brazen behavior wasn't the middy's fault. By brute force I made my tone gentle as I started down the path. "A caning?" Midshipmen and cadets were considered young gentlemen, and were subject to corporal punishment, unlike ordinary seamen.

"No, sir."

"What, then?"

"It's just . . ." He swallowed. "Yesterday I helped Santini into her suit. She always had trouble with her clamps. Always."

"You were . . . friends?" Fraternizing was discouraged, but I recalled a middy, long years past, who'd made my cadet days bearable.

Miserably, he nodded. "What do we do, sir?" It was an appeal.

"Our duty. It's the only answer I know." It wasn't near enough; my hands moved without my volition. "Come here, boy." Gently, I pulled his red locks close to my chest.

"It's not—we weren't—"

"I know."

"She tried so *hard!*"

"They all do."

After a time he pulled loose, scuffed the earth with a spit-shined boot. "She made fun of my hair."

"Daring, for a cadet." We resumed our walk.

"She knew I didn't mind." He sniffled. "Seeing her lie there . . ."

"I can imagine."

"Blood running from her mouth." He recoiled. "Why, sir? Why does it have to end like that?"

"I don't know, son."

His voice was almost too soft to hear. "I'll miss her."

We passed the Commandant's office.

"Sir?" He gestured. "The helipad's this way." A path forked to the left.

"I know." I headed onward.

"Where are you going?"

"To my duty." As we neared the wrought-iron gates, I smoothed my hair, tugged at my tie.

Ahead, a predatory swarm of mediamen focused through the iron rails. My face was a stone mask.

* * *

"We're home, sir."

Blinking myself awake, I peered through the foggy heli window. We'd set down on the dusty concrete pad in my Washington compound.

Outside the walls, red maples drooped in muggy July heat. Across the river from Old Washington, the compound nestled in the Virginia hills incorporated into the broadened District. Built to resemble an old southern estate, it was a gift raised by public subscription after the end of my first Administration.

A large home, with seven bedrooms and a plethora of verandas and porches, its outbuildings included sheds, a greenhouse, and a small cottage, all within protective stone walls.

I'd been adamant in refusing the unwarranted gift, but Arlene's good sense prevailed. We needed a home for P.T., and I'd had no savings whatever. "You deserve it," she'd insisted, and at length I acquiesced.

These days I found it a nuisance commuting to the Rotunda in New York, and I did so as seldom as possible. Naturally, when the General Assembly was in session I had to be present, at least on occasion, to defend my Government against the ruthless elitists of the Territorial Party, and those independents who would bolt us for personal gain. A vote of no-confidence in the Assembly would bring down an Administration.

But other times I brought work home, and met with delegations and political allies in my comfortable den. If the electorate didn't like it, they could vote me out.

Ours was a complicated system. Assemblymen were elected from districts corresponding to regions of constituent nations, and served terms of four years unless the Government lost a vote of no-confidence or failed to pass major legislation, or unless the SecGen dissolved the Senate and Assembly and called for new elections. The Senate, on the other hand, couldn't dismiss the Government with a motion of no-confidence, but could block legislation indefinitely. Senators were elected for six years and were maddeningly independent.

I rubbed my eyes. Despite all the amenities and care lavished on a SecGen, intercontinental travel was wearing. I'd slept two hours in the noisy suborbital from London, but my aging body craved more. With helpless envy I recalled the lithe form I'd possessed as middy, then Captain. I'd thrived on lack of sleep, or so it had seemed.

I yawned. "Where's Arlene?"

Mark Tilnitz whispered a query into his throat mike, cocked his head for the response. "Cleaning up after the Hollanders, I believe."

Supervising the staff, that meant. I'd throw a fit if I saw her toting trays of glasses herself. We'd done enough of that in our private years. There had to be *some* compensation for the misery of public office. These days we had help with cooking and gardening, though I refused to allow anyone but my midshipman aides to maintain an office in the compound. My Rotunda staff communicated from New York via caller, nets, and fax.

I tramped to the veranda. Glassed double doors from my inner office awaited me. I hesitated, chose instead the door to the sunlit hall where my aide's desk was placed.

"—like an old lion facing a pack of wolves. Look at him!"

"*Yes, I'm responsible. For my government, for the Navy, for the lives of those poor cadets. I take the obligation seriously.*"

"*What will you do now?*"

"*Go home, and set the investigation in motion.*"

"*And when you find the terrorists?*"

"*Lord God willing, I'll attend their execution.*"

"Oh, good line."

"He means it. Uh-oh, he's calling on Vince Canlo."

"Mr. SecGen, the Independents are demanding an investigation of Galactic's funding. Was there a deal between you and the Territorials?"

"Watch. He blew his answer."

"There was an understanding. We all agreed that a strong Navy was necessary, and funding ships was the way to achieve it."

A groan. "We're in for it. He admitted there's a deal."

"The old man won't lie, even if— Oh! Mr. SecGen!" Charlie Witrek, my earnest young middy, scrambled to his feet. Slower to rise was my chief of staff, Jerence Branstead. A sardonic wave.

"Hallo, Jerence." Safe from probing holocameras, I loosened my tie, took off my jacket. Charlie took it to hang.

"Mr. SecGen, will you make further concessions to enviro sentiment as a result of—"

"The question is offensive. No. We will not submit to terrorism. These people are glitched, throwbacks to a discredited age."

Branstead nodded his approval at the screen. "Well said."

"Do you support Reichschancelor Mundt's call for a worldwide reassessment of costly pollution measures?"

"No. The issue's been studied over and again. We're doing what we can. Mundt is protective of the Dresden chip works, but our measures won't cause a shutdown."

I'd tried to sound conciliatory, I recalled. Mundt was a Supranationalist, a member of my own governing party, but was obsessed with protecting his nation's industry from regulation. At times he could be difficult. And Widener, the British Prime Minister, pressed just as strongly for stiffer enviro legislation. My role as SecGen could only be to steer a middle course. The world had been debating environmental spoliation for centuries, and I saw no need to act rashly.

"Do you view the cracks in the Three Gorges Dam with greater alarm now that—"

"Turn that bloody thing off." Wearily, I slumped into a chair.

"—shifts in rain patterns filled the reservoir thirty percent above rated capacity?"

My image faded from the screen.

"You did well, sir." Witrek, my staff middy. He ran fingers through his hair, but as always, every strand was in place. He wouldn't allow it otherwise.

I glowered. "What would I do without your approval?"

He grinned, knowing me too well to be fazed. "How can you stand those vultures?"

"I hold my nose."

Charlie brought me a coffee, strong and black as I liked it.

"Thank you." A middy wasn't a butler, and shouldn't be treated as one. But Witrek, with quiet competence, found ways to make himself useful without being asked.

I would miss him.

As if reading my mind he asked, "Did you pick my successor, sir?"

"We're working on it."

"I imagine it's difficult."

If I said nothing, he would let it drop, but I knew he yearned for me to pursue it. "Do go on, Charlie."

"I mean, he'd need to be resourceful, motivated, as patient as Job . . ." His tone was bright.

"Yes, I've missed those qualities the last two years." Not so, but I enjoyed our byplay. "Any word on your posting?"

He grimaced. "Not yet." No doubt he'd be sent to a ship of the line. I could intervene, but wouldn't unless there was need. I wondered if he'd sought *Galactic*.

"What's on for this afternoon?"

Charlie consulted his console. "Mr. Carr's due at five. He'll stay the night."

"Good." Despite my weariness, my face softened to a smile.

Derek Carr, scion of an old Hope Nation family, had been an arrogant Uppie of sixteen when he'd first sailed as a passenger on *Hibernia*. After the death of our officers he'd answered my summons to become a cadet, a difficult role for him to fill, given my uncertainty and inexperience. Nonetheless, I'd promoted him to middy as soon as I could. We'd toured his colony together, and over the years had become steadfast friends.

Jerence Branstead said cautiously, "Arlene's laid on a small reception for Mr. Carr."

I groaned. My wife knew how little I enjoyed playing host. I could deal with visitors on business of state; as long as I stood for election I had no right to complain. But at a private party I felt as awkward as a middy in a gathering of Captains.

"But Jeff Thorne's invited."

"Oh." I smiled. Admiral Thorne, my mentor in Academy days, had been Branstead's predecessor as chief of staff. Now retired, he lived in London. I checked my watch. "I'd better get changed." Leaning on the banister, I made my way upstairs. They'd offered to put in an elevator, but I wouldn't hear of it. I was aged enough without acting the part of an old man. Next they'd have someone wiping drool from my lips.

"They say it's huge." A woman of thirty or so, resplendent in a mauve jumpsuit and amethyst bracelets. I was trying desperately to recall her name.

My eyes searched for Arlene. "By comparison, my first ship, *Hibernia*, had a hundred thirty passengers. *Galactic* carries over three thousand."

"That's a small city. Her Captain must feel like a colonial governor."

"Captain Stanger?" I'd only met him once; he'd spent

his early career in transit to one colony or another, and much of the rest of it at Admiralty in Lunapolis. "I don't really know him."

"Why'd you give him the posting?"

"I didn't. I'm just SecGen." The Board of Admiralty had selected Ulysses Stanger for *Galactic,* and I'd seen no reason to overrule them. They'd chosen him partly for his experience, and partly, I suspected, because he had political connections.

Again, I regretted the Navy's concentration of resources in one ship. At least she'd serve a myriad of functions. With full holds and a carefully selected complement of passengers, she could seed a new colony. Her armaments were enough to put down any colonial rebellion imaginable. And fitted with the latest model fusion drives, her interstellar speed was adequate, though not remotely approaching a fastship's. But that couldn't be helped; it was only the lack of mass that allowed fastships to cut months from a typical voyage.

Arlene's arm wrapped around mine. Her off-white gown dipped along her backbone, emphasizing the soft curves of her shoulder blades. "Nick will talk about his Navy forever," she said, rescuing me. "Let me circulate him, Lois."

We drifted away. "Thanks, hon."

"You had that glazed look."

She deposited me alongside a cluster of joeys grouped around the marble mantel. Businessmen, most of them, hoping to overhear a tidbit that would enhance their interstellar commerce. But among them were Derek Carr and Jeff Thorne.

A waiter proffered a tray, and I took a glass of sparkling wine.

"Hello, sir."

"Derek." My smile broadened. How typical of him, to call me "sir" after all these years, though head of a government coequal to mine. "Did your trade talks go well?"

"Bah," he grumbled. "My countrymen seem to forget why we fund their legation." A twinkle eased the creases on his lined face. "We're going to break your stranglehold on shipping, you know."

Thorne raised an eyebrow. "Over the Navy's dead body, Mr. Carr." His tone was affable.

That caught the attention of several listeners, so we three wandered off by ourselves. "You've been threatening that for years," I told Derek. There were private interplanetary vessels, many of them. But only Naval ships traveled interstellar. It was partly a function of cost, partly government policy.

"I saw you on holovid today, sir. You were wonderful."

I groaned. "Not you too."

"They still don't know how to treat someone who faces them and tells the simple truth." He grinned. "I've tried it from time to time. Trouble is, our planters are too devious. Prevarication is a way of life for us."

I grimaced. After the abomination I'd committed at Farside, I'd vowed I would not lie again, regardless of the cost. It helped keep me sane.

"Nick . . ." Derek was one of the few who could still call me that. His eyes had gone serious.

I raised an eyebrow.

"This Eco Action League. How seriously do you take it?"

Thorne bristled. "They murdered our cadets!"

"I don't mean that. Overall, how seriously do you judge their threat?"

I said cautiously, "I'm not sure. We know nothing about them." Yet.

"Have you read their manifesto?"

"On the suborbital."

"It's more about *Galactic* than the environment, did you notice?"

"The ship's a symbol, Derek. That's all."

"I won't tell you how to run your affairs, sir, but—"

"Please do." He was one of the few I'd listen to.

"There's an odd undercurrent to the conversations I've heard about her."

"How so?"

"As you say, *Galactic*'s become a symbol. Everyone's either violently opposed or very much in favor. For every enviro who bemoans her cost, I've heard a Navy man defend her, but with such contempt and hatred of the enviros—"

Thorne said, "Joeys get emotional. Pay no attention." I nodded agreement.

Derek studied me closely. "You're sure?"

"Yes." I spoke more confidently than I felt. Why in Lord God's name had I approved the expenditure? Even if *Galactic* hadn't gone over budget . . .

"I'm glad you built her," he said simply. Then, with a grin, "You'll learn *Galactic* and *Olympiad* are wasted as supply ships. Their best use will be to open new colonies." A wry smile. "And the outworlds need all the allies we can get."

Even as a jest, it troubled me. "Does Hope Nation need protection, Derek?" My attention wandered. The crowd was starting to thin; I really ought to circulate, at least to say good-byes.

"Not from you, sir. That goes without saying."

True. On my visit to Centraltown, their capital, I was feted as hero, revered almost as deity. I'd never gone back.

Derek's look was pensive. "But you won't be SecGen forever. And even in office, you can't manage affairs light-years from home."

I snorted. "I don't govern your Commonweal." Acknowledging a fait accompli, as a young Captain I'd granted Hope Nation its independence, after the Navy had abandoned the colony to alien attack.

"Some folk wish you did. Oh, not at home. Here." He

lowered his voice. "That new Bishop the Patriarchs sent to Centraltown. Know him?"

"No."

Thorne rubbed his chin. "Andori? He's Saythor's man, and conservative." He snagged a cocktail from a passing waiter.

Derek said, "We've locked horns half a dozen times. He's gone so far as to threaten me with disavowal."

I drew breath. Disavowal was one small step short of excommunication, a deadly matter. No citizen caring to preserve his soul could have dealings with a disavowed individual. And if one were excommunicated, even wife and children were expected to shun him. "Be careful."

"The Bishop has less support than he thinks. Religion has waned a bit; if it came to that, I might carry a vote to disestablish the Church."

"Derek!" I was scandalized, and not a little offended.

He held up a placating hand. "Only if it comes to it. Would you rather I wandered the plantations stealing corn?"

"Lord God." I drained my drink.

"It's worse on other worlds. What irks the colonies is how little you realize you need us. Your imports of food and raw materials have skyrocketed. Soon the balance of trade will be in our favor. You need our goodwill, Nick. And you won't get it with heavy-handed threats."

"I never once—"

"Not you personally, but your government. Really, you ought to visit more."

"He can't." Old habits die hard; Thorne rushed to my defense. Even in a fastship, Hope Nation was a nine-month cruise.

I said warily, "What haven't I been told?"

"In the colonies, there've been hangings from time to time, for treason and heresy." Derek shook his head. "In reality, for nothing more than political talk. No actual rebellion."

"I'll look into it."

"The Navy, of course, backs the colonial Governors. Some of your less temperate Captains urge mass executions, or boycott. There's a move in your Senate to rescind Detour's independence, return them to colonial status. They say—"

"That's gone nowhere. I've seen to that." Neanderthals, everywhere. Frightened of change.

"As I said, you won't be SecGen forever." Derek shot me a look of appraisal. "Though you have a few years left."

"We'll talk about it later." Derek would stay the night, as would my chief of staff. Jerence Branstead and I were old friends from Centraltown days, when he'd been but a boy.

The party was definitely winding down; Arlene's glances were ever more pointed. I drifted off to join her at the door.

"What a relief." I eased off my shoes, rested my feet on a hassock.

Wiping an end table, Arlene frowned. "Your shoes? They're your favorite—"

"The reception." I gestured vaguely at the nearly empty room. House staff joeys were quietly, efficiently gathering abandoned glasses and hors d'oeuvres.

Branstead settled himself comfortably on a sofa, near Derek. "By the way, about your Devon press conference—"

"Don't start. Please."

"—when Vince Canlo asks a hostile question, turn it aside. No need to alienate—"

"*Newsnet* hates us," I said sourly. "They're in the Terrie Party's pocket."

"All the more reason not to feed him. A diplomatic evasion now and then . . ."

Derek grunted. "That's not Nick. Never has been." He raised an eyebrow at Branstead. "You've been with him long enough to know."

"Would you have him play into their hands?"

"I'd have him tell the truth, as he does." Derek pursed his lips. "I concede they were harrying you, Nick. You don't personally dictate clean air policy."

"I didn't raise sea levels, either." I tried not to sound glum. "Or cause the Santa Monica mudslides."

Arlene handed a waiter the tray of glasses she'd collected, and perched on the arm of my chair. "Feeling sorry for ourselves, love?" Her fingers brushed the back of my neck.

"Not at all, hon, it's just . . ." I sighed. "I can't please everybody."

"You please me." Abruptly her mouth hovered before mine, and rewarded me with a long kiss. "They snapped and growled at your heels." Another kiss. "You stood up well. Sounded like the wrath of God. When Canlo brought up the ruins of Bangladesh . . ."

I'd nearly lost my temper. As I had when *Holoworld* asked about strengthening the New York Seawall. Didn't they know that their questions gave credence to the fulminations of the Eco Action League? How could mediamen support those ruthless murderers?

I growled, "You've all nothing better to do than stare at a holovid?"

"You're news, love." Arlene settled into my lap, a beautiful, slender woman. I felt myself stir.

"Um." I looked about helplessly. "We ought to help straighten the house."

"He's embarrassed," she told Jerence sweetly, getting to her feet. "Or he doesn't want me."

"Arlene!"

A wicked grin. "Tonight you'll have to show me otherwise."

I tried not to blush.

Chatting with Derek, I puttered about the room. It was amazing where joeys might set down drinks and food. Once, I was lighting a fire and found—

". . . the Patriarchs?" Jerence waited expectantly.

"Eh?" I wrenched my mind to the present.

"We ought to prepare for your meeting," he said patiently. He'd known me too many years to be offended.

"How can we?" I hadn't a clue why I'd been summoned. "It's probably the religious education budget. Get me next year's figures."

"Will do, but I doubt they'd hold a special session to—"

"Nicky." Arlene tapped my shoulder. Something in her tone gave me pause. "P.T.'s come."

I regarded her steadily.

"He wants to talk to you."

"No."

"Please, love."

"No." I turned away, but she caught my arm, swung me back. "Don't walk away from *me*, Nick Seafort!"

I tried to disengage her fingers. "What do you want of me?"

"Speak with your son."

Casually, Derek swung from his seat and drifted toward the hall. I stayed him with a gesture. He was my oldest friend; from him I need not have secrets.

"Not today of all days, Arlene. Not after Devon."

"Nick, this can't go on. The two of you are like little children."

"Don't call me a—"

"He's waiting in the hallway."

I looked to Derek and Branstead, but they said nothing. "Well?"

Derek shrugged. "Far be it from me to—"

"Damn it!"

"How long have you been estranged?"

I shrugged. "A year or so."

Arlene folded her arms. "Almost three."

Derek said, "And you're miserable."

"I'm no such thing. He deserves—"

"For God's sake, Nick. I've known you forty years."

I capitulated. "Even if I were, it's a matter of principle."

"Mr. SecGen, don't be an ass." His tone was light, but his eyes were not.

"You're the second person today to read me off." For a long moment I stared at the carpet. "I don't know if I should see him. It's been so long, and when he left—"

"Hello, Fath."

I whirled.

P.T. stood in the doorway.

At twenty-four he was everything I'd once hoped him to be. Brilliant, athletic, dedicated, and handsome, at least to a father's eyes.

"Philip." I yearned to sink into my favorite leather chair, but that would extend the conversation, and I wanted at all costs to do otherwise.

"You've been well?"

My tone was harsh. "Is that why you've come?"

Derek's eyes caught Branstead's, but neither man spoke.

"No, sir." Philip's hands fluttered, found his pockets. "When I heard the news from Academy . . ."

I waited, refusing to make conversational sounds that would help him.

His glance flitted to his mother. "Should I go?"

I said, "Perhaps another time would be . . ."

"Nick." Derek.

I knotted my fists. "Say what you came for."

P.T. said earnestly, "We had nothing to do with it. I swear by Lord God." His eyes searched mine for absolution.

"Philip, the Enviro Council is composed of fanatics that cause us no end of trouble. Did you plot the murder of my cadets? No. But you created the atmosphere that made it possible, and I find that unforgivable."

Jerence opened his mouth to speak, thought better of it. I rounded on him. "Well, they did! Their constant carping about our policy, the way they undermine us in the Assembly . . ."

"Fath, how can you oppose us? Have you seen holos of Bangladesh?"

"I've been there." In what little was left of that hapless swamp.

"Do you know what Holland is facing? Louisiana? For that matter, how's Micronesia holding up?"

"Is this about politics, you two?" Derek stood, hands on hips.

I ignored him. "Philip, it would take generations to reverse—"

"No it wouldn't! At the Council we've done studies of the economic cost. I've run the stats myself, in fact it's my project. In the long run, reversing the ecological damage will actually save—"

"Over how long?" I glared. "Generations."

"Stop it, both of you!" Derek looked every inch the Stadholder of Hope Nation.

"Thirty years," P.T. said stubbornly.

"Paid for out of this year's budget. Philip, we haven't the money." How many times had we been down this road, my intransigent son and I?

"South Atlantic fish yields are down again. It's the fifth summer—"

"And colonial food imports are up. We balance."

I looked past him to the doorway, hoping he'd take the hint, yearning for him to go.

"I won't watch this." Derek's eyes had a dangerous glint. "Jerence, let's leave them to their lunacy." He tugged at Branstead's sleeve. "Nick thinks he's in the Rotunda, arguing with a Territorial deputy." He brushed past. "And *you!"* He stopped short, to scowl at Philip. "You've nothing to be proud of this day. For a prodigy, you act like a dolt!" And he was gone.

Branstead followed, squeezing my arm in passing.

Silence.

"Is there anything else?" My tone was unyielding.

Arlene said softly, "Remember why you came."

Philip braced himself. "Yes, sir, there is."

"What, then?"

His voice was unsteady. "Fath, I love you."

I bolted past him to the door, but my fingers slipped on the knob, and then he was there, his hand over mine.

"Father, I'm begging you!" He sank to his knees.

"DON'T DO THAT!" With horror, I realized my fist was raised to club him into submission. Instead, I hauled him to his feet.

Once, in my youth, a man had begged me on his knees, and I'd refused to spare his life. It was a gesture I could no longer abide.

I covered my face. "P.T., leave, I beg you."

"Sir, it doesn't have to be this way between us."

"You made it so. Who was it rifled my office, copied my private environmental papers for the Territorials?"

He cried, "I was nineteen, and stupid! They said it would help." And sardonically, they'd betrayed him.

"You were never stupid. Over and again I've asked you to stay clear of the enviro fringe. You knew the political capital they made of your support. They still do!"

"We're not fringe, Fath." His tone was reasonable, but he abandoned it. "I love you so much, sir!" His voice cracked.

Unable to respond, I faced the door, hugging myself.

"Can't we be friends again? Please?"

"Yes, Nicky, can't you?" Arlene's voice was soft.

I swallowed, until I was sure I could speak. "How's Jared?"

P.T.'s tone was pitifully eager. "Fine, sir." Jared Tenere had lived with us once, as a boy, and caused all sorts of trouble. I'd disliked him intensely. Now he and Philip were paired.

"Still planning to adopt?"

"He wants to go monogenetic clone."

"Whose cells?"

"Mine."

"Derek is monogenetic clone."

"I know."

We were marking time.

I took a deep breath. "Will you give up enviro politics?"

He glanced at his mother, with resignation. "No, Fath." His tone was resolute.

It should have made me furious, but for some reason I was glad. I forced myself to turn, and faced my son. Something stung my eyes. Damned pollutants. Not that the enviros were right; there was nothing we could do about them.

Philip's hands began to pick at his shirt. His eyes darted. "Oh, God, I'm revving." It was a frenzy he'd often worked himself into as a child, when the breathtaking speed of his thoughts outpaced his ability to cope. He closed his eyes for a moment, tried to breathe deeply. "I can't stand— about the cadets, sir, I swear I'll do whatever you say to make it up. Don't shut me—"

Lord God, I can't bear any more.

His fingers scrabbled at the cotton of his tunic. "Oh, Fath, please don't cry!"

I opened my arms.

With a moan, he fell into them.

Arlene leaned against the door, silent. Surreptitiously, she wiped her eyes.

I yawned. It was late, but I treasured my time with Derek. Arlene nestled close, holding my hand. Branstead was in the den, communing with his caller. Derek slouched on a comfortable sofa. "So, it's done," he said.

I shrugged. "And then he went home." After our fervent embrace, Philip and I had chatted a while longer. Despite the emotion of the moment, three years of estrangement couldn't be so easily overcome. Our talk had veered again to politics, and become strained. Eventually, he'd left, with a vague promise that he'd visit soon, with Jared. With shame, I realized I was glad to see him go.

Arlene stirred the remains of her drink. "I'm glad you reconciled."

"Who said we did?"

She snorted.

"You could say we reconciled, after a fashion." My tone was grudging. I hadn't told Philip how I'd cherished cradling him in my arms. Perhaps my fragile, genius son already knew.

"Between the two of you . . ." She shook her head.

She must have been miserable, these last years. I'd been so caught up in my stubborn anger . . . . "I'm sorry. I didn't mean to keep you from him."

"Good heavens, did you think you had?" She looked at me quizzically, but squeezed my fingers.

"I don't—you and I haven't talked much about—" I sputtered to a halt.

"Not since that day you began shouting, at breakfast."

I cringed. It hadn't been one of my better days. Still, I felt betrayed. "All this time you've been seeing—"

"Of course. I'm his mother."

"And I'm his father!"

"Yes, love." She didn't quite make it sound an accusation.

Hastily, I retreated. As always, Arlene would do what she thought right.

"I'm glad it's over," said Derek. "You can bear only so much loneliness."

"You forget yourself, sir!" My tone was ice.

"Do I?" The Stadholder of the Commonweal of Hope Nation met my scowl, unflinching.

I struggled to hold on to my vexation. "If I want analysis of my feelings, I'll ask."

"Is he abusing you, Derek?" His calls completed, Branstead peered in from the door.

"No, but he's trying."

"Don't gang up on me," I said sourly.

Derek said quietly, "You've always been lonely, haven't you, Nick?"

Uncomfortable at the probe, I considered his question. "Not reall—I suppose so." Life in Father's cottage had been lonesome, except for my friendship with Jason, though I hadn't considered it so at the time. During my years on ship I endured the unyielding isolation of a Captain. Command of Academy wasn't much different. Then had come the monastery. I glanced quickly at Arlene, curled at my side. "Except for my marriage."

"If only it were true." She smiled to ease the hurt of her words.

"Arlene?"

Languidly, she rose to her feet, wrapped herself around the back of my chair to massage my shoulders. "You've been a loving husband, and attentive too. But nothing can penetrate the wall you've built. I blame your father for that."

"Bah." I waved it away. "What's come over you all tonight?" Gently, I set aside Arlene's fingers, struggled to my feet. "I have work to do. It's morning in Asia; Hiroto-san is waiting. And I want to call Hazen about that murderous sergeant. Has Charlie gone to bed?" My staff middy and I often worked into the night. It was a peaceable time, and productive.

"Witrek will be transferred in a week," Jerence reminded me.

"Call someone down. We have a list." The last thing on my mind was choosing a middy aide. Tomorrow, I'd have to fly to New York; the Council of Patriarchs waited. The day after, we had the Von Walthers banquet at Earthport Station.

I paused at the door, disconcerted. At last I muttered, "Derek . . . thank you." A quick wave good night, and I limped to my office.

In Father's cottage, tongue between my teeth, I bent over my desk, laboring over my balsa model of UNS Repulse. Jason and I had chosen it on one of our infrequent bicycle rides to Cardiff. I hoped to have it finished by his next visit, so we could paint it together.

I struggled to attach the disk of Level 3 to the central shaft. Repulse was, like most ships of the line, a three-decker.

Not that there was much chance I'd ever see her.

I was twelve, desperate for a year to pass so I'd be old enough to apply to U.N.N.S. Academy. Last year I'd managed, after months of scrimping and saving, to set aside enough coin for Neilsen's Naval Academy Entrance Exam Prep Guide, and at my stubborn insistence, Father now included a heavy measure of math in my home schoolwork.

"Nicholas, it's bedtime."

"Aye, Father." Reluctantly, I set down the model. If it was only possible . . . I closed my eyes, rested my forehead on the scarred desk.

I'd have to get past transcript evaluation, two interviews, and final cull, before I might ever see Academy. Each year many thousands applied, and fewer than five hundred were selected.

I busied myself making ready for bed, knelt next to the covers for my prayers.

"Lord God, I beg You, let me serve in the Navy. I'll be

noble, and good, I swear. I'll be true to You forever." I
took a deep breath, echoed earnestly, *"Forever."*

"Nick, you're kicking me."

"Wha—" Slowly, I came awake.

Arlene gently stroked my flank. "You were thrashing
about, love."

"I'm sorry." I put my head down, pretended sleep, felt
my eyes burn.

Could I start over, Lord? You gave me such a magnificent gift, this life. And I've made such a hash of it.

3

Whyat's that racket?" I paused at the heli door.

"Demonstrators, sir." Karen Burns, deputy chief of security. Her tone was disapproving.

From the helipad I couldn't see the protesters, of course. A high wall surrounded our compound. When P.T. was younger, it had been my dread that some crazed partisan would scramble over the wall and injure him. But then, as now, Security kept vigilant guard.

"Who now?" I wiped my face. The day was sweltering. It seemed summers were worse than ever.

"European Independencers by the cottages, Earth Firsters south of the gate."

"How many?"

"I'm not sure."

"Let's take a look."

"No, Mr. SecGen!" Karen grabbed my arm before I'd taken two paces.

I rapped her with my cane. "Belay that!"

"Mr. Seafort, how do you expect us to keep you alive?"

"Oh, come now. How many assassins come here expecting me to visit with them?" Obstinately, I moved toward the gate.

"Larry, Ezekiel, take the point! Suko, watch for darters."

Fuming, I let my nannies surround me as I strode past the gatehouse, along the path to the street. For a moment the clamor lulled. "Open the gate."

"Mr. SecGen . . ."

"Do it." But I did it myself, thrusting into the mass of Independencers. Five hundred or so, I guessed. Well enough dressed, most of them. "What's this about? What do you want?"

"Freedom for—"

"Hey, it's Seafort!"

"Get away from—"

"Bring back the E.C.!"

"Stand clear!" Karen's tone brooked no argument. I occupied the sidewalk; pressure from my guards slowly forced the demonstrators into the street.

I raised my voice. "How can I listen in this uproar?" I raised my hands for silence. "Have you a spokesman? *Will* you be quiet?" Slowly, the din subsided. "Mark, pass me that bullhorn."

A heavyset man pushed forward. "I'm in charge. We're here to—"

"I'm Nicholas Seafort. What's your name?"

"Uh, Franks. Maury Franks."

"What do you want?" I handed him the speaker.

"Independence for the European states."

"All of them?"

"I—yes."

I said, "Public opinion in Britain runs seventy percent in favor of union, last I looked. France is—"

"Polls can be faked. We want a plebiscite! People, the Government has conspired for decades to hide the truth. Ever since the Austrian-Italian Merger of 2170, Administration after Administration has—"

"Oh, no, you don't." I snatched back the bullhorn. "I'm willing to listen, but not if you besiege my home. Certainly not if you make speeches. Bring a petition to my U.N. office."

"We tried—"

"I guarantee you I'll personally deliver an answer within three days."

"We've heard that goofjuice before. Lies, all of it."

"You have my solemn oath. Before Lord God." It brought murmurs of astonishment.

Franks blustered, but a glance showed him his congregation wasn't with him.

"Deliver it whenever you're ready, Mr. Franks." I moved toward the Earth Firsters. "What are you joeys doing here?"

Below, Delaware merged into New Jersey. *U.N. One* would be landing on the East River strip in half an hour. Washington was too close to New York for a suborbital; we were reduced to old-fashioned jets, hi-trans rail, or a heli. My jet was equipped with every sort of luxury, which I never used. Nonetheless, we carried valets, a butler, security staff, my media secretary, putermen, a Naval liaison . . . I sighed.

Mark Tilnitz selected a bottle from the bin. "Wine, sir?" He had to raise his voice over the drone of the engines.

"And meet the Council of Patriarchs reeking of alcohol? Are you glitched?"

"It's not illegal, Mr. SecGen. You're a civilian." And I was ashore, to boot. Aboard Naval vessels, alcohol, like most drugs, was strictly forbidden. "The Beaujolais, do you think?" Tilnitz's voice was smooth.

Perhaps he was tweaking me to divert my disquiet; he was sensitive to my moods. I stared moodily out the window at the brown landscape below.

In the cockpit were two pilots, a navigator, a radar defenseman. Behind them in the galley, two uniformed stewards waited, hoping I'd press a call button. In the compartment aft of us, Jerence Branstead chatted with a few favored mediamen. Farther toward the tail lounged our press secretary, the valet, and the rest of my swollen entourage.

"It's ridiculous." I slapped the armrest. "An escort of seventy for a trip to the office."

"We've been through this." Tilnitz sounded resigned.

"Go through it again!"

Instead of answering me directly, he raised an eyebrow. "Sir, I'm sure the Council has no quarrel with you."

"Don't patronize me, Mark."

"Why not?"

I glared, but after a moment his mouth twitched. I grumbled, "Why do I put up with you?"

"Because Jeff Thorne retired." Admiral Thorne, my former chief of staff, had once been my superior, and was one of the few who knew how misplaced was the public's adulation. In consequence, he spoke to me without undue regard for my rank. During my second term I'd relied heavily on his judgment and discretion.

Perhaps Mark was right. I seemed to need a goad, to puncture my moods. In earlier days, I'd had Edgar Tolliver, but he was long gone from my life, first to a Captaincy, then to retirement.

Mark's tone was dry. "Karen's rather miffed with you."

"Why?" I knew full well why.

"Crowds are dangerous, sir."

"I'm no tyrant. If the people want to kill me, I should let them, or leave office."

"You don't believe that."

I was silent, not sure whether I did.

"You certainly startled them," Tilnitz admitted. "But what was the point?"

"I don't know. I was restless. To shake up their thinking, I suppose. Make them see me as a person, not an abstraction."

"Oh, great. At five hundred a pop, how long 'til you win over thirty billion citiz—"

"Enough, Mark." I keyed the caller. "Mr. Branstead, join me, please."

"You rang?" Jerence must have been standing at the entryway.

"Ask the puter for our budget for religious education for the last ten years."

"Surely that's not why the Patriarchs—"

"Do it!"

Jerence and Tilnitz exchanged sympathetic glances. If I'd carried a pistol I could have shot them both.

I strode down the mosaic walkway toward the Rotunda.

The new U.N. enclave—everyone called it that, though it hadn't been new for a hundred fifty years—stretched along the befouled East River from Thirty-eighth Street to Forty-seventh. Within its confines were housed the offices of Senators and Assemblymen, the numerous U.N. commissions, tribunals, and organizations, and envoys from our former and current colonies.

Many were in two huge towers whose lines suggested the original U.N. building, long demolished. Between them, surrounded by manicured walkways, was the magnificent marbled Rotunda that housed my Secretariat.

I panted, "Are we late?"

Jerence checked his watch. "We have twelve minutes."

"Hmpf." I strode faster, ignoring a warning twinge in my knee. Dutifully, my retinue kept pace. In younger days I would have increased my stride until the throng was forced to lope. It was absurd; even on the walkway I had at least twenty companions. Why hadn't I put a stop to it in my first term?

I glanced upward to the Von Walthers Administrative Center, on top of which sharpshooters doubtless maintained vigil.

The sun passed behind the shadow of a looming tower. No apparatus as vast as the world government could be housed in as small a space as the U.N. enclave; only the heads of each department—Treasury, Education, Planetary Trade, etc.—maintained offices in the Rotunda.

Unlike capitols of earlier days, we had no need to concentrate our principal offices, so departments were spread over several continents, and linked by net. Only six hundred thousand worked in the U.N. complex and its environs. Many of them were housed in huge towers, amid New York's wealthy Uppies.

Admiralty, as always, was based in London, and semi-independent. The Territorials had tried once to bring them into the fold, but the Navy had called in every political marker it possessed, and sent the administration reeling. No government had again attempted to rein them in.

We neared the Rotunda steps. Within, the Patriarchs waited.

The relationship between the United Nations and the Reunification Church was not fully defined. During the Era of Law that followed the Rebellious Ages, America and Japan had slowly lost their ability to dominate the world by financial strength. The U.N. became the only strong global institution, just as the Final War permanently changed the world balance of power by devastating Japan, China, and much of Africa.

At the same time, the miracle of Christian Reunification swept conservative Europe, now the most influential region of the globe. The United Nations explicitly governed in the name of Lord God and His Church. Rebellion was more than treason; it was apostasy.

"Easy, sir. Let them wait; you're head of Government."

"I owe them courtesy." They represented the Deity. On the other hand, so, by law, did I. I slowed my pace a trifle.

Despite the acknowledged relationship, the Church had no specific rights or duties under the U.N. Charter. The Council of Patriarchs, of which the head of every major Christian sect was a member, was the principal achievement of Reunification. It governed the Church. But it did not govern the United Nations.

Yet, what fate would befall a SecGen who openly defied the Council's command? Disavowal, surely. Only once in their history had the Patriarchs ever disavowed their own Government. Not that the infamous Van Rourke deserved any less.

Formal excommunication was also possible. In that event one would be barred from the rites of any member sect, and all must acknowledge that Lord God's face was turned from him. To consort with him would be treason.

Jerence waved jauntily to the mediamen gathered on the lawn. As was my wont, I ignored the holocams and the reporters' shouted questions. They'd learn soon enough why I was here, as would I.

Gritting my teeth, I climbed the innumerable white marble steps to the imposing entrance. It was a show for the holocams; I could have been whisked by tram through the tunnel from the landing strip, direct to the smooth, silent lifts. But Jerence had unearthed a poll that questioned my physical abilities, now that I carried a cane, and he took every opportunity to put the public's doubts to rest.

Within, all was marble dadoes and mahogany paneling, interspersed with solemn portraits of long-dead leaders. I couldn't imagine why a head of Government would want to work in such a tomb.

My staff dutifully following along, I made my way through echoing corridors to the reception room. Jerence Branstead whispered, "Stand up for your rights," and stood aside.

Anderson, chief of protocol, flung open the doors.

I stopped short. At the head of the vast oval table, where I'd expected to preside as host, sat Francis Saythor, First Bishop of the Protestant Episcopal Church, current Elder of the Council of Patriarchs. His hands were folded comfortably across his stomach.

Surrounding him, in the closest seats to the head of the table, were all thirteen of the colorfully dressed Patriarchs. I'd expected that the Executive, at most, would convene. Certainly not the full Council.

The dapper Archbishop of the Methodist Synod nodded. At his right was the Roman Catholic Bishop of Rome, robed in imperial purple and white. At his left, the elderly First President of the Church of Jesus Christ of Latter-day Saints, in an old-fashioned business suit. He glared across the polished table at his principal competitor, the President of the Reorganized Latter-day Saints.

Saythor, rotund and pale, stroking his charcoal beard, gestured to a seat.

Instead of taking the closest vacant chair, I strode to the foot of the table, took the seat opposite the Elder's. If confrontation was what he desired, confrontation he would have.

"Brother Nicholas." Saythor's voice was soft. "Let us pray."

I bowed my head. Even in conflict, Lord God must prevail.

After the benediction, Saythor made a temple of his fingers and smiled affably. "Thank you for joining us, Nicholas."

Religion was a serious matter; one ought not trifle with Lord God. But the Elder had always irked me, and his behavior today was no exception. So I said, "It's my pleasure, Francis."

As I expected, the use of his first name displeased him, but he made no overt gesture other than to raise an eyebrow. "The Council has concerns we wish to share." His manner was ponderous.

"By all means."

"Your Administration—you in particular—have shown unnecessary hostility to those who would protect Lord God's most cherished planet."

My jaw dropped. "You want me to favor the enviros?"

"Sarcasm is unnecessary," Saythor admonished. "We speak of those who'd protect Earth from the ravages of her selfish colonies."

I frowned, still not sure what he meant.

Stefan Wendrous, Patriarch of the Greek Orthodox Church, intervened in his heavily accented English. "Mr. Seafort, we're distressed that you persecute political groups whose sole purpose—"

"What groups? Please speak clearly."

Saythor shrugged at his colleagues, as if to demonstrate my obstinacy. "It's not necessary to list them by name. Your policies—"

"Toward whom?" I was sailing in a fog.

The Elder's temper frayed. "The Earth First Alliance, among others. The Committee Against Colonial Waste. The Council of Economic Realists." Conservatives, all of them. No, reactionaries, who demanded our funding of the colonies be curtailed. Why would the Patriarchs demand I support them?

"Now, wait a minute." I struggled to control my tone of voice. "The Patriarchs have always favored colonial expansion. In the process we spread the Gospel of Jesus Christ throughout—"

"Of course." Saythor's voice was bland. "But it's past time our colonial children began paying back our beneficence."

"Began?" Derek would have apoplexy, were I to repeat that remark. No doubt the other colonial governments felt likewise. "Do you realize we've crippled their economies, asking them to pay for our rebuilding?"

Andrew DeStoat, Elder of the Evangelical Lutheran Church, snorted in disdain. "The fish who attacked were instruments of Satan. It's appropriate to require all Christian nations to undo their mischief."

"So you want me to crack down on the colonies?" My

hand toyed with the silver head of my cane. What on earth had caused this shift in policy? I'd not met often with the Council, but they'd rarely interfered so blatantly. Their usual concerns were more likely to revolve around religious education, or criminal statutes they saw as overly lax.

"Certainly not." The Elder looked shocked. "However, considering the vast sums we've spent—"

"Our colonies provide foodstuffs, raw materials, manufactured—"

"—on gargantuan ships such as *Galactic,* it behooves us to use her well."

I fell silent, aghast. Never before had the Patriarchs interfered directly in Naval matters.

"Her early voyages should both transmit our goodwill, and our insistence that Earth's needs be met. After all, ours is the one planet in the known universe blessed by the sojourn of Jesus Christ." He leaned forward, spoke with grave emphasis. "The miracle of Reunification mustn't be squandered. In the colonies, unreconciled sects run wild; without our intervention, they'd do so here as well. To combat them takes funds. Our income mustn't be jeopardized."

I clamped my mouth shut. The Church was infallible, though I had my private doubts about its current Elder. Still, I had to say *something*. "I'll ask Admiralty to take your views into consideration."

"Favorably?"

"I can't speak for Admiralty." I'd begun to perspire.

"A maiden cruise to Belladonna would be a welcome start."

I swallowed. We'd just negotiated a new trade pact with Belladonna, giving the distant mining colony greater say in ore quotas, and granting liberal trade allowances.

It wasn't mere generosity on my part. Only by keeping our colonies content might we keep their support, and head off their yearning for self-government. Hope Nation was an example; years ago, I'd had to grant them independence, after suppressing a planters' revolution.

We couldn't afford another upheaval, economically or morally. Revolt against the U.N. was rebellion against Lord God. Millions of souls hung in the balance. My own understanding that I was damned caused me ceaseless misery.

Luckily for the Navy, I had an out. "*Galactic* Fuses in two months for Constantine. She's carrying the principal wave of colonists and supplies."

"A few months' postponement won't matter." Saythor's stern visage met mine.

I said evenly, "Delay would be unwise."

"Look, Seafort." The Elder's tone was now openly hostile. "We're in agreement on this." His gesture included his colleagues. "You understand what that signifies? Representatives of all His churches concur on His will, without dissent. We have no doubt that in this we speak for Lord God."

That was a warning, if anything was. If I defied the Church on a matter in which they spoke for the Deity, I could be charged with heresy. Unlikely, I supposed, but quite possible. Nonetheless, I waited in stubborn silence.

"Let me be frank," Saythor added. "We already know the Territorials will have no scruples in furthering His cause." No, they wouldn't. The opposition party saw the Navy as a club with which to strike its enemies. It always had. In the Transpop Rebellion, the Terrie government had used Naval lasers to blast city streets. And they were dead set against colonial independence. Ordering the Navy to hold the colonies by brute force would be a simple solution they'd eagerly endorse.

I hesitated, yearning to comply. But visions of the idyllic Hope Nation landscape drifted before me, and of the earnest, hard-working folk of Detour. I wouldn't let the greed of the Patriarchs corrupt U.N. colonial policy. "I will not send a Naval vessel to menace U.N. citizens who've done no wrong."

The Elder's fingers drummed the table. "As you wish."

"Brother Nicholas." The Bishop of Rome stayed Saythor with an upraised hand. "Review the matter without haste. I pray you, don't discard a life of service over a small issue."

"We speak of finance, Your Holiness." I fished in my pocket for a coin, found only a credit chip. I held it between two fingers. "This is of Caesar, not of God. Let temporal matters arrange themselves without your intervention."

"It's our duty to intervene." Pope Nicholai shook his head. "Still, Francis, wait a week. Give him time to consider."

A look of annoyance flitted over the Elder's pudgy face. "In deference to your wishes, so be it." He looked to me.

I was beyond tact. "I don't need a week. Let someone else besmirch the Navy."

"Nonetheless, we'll wait. The usual press statement, outside? Earnest exchange of views? Frank discussion?"

"Very well." What they told the mediamen was of no concern. Mechanically, I moved with the rest of them to the door.

I would be free at last. For years I'd sought release from the burden of office, and now it was at hand. So why did I feel not relief, but disappointment?

Because my beloved Navy would be used for dishonorable ends. For two hundred years courageous sailors had sailed the starlanes, not to threaten our colonies, but to nurture them.

On the other hand, the Council spoke for the Reunification Church, and the Church for Lord God. Who was I to set my will against that of the Deity? I couldn't believe the Patriarchs had actually threatened me with renunciation. Well, they hadn't, not in so many words. But what did Pope Nicholai mean, "discard a life of service over a small issue"? Discard my life itself? My service?

My lips tightened. When I couldn't reconcile my duty with the Church, it was time to leave office.

In the anteroom I nodded curtly to Branstead and Mark Tilnitz. Security men formed their customary ring as we began our walk through the rooms of state to the holocams waiting outside.

"Trouble, sir?" Jerence's voice was a whisper.

"Later." The Patriarchs and their retinues were near.

A hand touched my shoulder.

The Elder of the Lutheran Church said quietly, "Bishop Saythor isn't graced with soft speech, Brother Nicholas, but heed his words nonetheless." A short, graying man dressed in traditional black, he wiped his brow with a starched handkerchief.

I leaned against a marble column, letting the procession pass me by. "I'm puzzled, Reverend DeStoat. What brought on the Council's sudden anxiety about our colonies?" I could guess the answer: the Territorials, out of office for twelve years, had been whispering in their collective ear. The Catholic sect, among others, had always favored the Terries.

"They have more than economics on their mind." DeStoat's smile was wry. "In the colonies, too many wayward cults have sprung up, in disregard of the one true way."

"Couldn't you settle those matters ecclesiastically?"

His mouth tightened. "Only when colonial affairs are firmly in hand." He lowered his voice. "The Reunification is a precious gift. If we make demands of the colonial churches we can't enforce, our unity might be shattered. It's a risk we can't take. We *must* keep them under firm control, and the Navy is Lord God's instrument. Take care, Brother Nicholas." His mouth smiled, but his eyes did not. "Defiance could jeopardize more than your Administration."

A warning, or a threat, barely disguised. We reached the door. Dutifully, I took my place beside Elder Saythor, letting my presence endorse his platitudes to the mediamen.

* * *

"I hope it's not *Galactic*," said Charlie Witrek. He put another chip in the holovid, scanned it. We were in my Washington study, attacking my endless paperwork.

I snorted. "You're probably the only middy in the U.N. Navy who doesn't want her. Why?"

"She's too big. Too many middies. I'd never be first." The first midshipman, on any Naval vessel, had special privileges, and was in charge of his fellows. But seniority applied; the midshipman with the longest service was automatically first.

Charlie was no doubt right; on a ship such as *Galactic* it would be years before he'd have hope of making first middy.

"You're how old? Eighteen?"

"Nineteen in September." Young, by civilian reckoning, but not for a middy. Witrek would have joined at fourteen or so, as a cadet. He filed his chip, reached for another. "It's not like they'll have a lot of ships to choose from."

I grunted. UNS *Wellington* had just left for Casanova, and *Braeburn* was already en route to Vega. Over seventy starships, but not more than two were in home system. A far cry from the days of the fish war, when we'd recalled nearly our entire fleet. Nowadays the Navy was desperately busy ferrying colonists outward, hauling their produce back home.

"Mr. Seafort?" For once, he sounded tentative, unsure. "I don't want to take advantage, but . . ." He steeled himself. "Could you see that I get a ship? Not an administrative posting?"

I could have sworn he held his breath. Any thought of twitting him vanished. "Yes, Charlie. You deserve that much."

A sigh. I was right. He *had* been holding his breath.

Arlene faced me, hands on hips, a disapproving frown creasing her lined face.

"For heaven's sake," I said. "I *have* to go; it's the Von

Walthers Award, and I'm the guest of honor." They'd named the moral leadership award for Hugo Von Walthers, the legendary Captain who'd discovered the wreck of *Celestina*, gone on to be a colonial Governor, and ended his career as Secretary-General over a century before.

Canceling the trip was impossible. They'd laid on the awards banquet at the Earthport Hilton. I felt vaguely uneasy about it; I knew our easing of the Charities Tax Act had played a significant role in their selection of me as this year's recipient, though there hadn't exactly been a quid pro quo. Not really, although Jerence had discussed it with the nominations committee. In any event, while I was aloft, I wanted to consult with Naval brass; the Council's ultimatum made doing so even more urgent.

Of course, now that my tenure as SecGen was about to come to an ignominious end, perhaps my consultations didn't much matter. Regardless of what Admiralty said, I wouldn't carry out Saythor's policy.

"Nicky, you've been pushing yourself. And the acceleration—"

I snorted. "Since when have I had problem with liftoff?" I'd spent my life clawing my way out of one planetary gravity well or another.

"You're getting older."

"I'll be fine." I sought to mollify her. "I'll have Branstead make time for a nap after we dock."

That brought a smile, as I hoped it would. But it faded. She said, "Don't mock my worries."

"I'm not, hon, but as long as I'm SecGen, I have to keep up appearances." I checked her expression; my reassurance seemed to have little effect. "Care to change your mind and come along?"

"Well . . . yes."

I did my best to hide my surprise. "Very well, get packed; we leave in two hours." In truth, I was finding liftoff more difficult each trip, and I didn't want Arlene along to observe me. She herself seemed to bear acceleration as easily as when she'd been a cadet eager for her first trip to Farside. On the other hand, she'd always been a fitness fanatic. She taught Philip self-defense, far more competently than I could have. She'd have made a formidable drill instructor. Even today she kept herself in fine shape.

Normally we'd lift from Potomac Shuttleport. About half the size of New York Von Walthers, it was North America's fourth largest spaceport. It handled suborbitals to Europe and Asia as well as the massive shuttlebuses that lifted cargo and personnel to Earthport Station and beyond.

Unfortunately, our Secretarial shuttle was docked in New York, and Tilnitz merely laughed at my suggestion that we book a commercial flight. So we trooped into a heli, heading for Potomac Shuttleport, where we would board the jetliner that would save an hour compared to a heli flight to New York. I bore it with ill grace; I'd have preferred flying the jet heli directly to Von Walthers Shuttleport, but it couldn't have carried the entourage mustered for my visit aloft.

We flew over the old White House, where the American President still reigned over his regional government. Washington still bore the scars of the huge bureaucracy that had throttled it: vast white stone buildings in federal style and glass monstrosities littered the landscape. The remains of the Pentagon scarred miles of lowland.

At Potomac Shuttleport Arlene and I walked the red carpet to the jetliner, followed by my numerous aides. I seethed at the fuss.

Perhaps sensing my mood, my staff gave us a wide berth once the doors were sealed. Carlotti, my press secretary, made himself comfortable in the aft compartment; Mark Tilnitz settled with the crew in the cockpit. Arlene, knowing my moods, sat peaceably across the aisle scanning a holozine. Only Jerence Branstead, with the ease of long familiarity, sat near me, holovid in hand.

"You wanted to review the Von Walthers seating, sir?"

Seating approval for the banquet was one of the terms we'd negotiated.

"Oh, yes. The chart?" I peered at the arrangements. The Von Walthers affair would be among my last public appearances; I might as well enjoy myself. "Have them put Kahn elsewhere. We've never been friends." Besides, a seat other than at the center of the dais would thoroughly annoy the former SecGen. That sort of power was a perk of office I'd rarely exercised. "Where's Metzner? No, put him on the dais. He supported our cuts to the U.N.A.F. budget."

The engine whine grew louder. Almost imperceptibly, we began our taxi.

"Now, make sure Boland's seat is near mine. It'll make him happy, and irritate the devil out of Rothstein."

My chief of staff looked askance. "Are you sure, sir?"

"If the Terries don't like it, they can eat in the lobby." My tone was gleeful. After a moment Branstead smiled too.

At last, we began our takeoff roll.

"Now, as to the Naval brass—"

An unexpected bump lifted me from my seat. Almost instantly, the craft braked, rocking side to side. I braced myself.

Mark Tilnitz darted out of the cockpit. He reached past Jerence, tore off my seat belt, threw me to the deck.

He whipped across the aisle, pulled Arlene clear. He hauled her to a seat several rows forward. He dived back to the chair I'd vacated, scrambled to lower the porthole shades.

Swerving, the craft slowed.

I snarled, "What in God's—"

Ignoring me, Tilnitz barked into his shoulder mike. "Ground team, we've got a scramble! Shots fired from the west. Seal the terminal!" He whirled to the cockpit. "Pilot, stay away from buildings! Roll to the far end of the field!"

The door to the aft compartment flew open. Two burly security men dashed in. One knelt over me, protectively.

"Stay clear of windows, Branstead! Get down!" Mark drew his pistol, peered cautiously past a shade. "No one in sight. Anyone hurt?" He glanced about. "They shot out a tire."

I pushed the security agent aside, hauled myself to a seat on the far side of the craft. "How do you know?" The rush of adrenaline left me shaky.

"I saw sparks on the tarmac. Their first two shots missed. Get down, sir!" He tugged at my arm. Again, he keyed his caller. "Armored vehicle to the north end of the field. I want troops, a heli, full air support."

I twisted free from his grasp. "I'm as safe here as anywhere. Arlene?"

"I'm all right." Her face was grim. "Mark, catch them."

"Our joeys know the drill." He muttered into his caller. "Mr. SecGen, we'll take you home to the compound."

I slammed the armrest. "The hell you will." I felt a moment's guilt for my language. "I'll not be made a prisoner by some lunatic with a rifle."

"Nicky—"

"No, Arlene, I'm going to Earthport. Stay home if you're afraid." I could have bitten my tongue off, but it was too late. Instead of erupting, though, Arlene compressed her mouth and said nothing. I knew her outrage would be slow in cooling.

I tried to sound reasonable. "Mark, I'll accept protection while you sort this out. An hour. Two, no more. Then we go on to New York."

"This is my show, sir. Shots were fired."

"You heard me."

"And you heard me. Or I'll resign." We exchanged glares.

Jerence growled, "Enough, the both of you."

I gaped. My chief of staff never spoke to me so.

"Mark, he's the boss, whether we like it or not. Mr. Sec-

Gen, stop throwing your weight around. Mark knows what he's doing."

"I never said he didn't." Why did I sound peevish?

In the distance, sirens screamed. Flashing lights drew close, wheeled to surround us.

Mark's gaze grew distant as he listened to his earplug. "Area secured. Off the plane, Mr. SecGen."

"Very well. Arlene?" I held out a hand, but she stalked past me.

Tilnitz led the way, pistol drawn and ready. Surrounding me, security agents hustled me down the steps. In seconds, I was huddled inside a dim-lit armored truck.

Mark snapped, "Go!"

"Not without Arlene."

"She's in the next car. Go go go!" We lurched off, gained speed rapidly.

"Where are we headed?"

"A hangar."

"Why there?"

His tone held resignation. "It's by the book, sir."

An hour later, I paced the cold concrete of the hangar. "I want to see the body."

" 'Til we search every inch, the terminal's not secure."

My mood was foul. Arlene was barely willing to acknowledge my existence, despite my apology. I knew my comment had been inexcusable; on *Wellington,* Arlene had faced attack by the alien fish without qualms. To question her courage . . .

Jerence Branstead stood by the truck, arms folded, disgusted with my resolve to be on our way to Earthport.

I took a deep breath. Then another. I'd have to practice patience.

Jerence sighed loudly, for the third time.

No, by Lord God, I would not. I was about to be disavowed by the Patriarchs; I would do as I wished. "Mark, look at me." I took his hand, placed it on my chest. "Who do you think I am?"

"The Secretary-General." He sounded puzzled.

"Not Lord Christ? I'm just a man, do you agree?" He nodded. "So I can be killed despite all your efforts. I spent all my Navy years in one sort of danger or another. They shot at me aboard *Hibernia*, and on Hope Nation. They wounded me on *Challenger*. Fish hurled acid at my ships. I damn near died in the Rebellion." I was skirting blasphemy; I'd have to rein in my tongue. I made a short prayer of contrition.

He said, "Those days are past."

"Not if Lord God wills it!" I brandished my cane as if it were a laser. "I won't go skulking about, do you hear? Show me the damn—the blessed body."

Mark threw up his hands in defeat. "Very well." We piled back into the truck.

The terminal lobby had been cordoned off. I knelt by the bloody corpse still clutching its ancient rifle. A sallow blond-haired joey, about thirty. Faded jumpsuit, with a scorched hole in the chest. Receding hair, sallow cheeks. No one I'd ever met. I hadn't really expected otherwise.

Around us, civilian police and U.N. security staff milled about recording the scene, note-taking, interviewing. Thank heaven, Carlotti was keeping the mediamen at bay. It was the only reason I tolerated him.

I looked down at the vacant eyes. "Was he alone?"

"Except for his driver."

"ID?"

"We've taken prints and DNA. It shouldn't be long. He's E.A.L., though." Mark saw my mystified look. "Eco Action League. Had a manifesto in his pocket."

"A new one?"

"Fairly similar to the first." He grimaced. "We should have been prepared. At Devon they warned they'd strike again."

"Where is it?"

"Forensics has it; I'll get you a copy."

I fingered the scorched jumpsuit. "Was your enviro goofjuice worth dying for, joey?"

"I don't think he expected to die." Mark gestured to the outer door. "He almost got away. A car was waiting."

"Did you get a description?"

"Oh, we have it. But in the confusion the driver bolted and escaped. I want you out of here. Have you seen enough?"

"Yes." I was profoundly disturbed. How could the ecos murder innocent children, attack my transport? The Rebellious Ages were long past, thank Lord God. Our population wasn't under the heel of a tyranny; across the world, the public embraced the strictures that bound us together and made war and terror relics of history. Yes, the urban transpops had once rebelled, but they'd been driven to it by desperation, by the threat of extinction.

Acts of terrorism were punishable by death, regardless of their success or failure. That was just. But when had the penalty last been meted? Public dissension was so rare these days . . . and since the upgrade of the laser installation at Lunapolis, what point in insurrection? America's eastern seaboard, seat of government and our primary industrial base, was so heavily protected that no earthly force could threaten it.

I sighed. What was the world coming to? Well, it wouldn't be my problem for long. "Get us to Von Walthers."

Mark led me to a heli.

Earthport was the largest orbiting station ever built. In geosync orbit over the eastern U.S., its bays moored interplanetary vessels for Lunapolis, Deimos, and other nearby settlements and, more importantly, vast Naval starships for our more distant colonies. Its bonded warehouses stored cargo for transshipment as well as ores and grains ferried home from distant provinces awaiting transfer to Earth or other local ports. Earthport's numerous hotels and restaurants served throngs of passengers en route to and from the sixty-seven planets and satellites on which the human race had established beachheads.

Eleven of those outposts had been colonized during my terms of office.

Surreptitiously I rubbed my chest, not yet recovered from liftoff. For decades, ever since my lung replacement . . . ah, well.

"Welcome, sir," said Geoffrey Rand, civilian administrator of Earthport. "Thank Lord God you're safe."

I frowned. No doubt the news zines were already trumpeting the shuttleport fiasco. "Have you met Ms. Seafort? Arlene . . ." She nodded curtly, still miffed.

Rand gestured toward the waiting electricart. "This way, sir." As I passed the sparse line of officials, Fleet Admiral McKay saluted stiffly.

At my side, Mark Tilnitz eyed each face, his glance flickering down to the hands. I supposed I couldn't blame him, given the day's events. I beckoned Branstead. "What's the drill?"

"I scheduled you a couple of hours in your Hilton suite, but that was before the, um, delay. I'll cancel the Naval tour so you'll have time to rest before the banquet."

"Nonsense." I took a deep breath, tried not to wince. "I'll skip the nap."

"You need it, Nick." Arlene's voice was acid.

"I'll decide that." I pressed my lips tight, unwilling to quarrel in front of strangers.

The cart rolled through bright-lit corridors, each punctuated by emergency hatches that would slam shut at the first sign of decompression. For security reasons we'd docked on Level 5, near the Naval wing, far from the civilian concourses and their shops.

As a Captain, I'd oft walked these corridors and thought nothing of it. My knuckles tightened on my cane. I could do so again, if need be. My staff coddled me too much, and I suspected I was becoming soft as a result. I had half a mind to stop the cart and walk. In fact—

I raised my cane. "Hold it." Startled, the driver carefully braked. I slid off the cart. Hurriedly, Mark followed.

All were staring at me. I couldn't very well demand to walk, could I? I'd inconvenience Rand, the Admiral, my staff . . .

I had to give a reason for stopping. "What's this?" I pointed to a hatch.

"Traffic control, Mr. SecGen." If Rand was surprised at my abrupt diversion, he gave no sign.

"Let's see." I slapped open the hatch, from the access pad at its side.

Within, a small anteroom. I peered past the startled guard. Beyond, a row of consoles, manned by techs. "Why aren't they in uniform?"

"They're civilians, sir."

"Oh. Of course." I felt an idiot. If I'd visited Earthport as often as I ought, I'd know better. The Navy operated out of its own wing, and the rest of the station was under the administrator's control. "Very well." Casually, I eased myself onto the cart. "Carry on."

In moments, we rolled to a stop at the closed and guarded hatch to the Naval wing. I shook hands with Rand, the station administrator, and confronted Tilnitz. "Mark, I'm in Navy territory. Get some rest. Take Arlene to the hotel. Unless . . . ?" I gestured to the hatch.

Arlene shook her head. "The hotel."

"Mr. SecGen—"

"Jerence, tell Mark I'm safe with the Navy. Admiral, let's go." I left Tilnitz protesting.

The conference room was spacious enough to hold the entire Board of Admiralty, fifteen in all, but we were only five, including a Captain. Gray-flecked Admiral McKay took a place across from me. Farther down the table was Admiral

Hoi of BuPers, thin of face, his expression somber. Johanson of the Governmental Affairs Office was there also, and an officer I didn't recall, whose stern blue eyes regarded me steadily.

"Mr. SecGen, may I present Captain Stanger."

Oh, of course. I'd seen his holo, spread across the zines. "How do you find *Galactic*, Mr. Stanger?"

"She's wonderful, sir." His gaze softened in a brief smile.

I grunted. She ought to be, for what she cost. But I owed him more courtesy than that. "And the loading?" *Galactic*'s cargo holds were huge, and most of her stores had to be hauled from groundside, a shuttle load at a time.

"We're coming along well. Two months, according to schedule." He saw me grimace, added quickly, "It's all right, sir, really. We're using the time to whip the crew into shape."

That, at least, I understood. As difficult as it was to train new crewmen, it was twice as hard when the entire ship's company had been transferred from other vessels, and had to learn the quirks and peculiarities of a new craft.

Admiral McKay cleared his throat, switched on his holovid. "Well, then—"

"Would you like a tour, Mr. SecGen? We'd be honored." Stanger waited expectantly.

"I wish I could. I have the Von Walthers banquet—" On the other hand, my schedule tomorrow held nothing of great importance, and it was time I saw the great behemoth that was such a bone of contention. Besides, after I next met with the Patriarchs, I doubted I'd have another chance.

I'd delay my return shuttle. Tilnitz and Branstead didn't have to like it. "Very well, in the morning. I'll look forward to it." I saw McKay's eyes were frosty. "Sorry, Admiral, on to business."

We ran through half a dozen routine items: staffing concerns, out-of-budget special appropriations, home fleet dispositions.

There was an awkward pause.

"Well?" I looked from one to another. "What is this meeting really about?"

"Mr. SecGen . . ." Admiral Hoi's tone was cautious. "We wanted you to be cognizant of concerns shared by a great number of Naval officers."

I'd endured similar mind-numbing circumspection from the Patriarchs, and was thoroughly sick of it. "Speak plainly."

"We all love the Navy; that goes without saying. We're concerned about Administration priorities."

I stirred. Why was it so difficult for him to reveal his thoughts? Perhaps Captain Stanger sensed my impatience. He coughed discreetly, and Hoi nodded in relief.

Stanger leaned forward, his blue eyes serious. "There's little enough money to rebuild New York, aid the ravaged Netherlands, and support the expansion of the Navy to protect us from colonial dissolution. The Navy doesn't want funds squandered on ecological boondoggles. There, it's said."

"What boon—how is this your business?"

"Officially, it isn't." For a moment he dropped his eyes. "Would you prefer we didn't speak?"

Yes. "No, of course not. It's just . . ." I was floundering. "Go ahead."

Stanger's smile was grim. "All of us here are loyal to our last breath, as are all the officers we've spoken to."

"Naturally." Why did I feel a chill?

"Nonetheless, officers throughout the Service are troubled. I believe you'll confirm, Admiral Hoi, will you not? Just so. The Seafort Administration hasn't opposed the Greenhouse Gases Reduction Act, for exam—"

"Cutting industrial emission of greenhouse gases will slow global warming, at least to a degree. And it's only five percent."

"On top of four percent three years ago. But any reduction

cripples our industry and will slash Government revenues. And to what purpose? Frankly, Holland is beyond saving. Cut our losses."

I shook my head. "It's not just the Dutch. The same tides roil across Florida, Louisiana, Japan—"

"A seawall is a hell of a lot cheaper, Mr. SecGen, than foolish enviro fantasy on a global scale. You see, sir"— Stanger waited for my nod to proceed—"expansion of the fleet is vital. Surely you must agree. The colonials are restless, but if trade with a single colony is disrupted, our economy could tailspin. Now, if ever, we need a firm presence among the worlds, and that means more ships. And it's not just factory emission controls that hamper us. There's no real proof ozone reseeding works, or—"

"But we ought to try." Why did I feel I was parroting the enviro line? Essentially, Stanger was right. There was little we could do to change the course Lord God had set for us. But I mustn't tell Stanger that; he was challenging Administration policy. "We're under increasing pressure from the enviros. Not just Winstead and his Council; now there's the loonies of the Eco Action League. Casting aside enviro programs would be as bad as giving in to their terrorism. Can't you see we have to maintain a steady course?"

"I see the Naval budget in disarray. Don't make it worse with useless enviro—"

I said, "The Navy spent more this year than last."

"Yes, we had an increase, but almost all of it went to *Galactic* and *Olympiad*."

I slammed the table. "You wanted those ships!"

"Of course we do." Stanger's tone was soothing. "They can carry thousands of troops, if it comes to that. No colony will—"

"We won't use them to browbeat other worlds!" I reined myself in. We were far off topic. "I won't abandon the Greenhouse Gases bill. It's not expedient." We'd decided,

Branstead and I, to give the enviros what little we must, to keep them quiescent.

"You'll continue playing into the Enviro Council's hands?"

"I didn't say that." A pause. "How many officers agree with your sentiment?"

"Most I've spoken to." He passed the ball to McKay. "Sir, what is Admiralty's view?"

The Admiral looked uncomfortable. "On the whole, we've little disagreement. Mr. SecGen . . ." He looked to me in appeal. "You've been the Navy's staunch supporter all your life. Can you not see that this is no moment to falter?"

I got slowly to my feet. "Is that what I'm doing?"

Johanson of Governmental Affairs spoke for the first time. "Absolutely not, sir. But we're worried about the immense pressure put on you by the enviro fringe. They're totally unrealistic on budgetary constraints."

"What if . . ." I was almost afraid to ask, "I don't do as you ask?"

"Why, sir." Stanger's guileless eyes met mine. "We'll do our duty, as always. But we'll be disappointed."

"Very well. See that it comes to no more than that." My skin was clammy. "I'll think carefully on what you've said. Next month when I meet with Admiralty on the budget—" But I wouldn't be meeting with Admiralty next month. At best, I'd be retired. Or facing a heresy charge if the Patriarchs were so minded.

"I'll think hard on it," I finished lamely. "Believe me, I too want the Navy strong and vigilant." On that note, we adjourned.

The confrontation left me troubled. Whether I viewed their remarks as threat or warning, they made clear I'd been too long out of touch with the working officers. Well, it would be my successor's problem, not mine. Unless I chose to throw my lot in with the conservatives, mount a show of force for the colonies, and by doing so win the Patriarchs' favor.

"Oh, Mr. SecGen." Admiral Hoi seemed cordial. "Could we stop at my private office? I've something to show you."

"Very well." In the corridor, Jerence Branstead waited with my security chief. I scowled. "I thought I told you to rest."

Tilnitz waved it away. "My job's to keep an eye on you."

Hoi was present, so I held my peace. I followed him to his hatch.

"That way, sir."

"I know." My tone was curt. A decade ago, I'd come aloft to this very office to demand Admiral Jeff Thorne put an end to the decimation of the transpops. The place reminded me of tragedies I'd as soon leave buried, of days before P.T. and I had grown apart.

Hoi stood aside. I limped in, caught a glimpse of the huge holoscreen dominating the far bulkhead. "It hasn't chang— Lord in heaven!"

The Naval officer who came to his feet wore a shy grin. "We wanted to surprise—sir, are you all right?"

I steadied myself at the console. "Yes, I . . . Alexi, how have you—it's so good to—I didn't know—" I swallowed. "Come!"

He extended his hand; I started to take it, pulled him instead into an embrace. "Oh, God. Lord God." I could say no more.

Alexi Tamarov had been a fellow middy on *Hibernia* when I first reported to her wardroom, a hopeful boy with the ruin of my life still ahead. Afterward, I'd made him lieutenant, sailed with him again years later, seen him through a terrible wound and the anguish of amnesia.

I wiped my eyes. "How did . . . where did you . . ."

"*Melbourne* docked two days ago, sir."

"It's been how long?"

"Twelve years." Several cruises, on his part, elections and politics, on mine.

I closed my eyes. How could it be? Where did a life go? "Let's have a look at you." Still slim, a finely chiseled face, wavy hair only now showing a touch of gray. "You're Captain." His shoulder patches told me that, but I'd already known. From time to time I watched the few names I still recalled, as they climbed the Captains' list.

"For six years. I've been out of system a year and a half. I arranged extra leave; Josh Fenner has *Melbourne* for the Titan run. Moira is a bit unhappy I left her with the joeykids, especially as Mikhael—is Ms. Seafort along?"

My smile vanished at the thought of the amends I must make. "At the hotel. She'll be delighted to see you. And we'll have you down to—oh!"

"What, sir?"

"Derek's in town!"

His face lit in delight. "The three musketeers, together at last!" Barely more than boys, together we'd endured Centraltown's upheavals.

I giggled. Somehow, his presence swept away my burdens. Alexi was a good-hearted joey, and steadfast unto death. If only I'd had him with me, these cheerless years.

Someone coughed. Dimly, I realized we weren't alone. "Ah, Mark, you've never met . . . Admiral Hoi, would you do the introductions?" I sank into a chair, my head in my hands.

Once, in Hope Nation, Alexi and I had shared a tent outside the Plantation Zone. *"Sir?"* I'd been young, still eager, struggling to know my duty. *"Sir, are you well?"*

"Of course, Jerence." I groped for his arm. "Make time for Alexi. Fit him in, regardless of what else I have on my plate. And put him on the dais tonight."

"Done."

* * *

Two levels below, Earthport's corridors were wider, the fittings more stylish, as befit public areas. Our cart slid to a halt at the Hilton's main hatch, resplendent in gold trim.

I waved cordially to the gawkers, delighted to have Alexi at my side. We made our way into the crowded auditorium. The audience had undergone stringent security checks, beyond those they'd already endured to reach the Station.

Half an hour later, in view of the hundreds who'd paid astronomical sums for the privilege, and watched by millions on worldwide nets, I toyed with my roast chicken and peas. I was thinking of Arlene, wishing I could discuss with her Stanger's assertions, and regretting my vile accusation of cowardice, but she was in the front row, having steadfastly refused the dais.

Somehow, I'd have to undo my folly.

Senator Rob Boland leaned close. "I hope I won't embarrass you tonight."

"You won't if you tell truth." If he weren't up for reelection, I wouldn't have agreed to his giving the principal address. But Robbie Boland had served well in his father's old Senate seat, and deserved another term.

We'd long since set aside our differences over the transpops, and his moral failure to support them. Politics required me to be practical. His help was instrumental in shepherding through the Senate many bills that our party thought important.

At the far end of the dais, former SecGen Kahn chewed stolidly.

Robbie reached across my plate to offer Alexi a hand. "Mr. Tamarov, I don't believe we've met."

"A pleasure, Senator."

"You served on his first ship, right? How I envy you."

"How so?" Alexi shot me an apologetic glance, but I didn't really mind them talking past me.

"I met Mr. Seafort when he was Commandant." Boland

had been a cadet then, in my care. "But you knew him when he was young."

"We were all young then." Alexi smiled at the memory, turning to me. "And now, look at you." He read from the glittering emblem on the screen behind the dais. "The Von Walthers Award for Moral Leadership."

"Lord Christ, Alexi. Er, sorry." For an instant I bowed my head in contrition. "Don't you realize it's all political? How could I actually deserve this?"

"How could you not?"

The lights dimmed; the chairman rapped on the podium, began his introduction. I tried to achieve a look of polite interest.

First he had to thank the event's organizers. Then he handed off to Anton Bourse, the world-famous holo star, who gave the world's millions a capsule biography of Captain Von Walthers. Next, the head of the Von Walthers Foundation spoke of their charitable work, and of the award they sponsored.

My polite smile began to congeal. I covered my mouth with my napkin.

Alexi whispered, "Patience, sir. It won't be long."

I grunted.

His eyes glowed. "I had no idea when *Melbourne* docked that you were getting the Von Walthers. It's so fitting."

"You're an innocent."

"Don't you understand, sir? I'd have dropped out years ago if not for your example. Even today, middies revere you. I can't tell you how good it feels to know the public feels the same."

"Alexi, how often must I tell you? We engineered this, Branstead and I." I turned away, took a cautious sip of wine. Through the glass, one of the lights looked like a porthole. I toyed with my goblet. Like a porthole at UNS *Helsinki*'s aft airlock.

I strode down the Level 2 corridor. Up the ladder, turn

left. Sixteen, green and awkward, I was a nervous young middy reporting for the first time to the bridge. I'd not yet met Mr. Hager, the first midshipman who'd control my destiny, or the Captain, so far advanced on the ladder of life that I was sweating in anticipation of our coming encounter.

I had to make a good impression. My whole career depended on it. All my striving, all my training, had led to this interview.

Help me, Lord God. I am Yours, wholly. I dedicate my service to You.

My footsteps slowed. I was outside the bridge.

Clutching my orders, I smoothed my jacket, ran a hand through my close-cropped hair. This is it, Lord. My career starts in this moment.

Help me make it right.

Help me to be proud.

A round of applause. I looked up, startled. Robbie Boland slid back his chair, strode to the podium.

"Ladies and gentlemen, it is a sobering honor to be here tonight. For our honoree is a comrade, an old friend, my late father's long ally, my . . ." He hesitated. "My mentor. The man who showed me right from wrong, who was"—a rueful smile—"responsible for my political eclipse." That brought friendly laughter.

Boland, distraught at the death of his friend Adam Tenere that he'd done nothing to prevent, had resigned as Assemblyman to raise Adam's troubled son Jared. It was five years before he reemerged into political life.

"Nicholas Seafort is a man who will not lie. A man who will not prevaricate. A man who hates falsehood. A man who does right, as he sees it, no matter what the cost."

Alexi squeezed my arm. "I'm so proud of you! I wouldn't miss this for the world."

I stared at my goblet, but the bridge of *Helsinki* had faded beyond recall.

Lord, why must it be so? Why cannot I go back, be again that earnest boy?

At the far left, SecGen Kahn looked fixedly at his plate.

Why am I here, Lord?

". . . a man who is at once kind, resolute, brilliant, innovative, and a moral beacon for all mankind. I give you the Captain of *Hibernia, Challenger,* and *Trafalgar,* the recipient of this year's Hugo Von Walthers Award, Secretary-General Nicholas Ewing Seafort!" Boland turned, led the thunderous applause.

Lord, take me back to boyhood. I'd beg on my knees, if it would sway Thee. Give me another chance.

"Sir, it's time."

Please. How could I have gone so wrong?

"They're waiting!"

There was nothing but to go through with it. A few words of thanks, and it would be over. Slowly, reluctantly, I got to my feet. The thunder hadn't abated. Across the hall, guests had risen, offering a standing ovation.

It was intolerable.

I reached the podium, leaned my cane against the stand. Smiling widely, eyes shining, Robbie Boland offered me his hand.

Waiting for the applause to subside, I scanned the hall. Arvin Rothstein was banished to the second row of tables, as I'd planned. He'd paid over a thousand Unies to participate. Lord God, he looked elegant in his black dinner apparel.

I raised both hands, waved the multitude to their seats. How many of the attendees did I know? Admiral Hoi, of course. Deputy SecGen Cisno Valera, with a table of his aides. Connie Histung, of *Holoworld.* Vince Canlo from *Newsnet,* so many others.

Slowly, the applause dwindled.

I squinted past the lights, past the banks of holocams that would send my words to the world.

In the front row, joeys were waving, as if to attract my attention.

Oh, no.

My son Philip and Jared Tenere grinned up at me, delighted at my shock.

No, Lord. Not this. I glanced back to Alexi. His mouth formed silent words. "Bravo, sir!"

The scrape of a thousand chairs. At last, the hall quieted. Only a few words. Then it would be done.

"Ladies and gentlemen, I thank you—"

"Midshipman Nicholas Seafort reporting, sir!" The eager young boy's voice cracked. He stiffened to attention. The Captain of Helsinki turned piercing gray eyes upon him.

"—thank—" I faltered.

No.

I stood a long moment, staring at the podium.

In the hall, murmurs of unease.

I gripped the lectern, with knuckles turned white. At the front table, my son P.T. gazed upward, trusting and proud.

I raised my head. "—thank you for the honor you wish to confer." I searched the audience, for a face that might understand.

"You would fete my moral leadership. Yet last winter I approved revision of the Charities Tax Act, benefiting the Von Walthers Foundation, among others. I knew that bestowal of this award was contemplated as a result. In what I can only describe as an act of moral negligence, I allowed my nomination to proceed."

Gasps, from throughout the hall.

In the front row, Philip watched, his lips parted as if to protest. Jared's hand slid across, protectively grasped his.

"Am I, overall, an evil man? I think not, yet I allowed political revenge to dictate the seating of this banquet. Mr. Sec-Gen Kahn, you should have been seated more prominently, and would have been, had I not interfered. Mr. Rothstein, though you are a director of the Von Walthers Foundation, I had you removed from the dais for your opposition to the wheat tariff bill. I apologize to you both for my moral lapse."

"Mr. SecGen, don't!" Jerence Branstead's hiss carried from the dais.

"Rumor has it that the Von Walthers Award has been politicized before. So be it. That is no excuse for my participating in a tawdry sham."

Murmurs, that stilled to shocked silence.

I swallowed a lump in my throat. "As I've sat here with an old shipmate, in the presence of my son of whom I'm immensely proud, and a fine boy who was once my cadet, I've been reminded of what once, decades past, I strove to become. It's too late to be that person. But I can make a token effort to redeem myself. So, you see, if I have any pretense to moral decency, I cannot accept an award for moral leadership. I decline the honor you would do me tonight."

I gazed serenely at the holocams. "Thank you for your intentions. May Lord God bless you all."

Grasping my cane, I limped from the silent hall.

4

We were gathered in my luxurious Hilton suite. Spacious portholes overlooked UNS *Galactic*, and beyond it, the immense sphere of Earth.

Jerence Branstead slumped, head in hands.

Arlene made a place for herself on the arm of my settee. "Ah, Nicky. Will you ever change?"

I snorted. "Not likely." Not at this late date.

"It's a shame. Aside from your Puritan morals you're a pretty decent joey."

Scandalized, I glanced about. Though I respected her criticism, she rarely went at me in public. True, I thought of Branstead and Alexi almost as family, but . . .

Alexi blew his nose.

I snapped, "For heaven's—this isn't a wake!"

"It might as well be," said Branstead. "Politically." His penetrating gray eyes settled on mine.

I waved it away. "It doesn't matter." The Patriarchs would put paid to my account in a very few days. But Jerence and Arlene didn't know, and I didn't care to tell them. There was no way I could criticize the Elder without disparaging the Church itself, and that I was loath to do. It would put me in conflict with Lord God Himself.

"It was such a fine moment, sir." Alexi. "Why ruin it?"

"It's not your concern." I spoke before thinking. "Sorry, you deserve better." Wearily, I leaned back, resting my head, wishing Philip had chosen to join our gathering, but he'd told Arlene he wanted to be alone, and disappeared from the auditorium. "I've become rather imperious of late. Surely you've all noticed. You should have stopped me."

"We tried." Branstead's tone was wry.

"It's as if I treat my office as a right. I get so impatient with the fools who block our progress." I sighed, wishing I had words to explain. "When I first took office, the scars of the alien bombing were still raw." Cities obliterated, the populace in shock that our brave conquest of the stars had sown such havoc.

"And then, my second Administration, after the Transpop Rebellion . . ." New York had been in flames, and unrest had spread to Chicago, Detroit, London.

As a Naval officer, as a civilian, I'd been a war hero, then peacemaker. But as SecGen I'd labored to restore the damage, ease the world's economic strains. To quell emotion, to keep us on the steady path to recovery. In the process I constantly traveled the globe, offering myself as solace to those overcome by incessant disaster. The Berlin spew, the New Orleans flood, the Kiev meltdown . . . would it never cease?

No. It seemed a crowded, injured world took chances, too many of them, to restore its faltering economy. But I showed myself, exposing myself to fouled air, cholera-ravaged homeless, polluted waters, raging fires, doing what I could to galvanize the machinery of Government. Over and again I'd toured the cities of Earth, letting myself be seen, touched, heard, in contrast to my aloof predecessor, SecGen Kahn.

In foreign affairs, I rebuilt our relations with our many colonies, disgruntled at abandonment in their moment of need when the remorseless fish were attacking so many outposts. I'd altered the exchange rate in their favor, to encourage their industries and promote trade.

And, throughout, I'd told the truth, an unvarying policy that eventually earned the world's begrudging trust.

And yet, I'd handled so many matters so poorly. "I suppose, as we age," I said, "we all yearn to be young again, to have more life before us. But that's not quite how I feel. What I really want is to go back and change whom I've become. But that's impossible, and it drives me mad."

"Someone tell him." Alexi spoke to the wall, as if afraid to meet my eye. "If anyone should have pride in whom he's become, it's he."

"I'm not proud of myself of late."

"Bah. You never have been."

"Those acts you call heroic—"

Jerence said, "You're as wrong about yourself now as you ever were."

"Oh, nonsense. I know I abused you as a child, and as for *Trafalgar*—"

"God damn it, you listen to me!" Branstead's voice was hard. I gaped at his blasphemy, but he paid no heed. "Where would I be if not for you? Dead, or in a prison colony pining for goofjuice!" The horribly addictive drug had seized him as a boy, and he'd writhed in its clutches, until I'd encouraged his escape.

A fourteen-year-old joeykid swam before me, on the fastship *Victoria*. He put his hand for comfort in mine. "I swear on my immortal soul that I . . . won't . . . ever use . . . goofjuice again." He was weeping. "It was so hard, Mr. Seafort. So hard!"

But he'd done it. And made a life to be proud of.

"And me." Alexi's voice was soft. "If not for you, Mr. Seafort, what would I be?"

"As you are now. Recovered from your troubles, a successful officer—"

"You taught me how to be an officer. Then you taught me again."

"Alexi, I had little to do—"

His words were almost a whisper. "Don't discredit what you were to me. And still are."

I threw up my arms. "I don't know what to say."

Arlene tentatively raised a hand, like a joeykid at school. "That you're wrong, and you're sorry?"

Lord God, how do I deserve friends such as these?

I bowed my head.

An hour later, our company gone, Arlene settled across the room. She regarded me warily. "Nicky, what in God's name is troubling you? No, don't look away. It's time we . . ." She swallowed. "Tell me."

"It's . . ." My heart pounded.

"Say it."

"There's a woman. I—we've been in love."

For a moment her eyes closed, as if in some unbearable pain. Then, with resolve, "Is she beautiful?"

I studied her, wondering how much more she could be hurt. "Yes. Lord God, yes."

A moan.

"Blue eyes, auburn hair . . ."

Her tone was bitter. "You've known her long?"

I forced myself to meet her eyes. "Finding her was the miracle of my . . ." My throat caught. "I abhor myself for not doing more for her. I've loved her since I was sixteen, and I still don't know what I'd do without—"

"Oh, Nicky!" She flew across the carpet, threw herself into my arms.

I wrapped myself around her, breathing in her fragrance, exulting in the sturdy beat of her heart. "I'm sorry, my love. I'm so sorry." I could say no more. "So sorry."

From the porthole of our launch, UNS *Galactic* was a disappointment. She was large, but not all that immense. Her lights beamed from her mooring a kilometer or so from Earthport Station. Actually, she wasn't moored; she merely floated at rest relative to the Station.

Galactic was too vast to be accommodated at Earthport's usual locks; she would block five bays at a time. The Station's extension bay at which she and her sister ship would dock wasn't completed yet. A minor inconvenience, all told.

The starship had four launches and two gigs, to carry passengers back and forth. Her middies must be beside themselves, striving to earn the boon of piloting between Station and ship. In fact, a gig was just setting off; its running lights glowed green and white. Utterly dwarfed by *Galactic*, it steered a course for a Station bay.

Alexi, Arlene, and I had boarded *Galactic*'s launch from one of the Naval locks. A night's sleep hadn't changed my mind that I'd acted appropriately at the Von Walthers banquet. A pity I hadn't come to my senses earlier, and refused the nomination.

Some idiot had arranged for mediamen to record our jaunt from Earthport, and their shouted questions still echoed in my ears.

"Mr. SecGen, have you seen the polls?"

"How long did you plan—"

"Is this the start of your reelection camp—"

"Did you mean to set an example for the Assembly?"

The hiss of a sliding hatch had restored blessed silence.

We decelerated, as our pilot began his approach to *Galactic*'s launch bay. Off our starboard bow, the gig floated toward the Station.

I caught my breath. That wasn't a gig, it was another launch, several times a gig's size. That meant . . .

Suddenly, I saw *Galactic* in perspective. If her launch looked like a gnat on a bison, she was truly gigantic. I pressed my forehead to the porthole, straining to take in her glory. At last, I leaned back, assimilating what I'd seen. Arlene squeezed my hand.

"What I'd give to have her," said Alexi.

I nodded agreement. Any Captain would give his right arm for the posting; I wondered again what influence had swayed Admiralty in Stanger's favor. Perhaps I should have taken a stronger role in the selection. *Galactic* was the Navy's greatest vessel, the largest ever built. Only her sister ship *Olympiad*, still under construction, would be comparable.

As if reading my mind, Alexi said, "They could have built ten starships for the cost."

I nodded.

"Well, no doubt she'll satisfy the hotheads." He turned to the porthole. "Sorry, shouldn't meddle in politics."

Almost, I let it go. "What are you saying, Alexi?"

"Surely you've heard the talk. The Navy's mission of destiny. Lifeline to the colonies. Earth's ungrateful children, that sort of rubbish." His eyes roamed the distant hull. "Lord, she's big."

"How will *Galactic*—"

"Oh, just by being there. An unstated threat, should one be necessary." He made a vague gesture.

"Is that sort of talk common?"

"Common enough. I didn't mean to tell tales out of school." A placating gesture. "It's just . . . well, we've grown so dependent on imports, it makes joeys nervous." He smiled. "Captains on a long cruise have too much time to brood."

I knew that was so.

"Look, sir, the launch bay hatches are open. The ship's so massive you can barely see the bay."

I joined him at the porthole. Behind us, Arlene watched quietly, her face without expression.

The pilot began braking maneuvers.

Soon our vessel inched into the launch bay. At last the capture latches clicked into place, and the huge outer hatch slid shut behind us. A short wait, while the bay was pressurized. Naturally, as on any ship, there was a lock between the bay and the working areas of the ship, but one didn't want to herd passengers about in suits if it was avoidable, so the bay was normally kept aired.

We climbed down, cycled through the lock to the Level 3 corridor.

A voice roared, "Stand to!"

Twenty-two officers resplendent in dress whites stiffened to attention. At their head, Captain Stanger snapped an Academy salute. Despite myself, my heart quickened.

"Gentlemen, as you were."

Stanger stepped forward smartly. "Welcome to *Galactic*, Mr. SecGen."

"Thank you." I glanced about. All circumference corridors had a curve, but *Galactic*'s was far less pronounced than on any ship I'd known. Her disks were far wider, so that was to be expected, but it gave the ship a sense of grandeur and luxury I hadn't expected.

Arlene's eye flitted about. "Good Lord."

I understood her awe. The typical ship's corridors were painted Naval gray, but here the corridor was richly detailed in wood tones, with an astonishing amount of intricately molded trim. Hatch surrounds were outlined in gold.

I looked down, scandalized. "Carpeting? On a corridor deck?" Corridors had riveted plates throughout. Always.

"We're on Level 3, sir. Passenger country. Level 1 is more what you're used to."

I scuffed my feet on the obscenely soft material. After a moment I relaxed enough to grin at Arlene. "She's something, isn't she?" Almost, I didn't regret the cost.

Alexi said, "She puts *Hibernia* to shame."

"Hmpff." Loyalty made me frown.

The officers seemed suspiciously young. My eye flitted among shoulder stripes and length of service pins. "Lord in heaven, how many middies do you berth?"

"Eleven, sir."

"All in a wardroom?"

"Not exactly. We call it one, but it's divvied into two compartments."

The first middy would have his hands full, if *Galactic* was like any ship I'd ever known. I'd found it a trial to keep track of three middies. Ten subordinates would be . . .

"Who's first?"

"Mr. Speke, step forward."

A lanky joey strode from among his fellows, saluted. "Midshipman Edwin Speke reporting, sir."

I glanced at his service pins. "Six years." Plenty of experience. Useful. But why hadn't he made lieutenant? Well, six years as middy wasn't all that long. Eyebrows wouldn't begin to be raised for another year or so.

One by one Captain Stanger introduced his lieutenants, who all seemed eager to shake my hand. I wondered how many of them would still brag of meeting me, after my coming disgrace by the Patriarchs.

"Shall we visit the bridge, sir?"

"Please." I had to negotiate the shoals of protocol. Even as SecGen, I had no right of command in Stanger's ship; the Navy took its chain of command most seriously indeed. He and his crew had come to attention before me as a courtesy, not an obligation.

A ship could have but one Captain, and Stanger was he. No civilian, even the Commander in Chief and head of Government, could legitimately issue a direct order on ship. Even an Admiral was required to operate through his subordinate Captain, who had actual responsibility for the vessel. The Admiral's recourse was to remove a Captain who offended; even an Admiral couldn't countermand his Captain's orders.

It was well this was so. The Navy survived by maintaining an absolutely clear line of authority.

Ultimately, I could have *Galactic*'s crew do as I wished, but only by issuing directives to Admiralty, and having their orders filter through the chain of command. Of course, in practical terms a request from me had the effect of a direct order. No sailor in his right mind would alienate the SecGen.

We started down the corridor, several officers trailing behind.

Like any starship, *Galactic* was composed of disks. Imagine a series of foam rubber circles, stacked one on top of another. Then picture a rather thick old-fashioned pencil stuck through the center of the disks. The part of the pencil forward of the disks contained the voluminous cargo holds that justified the ship's existence. Aft, below the disks, were the fusion drive chambers that generated the N-wave that drove the ship. But the disks were where passengers and crew worked and lived.

Most starships contained two levels, or three. *Galactic* had six, and they were huge. Through the middle of each disk ran a circular circumference corridor, divided into nominal east and west. The disks were connected by stairwells, which by Naval terminology were ladders.

"I feel . . ." I couldn't say it aloud, even to Arlene. I felt more at home on this ship, unfamiliar as she was, than ever I'd be in the corridors of the Rotunda.

Why can we not retreat to what was? More to the point, why had I ever abandoned life as a Captain? I sighed.

Stanger stopped abruptly at a hatch, slapped the panel. The midshipmen continued on until they were beyond the corridor curve.

A hatch slid open. I gaped. "Elevators, in a starship?"

"For passengers, mostly. Remember, we have six levels." He smiled. "The lifts are off-limits to middies."

"I would hope." How soft would the Navy grow, if middies rode elevators from level to level? Why, in my day . . .

"Shall we?"

I asked brusquely, "Do you normally ride?"

"No, sir. But . . ." His eye flicked to my cane.

That did it. "Neither do I." I stalked down the corridor.

The ladder was farther than I'd thought. Surely the stair to

Level 2 was no steeper than usual. Lips tight, I negotiated the steps, transferring as much weight to the rail as I could. As I climbed, though, my discomfort lessened. At the top of the ladder, on Level 2, I felt almost light-headed.

Stanger read my mind. "We have three gravitron units. They're intended to mesh, but I keep the bow units set low. About a third gee. It's better for our health."

"Is it?"

He shrugged. "I like it that way." As Captain, he could set them as he chose. Light gravity *was* rather refreshing, once you got used to it. Most unusual; a ship such as *Hibernia* had but one set of gravitrons.

We climbed to Level 1. It was, as Stanger had said, more as I'd expected. Gray bulkheads, alloy plate decking. Utilitarian. To my eye, comfortable.

A quarter of the way around the long corridor, we came to the bridge. Stanger slapped open the thickened hatch. A bridge was built like a fortress; if sealed from within, only a heavy cutting rig could penetrate it.

The watch officer jumped from his console, stood at attention.

"As you were." Automatically, Stanger glanced at the console readouts. My own eye was drawn to the simulscreen that dominated the front bulkhead. As on any bridge, it provided a view of the stars, as seen from the ship's prow. But most ships weren't moored just off Earthport Station. The view from *Galactic* was beyond spectacular. It was breathtaking.

"Mr. SecGen, Ms. Seafort: First Lieutenant Garrow."

I grunted, still lost in the Station's blaze of lights.

"An honor to meet you, sir."

"Of course." After a moment I tore myself from the simulscreen, realized what I'd said. "I mean . . ." I flushed. "Sorry. You've been on ship long, Lieutenant?"

"I came from *Seville* two weeks before commissioning."

I forced myself to concentrate. "Captain Stanger's last command." I'd read as much, in a briefing.

Stanger drifted to the hatch. "I brought Garrow with me. A good man. Would you like a brief tour, Mr. SecGen?"

"Very well." Reluctantly, glancing behind, we followed him from the bridge. Two middies tagged along, apparently at the Captain's behest.

The dining hall on Level 2 was elegant beyond words; its decor would have been suitable in the finest French restaurant in Lunapolis. Alexi and I exchanged skeptical glances. "Rather ornate," he allowed.

I tried to count the tables. If *Galactic* carried three thousand passengers . . . "Mr. Stanger, surely you don't hold two seatings?"

"No, this is only first class. Most passengers are served in the second dining hall below. We—"

I spluttered, "First *class?*" In all my Naval years, it had been a proud axiom: the Navy traveled with but one class of passenger. While wealthier joeys could buy certain amenities, such as parties and receptions in the lounges, passenger cabins were all the same size, and meals were alike.

"It's not really a class, sir, it's—"

"Why wasn't I told of this?"

"I don't know, sir."

"Show me the other dining hall."

Grimly, we proceeded two levels down the ladder.

Alexi scowled at the pressed celulex tables, the rows of straight chairs. "Hah. Not really a class?"

I muttered, "Inexcusable." Compared to the opulent first class dining hall, the compartment was dreary and utilitarian.

Arlene gave my hand a warning squeeze, but her eyes said she was as disgusted as I.

I shook my head. "I'll be paying Admiralty a visit." I rounded on Captain Stanger. "I suppose the cabins are equally classless?"

"There are differences among them." Stanger's tone was frosty. "Remember, Mr. SecGen, that I'm not the architect."

I wasn't about to be mollified. "You, of course, dine on Level 2?"

"It's nearer the bridge."

"But of course." My tone dripped contempt.

The two middies exchanged glances.

"Easy, sir." Alexi touched my arm.

"It's an outrage." He and Arlene were right: there was no point in alienating Stanger, but . . . the Captain wasn't even ashamed of the disgraceful arrangements. Still, I'd treated him poorly in front of his own midshipmen. For the sake of ship's discipline I tried to rein in my ire. "No need to drag you about the ship; a middy will suffice. You, there. Speke, is it? Would you care to show us the engine room?"

"With the Captain's permission." A touch insolent, perhaps, but technically correct. It was Stanger's ship, not mine.

Stanger nodded his consent. Then, to me, "Would you care to lunch with us before you leave?"

"No, thank you. We have a shuttle to catch." Not quite true; our shuttle for Von Walthers would depart when we were ready. Earthport was in geosync over the southeastern Americas, so we need not be concerned with an entry window. Still, I doubted I'd enjoy a meal in a galley masquerading as a luxury hotel.

The Captain's face was wooden. "As you wish. I'll have the launch crew stand by." Another salute, and he left us.

Perhaps Midshipman Speke had taken umbrage at my dismissal of Stanger; he was distinctly cool as we went about our tour. It annoyed me enough so that obstinately, after the engine room, I asked to see more. Arlene looked about with interest; she'd been a lieutenant for a number of years in one of the Navy's proudest ships.

"This way, sir." Speke's tone was sullen. Well, if that was his attitude, no wonder he hadn't made lieutenant.

I had the middy lead us to the comm room—an impressive establishment, bristling with radionics and sensors—and then an elegant passenger lounge, complete with ornate bronze statuary. With every step, I was more uneasy, more sure the Navy had made a grave miscalculation.

Galactic was stunning, there was no denying it. But the Navy was in the transport business, not the hotel trade. A voyage could last well over a year; *Galactic*'s cruise to the new colony of Constantine would take a full nineteen months. On such long voyages class distinctions ought to be suppressed, not encouraged, else they would fester, and resentments burst forth.

I asked, "Where are hydros?" Despite her capacious holds, the starship would depend to a large degree on the produce of her hydroponics chambers.

Speke said, "Below, on Level 6."

I gaped at Alexi, but he had seen it too. The impatient middy had rolled his eyes. Alexi shook his head. I knew what he was thinking: on *Melbourne,* or for that matter, on any ship of mine, a middy who showed such disrespect would be brought up short. Well, *Galactic* was Stanger's to command. I wouldn't interfere.

Passing cabin after cabin, we trudged down the sumptuous corridor toward the hydroponics chamber, my knee aching. We passed an airlock, one of half a dozen the ship boasted. Two seamen waited for the entry light to go green, stiff and awkward in their pressure suits.

Alexi said, "Hullo, what's this?"

The young middy's voice was cool. "Machinist's mates, sir. I believe they're checking another sensor."

"Problems?"

"Four external airlock sensors have gone bad so far." That sort of thing happened, especially on a new ship. That's why *Galactic* tarried so long in home system after her commissioning. Speke shook his head. "Shoddy Navy parts." I bit back a savage reply.

By the time we'd looked at the rows of tomatoes, legumes, and greens growing in East Hydros, I'd walked as much as I could tolerate. We started back to the launch berth.

At the Level 3 launch bay lock, I opened the inner hatch from the corridor panel. "That will be all, Mr. Speke."

Alexi cleared his throat. "Middy, please give Mr. Stanger a message."

"Yes, sir?" The boy waited.

Alexi's voice was stern. "Tell him Captain Tamarov is offended by your behavior, and wishes to call it to his attention."

The middy gulped. "Aye, sir."

I whistled under my breath. The boy was in for it now. At twenty, he was by custom too old to be caned, but he'd have to work off demerits as would any other middy. If I were his commander, he'd get a full ten demerits, for the folly of irking a fellow Captain. Each required two hours of hard exercise.

I'd been prepared to let the matter go, but Alexi wasn't so charitable. Well, coming off a ship of the line, he expected shipboard discipline. No doubt, on *Melbourne,* he got it, though Alexi was one of the most kindhearted souls I knew.

Still, I hesitated. It was I who'd kindled Speke's resentment in the first place, by being so brusque with Stanger. Nonetheless, I'd see ten midshipmen caned before I'd alienate my oldest friend. I flashed Alexi a glance of apology. "Your outrage is warranted, Captain Tamarov." I favored the hapless middy with a steely glare. "Tell me, Mr., ah, Speke. Can you imagine making Captain?"

"Um—I . . ." It was every midshipman's dream. "Yes, sir."

"And if one of your middies—no doubt a good joey at heart—went about sulky and sullen, sighing under his breath, rolling his eyes . . . You'd be pleased?"

"No, sir." He reddened.

"And this in front of a distinguished Captain and the Sec-Gen?"

"No, sir." He was sweating.

"You were annoyed, perhaps, that I was curt with Captain Stanger?"

"I—there was no—it's none of my business, sir."

"Ahh." My glance softened. "Perhaps I might prevail on Mr. Tamarov to countermand his order?"

Glowering, Alexi nodded.

"Very well, no need to report the matter to Stanger. But joey . . . think on it."

The boy's gratitude was pathetic. "I will, sir. Thank you. Please forgive me."

"Good lad." Out of habit, I saluted, and automatically, he stiffened to return it.

In silence, we passed through the lock.

"I wish I'd been at the banquet." Derek Carr lounged on the soft blue divan in my Washington living room, swirling his drink. "After you left the hall, the media were at a loss. I've never heard such blather on the nets." His sharp blue eyes met mine. "Though you shouldn't have done it."

"I had to."

"Why? Because you're not perfect?"

"I'm much less than that."

On the couch opposite, Arlene lounged with Alexi. Though they'd never known each other in the Service, they'd hit it off from the moment they'd met, years ago. In fact, during the Transpop Rebellion, we'd stayed with Alexi and his wife, Moira, while searching for Philip. They'd had one toddler, I recalled, and another joeykid on the way.

Again I wished P.T. were with us, but he'd left word in response to my query. He needed time, he said, to assimilate what I'd done. I knew my refusal of the Von Walthers hurt him deeply, though I wasn't sure why.

Alexi sipped at his scotch. "I haven't followed the news. What's the line?"

Derek grinned. "First word was that the SecGen's glitched and should resign. But then they read the early polls."

"And?"

"I'd say he got away with it. The newsies go on about his unyielding moral rectitude, his refusal to compromise, his—"

"So, Mr. SecGen." Alexi raised his glass in mock salute. "You'll hold the Rotunda awhile yet."

"No." It was time I told them. "In a few days it'll be over."

Arlene gazed at my face, silent, waiting.

"I—it's—you see . . ." I hadn't expected it to be so hard. A deep breath. "The Patriarchs intend to disavow me."

"Why?"

"Because of the Navy. Colonial affairs. No, that's not it. The real issue is that I refuse to support Mother Church. They want me to coerce the colonies into economic and social submission, and I refused. But they're right, you see. They have to be." For some unfathomable reason, my eyes stung. "They represent Lord God. Only a fool would oppose His will."

"But you're not that." Alexi set down his drink. "Sir, they've no right to—"

"Be silent!" I slapped the table with open palm. "Not another word!" He'd come close to blasphemy, and perhaps damnation.

"No." Alexi gave an apologetic smile. "We're past that, you and I. I'm long since adult, and a Captain. I take responsibility for my acts. If the Patriarchs condemn you, they're wrong. It's that simple."

Derek uncurled himself from the divan. "Does Branstead know? Has he started to fight? Plant stories in zines, get out the word that—"

"He doesn't know, and we'll do no such thing." My tone was firm. "They've every right to censure me. And even— no, let me finish—even supposing they're wrong, if you think I'd raise my hand against them, you know me not at all."

Silence.

"Besides . . ." I made my tone more reasonable. "I'll re- tire at last. You've no idea how much I want out of office."

Abruptly, Arlene got to her feet, padded to the door.

"What's up, hon?"

"I'll make tea." She disappeared into the hall.

"Excuse me." Perhaps she wanted tea, but that wasn't all. "Hon?" I followed into the bright-lit kitchen. "What is it?"

"Nothing, Nick. You have enough troubles." She set a ce- ramic pot in the micro. "Until it boils," she told it.

"Go on, hon."

"Retirement."

"I look forward to it so much."

Her gaze was speculative. "You've said that for years. When did it stop being true?"

"What? How can—I've always dreamed of—"

"You meant it at first. The night you announced for re- election, atop the Franjee Tower, you almost wept. When did it change?"

"It didn't!"

"Swear it, Nick. By Lord God."

"Of course I do. I—"

"Say the words."

"Oh, Arlene . . . By Lord God Himself, I swear to you, I yearn . . ." I faltered.

"Water boiling." The micro lapsed silent.

I blurted, "I don't know when. Until tonight, I didn't real- ize . . ." I met her gaze. "I like being SecGen. I want to hold on to office. I like the power. And I'm good at it; I make de- cisions and get them carried out. It's like being Captain

again; when I speak, joeys jump. That's Lord God's truth."
My smile was bitter. "See what I've become?"

"It's important you see also."

"Why?"

"So you can have what you want. Let's fight them."

"No. Tell me, what do *you* want?"

"A cup of Darjeeling." She busied herself with the pot.
"All right, that's not honest. I hoped you'd retire, because I
thought that's what you wanted. I can make a life for myself
either way, Nick." Suddenly her eyes teared. "I always
have."

"Oh, hon." I drew close.

She fended me off with a palm. "If we're to tell truth . . .
You love me, I think, though sometimes I'm not sure. But
you don't need me. I've stayed busy. I raised Philip, and did
a damn fine job of it. So did you; we were good parents,
weren't we? I wish he were still young."

She sipped at her tea, made a face. "I played at First Lady
when I had to. I've read, and gone back to school; you know
how proud I was of my doctorate." She paused, reflecting.

"Arlene . . ."

"But for years . . . I've been marking time. I have a few
friends, but not many." She stared into her cup. "So we'll
leave the Rotunda for good. It's all right. It's just . . . *Galactic* reminded me of my years on *Wellington*, and what it was
like to see other worlds. Of the life I lost."

I whispered, "You too?"

"More than you'll ever know." She lifted her tea, splashed
the counter, set it down. "Damn. Sorry. But—damn!" She
fled to the hall. "Say good night for me."

"Hon—"

"Please, Nick!" She was gone.

"Booker's disappeared from the face of the Earth." Mark
Tilnitz looked grim. "We've searched, Naval Intelligence is
hunting, U.N. Security has pulled out all the stops."

"And?" I tapped my desk, wishing I'd held the meeting in the comfort of my Washington compound, but I'd hoped the formality of my Rotunda office would spur the world's security forces to greater effort.

"We're falling all over each other," Karen Burns said, "and getting nowhere."

General Donner glowered. As head of U.N. Security Forces, he was nominally Mark's boss, but he knew that in reality Mark was answerable only to me. "We've run analyses on the two manifestos. We think one person wrote them both."

"That's a great help." I sounded too sarcastic, and regretted it.

"The joey in the terminal was Brian Keltek," said Tilnitz. "From Vancouver, a metallurgist for BP Shell. A loner, no surviving family. Father was a fisherman until the North Pacific die-off."

"The fish kill wasn't our fault. The temperature inversion had nothing to do with global warming." Why did I sound defensive?

"A number of scientists agree with you. Keltek contributed to the Enviro Council for seven years." Mark regarded me steadily.

"It figures." Let them claim what they might; Winstead headed a gang of loonies.

Captain Binn of U.N.A.F. Security asked, "Does this Keltek have friends? Associates?"

"Neighbors. Naturally, they saw nothing."

"Now, look." My tone was sharp. "A man can't just disappear unless he goes transpop. There's hotel records, travel vouchers, credit billings—"

"Don't tell me my job." Donner was blunt. "We're working on it."

Captain Binn demanded, "Who knew the SecGen would visit Academy?"

Tilnitz said, "We've been over that. The Commandant,

two of his lieutenants, the SecGen's security detail. The media wasn't informed until he was on the way. That's routine."

"The Eco Action League manifesto referred to the Sec-Gen at Academy. That means a leak."

I rubbed my temples, hoping to soothe the first intimations of a headache. "Anyone could have known. Once we announced it to the media . . ."

"Lots of enviro sympathizers in that bunch." Mark sounded gloomy. "We're checking."

"This is nonsense." I flipped off my holovid. "These Eco League joeys are glitched. They're throwbacks to some other century. We simply don't *have* terrorism anymore."

"I know, sir. Perhaps we imagined the gunshots." Tilnitz withstood my withering glare.

I suppressed an urge to pull out my hair. "What about the airport joey's car? The driver?"

"The electricar was stolen the morning of the attack. No clues. We've taken it apart looking for prints or DNA, but all we get is the owner's."

"Find the Eco League. We're running out of time."

"Time?" Mark looked puzzled. "How so?"

I cursed under my breath. Nobody in the room knew about my impending dismissal, and I couldn't tell them. Only fear of my impatience would spur them on. "The E.A.L. may attack again," I said. "Worse, every day that passes sends a message to the public that we can't catch fugitives. This isn't some untamed colony, it's Earth itself." I stood. "We meet again in two days. I want results."

The massive jet droned toward New York, my third trip this week. I might as well move there, I thought disgustedly.

Charlie Witrek, my middy, sat across from us, reading a holozine. As always, he was immaculately groomed.

Alexi sat comfortably at my side. He was hitching a ride back to Moira, he said, though I knew he had come along to provide moral support for my showdown with the Patriarchs.

Derek would have joined us as well, but with the Patriarchs' attitude toward our colonies, I wanted him out of harm's way. Lord knew what the Elders might do at the sight of him.

Hope Nation was no longer a colony, thanks to my highhandedness years before. Derek's government had maintained its independence through several SecGens, despite unrelenting pressure from the Church. Perhaps, if the Patriarchs had their way, *Galactic* might someday appear over Centraltown, bristling with lasers, to reassert our control over a free people.

I sighed.

Alexi said, "What's wrong, sir?"

"It won't be my problem much longer."

A pause. "Sometimes you're too cryptic even for me."

Across the aisle, Charlie Witrek nodded emphatically.

I couldn't help but smile. "Hope Nation, I meant."

Alexi said, "What will you do after, ah, you retire?"

"After I'm dismissed? Travel, I suppose." If they let me.

"Sir, I know you're worried they might—"

"Why do you keep calling me 'sir'? You have more seniority than I ever did."

"Would you rather I called you 'Mr. SecGen'?"

" 'Nick.' "

A moment's silence. "I never called you that."

"Start."

"I don't think I could." He waved his glass at a steward, waited until his drink was poured. "It'd be sacrilege."

I frowned. Lord God shouldn't be taken lightly.

"You never cease to amaze me, you know." A long sip. "When we were young, you'd have reamed that middy Speke so he never dared to be rude again." He stared at his liquor. "We were terrified of crossing you, back on *Hibernia*. You had a way about you."

Charlie slowly put down his holovid, all ears.

"I was harsh."

"When needed. But you were gentle with Captain Stanger's middy."

I stirred uncomfortably, as if at an accusation. "We'd provoked him, and he was too young to deal with it."

"He'll revere you now." A bleak smile. "You've mellowed, sir. Kindness comes easily to you."

"Preposterous." I frowned at the porthole, while we droned over billowy clouds.

"Those joeys who come to stare at your compound wall—why do you think they do it?"

"They're deluded."

"You offer them a hope. Of what they might be."

"Bah. All this from not making Speke turn himself in?"

"Of course not. It's your honesty, your refusal to dodge blame . . . I've tried to raise my Mikhael in that mold." Alexi sighed. "I've work to do yet."

"Problems?"

"He's fifteen. Should I have brought him on *Melbourne*? I wanted him to have a normal life. After my last cruise, Moira and I agreed to raise the joeykids at home." His eyes were moody. "I don't think it worked."

"If there's anything I—"

"It's my problem." But he brightened. "There, you see, sir? You're SecGen, the busiest man in the world, and without thinking, you offer yourself."

"It's only words." There was nothing I could do for his son, and I knew it. People made too much of polite phrases. Then, before I had time to stop myself, "Alexi, why don't you bring the family to Washington? Stay with us awhile." What was I doing? He needed time alone with them, to rebuild relations. "You could stay in the cottage, if you prefer."

He brightened. "I'll ask Moira." Then, after a pause, "For

all these years I've treasured you as a friend, more than you can ever know. But I'll continue to call you 'sir.' "

I stared out the porthole. Slowly, as if by its own volition, my hand stole across and settled on his arm.

"I thought you were going home to Moira." We clumped along the walkway, in the shadows of the U.N. towers.

"After you meet with Bishop Saythor."

"I've Jerence, Carlotti, and Witrek, here—a whole bloody squadron. Look at them!" Behind us, ahead, alongside, some twenty-five aides, security joeys, and flunkies hurried to keep pace.

Charlie said brightly, "I could have stayed home, sir. You wanted me along to—"

"I was wrong." My tone was gentle.

Alexi's face closed into a stubborn mask. "I'll see you through your meeting."

I nodded, knowing what outcome he feared. It would, no doubt, be a short conclave. This time, I'd have no choice but to face the baying pack of media gathered on the front steps. My disavowal by the Patriarchs would be world news. Many in my own Supranationalist Party, I suspected, would be glad. Too long, I'd barred the way to their ambition.

We negotiated the steps. Perhaps I should let the doctors have at my knee. Old age would soon be upon me. There was no reason to go through it in pain. I nodded grimly at the mediamen.

"Sir?" Alexi paused, to let me go first through the massive doors Charlie held. We strode down the ornate hall. "You could buy time, you know."

I stopped, leaned against a marble column. "I won't prevaricate." And if I found Elder Saythor in my seat, I'd evict him. By force, if necessary. I gripped my cane.

"Consider a strategic retreat." Alexi spoke with urgency. "Tell them you'll look favorably . . . hell, you know the words better than I. Tell them you'll—"

Whump!

Alexi receded toward the far wall, as if seen through a zoom lens in reverse. A thump shook my chest. I sought breath, found none. The room tilted. I slammed into a lamp, crashed to the floor, skidded to the wall. My head slammed into a panel. The day dimmed.

Pandemonium.

It was time to get up. I had chores to do, and Father would be annoyed. I reached for my shoes.

"Don't try to move, sir." The voice was far distant.

My arms flailed as I struggled to get out of bed. Pain lanced my side. I tried to wiggle my toes. My legs were asleep.

Blood dripped onto my forehead. *"DON'T MOVE, MR. SECGEN!"* Why was Mark Tilnitz in Father's house? Why was he bleeding? I wiped my brow.

"Where's the fucking ambulance?"

I strained to hear. My ears were clogged.

"It's landing on the lawn." Jerence Branstead, weeping.

"Shape up, Cadet." My growl was barely audible.

"Stand back, all of you! Give him room! Karen, how many dead?"

I blinked, trying to bring the room into focus. Gingerly, my fingers probed my side, came away red.

"Four, so far."

"The SecGen gets the first ambulance."

"The med helis hold three—"

"You heard me. Where in God's name is a gurney?"

"They'll have their own. Easy, Mr. Tilnitz."

"Easy, hell! If I'd shielded him as I was supposed to . . ."

"Mark . . ." I struggled for breath. "What happened?"

"You're hurt, sir. A bomb."

I laughed, and coughed up salty blood. "And they missed? Incompetent idiots."

The clatter of running footsteps.

"The column blocked the blast. Please, sir, don't try to talk."

"Why not? It may be my last chance."

"Don't say that!" His tone was agonized. "You, this way! It's the SecGen!"

Strangers bent over me. "His side, any foreign objects protruding? Bind it. Sir, can you feel this?"

I gasped. "Christ, yes!" Sorry, Lord, but it hurt so.

"Move your fingers, if you would."

I did.

"And your toes."

I did.

"Try again." A pause. "Don't lift him. Slip the stretcher underneath. Careful, an inch at a time. Sir, you've lost blood, we're starting an IV."

"Tell Arlene I . . ." It seemed too much trouble. Anyway, she knew. I closed my eyes, let black claim me.

5

My mind was clouded. Joeys leaned over me to ask incomprehensible questions. I slept, woke again. Arlene sat alongside me, holding my hand. Sharp pain. I groaned. Someone adjusted a tube. I slept.

I drifted back from a far place.

"Where am I?" My throat was so dry I could barely make a sound. I licked my lips.

A white-clad nurse turned from the holovid that helped pass her vigil. "At Boland Memorial, sir." She held a cup so I could drink from a straw. Never had water tasted so good.

I struggled for memory. "A bomb went off." A sudden panic. "Mark Tilnitz?"

"Outside. He's taken over the floor. We all have special passes." She showed me hers, pinned to her tunic.

"How long have I . . ."

"Four days."

"Lord God above." I tried to throw off the covers. Something stabbed at my side. "I have work waiting."

"Lie back, Mr. SecGen." She spoke urgently into a caller.

"Where's Branstead? What's on my schedule?" Tubes snaked from under the covers. Others were attached to my veins. "Unhook me."

"Wait, sir. I've called the doctor."

I tried to swing my legs out of bed, but couldn't. "Am I tied? Help me up."

The door burst open. "He's awake? Good. Sir, I'm Dr. Rains." He wore the white coat that was the uniform of his profession.

"Hello. Let me out of here."

"Sit back, Mr. Seafort." It was a command, sharp enough to give me pause. Gently but firmly, he helped me ease back onto my pillows. "You've been hurt."

"How badly?"

"Your forehead is only bruised, and your concussion is fading. You've regained most of your hearing. The hole in your side is repaired with skintape. Two broken ribs, but we've applied the bone growth stimulator every morning."

"So, then." I had no patience with his recital.

He flung off my covers, revealing my nakedness and the catheters invading my body. I flinched. "Mr. SecGen . . ." His voice was unexpectedly gentle. "Move your right foot."

"What is this nons—" I couldn't. I tried again.

"Your left."

I grunted with the effort.

He tapped my ankle. "Feel this?"

"No." Suddenly, I was clammy with sweat.

"There's been, uh, spinal damage. We operated to stabilize you, to fuse the cracked vertebrae that—"

"How long 'til it heals?"

"It won't heal," said Dr. Rains.

I gagged. Nothing but spittle came up; I hadn't eaten for days. I fought back terror.

"Mr. Seafort, there may be hope. We've procedures that—"

"Get out!"

"Neurosurgery has come a long way."

"I don't want to hear." I twisted wildly, trying to move my legs.

"We can help you adjust—"

I pulled myself to a sitting position, pounded my knees. No sensation. I was numb nearly to the hips.

Dr. Rains caught my hand. "You'll do yourself damage."

"Let me go!"

"Nurse, twenty cc's of Almonel, stat."

"What's that?" Desperately, I tried to twist free.

"A calmative."

"No!" I struck at his wrist. "Don't put me to sleep!"

He grabbed my forearm, held me still, brought the hypo to bear.

"Mark! MARK, HELP!"

The door crashed open. My security chief skidded in, laser ready. "Get away from him!"

"He needs a sedative."

"For God's sake, don't let him do it!" I scrabbled to twist free.

"GET AWAY!" Mark's face was like death. Gaunt, unshaven, a jagged scab crossed his forehead. He knelt, aimed two-handed.

Hastily, Dr. Rains stood clear. In the hall, running steps.

"Put that down." Tilnitz slammed the door in the startled faces of a pair of orderlies.

"He needs—"

"Now!"

Carefully, Dr. Rains set down the hypo. "This man is my patient."

"He was going to . . ." I tried to bring my voice under control. "Get him out!"

"Do you need a sedative, sir?"

With more effort than anyone would ever know, I made my tone calm. "No, I need to be left alone."

"You've got it, Mr. SecGen." He herded Dr. Rains and the nurse toward the door. "I'll be outside."

Before the door closed I called him back. "How long have you been on duty?"

"Four days."

"I thought as much."

"When I go to the bathroom Karen and Tommy take over. The security zone is two floors below, two above. You're safe."

"Thank you." My tone was tremulous. "Get some sleep. Call Alexi, he'll sit with me."

Mark came to the bed, knelt by my side, as if a child seeking his father's blessing. His eyes sought mine, fled quickly to the distance. Nonetheless, his tone was resolute. "Captain Tamarov is dead."

An awful cry, that echoed from the cold unforgiving walls. After a time, I realized the wail was mine. "How . . . when—"

"The bomb, sir. He felt no pain."

I feel it. My eyes darted to the door. He took the hint, patted my shoulder, and left.

Over and again I pounded the mattress. *Let it have been me, Lord.* He *deserved* to live.

I stifled a moan. Lord God still toyed with me. Bereft of my truest friend, helpless, bedridden, with no reprieve in sight. A pitiful old man. In the open closet, near what was left of my clothes, lay my silver-tipped cane. I'd not need it again. I retched. *Come, night. Take me to your bosom.*

I don't know how long I lay, lost in misery. Across the room, the holovid chattered softly. It was set to a newsnet.

"*—according to the latest bulletin from Boland Memorial.*"

"*Any word on when he'll be up and around?*"

"*A highly placed source says within days, despite the rumor of serious injuries that would keep the SecGen bedridden for months. Phil Bansel, reporting live from Boland Memorial Hospital. Back to you, Dan.*"

"*Meanwhile, Acting SecGen Valera confirms that little progress has been made in identifying the Eco Action League, which claims it carried out this third terrorist attack on the—*"

A soft knock. Arlene peered through the half-open door. "You're back with us." She came to the bed.

I tried to turn away, but only the upper half of my body moved.

"Nick . . ." She rested her hand on mine. I flinched, and her eyes widened. "What is it, love?"

I pulled my hand free. "I can't abide pity."

"What on earth . . ." She sat, a tired expression flitting across her lined face.

"It's just . . . I . . ." I tried to turn away. "Not now, Arlene. Please." I prayed she would leave, before I lost control.

"Nick, whatever happens, we'll get through this. I'll be with you."

"Can't you see I—" My voice was ragged. "Arlene, if you love me, leave me alone! For the sake of Lord God!"

When at last I looked up, she was gone.

For days I lay abed, mindlessly staring at the holovid. I left most of my food uneaten. Dully, I answered doctors' questions, tried to move my limbs on their demand, allowed them to manhandle me into a wheelchair to change the bed.

Jerence Branstead came to sit with me, tried to talk business of state, but I paid no mind. "It doesn't matter, Jer. I'm done."

"With what?"

"Office. Life." Wearily, I shut my eyes.

"Oh, you've come a long way." His voice held something that might have been contempt.

"From?" I wouldn't let him goad me.

"From *Victoria,* you sad son of a bitch." From the fastship, on which we'd sped home from Hope Nation, decades past.

I gaped. "How dare—"

"Yes, how dare I! I know all your lines." Jerence flung his holovid to the bed, barely missing my legs.

"Get out!"

"Gladly." He stalked to the door.

"And take your bloody holovid!"

He strode back, snatched it from the sheets. I grabbed his wrist, stayed him. "What did you mean about *Victoria*?"

"It wasn't for the Navy that I gave up juice. It was for you."

I reddened. "I know." In all the years, we'd never spoken of the mighty effort by which he'd mastered his craving.

"I yearned to be like you. You never quit. Whatever cards life dealt, you played on." His gaze found mine. "You always have."

"Thank you." My tone was gruff.

" 'Til now."

"I have nothing to live for."

"That's how I felt." He'd drowned himself in juice, careless of his own destruction.

"You were a boy, your whole life ahead—"

"Coward!" His eyes blazed. He jerked his thumb at the window. "If only they knew."

"Who?"

His brow wrinkled. "No one told you?"

"Told me what, damn you?" An offense to Lord God, but I was beyond caring.

He strode to the door, flung it open. "Mark, Karen, give me a hand." He fished in the bedside drawer. "Comb your hair."

"Why?"

"Do it!"

Meekly, I complied. This was a Jerence I'd never seen.

"Help hoist him." He rolled a huge, heavy wheelchair to the bedside.

"Where are we taking him?" Tilnitz positioned himself at my arm.

"To the window." Together, they manhandled me into the chair.

Jerence flung open the shades. "Look outside, you selfish bastard."

"Easy, there." Mark's tone was cold.

"Shut up. Look, damn you."

I peered down. My room was on the fifth floor of the hospital, in what had once been a miserable transpop slum. Twelve years ago, Earthport's lasers had crumbled buildings, buckled streets, sent untold thousands in the district fleeing to their deaths. Now it was a mixed area, and business and middle-class immigrants were slowly taking hold, a harbinger of the city's rebirth.

I caught my breath. Streetside, outside the hospital gates, hundreds—thousands—of joeys had gathered. Some wore the colorful costumes of the Sub or Mid tribes, others were in casual jumpsuits. Many carried signs that were too distant to read.

Someone pointed. The word spread. In moments they were all gazing upward. A clamor swelled to a roar.

"Wave."

"Take me back."

"Wave. You owe them that."

I did. "How long have they been . . ."

"All week. More each day."

I waved again, pretending cheer, while my soul lay charred and lifeless. "Put me in bed."

"Sir, it's time you thought about—"

"NOW!" My tone brooked no refusal.

It was as if air had gone out of a balloon. Defeated, Jerence pushed the chair to my bedside. I clawed at the mattress. Mark helped lift me in.

I grabbed my leg, hauled it on top of the other so I could face the other way. "Good-bye."

I didn't hear them leave.

After a time, the nurse brought dinner. I left it untouched. Slowly, the room darkened.

A soft knock at the door.

"Take it away. I'm not hungry."

"It's me, Fath." Philip shut the door behind him, pulled up a chair.

I said nothing.

"I hear you've been difficult." His tone was light. He waited, got no answer. "I'll be staying awhile. Shall I read to you?"

"I'm in no mood for visitors."

"So I hear."

"Please leave."

"No, sir."

I grasped his arm, hauled him close, transferred my grip to his collar. "Do as I tell you."

"Not today." Without rancor, he loosened my fingers. "Before I forget, I apologize for leaving after the awards banquet. I was . . . upset."

"Thank you." I tried to make my voice cold.

He regarded me. "You've lost weight. Have some soup."

"Damn it, Philip, get out or I'll have Tilnitz throw you out."

"Do it." His tone matched mine. "He'll have to hurt me."

"Mark!"

After a moment the door opened.

P.T. said, "My father wants you to eject me, sir. I'm going to resist." He peeled off his jacket, took the defensive stance his mother had taught him, years past.

"Mr. SecGen?" Tilnitz looked helplessly between us.

I pounded the bed. This was absurd. "Enough, both of you."

Mark asked, "Do you want me to . . ."

"No." I lay back, defeated. "Let him stay." Why did my heart beat faster, more eagerly? Tilnitz left, shaking his head.

"Eat your soup." Philip held a spoon to my mouth.

"I'm no child."

"I know, sir. Stop acting like one."

Grumbling, I ate, surprised at how hungry I felt.

Afterward, P.T. read from *Holoworld,* then *Newsnet.* I lay back on my pillow, drowsing. After a time I said, "Where's your mother?"

"Home, in the compound." He looked to the floor.

"I hurt her."

"Oh, yes."

"I'm sorry."

His hand rested on mine. "I think she understands."

"It's just that . . . Philip, do you remember when Mr. Chang was dying?" We'd all assumed it would be his heart that took the old transpop, but it was a stroke that felled him. "He lay in that forlorn bed, unable to move, only his eyes showing his misery."

"You're not in that condition, Fath."

"Close enough." How could I explain what I dreaded more than anything else in the world? If Dr. Rains wanted to subdue me, he had but to grab my arm. I couldn't flee, couldn't fight. "Philip, I'm ready for the end." I could face death, and my long delayed reckoning with Lord God, but helplessness . . .

"Goofjuice. No, that's not strong enough. Bullshit."

"P.T.!" I grimaced. "You never used such language."

He grinned. "Jared taught me."

"Ah, Jared." I tried not to flinch at the mention of his lover. After a moment, "How is he?" Hormone rebalancing was losing some of its stigma, but the thought of Jared's treatments still made me uncomfortable. On the other hand, in his case they'd been utterly necessary.

P.T. misunderstood the source of my discomfort. "Fath, I'm omni, not gay." His last attachment had been with an earnest art student, who was as fascinated with Rodin as he. She'd been determinedly pleasant, but I'd never warmed to her.

"I know, son." My hand crept over his. I was ashamed of what I'd let him feel.

"I know you don't like him."

Jared had caused all sorts of havoc with the nets in the Transpop Rebellion. His lawlessness had led to the death of his father, my aide and friend. Only Robbie Boland's influence had saved Jared from a prison colony, even at fifteen.

"I never said . . . It's just . . ." I sighed. "Tell him I said hello."

"You could do that yourself. He's downstairs." P.T. said nothing more, but his eyes watched, waiting.

"Arghhh." What had I gotten myself into? "Not like this." I wouldn't have Philip's mate see me flat on my back, helpless. "You'll have to get me out of bed."

"If you wish, Fath."

I frowned. He made it sound my idea.

"Where's Charlie Witrek? He'll help."

Philip's mouth tightened.

I hadn't seen Charlie since the blast. "He isn't dead!" It was a plea, to Philip, or Lord God.

"No. Blinded." He wheeled the chair alongside.

"Oh, Charlie!" For a moment, I forgot about my useless legs. "Where's his room? Take me there."

"They flew him to Johns Hopkins." P.T.'s tone was gentle. "Lean toward the edge of the bed. We'll see him another day."

Karen and Mark helped prop me in the chair. Someone gave me a mirror, and I agreed I looked like hell. A nurse fussed at helping me shave. I ordered Philip to fetch a shirt to replace the hospital gown. Someone handed me a tie. Mechanically, I knotted it, tugged it tight.

While P.T. went to get Jared, I smoothed a blanket over my legs. "How do I look?"

"Like yourself again." Mark Tilnitz stifled a yawn.

"Is my hair smoothed? I'm not an idiot, by the way. I know I've been manipulated."

"Not by me, sir." He opened the door. "Do you want Tenere on the permanent access list?"

It was of no consequence; I didn't expect to be in office long. "When he's with Philip." A silence. "Where's Branstead?"

"At the Rotunda."

"At this hour?"

"He said there was work to be done. Is there anything else?"

"Call him." Abruptly, my voice was husky. "Ask him to forgive me."

The door opened. "Hello, sir." Jared Tenere sounded nervous, as well he ought.

I thrust out a hand. "Good to see you." If I spoke too heartily, no one seemed to notice.

P.T.'s eyes met mine. They glowed with gratitude.

I said reluctantly, "All right, I'm ready for Dr. Rains." I sat in the motorized chair, propped with pillows so my hands were free. I'd never known, until a few days past, how essential one's leg and thigh muscles were in sitting upright. I had a great deal to learn, most of it insufferable.

P.T. went out, spoke to the nurse. He had stayed in New York, camping out at Robbie Boland's apartment, since the night of his visit. My suggestion that he resume his own life fell on deaf ears, and I couldn't reveal how pleased I was.

Arlene remained in Washington. Over the caller she was cordial, but said she'd wait to see me at home. Time and sincerity, I knew, would earn her forgiveness. I resolved to do whatever it took. I began by sending her a note of apology, of which I meant every word.

I fidgeted, but it was only a few moments before Dr. Rains appeared. With him were three other doctors, one of whom I'd already met.

Rains introduced his colleagues: a radiologist, another neurologist, and Dr. Knorr, an expert in space medicine. Rains regarded me warily.

"Well?" My tone was frosty. "What news do you have?"

He cleared his throat. "Mr. SecGen, you have a partial spinal cord transsection at the T-12, L-1 level, resulting in paralysis of the lower extremities, but—"

"Is there any *good* news?"

"Quite a bit, actually. First, as you're aware, your paralysis is from the thighs down. A portion of the bomb casing hit you like a piece of shrapnel, but didn't quite sever the cord. There's partial sparing of sensation in groin and hips. That's one reason you aren't incontinent."

If I were, I would be facing Lord God's judgment. My life was not worth preserving if it meant that indignity.

"Nor are you impotent."

"Get on with it."

"Listen, Fath."

"It hasn't left you—"

"Tell me what it *has* done!" I ignored P.T.'s silent rebuke. I wasn't about to answer to a child I'd raised.

"You have no feeling in your legs. You can't walk."

"I know that. Will there be any improvement?" I tried to sound casual, but betrayed myself by holding my breath.

"No. The nerves are too crushed to heal. I can show you just where." He flipped on a holovid, dialed up my chart. "Here, just below your rib cage. Look where—"

"I believe you." Lord God, damn those enviro terrorists to Your ultimate Hell.

His colleague Dr. Knorr pulled up a chair, leaned forward. "Mr. SecGen, you won't heal, but there *is* some hope. Not much, I'll grant you, but have you heard of the Ghenili procedure? No? Well, occasionally nerve tissue can be replicated. In some cases it's possible to insert replacement nerve tissue and, ah, reestablish the connection."

My heart leaped. "Some cases?"

"Yours might be one."

"Do it." Anything to be out of this hated chair.

"It's not that simple. First, we have to wait for the trauma to dissipate. Then—"

"How long?"

"Months." He saw my despair. "A few weeks, at any rate. Tissues are swollen, the nerve ends are still dying. When that's settled, as it were . . ."

They'd examine me again. If the gap wasn't too wide, they would operate. In most operative cases, over time, the subject would regain sensation and motor function. The procedure had been discovered by researchers in Lunapolis trying to aid survivors of the fish war. When the warrens had been bombed, the result was similar to the collapse of coal mines. Spinal injuries were common. Loath to transport paraplegics groundside by shuttle, the medical community treated many survivors locally.

Dr. Ghenili and his team tried their new procedure on hopeless cases, and found encouraging results. They'd refined their techniques, studied how the nerve tissues slowly reknit. Eventually they'd devised protocols to determine which patients were suitable candidates.

"And I might be one of them?" Despite myself, my pulse quickened.

"There's a possibility. We have no way to tell. But there's a catch."

I shot P.T. a glance of dismay. There was always a catch.

Ghenili's achievement galvanized the neurological profession. Eagerly, surgeons all over Earth tried to replicate his results. And failed.

Yet, on Lunapolis, he continued to have success. They finally discovered the cause. Nerves reknit only in zero to one-third Terran gravity. At one gee, Earth normal, the inserts slowly died.

"What about after? Can the patients go home?"

"After full recovery, yes."

Dr. Rains intervened. "We're way ahead of ourselves, you understand; you may not be a candidate at all. If you are, the period after the operation is critical. You'd be bedridden for weeks. Then very limited movement. Any strain . . ." He shook his head.

"That's fine." I'd soon be done with public life, and if they'd operate, I'd be free to devote myself to recovery. "How soon can I leave the hospital?"

"You've been resisting physical therapy. We need to—"

"Answer my father's question." P.T. spoke softly, but in a tone edged with steel. I'd known a drill sergeant to speak so to cadets. They'd leaped to obey.

"In a few days. He needs to bond with his chair, to learn the mechanics of daily—"

"Very well." I waved it away. I would undergo Ghenili's operation, or kill myself and go to Hell. "Bring in the therapists."

I passed two days in a haze of impatience. I learned to hoist myself from chair to bed, bed to chair. I found out why the motorized chair was so massive, so heavy. Fitted with Valdez permabatteries under the seat, visual sensors fore and aft, it had a speaker in one arm, a pickup in the other. The chair's frame itself incorporated the cybernetic brain. It would take me where I told it to go. The contraption was more puter than chair.

Not as versatile as a ship's puter, it had to learn to understand me. Naturally, it had a program for that. "Say a few sentences, please."

"What?"

"Anything."

"My name is Nick Seafort."

"More."

"I was born in—this is bloody nonsense!"

"Referent not understood. Say a few sentences, please."

I swore. "What can I—all right. I, Nicholas Ewing Seafort, do swear upon my immortal soul to preserve and protect the Charter of the General Assembly of the United Nations, to give loyalty and obedience for the term of my enlistment to the Naval Service of the United Nations and to obey all its lawful orders and regulations, so help me Lord God Almighty."

A pause. "Syntax integrated. Linguistic idiosyncracies assimilated."

"Whatever the hell that means."

"It means I understand you. Waiting for input."

I practiced dressing, hygiene, all the tricks that the normal world was unaware paraplegics had to master. At night, I had unbearable dreams of loping through the wind, though my knee hadn't allowed me more than a steady, painful walk for years.

Yet, slowly, I began to accept that life would go on. I called Baltimore, got through to Charlie Witrek's room. Over the phone he was determinedly cheerful, though Lord God knew what it cost him. Transplants might be possible, he said. They were waiting for a match.

After a time, I found myself looking forward to going home. I called Moira Tamarov, asked if there was any way I might help ease her loss. There wasn't. Impulsively, I invited her to bring the family to Washington, as I'd invited Alexi. Listlessly, she accepted, but we left the date unsettled.

When I'd been in the hospital some three weeks, and was thoroughly restless, I summoned my staff for a long overdue conference to wrap up our Administration. Branstead, Tilnitz, Philip, Karen Burns, and General Donner, the U.N.A.F. security specialist, met with me in a secluded room.

I asked, "Have the Patriarchs made their announcement?" Ample time had passed since my defiance of Lord God's authority on Earth. I assumed Mark and Branstead were conspiring to shield me from the details.

Jerence said gravely, "I have some bad news." He glanced at Mark.

"Did Saythor call for excommunication?" Arlene would

stand by me, if no one else, though I wasn't sure I'd let her risk her immortal soul.

"Not quite." He handed me a *Holoworld* chip.

I fitted it to my holovid. "Good Lord!"

The Elder had expressed, on behalf of the Patriarchs, outrage at the Rotunda bombing, and full confidence in my Administration. His praise was more than perfunctory, it was effusive. "What's this about?"

"Renouncing you now would endorse terrorism. Besides, Saythor's seen the polls." Branstead's tone was sardonic.

"I—what?"

"It's not just the crowds outside, you know. We're overwhelmed with letters. I put Warren to answer the E-mail, else it would have taken months." Warren was our chief puter, who had something of a literary gift. "It started with the Von Walthers banquet, and since the bombing . . . your approval ratings have never been so high." A grin wiped the exhaustion from his eyes.

I slammed my fist on the table. "Alexi died, and three good souls with him. Six more gravely hurt, to attain the esteem of fools. Don't mock the dead! It's obscene!"

Across the table, Branstead got to his feet, loomed over me, his fingers spread on the gleaming wood. "Don't call them fools, Mr. SecGen! I won't have it. They respect you. Some even love you. The least you can do is respect their intelligence."

Taken aback, I swallowed. "Well. Um."

No one spoke.

So, I would continue my labors. From a Lunapolis hospital bed, perhaps. My mind whirled. If I was to stay in office we had work to do. I asked Tilnitz, "What have we learned about the ecos?"

"Still no sign of Academy's Sergeant Booker. And clues in the bombing are scarce."

"Mark, it's the *Rotunda*." How could terrorists manage to plant a bomb in so heavily guarded a place?

"I know, sir. We interrogated the staff and got nowhere. Valera wants to declare a state of emergency, to suspend defendants' rights."

That would allow P and D questioning, without evidence of guilt. I pursed my lips. Why not? Killing cadets was horrible enough, but when the enviros bombed the U.N. enclave itself . . .

"Don't, sir." Branstead.

I raised an eyebrow.

"When terrorists force Government to curtail civil rights, they win."

"You know so much about the subject?" My tone was sour. For generations, since the Rebellious Ages had given way to the Era of Law, civil disobedience, to say nothing of terrorism, had been almost unheard of.

"Hope Nation had its dissidents, when I was a boy."

I flushed. In his distant colony, I had set civil liberties aside without cavil, to put down the colonial rebellion. "What information *do* we have?"

General Donner stirred. "The bomb was old-fashioned plastique. We're trying to trace its chemical signature. It's in my report."

"Which I haven't read. Was I the target?"

"According to their communiqué, yes."

"Why so small a bomb, then? For that matter, why not a missile, or a . . ." I trailed off. I'd been about to say "a nuke," but one had to watch one's language. Since the days of the Belfast nuke, even to suggest the use of nuclear weapons in home system was treason.

"Lack of access, I assume."

"General Donner?" Philip looked apologetic. "If Father goes home . . ."

"Yes?"

"Can you protect him?"

I growled, "Now wait a minute—"

"Of course." Donner.

Mark Tilnitz rapped the table. "That's *our* responsibility."

"You failed. He's lucky he wasn't—"

"We didn't fail!" Karen Burns overrode the two of them. "But we're lucky you survived, Mr. SecGen. It's time you cracked down. Go with Valera's declaration. Have Donner arrest the leaders of the enviro fringe. Only by showing the world we won't knuckle under can we—"

"Nonsense!" Branstead.

"You can't just—"

"The law doesn't allow—"

I raised my voice. "Enough!" They subsided. "Karen, I won't let the ecos push me into repression. That would play into their hands."

"But—"

"Subject closed."

"I never got an answer." P.T. sounded apologetic. "Can you protect Father? The ecos have struck both times in your presence."

"Actually, sir . . ." Mark Tilnitz looked abashed. "It's easier now that you're less mobile. You have—had—a habit of darting off unexpectedly."

I fought an icy rage. P.T. clasped my hand, but I pulled loose. Mark saw my paralysis as an advantage, did he? I'd break him. I'd have him pounding a beat in Senegal. No, Eritrea was more remote.

Somehow, before I ruined another companionship, I restrained myself. "Get me a coffee."

Philip jumped to comply.

"Thank you." But my annoyance flared anew. "Now Charlie's gone, I need a middy. He should be doing this."

Branstead said, "I meant to ask Admiralty for a replacement, but I've had a lot to deal with."

I flushed. My sulky refusal to deal with matters of state had added to his burdens.

"I don't mind, Fath." My son headed for the door.

"I do. Jerence, get me our list of candidates. No, by

heaven, let that bloody enviro cadet fetch and carry for a while. Show him what havoc his politics cause."

"Sir?" Jerence looked blank.

"The cadet, don't you—oh, you weren't there. Bivan, or whatever. Bevin, that's it, from Academy. Tell Hazen I want him seconded for special duty."

"Mr. SecGen, are you sure—"

"Quite." I allowed myself a small smile of satisfaction. The boy would learn the hard way the effect of his enviro fantasies.

Mark asked, "When will the hospital release you, sir?"

"Tomorrow." I would wait no longer. Arlene hadn't replied to my note.

6

Are you sure you want to do this, Fath?" From the wings, Philip cast a dubious eye on the mediamen gathered in the hospital auditorium.

"No, but I must." I knotted my tie, smoothed my jacket.

Facing the mediamen would be, as always, a nightmare. Branstead had suggested they sneak me out in an ambulance, and announce the fact afterward. The public should be introduced to my handicap slowly, so they wouldn't see me as a cripple.

But I *was* crippled. To suggest otherwise was a lie. Disabled, handicapped, differently abled, impaired, minimally limbed, maimed, physically glitched . . . all the weasel words of the past two centuries wouldn't lift me out of this hated chair. I yearned for the day I might be free of it.

"I'm ready." At my own insistence I would wheel myself onto the stage alone, without the help of the puterized chair. Crippled didn't have to mean dependent. I caught a glimpse of my security chief's disapproval. "You inspected their gear, Mark."

"And we'll be standing in front, between you and them. It's not enough."

"Shoot the lot of them, then. It's fine with me." On that

note I rolled myself onstage, maneuvered myself to the center of the battery of mikes and speakers.

A blaze of lights, the whir of holocams, as the world got its first view of the new, improved SecGen. For a stunned moment there was silence. Then, cacophony.

"Mr. Seafort, do you—"

"Mr. SecGen!"

"Will you be able to walk?"

"Have you located the—"

"MR. SECGEN!"

They were always like that. I simply waited. When at long last the din abated, I pointed to the second row. "Ms. Searles?"

"Sir, do you have a comment about the Eco Action League?"

"The terrorists known as the Eco Action League will be caught and tried. I presume execution will follow." As was fitting, the law provided no lesser penalty.

I pointed elsewhere.

"Does the government know who they are?"

General Donner wanted me to claim we did, but that was nonsense. The killers knew otherwise. "Not yet."

"Sir, there's a rumor you'll declare martial law. Is that—"

"We will not." My voice was a lash.

"Mr. Valera said yesterday a martial law bill was being drafted."

My Deputy SecGen had always been impetuous. I said firmly, "The bill will not be introduced." A shocked murmur; I'd publicly cut the legs from under him. He—and the party—would be outraged. It served them right for not getting my approval.

"Does this indicate a rift within the Supranationalists?"

I hesitated. "No, it indicates that I'm still SecGen."

A wave of mirth swirled around the hall. Suddenly, I had them, and the tone of the questioning changed.

"When will you leave the hospital?"

"Today." I nodded to the correspondent for *Holoworld*.

"Sir, when will you resume work at the Rotunda?"

"When there's a meeting I can't avoid. I prefer to work from home."

"Mr. SecGen, will you ever walk again?"

I tried to look at all the holocams at once. "I don't know." Offstage, Branstead flinched. Well, too bad. He'd become too political. Best he remember he was a Navy man. With reluctance, I turned to an old adversary from *Newsnet*. "Mr. Canlo?" He, too, was entitled to a question.

"Sir, what do you say to charges that you were negligent in the deaths of your aides?" From elsewhere, a sharp intake of breath.

I'd learned over time that answering his questions directly got me nowhere. "I haven't heard any such charges. Have you?"

"Yes."

"From other reporters in a bar?"

Nervous laughter, here and there through the hall.

Canlo held his ground. "Will you answer the question, sir?"

"Detail your charges. How am I responsible?"

"A bomb was placed in the Rotunda. Isn't the Secretary-General responsible for the U.N. complex?"

"I'm responsible for the entire United Nations." I paused, to rein in my disgust. Lord, I hated press conferences. "That doesn't let you sue me personally if you trip in the General Assembly."

Gales of laughter. Was I turning political at this late date? Heaven forbid. I added, "I take seriously the deaths of Press Secretary Carlotti and Security Officer Bailes, as well as my great friend Captain Tamarov and communications aide VanderVort. I don't hold myself responsible." Or was I? Had the ecos not gone after me, Alexi would be home with Moira and the joeykids. And Charlie would be on his coveted starship. Quickly, I found another hand. "Ms. Gier?"

Canlo stayed on his feet. "What do you say to calls for your resignation?"

"I'll resign when the public so demands." Or the Patriarchs. Under my jacket, I was sweating. I glanced to the wing, where P.T., unseen, was earnestly giving the media a sustained finger. Abruptly, my equanimity was restored. "Ms. Gier?"

"What measures are you taking to find the terrorists?"

"We're analyzing their writings, sifting the rubble for clues, determining who had access to the Rotunda, questioning witnesses. We've sought the cooperation of"—I tried not to let my lip curl—"legitimate enviro groups, to identify who among the fanatic fringe might have committed these despicable acts." As far as I was concerned, they were all the fanatic fringe, but I wouldn't say that. Not now.

"Mr. SecGen, do you—"

"I'm not finished. I appeal to every citizen, wherever located, to come to our aid. To attack the United Nations, the Government of Lord God, is an assault on Lord God Himself." My voice trembled. "It is worse than treason. It is abominable beyond words. *'The powers that be are ordained of God. Whosoever resisteth the power, resisteth the ordinance of God: and they shall receive to themselves damnation.'* Any of you who have useful information, I beg your assistance. In the holy name of the Lord Almighty, as you cherish your immortal soul, I beseech you to come forward, to escape the fires of Hell." Throughout the hall, absolute silence. "Good day." I turned my chair, wheeled slowly off the stage.

P.T. met me in the wing, his eyes glistening. Without a word, he bent and kissed my cheek.

"Son, take me home."

"Wait, sir. Another few minutes." Mark Tilnitz held up a placating hand.

"Now what?" My chair was parked just inside the hospital door.

"Joeys are swarming out there. It's not safe. Karen has jerries setting barriers."

"What do they want?"

P.T. patted my shoulder. "To see you."

"Why?" A foolish question. Crowds haunted me everywhere. It was the reason my compound needed walls. Ever since I'd sailed *Hibernia* home . . . I'd spent my life trying to escape them.

And look where it got me. I snapped, "Open the door."

Mark shook his head. "Not yet."

"Now." I rolled to the entry. "Let them have me."

"Fath?"

"It's all right, Philip. Onward, chair." Before they could stop me, I pushed open the door, rolled into the dusk.

Karen and her detail raced across the lawn. "Mr. Sec-Gen—"

They'd strung police barriers from the door to the lot in which my heli waited.

A muted roar. The throng surged forward, broke through the barricades. My security joeys formed a circle around my chair, faced outward with lasers drawn.

I clawed at Karen. "Don't fire! Hold!" Desperately, I slammed my chair through the wall of my guards. "On, chair. To the street." I risked a glance back. With looks of horror, Karen and Mark scrambled after me, the rest of the detail trailing behind.

I rolled to a stop. A blizzard of frantic hands. Someone held out his arms, made a barrier. "Give him air!"

I clutched at fingers. "It's all right. Thank you for coming."

"*Mr. SecGen—*"

"*We're praying for—*"

"*I waited all day—*" His hand darted out, back again. I offered mine, and he seized it.

"I'm all right. Thank you."

"I'm so sorry, what they did—"

"Go with God." I squeezed a wrist. An elderly man blinked back tears.

Mark cannoned into a stocky joey looming over me, shoved him aside.

"NO!" Somehow I made myself heard. "Surround me if you must, but leave a space open. Let them through a few at a time." I adjusted the blanket over my useless knees. "Thank you. I'm all right." I grasped eager hands with both of mine. "Thanks for coming, joey."

Slowly, with curses, with rage, my security organized the chaos into an impromptu reception. The word was passed down a line of awed well-wishers, and a line formed, impatient at first, but calmer, as it became known I would remain.

Two full hours and then some, I sat in the misty lot, until the last hand was clasped, the last shoulder squeezed with silent reassurance.

Wearily, I flexed my fingers.

P.T. stared down at me with respect, and something more. "What is it, son?"

"It's as if . . . You've heard of the king's touch?"

"I didn't heal these poor joeys."

"Perhaps inwardly."

Mark said heavily, "As SecGen you have no business exposing yourself."

I thought a moment. "As SecGen I have no business not."

In the compound, all was familiar, yet strange. Simple tasks such as getting me upstairs to my bedroom had become immensely complicated. I bore it, determined I wouldn't be forced to live out my life in the cursed chair.

Still, bit by bit, I learned to get around, to maneuver through doorways. Sometimes I let the chair do the work, other times, stubbornly, I insisted on navigating myself. We rearranged furniture to ease my passage. My body seemed healed, except within. Lower back pain made me irritable, and I tried not to lash out. It would fade in a while, they'd told me, and in the meantime I had pills, though I'd vowed not to use them.

Arlene was stiff at first. "You recall denying you built a wall I couldn't penetrate?"

"You said that at Derek's reception." I paused. "Hon, in the hospital, when I found I was paralyzed, I was beside myself. I'm truly sorry."

"I tried to give you space. You needed to lick your wounds in solitude." A pause. "And I was hurt. You thrust me away, when I wanted to give you ease."

"Can you forgive me?"

At length, her hand crept to mine.

Over time, the calm she offered was her greatest gift. I let myself go, muttering and wincing at the wearisome pain, until I saw her rubbing her own spine in unconscious sympathy. From that moment on, I tried to hide my discomfort, and hers seemed to ease.

My relief at returning home faded. I longed for recovery, and worked dutifully with the two therapists who made daily visits. Mark Tilnitz scrutinized their security files, and refused to leave the room when they were present. I made a note to give him my special thanks, and asked Arlene to find a suitable gift. Since I'd been rushed to the hospital, he'd devoted himself to me utterly. These days dark circles lined his eyes, and he bore a haunted look.

I wrote to Moira Tamarov, repeating my invitation.

Philip visited the compound almost daily, from his flat in Maryland. Slowly, finally, we began to grow at ease with each other, as once we'd been. From time to time he stayed for dinner.

"No, Fath, it was the year you hurt your knee." We were in a bright-lit nook in the kitchen, just the three of us. Arlene had chased out the servants, and in unaccustomed intimacy we dined on lasagna we'd prepared ourselves. Confined to my chair, I was graciously allowed to cut and mix a salad.

"Hon, when did you teach him to shoot? Wasn't it earlier?"

"If P.T. says he was fifteen . . ." She shrugged. Philip had an uncanny accuracy with numbers, with data of any kind. His mental gymnastics no longer surprised me.

"You came home when I was thirteen, Mom." Philip glanced between us. Arlene and I had separated, briefly, after the Transpop Rebellion.

She raised an eyebrow. "Shouldn't I have?"

Dutifully, he gave her a hug.

She released him, pushed him gently toward his seat. "Twenty-four, a grown man . . . where did the time go?"

"Would you rather I was still a child?"

"No, but . . ." She looked thoughtful. "Parenting was fun, damn it. And now you don't need me."

"Of course I do." He tried to look injured. "Don't I call you from work? Don't I ask your advice—"

"Yes, love. But you don't need it."

"I'm sorry. I'll try to be more dependent." He held the lasagna for me to scoop. "If you don't like my growing up, have another child."

I snorted. At least Philip was young enough to be thoroughly unrealistic.

I threw myself into long-neglected affairs of state. I was working on the hefty U.N.A.F. budget when there came a knock on my study door. With a sigh, I set down the file, massaged my back. "Yes?"

A red-haired midshipman marched in, came to attention, a gray-clad cadet following suit. "Midshipman Thadeus Anselm reporting, sir!" He snapped a salute.

"At ease."

Smartly, he assumed the at-ease position, hands clasped behind him.

"Who's your . . . ahh. Mr. Bivan."

"Danil Bevin, sir." The boy's voice still hadn't settled entirely into the lower registers.

I ignored the cadet. "What brings you here, Mr. Anselm?"

"I'm the cadet's escort, sir!"

"Very well, consider him escorted."

"Yes, sir." The middy hesitated. "Am I dismissed?"

I unbent. "What are your orders?"

"To return to Devon base when released, sir."

If he was like every middy I'd ever known—like myself, at his age—he'd cherish leave in a foreign town. "Very well, you're not dismissed just yet. Have you an overnight travel allowance?"

"No, sir." Hazen had been stingy with his budget, it appeared.

Well, it was my own fault, for meddling. I buzzed security. "Show the midshipman a guest room. Mr. Anselm, I require your presence over the next few days, in case"—I glowered—"the cadet needs rebuke." If Bevin had any sense, he wouldn't take me seriously; cadets should expect a modicum of verbal hazing. "However, you'll not be needed until midnight each day. You need not stay on the grounds."

Anselm's face lit. "Yes, sir!"

"That's all."

With Academy precision, the middy about-faced and marched out.

"Chair, go around—oh, never mind." I wheeled from behind my desk, faced Bevin. "See what your enviro friends did to me?"

"They're not my friends!"

I rasped, "Are you looking to be caned?"

"Not again, sir."

"Then watch your mouth." I paused. "Again?"

He flushed. "After you left, Sarge wrote me up."

"For?"

"Arguing with—with my betters." The words came reluctantly.

"It's not what you say, Bevin." I had to admit the boy had courage. "It's how you say it." No need to chew him out, at our first meeting. "So. Tell me about yourself. You're English?"

"From Manchester." A shy smile.

"I was a Cardiff boy." But of course he knew that. Everyone did. "A Naval family?" Many of our officers were third generation, or more.

"Why, no." He looked puzzled.

"What's your father's occupation, then? Or is it your mother?"

He said tentatively, "Are you teasing me, sir?"

"No." I glowered. "If you don't want to tell me—"

"My father is Andrus Bevin, of the Enviro Council. He's Mr. Winstead's deputy."

I recoiled. "He's *that* Bevin?" I *knew* the name had sounded familiar.

"Yes, sir."

"Why didn't you tell me? Sneaking into my house without—"

"I never asked to be posted here!" His face was hot. "Besides, I told you the first time we met."

Dimly, I tried to recall. I'm enviro, the boy had said. And so's my father. I cursed under my breath. I would send him home to Devon, of course; I couldn't have a spy underfoot.

I colored. Do you want *my* resignation, Hazen had asked. He, too, had enviro sympathies. Not every enviro supporter was glitched.

"He's what, Winstead's assistant?" Perhaps if I kept Bevin from sensitive data . . .

The boy's head shot up proudly. "First vice president of the Enviro Council."

"Vice president."

"Yes, sir. He's your son Philip's boss."

If I dismissed the cadet, surely it would cause repercussions for Philip. Dismayed, I searched for a solution. Let the boy go, with orders not to tell anyone that . . . Call Winstead, explain that the posting had nothing to do with . . .

No. I would have to make the best of it. I took a deep breath. "Did Haz— Did the Commandant explain why you were sent here?"

"No, sir. Sarge said you wanted to keep an eye on me."

I smiled. "Not quite." I explained my custom of young Naval aides. "I won't keep you more than a few months. You'll graduate with your bunkies." Some of them, at least. Academy had no set graduation day; cadets were released when deemed ready.

Bevin opened his mouth, shut it again. A cadet didn't question his officers.

I sighed. I really should have selected a middy; look where pique got me. "While you're here, you may speak before being spoken to. There'll be no penalties."

"Thank you, sir. If you didn't know my background, may I ask why you picked me?"

"I knew you were enviro. I meant to show you what your enviro cohorts did." I grimaced. That wasn't the only reason. "Because you stood up to me in barracks. I loathe yesmen."

He regarded me quizzically. "You chose me for what Sarge caned me for?"

"Life's like that."

"After I'm done here, sir . . ."

"Yes?" Impatiently, I tapped the desk.

"Do you think— If I do well, could I be posted to *Galactic* when I make middy?"

"Of all the gall!" Was there no end to his effrontery? *Galactic* was the prize posting of the Navy; it had the finest accommodations, the most modern instruments, the most powerful lasers, the best-equipped bridge. No doubt seasoned middies from every ship in home system were vying for a berth on her. I growled, "Have Security show you your quarters. Dismissed."

He saluted smartly.

"Bevin!"

He paused at the door.

"Don't ah ... it would be better ... Perhaps you shouldn't tell anyone here you're related to *the* Andrus Bevin. Some of the joeys I work with might not understand." Why was I perspiring?

"Aye aye, sir." He left.

"To the veranda, chair." The motor purred. I struggled with the door, managed finally to help the chair maneuver outside.

My back throbbed. I'd been hoping to find Arlene, tell her of my fiasco, but she was nowhere in sight. I went back to my office, buried myself in chipfiles.

Later, I wandered to the living room. Arlene lay curled on the couch, reading a holovid. *Newsnet,* it was.

I tried to negotiate the narrow path between settee and chair. Muttering, I tried to haul the settee out of the way and nearly dislodged myself from my seat. I swore under my breath. "Hon?" I gestured at the obstacle.

Arlene purred, "Yes, Nicky?"

She knew bloody well what I wanted. Nonetheless, I said humbly, "I need your help."

"Very well." She moved the chair.

"Thank you." I rolled past. "Do I get points for asking?" My tone was hopeful. "You know I hate to be dependent."

The corners of her mouth turned up. "Is that another apology?"

"Yes, if it's needed."

She kissed the fading scar on my forehead.

After a moment I asked, "What's in *Newsnet?*"

"Your political obituary." She scrolled to the head of the article. "They say you'll resign within a month."

"Wishful thinking."

"Nick . . ." Suddenly she was serious. "How long will you stay in office?"

"Until . . ." I ground to a stop. How long, indeed? I'd been sure each term would be my last, but my second Administration had been in office twelve years, through three elections. Despite my contempt for the political process—Jerence claimed it was *because* of it—the electorate kept my Supranationalists in power, and the party wasn't about to abandon me. I wasn't sure why. All too often, for their taste, I appointed Indies or Terries to vacant posts.

If Bishop Saythor had carried out his threat, the question would be moot.

"I don't know. Every day, a small, quiet part of me still yearns to quit. Especially now I'm paralyzed." I paused. "But as I told you once, I've grown to like power. Isn't that despicable?"

"Have you used it well?"

"Yes, of cour—no, not really. I appoint my friends to office, bully the Navy, squelch the Earth Firsters every chance I get."

"What's the despicable part?"

"I ignore the wants of my party. I'm rude to the Senate."

"I'm still waiting."

"I break the rules when it suits me."

"Not for your own benefit. For the public good."

"Who am I to decide that?"

"Who else should?"

"The public. That's what a democracy is about."

"The public is—are—fools."

I smiled sourly. "Jerence tells me to respect them for loving me. You tell me they're fools."

Her smile was lighter than mine. "We might both be right."

I leaned forward to kiss her, lost my balance, ended up sprawled on her bosom.

"Is this an advance, sailor?" Her tone was wry.

I was helpless, and it enraged me. How else might I find myself incompetent? "God damn—" I caught myself, but my mood was shattered. I hauled my legs back onto the footpads, spun the cursed wheelchair.

"Nick, what . . ."

"Out, chair." I fled to my office.

7

Philip moved back home. He spent two energetic hours hauling his belongings upstairs to his old room, and rushed back to work. Subdued, I realized that in the years he'd been with the Enviro Council, I'd never visited his office, or even asked his duties. How must he see my indifference? Was I truly so cruel? I slipped into the den, closed the door to be alone with my turmoil.

I'd named P.T. after Philip Tyre, a heroic young middy I'd known.

We'd been so close, when he was young.

One day, when my son was five or so, I had him on my lap, showing him holos of Father and the run-down Cardiff farm on which I was raised. In those far gone days, P.T. had called me "Daddy." Solemnly, in his babyish voice, he asked if I'd like him to call me "Father," as I had my own parent. "If you'd like," I'd said.

Thereafter, I was "Fath." "Father," when he wanted to be formal.

With wonder and delight, I'd watched him grow toward adolescence. His goodwill was boundless, his intelligence awesome.

He was Lord God's undeserved gift.

The Transpop Rebellion scarred him, in some way I never

fully understood. We didn't quite grow apart, but he became ever more moody. In his teens he adopted the enviro cause with dismaying fervor, and finally left my home in a swirl of mutual recriminations. I was heartsick over his invasion of my files. If there was anything I'd hoped to teach him, it was inflexible honesty, and the honor I'd tried to espouse before my fall.

I'd hoped that he'd be better than I.

My joy at his return was tempered somewhat in that he brought Jared Tenere home. I couldn't well refuse; it would jeopardize our reconciliation.

Well, perhaps hormone rebalancing had stabilized the Tenere boy. Time would tell. At least, he'd lost the unbearable cockiness he'd flaunted as a youth.

What with the newcomers and other changes, my home life had developed an outlandish aspect. Each night, to my infinite disgust, security joeys hauled my weighty wheelchair up the stairs a step at a time, while I prayed fervently that nobody slipped. I was even tempted to install an elevator. Pride was one thing, a broken neck quite another.

Danil Bevin quickly learned his way around the house, and tried to make himself useful, in his less-than-timid fashion.

His second night with us, Thadeus Anselm, the middy, came staggering home past midnight, crooning a ribald ballad as he negotiated the stairs. Arlene merely giggled and went back to sleep, but if it hadn't been too much trouble I'd have hauled myself out of bed and given him a piece of my mind. I resolved to do so in the morning, but his pale and shaken countenance dissuaded me. Some lessons were self-taught.

Besides, his conduct wasn't my concern. Another day or so and I'd send him home to Devon.

Meanwhile, crowds gathered each day outside the walls. I didn't know what they sought. No doubt they came because

I was a public figure, and my injury unsettled them as a private person's would not.

Confined to my relentlessly helpful chair, restless and irritable, I buried myself in work. Luckily, there was plenty of that. I pored over budgets, arbitrated colonial disputes, struggled with the Dutch relief situation.

The overriding problem was where to settle the refugees, now that most of Holland was reclaimed by the sea. Pakistan had taken in most of the Bangladeshis, but the Netherlands had no ethnic sister, and Belgium's patience was wearing thin; she'd absorbed as many as her local economy would handle.

Across the globe, lowlands were swamped as never before in human memory.

The Dutch could be absorbed; even teeming Earth could find room for its refugees. But dispersal would cost the Dutch their national identity, and their leaders strenuously fought for other solutions.

I'd already authorized putting the Hollanders at the top of the list for emigration to Constantine, the newest of our colonies. But I didn't see how we could ship more than fifty thousand refugees over the next few years, and though that would make Constantine thoroughly Dutch, it wouldn't make a dent in the refugee problem. Besides, the Colonial Affairs office argued vehemently against allowing ethnic concentrations in our colonies.

A knock. "Cadet Bevin reporting for duty, sir."

"As you were. I'm a civilian, so we'll relax military courtesies."

"Sir?"

"Don't come to attention each time you come into my bloody office!"

"Aye aye, sir."

"Take these chips, file them in the case next to the holovid, where—"

The caller buzzed. General Donner, of U.N.A.F. Security.

I left the desk speaker on. If I couldn't trust my aide's discretion, I'd best find out now.

"Mr. SecGen, we may have a break in the Academy matter."

"Go on."

"We've had that Sergeant Booker's family under intense surveillance. Sisters, cousins, the works."

"And?"

"His father's niece Sara had a couple of odd calls. Nothing overtly incriminating, but the conversation was out of focus, as if it was in code. Discussing groceries for no reason, for example."

"You traced?"

"Public callers. The first in London, the second in Manchester."

"So he's in England."

"Sorry, sir, the voice wasn't Booker's."

"How would you know?"

"We ran the recording past your Commandant. He's under surveillance too, by the way."

I reared up in my chair. "That's an outrage!"

"You think so, Mr. SecGen? Who'd be better placed to arrange an accident?"

I spluttered. "I would. Is my caller tapped too?"

"Of course not." The General chuckled, unconvincingly.

If the Navy heard that its rival, U.N.A.F., had one of its officers under surveillance, there'd be hell to pay. "The Commandant was shocked when we heard about the murdered cadets. I was with him, and it was no act." I'd stake my life on it. I hesitated. Or would I? What if . . . no, I was becoming as paranoid as Donner. "Remove Hazen from your suspect list. We won't spy on the Navy."

"Sir, if he's involved in any way, even in covering up the—"

"I'll take responsibility."

His voice fell. "Yes, sir. About the cousin . . . we're going for P and D."

"You have an order?"

"This evening. We have a tame judge."

I opened my mouth to object, thought better of it. The less I knew of our investigative techniques, the better. Sometimes these things had to be done, and no one would really be hurt. I had the rights of our cadets to consider, as well as Booker's cousin. "Very well. Proceed." I rang off.

Bevin turned from the holovid. "We all want the murderers caught, but how can you send joeys to P and D with no evidence?"

"Mind your business."

"A tame judge? Is that honorable?"

I'd had enough. "You're asking for a caning."

"Fine, if it would get me home to Academy." His cheeks were flushed. "I thought, whatever else you are, you're an honest man."

"Whatever else I—you impudent young joeykid! What's that supposed to mean?" I wheeled around the desk, planted my chair inches from his legs.

"You're a— I'm sorry, sir. I'd better keep quiet."

"Far too late. Finish the thought. I'm a what?"

"A bigot. You hate your political enemies. You hate all enviros, without thought."

I was more scandalized than offended. "Bevin, don't you see that working with the SecGen is an honor? Well? Don't just gape, answer!"

"Is that why you hauled me from Academy? To watch you play favorites, trample public rights, bully your staff—"

"ENOUGH!" I turned to the desk, clawed for my caller, thumbed it to the upstairs speakers. "Anselm! Get down here!" I waited, seething.

The thud of racing footsteps. A knock, and the door crashed open. "Sir, Midshipman Anselm repor—"

"Take this lout and thrash him! I want him to remember—

Now, Middy!" If I'd had the use of my legs, I'd do it myself, with joy.

Bevin shot me a look of contempt. "Truth is no defense?"

"Not for an insolent, cocky—what do you mean?" Anselm had the cadet nearly to the door. I raised a hand to stay him.

Bevin rubbed his pinched forearm. "You canceled surveillance on Mr. Hazen because he was Navy, but you didn't on Sara because she was a civilian, and Booker's cousin. That's playing favorites. You're sending a girl to P and D for talking about groceries. They're bastards, whoever killed Santini and the others, but they have rights too. You couldn't get away with that with an honest judge."

"Go on." My voice was ominously low.

"I'm staff, and you bully me. My thoughts are my private affair, but you order me to tell them to you. Then you punish me because you don't like them."

"You were insolent beforehand."

"Yes, I was."

"Why?"

His eyes teared. "Because I wanted to believe better of the SecGen!"

A long time passed.

I said, "Anselm, let him go." I wheeled to my desk, got myself behind it.

Now what?

You're the SecGen, come up with answers.

Sighing, I picked up the caller. "Get me General Donner." I waited. "This is Seafort. Cancel the P and D on Booker's relatives until you have more evidence. No, you heard me." I listened to his protest, repeated my instructions, and rang off.

"Middy, get me a coffee, if you'd please."

Anselm left.

"Are you satisfied, Cadet?"

"That's not for me to say."

"Modesty, at this stage?"

He opened his mouth, thought better of it, bit his lip. "How should I answer? I'm in trouble if I keep silent, and in trouble if I speak."

"Arghh." There was a certain justice in that. I asked, "How is it you're not afraid of me?"

"I am!" He squirmed. "Do you think I like a caning? It hurts!"

"I know." I too had been a cadet. "Yet you don't hesitate to reprimand my conduct."

"I'm sorry." His face was red. "But . . . isn't that why you chose me?"

We eyed each other warily.

Anselm returned, bearing coffee. I sipped from the steaming cup. To Bevin, "I'm several times your age, and SecGen. Don't you think it inappropriate to admonish me?"

"Yes, sir. Please send me home." His eyes beseeched me.

"Very well, if that's what—"

Again, the caller buzzed.

"Branstead here." His voice was tense.

"Not now, I'm in the middle of—"

"There's been an incident in London. They attacked the Victoria and Albert Museum."

"Christ Almighty." I didn't know I said it, until Anselm's eyes widened. "Amen," I added quickly.

"They weren't well armed, thank the Lord. Still, eleven casualties, and they managed to set the place on fire. The enviros left two of their own among the dead."

"The London garrison—"

"Details are still sketchy. It seems U.N.A.F. was caught off guard."

"Typical. Keep me informed." I rang off, keyed the caller to Mark Tilnitz, told him the news. "Ready my plane. I'm off to Britain this afternoon."

"The hell you are." His voice sharpened. "Mr. SecGen, you're not mobile. You can't fly into a war zone when—"

"Yes, I can. We'd better show the flag, and I need a first-hand look at this mess." I set down the caller. "Anselm, find Arlene, help her get me packed. Bevin, gather your gear."

The two scurried off. I began putting away my holochips.

Mark met me at the helipad. His voice was maddeningly reasonable, as if dealing with a small child. "We can't arrange secure travel on short notice. The plane has to be fueled and prepped, we have to run security sweeps, arrange logistical support for forty people—"

"And make hotel reservations, gather my far-flung staff. I know." Suddenly I was fed up. For twelve years I'd traveled trailing a flock of joeys I didn't need, or even like. Some, I barely knew. Now that I was paralyzed, perhaps for life, I would do as I wished. "Skip the lot of it."

"What nonsense are you—"

"This heli." I jabbed at the fuselage. "It's got Valdez permabatteries, right? It could fly to London, or around the world."

"So? We couldn't all fit—"

"We won't need to." I cast caution to the winds. "Darius of Persia didn't travel with as huge a retinue as mine. No more, do you hear? I'm done with it." I forced myself to stop pounding the chair arm. I wouldn't get his help by sounding a spoiled child.

His voice was scornful. "Whom will you leave behind? The press crew? Security? Your therapists?"

He'd goaded me beyond endurance. "All of them! Help Anselm and Bevin lift me into the heli. I'll take the two boys to help with my chair. You can pilot. That's it."

"You're out of your mind." Mark folded his arms.

Again, I pounded the chair. "Put me in the heli! Middy, take one end. Jump when I give an order!"

"Aye aye, sir." Anselm struggled with the chair.

"Wait, slide me in first, lift the chair after. Mark, help me, or find another job!"

Abashed, Bevin stood aside, trying to make himself small.

"You're asking for my resignation?" Mark withstood my glare. "Damn it, I'm responsible for your safety."

"A fat lot of good you've done." Immediately I was sorry, but it couldn't be helped. "When we sally out in force, in a huge jet swollen with staff, the whole world knows. We'll be just as safe traveling incognito. Who's to know I'm in this heli?"

"It's a breach of protocol. Go abroad with only one security man? Donner would fire me, and he'd have cause."

"I suspend the protocol. We'll put it in writing to protect you."

"You're risking more than your life!" His face was red. "If you're assassinated, there'll be chaos."

"Let it be so. Mark, you know me. I tell you, I'm going, and I won't let you persuade me otherwise. Will you help or not?"

He wavered, but convincing him wasn't that easy. It took nearly an hour before he strapped me in. Even then, he passed our first hundred kilometers trying to persuade me to turn back to Potomac Shuttleport.

Anselm sat beside me during the long sullen ride.

I sniffed. "What's that I smell? Alcohol?"

The middy flushed. "I . . . had a drink." Seeing my look he blurted, "I was off duty, sir. You told me last night . . ."

"Very well." I folded my arms. I had more on my mind than a miscreant middy. The Eco League's attacks were escalating at an alarming rate. First cadets at Academy, then a bold attack on my plane that failed, then a bomb that nearly killed me. Now an outrage on civilians, in broad daylight. What next?

It also troubled me how well organized the ecos seemed. We'd run into a wall, tracking them. How could such a well-knit organization have formed under our very noses? Where did they get their arms? Rifles and lasers weren't readily available; mere possession of an unlicensed laser warranted the death sentence.

We droned on over the Atlantic. From time to time Mark made calls over the secure line. Lord God knew what sort of fit Security was throwing.

"Do we return tonight, sir?" At least, Mark's tone was civil.

"It depends what we find." I wasn't sure why I had to visit the bomb site, but I knew it was so. If Londoners had endured their first taste of war in over a century, my presence would be reassuring. Or perhaps not; the sight of my chair wheeling itself through the rubble of a national monument might give them pause.

"Sir?" Bevin sounded timid.

Anselm's voice was sharp. "Don't bother him."

A boy who drank in daylight, presuming to tell the cadet his place? I'd have none of it. "What, Danil?"

"We'll be so near Devon . . . while we're there, could you post me back to Academy?"

"I'm fretting about terrorists, and you whine to go back to Academy? Joeys died!" I grabbed his collar, hauled him close. "I need your help to get about. Not another word or—" I shook him.

"Aye aye, sir! No, sir!" Almost, he raised his hand to mine, but he came to his senses. "I'm sorry, sir!"

"Four demerits." As a civilian, I wasn't sure I had authority to log them, but he wouldn't contest the matter.

"I'm sorry." Bevin's voice was small. He stared at his lap. I stole a glance; he was near tears. It served me right for snatching a callow youngster out of school. In my desk I'd had a list of perfectly suitable middies.

We let the heli guide itself to Kensington. I'd have preferred navigating my way via the Thames, but I sensed Mark Tilnitz was at the limit of his endurance.

I'd intended to set down at the V & A's imposing entry on

Exhibition Road, but the street was filled with military and emergency vehicles. We circled.

I'd expected more damage than was visible. A section of wall was shattered, a number of windows were in shards, and the east facade was badly smoke-stained. But the building still stood.

"Set down there, on Cromwell."

"And then what? Wheel up and announce you're the Sec-Gen?"

"Why not?"

Mark seethed, but did as he was told.

A uniformed jerry bustled over while Mark and the boys manhandled my chair to the pavement. "Move that machine, mate! You're in a security zone!"

"Help me out." I clutched Anselm's shoulder, slid myself from the seat of the heli. "You there, name and rank!"

The jerry blinked. "By what authority?"

"Take a good look. I'm SecGen Seafort. Chair, back up." I wrapped an arm around each boy's shoulder; together they dragged me to the waiting chair. "Careful, Bevin!" They eased me down. "Name and rank, I said."

"I—Sergeant Rourke, uniformed division. Are you really the Sec—let me see some ID."

Mark bristled.

"No, it's a reasonable request." I leaned to one side, managed to extricate my wallet, flashed him my chipcard. "Satisfied? Chair, to the front door, that's to my right. Find a ramp and take me in." We rolled forward. "Come along, Sergeant. You'll help explain."

Tilnitz loped alongside. "Sir, this is insane. How can I watch for—"

"Don't bother. You think assassins are standing by, in case I show up? Go lock the heli; I don't want my suitcase stolen. I have the boys if I need any—whoof!" The chair lurched over a chunk of debris. I hung on. "While you're at it, reserve three rooms at a decent hotel."

"Government House is—"

"The atmosphere's like a tomb. A good hotel, I said. Chair, halt. Mark, we're doing this my way. Glare again and I *will* accept your resignation. On, chair."

"On what?"

"On. Forward. Continue."

"I think I bent a wheel." The chair's tone was plaintive. We wobbled on our way.

The bodies were gone, but the inside remained a scene of carnage. When my wheels skidded in a sticky pool of drying blood, Anselm turned green. I swallowed bile over and again, battling not to disgrace myself and dishonor the dead.

The survivors among the staff clutched at the reassurance of my visit. Over and again they repeated their ghastly tale.

Five joeys, hooded and armed, had burst through the front gate. They'd cut down the guards with lasers, set off an incendiary bomb in the principal exhibit, Colonial Dress Through the Ages from India to Belladonna. Sprinklers went off and alarms clanged.

Perhaps the din unnerved the invaders, or perhaps they'd intended a bloodbath all along. For whatever reason, they barred the front lobby and fired indiscriminately at fleeing visitors and staff. Among the slaughtered were a five-year-old boy and three nuns from Lahore.

When the first sirens wailed in the distance, their leader blew a whistle. They escaped to the street, where they met the heroine of the day.

Her name was Indira Raj. A museum guard, she'd crouched behind a parked lorry, waiting for reinforcements. When the gunmen raced down the steps, she'd come to her feet, coolly opened fire. She downed two terrorists, winged another before their comrades snuffed out her life. They fled to a waiting car, drove off.

I heard out the grisly recital. By now the lobby was full. The Lord Mayor had arrived, along with several MPs and the local U.N. Assemblyman.

I rolled to the waiting mediamen, gave a grim statement sent live over the nets, while Mark Tilnitz, despairing of my safety, had quiet paroxysms. I understood his misgivings; there was no point in arriving incognito, then announcing my presence to the world. On the other hand, there was no way to show my support if I didn't let Londoners know of it.

When we emerged, young Bevin was pale and shaken. I felt a moment's regret at exposing a cadet to such a scene. But still, he was an officer in training, and Naval life had its perils. Sooner or later he'd have to face death. The sight of a sailor exposed to vacuum was every bit as horrific as the carnage in the museum.

Mark had taken me at my word when I'd said "a good hotel"; he'd booked us into the New Dorchester. We landed on the rooftop heliport and rode down to the lobby. As a security precaution he'd used his own name for all three rooms, but I was recognized immediately.

There was a brief delay, no doubt to assign us better rooms, while the awestruck middy and cadet peered about at the immaculately uniformed bellmen, the brass rails salvaged a century ago from the old edifice, the paneled and dadoed walls. Then we were ushered to a three-bedroom, four-bath suite strewn with fruit and flower baskets. Jaded as I'd become, it took my breath away.

Well, I was on U.N. business. The government would cover the bill.

For two hours I lay on my bed, making calls. There was the family of the slain guard; I made sure they'd be well provided for. I conferred with Metropolitan Police; their investigation would need coordination with ours, but U.N.A.F. had a way of brushing aside local constabularies that left bad feelings.

I called Moira Tamarov, for the third time since Alexi's death. I urged her to bring their son and daughter to Washington the next day, to stay a week at our compound. I'd hardly known Alexi's wife, but perhaps Arlene and I, together, could offer solace.

The moment I rang off, Jerence Branstead was on the line. "Are you glitched, Mr. SecGen? A private heli? No staff?"

"Not you too."

"A public hotel?"

As usual, I had visuals off, but I could picture his expression. "Stop spluttering."

"Sir, your erratic behavior plays right into the hands of Valera. One of these days the Deputy SecGen will engineer a vote of no-confidence."

"Let him. Is this why you called?"

"No. Bishop Saythor wants a meeting."

I groaned. "The Patriarchs, again? So soon?"

"Just the two of you, private and unofficial. And promptly."

Interesting, but I had no idea why. "I'll be home tomorrow."

"I'll set it up at the Rotunda."

"No." I shook my head, forgetting he couldn't see.

"You prefer the Cathedral?"

"If he's so anxious, let him come to my compound."

"Sir, he's the Elder."

"And I'm the SecGen. Good night, Jerence." I rang off.

I glared balefully at my overnight bag, across the room. It seemed too much trouble to work myself into the chair to retrieve it. For a moment I was tempted to let myself sleep as I was, fully dressed, atop the covers.

Well, why had I brought along the middy and cadet? I struggled to a sitting position, rang their room. "Anselm? Come over, I need you."

In a moment he popped through the connecting door. His collar was awry, as if he'd adjusted it in haste. "Yessir?"

"My bag."

"What about it?"

I pointed angrily to the dresser. "Get it."

"Aye aye, sir." He strode across the room, stumbled, caught himself. Face flushed, he dropped my gear on the bed. "Anything else?"

"Would you hang my jacket, please?" I tried to shrug loose an arm.

"While you're wearing it?" He giggled.

I peered suspiciously. "Let me smell—you're drinking!"

"I am," he said with dignity, "off duty." A belch. He clutched his stomach, folded slowly, vomited on my shoes.

"Anselm!" I tried to spin away, could not; my lower limbs were encased in cement. The middy fell against me, moaning. Desperately, I held him off. *"Danil, get in here, flank! Bevin!"* I could have been heard in the lobby, twenty floors above.

The cadet dashed in, wearing only shorts and T-shirt. He stopped short. "Cadet Bevin repor— oh, my God!"

"Take this—this *person* out of here! Don't let—*hold him!*" Too late. Anselm sagged, upsetting my precarious balance. He flopped atop me, pulling Bevin onto the pile.

Beside myself, I flailed at any available limbs. In a moment Bevin recovered his balance, dragged Anselm off the bed. He thrust out his hand; I seized it, hauled myself upright. "Get that joey out of my room!" The cadet struggled, to no avail. "Don't you see he can't walk? Drag him!" With a mighty effort, Bevin complied.

My shoes and cuffs were soaked with vomit. The stench was vile. I bit back a sob. Please, Lord, don't let this be my life. I'm covered with a middy's puke, unable to clean myself.

Bevin poked his head through the door. "Shall I—do you want help?"

I screamed, "Put your clothes on!" He disappeared. In moments he was back, hopping from foot to foot as he slipped into his carefully polished shoes.

By then I had my pants unbuckled. Straining, I lifted my

buttocks off the bed. "Pull them down—help me get—*Jesus, Lord Christ!*" I was shaking.

"Sir, it's all right." His voice was soothing. "It's only—here, let me do that." He worked my pants to my ankles, got them off. He ran to the bathroom, returned with towels, covered the mess on the rug. "We'll get you into the chair, sir. It'll only be a moment." He spoke in the same tones I'd used to Philip, when he revved.

A few minutes later, I emerged cleaned and calmed from the lavatory. Danil sat calmly, watching a hotel servitor clean and dry the rug. "I hope you don't mind my calling them, sir."

"No, I—thank you." I found it difficult to meet his eyes. While I'd thrown a tantrum, he'd taken care of my needs.

When the houseman had gone, I rolled my chair close. I spoke quietly. "How long has this been going on?" I gestured to Anselm's room.

"I've only known Mr. Anselm a short time," he said carefully. "Since he brought me to Washington."

I flushed; I'd asked him to betray a mate, no, worse, a superior officer. In the Navy that was not done. "Sorry, Mr. Bev—Danil. I wish . . ." I patted his knee, as if to give him comfort. "It's difficult."

"What is, sir?"

"Being paralyzed." Being SecGen. Growing old and impatient. Living apart from Lord God.

He waited.

"Danil, help me out of the chair. No, not to the bed." I pointed to the floor, near enough to lean on the mattress. Else, I would topple.

"What are you going to do, sir?"

"Pray."

"On your knees?"

"I don't think Lord God hears me any other way." As a joeykid, Father had made me pray on my knees. These days, it was out of fashion, and I felt self-conscious before the boy, but I was determined.

I had no muscle control at all; I wasn't really kneeling, but sitting on my legs. It would do. I leaned forward, made a tent of my fingers.

To my utter astonishment, Danil Bevin slipped down, knelt by my side. He bowed his head.

"I thought you enviros were freethinkers."

"Well, I'm not." He sounded defiant.

It had been too long. *I'm sorry, Lord. Sorry for what I've done, and who I am. But You know that. If You hear me—if You listen despite my abominations—I beg You to help me.* I thought of asking to walk again, blushed at the effrontery. *Help me to be just, to deal wisely with those in my care, to catch the mad eco anarchists who would lead Your people astray. Bless Indira Raj, who died doing her duty, and Alexi, who died for no reason I can discern. And bless this passionate young joey at my side, with whom I've been so impatient. And if, somehow, You could grant me—I don't deserve it, but I long for it so—a little peace . . .*

"Amen." I didn't realize I'd spoken aloud. I blinked away a sting.

Bevin helped me to the bed, took a nearby chair. I sat quietly, eyes on the floor. It had been a long day.

A knock. Midshipman Anselm, his face red. "I'm terribly sorry."

"Danil, go to your room. This is between us alone."

"Aye aye, sir."

"And thank you. For everything."

A shy smile. He disappeared.

I pointed sternly to the chair. Meekly, Anselm sat.

"Did you know you're an alcoholic?" My voice was cold.

"I'm not, sir, I just—"

"Did you bring the wet stuff with you?" Normally, a boy his age couldn't order a drink, without risking a penal colony both for himself and the server. But, by act of the

General Assembly, a midshipman was a gentleman and an adult. He could vote, drink, and bring his life to ruin.

"Yes—no, I . . . no, sir."

"Which is it?" The comparison between him and Bevin was odious. The cadet, impetuous though he was, had a good heart and a sense of decency. This drunken lout was a disgrace to the Navy.

He squirmed. "Both. I had some in my gear, but it was— I ordered it from the hotel."

"And you claim you're not alcoholic?"

"I didn't break the law." His tone was sullen. "And I wait 'til I'm off duty."

I was relentless. "Since you came to Washington, has there been a day you didn't drink?"

He stared into the middle distance. His eyes seemed troubled. "I guess not. It's just that . . . with a couple of drinks, the world seems brighter."

"I imagine you worked hard to make middy."

He gulped. "Oh, God, you're cashiering me."

"Only your commander can do that." As a civilian I couldn't do much about him, other than send him home to Devon.

I sighed. At Academy, Anselm would be fortunate to escape with a caning; Hazen would be more likely to dismiss him from the Service, as the boy feared. Why should that trouble me? It was what he deserved. Not only had he been drunk, he'd sullied the Navy's cherished relationship with the SecGen. And if word ever got out that he'd vomited on me . . . I'd never hold up my head.

"Sir, I . . ." Abruptly, he began to weep. "I'm so ashamed."

"You should be."

"Your shoes"—a sob—"I'll pay for them. If there's anything I can do, any way to . . ." He raised a tear-streaked face. "You're the SecGen, and once you were our Comman-

dant. I was so proud to meet you. And I threw up on you."
He began to rock, hugging himself. "Oh, God, dear God."

If he thought his performance would move me, he was
sadly mistaken. I had no sympathy for a stupid young jack-
anapes who . . . dimly, I recalled a horribly sick young
middy, on his first leave, hugging a toilet in a bar in Lunapolis.

I cleared my throat. "To start with, you're not to drink
again, for six months. Not a drop."

He paled, but said only, "Aye aye, sir."

"You've dishonored the Navy."

He looked to the floor, and blushed anew. "Yes, sir."

"Call Mr. Tilnitz. He's in the next room."

In a few moments, Mark stood in the doorway, arms
folded.

"Mr. Anselm, you'll be caned." I leaned forward, steadying myself with one hand. With the other, I raised the boy's
chin. "I'd do it myself, if I could."

His eyes pleaded, but he said only, "Yes, sir."

"As a civilian, I'm not sure I have the authority. If you
contest it, I'll deliver you to Commandant Hazen with a note
of explanation."

"Oh, no, sir!"

"Very well. Mark, you'll do the honors. We have no barrel and no cane, so use your belt. Go, boy, and consider
yourself lucky."

Anselm stood unsteadily, brought himself to attention.
With reluctant resolve, he marched to Mark's bedroom.

I lay back in bed, turned off the light, and listened to the
middy's anguished yelps.

8

I yawned; the day had started early, I'd had a long transatlantic trip with a sleepy cadet and a subdued middy. Then, brunch with Arlene, Philip, and Jared Tenere. I'd had to make small talk, which I found difficult in their presence, all the more so because my mind still swam with images of blood and destruction. It didn't improve my mood that Jared's manner was inoffensive, almost deferential.

Afterward, in my office, I glowered at the caller. I hated holoconferencing. Karen Burns was at my side, Branstead at the Rotunda, and General Donner in Paris.

"You call that progress? Bah." I glared into the screen. On top of my other troubles, my back ached.

Donner drummed his fingers, causing his image to flutter. "We've identified both their museum casualties. That's a breakthrough."

"The one was already dead."

"Obviously not. I said he'd been *reported* dead, four years ago."

Karen listened to our byplay, silent.

Branstead rapped his desk for attention. "What disturbs me even more than the attack . . ." He rubbed his eyes. "The terrorists are too well organized. They can smuggle a bomb into the Rotunda, gather weapons, track the SecGen's movements, provide false identities for their cohorts. How big a group does that imply?"

"Huge." Karen leaned forward. "Too large to let them continue flaunting us. Crack down, Mr. SecGen. With P and D we'll break them."

I said, "If they're so many . . ." Why had we found no trace of them?

Branstead cleared his throat. "The public won't support this sort of thing; it's right out of the Rebellious Ages. It takes just one loose mouth in a bar. One braggart, and someone calls us with an anonymous tip. A dozen joeys would be their secure limit, I'd guess. So why haven't we gotten so much as a hint?"

We traded glances, each hoping another would speak.

I mused aloud. "We're looking for the wrong sort of group." It brought stares of surprise. "I mean . . . what if they aren't as many as we think?"

Jerence said, "So many separate attacks—"

"I was in London last night, and I'm back home today. We can move; why can't they? No, hear me out, Jerence. How many of these joeys do we actually know about? One in the airport; he's dead now. Sergeant Booker at Academy. Someone to smuggle a bomb into the Rotunda. Five in the museum, but they lost two. They could be as few as half a dozen." I shifted, trying to ease my spine.

"The false identities, the canister of nerve gas?"

"Think how much easier to hide two or three men than a large force. Assume Booker smuggled out a canister and his friends filled it."

"How'd they get the toxin?"

"How'd they build a bomb?" Karen Burns.

"How'd they get it in?"

I said, "What if we're making this too complicated? We know how the nerve gas got to Academy: Sergeant Booker. The airport was easy; they drove up to the gate. Concentrate on the bomb. List every joey who in the three days before the bombing had, or could have had, access to the Rotunda. One of them is our terrorist."

"There's hundreds," said Donner. "Senators, Assemblymen, their staffs . . ."

Karen looked grim. "P and D would tell us."

I said, "Not again, Karen. We haven't the authority."

"You would under martial law."

I felt a chill. "Out of the question." She was outraged at the bombing, no doubt, but even so, her urge to crack down seemed almost vindictive.

"How many more would you see die?"

"That's not—" A knock at the door. "Yes?"

Midshipman Anselm, his uniform immaculate, his hair brushed, his face scrubbed. A crisp salute. "Pardon, sir, but Bishop Saythor's arrived. Two helis on the pad."

"Why are *you* telling me? You have no duties here."

"Yes, sir. I mean, no, sir. I had Cadet Bevin stay to greet them. I thought you'd want to know right away."

"Very well. Who's with him?"

"I don't know, but three of the joeys had guns."

Karen keyed her caller. "Arnie? Who's out there, Church security? Can you disarm them? Well, keep them out of the house. No, that's final. I'll be right along." She strode to the door.

"Middy, show the Elder inside. Try not to vomit on him."

Anselm flushed beet red. "Aye aye, sir."

From the screen Branstead asked, "What was that about?"

"Last night something came up. Never mind."

"Mr. SecGen . . ." Jerence hesitated. "Last time I argued against P and D, but after the museum . . . I agree with Karen."

"I won't declare martial law. Whatever I'm remembered for, it won't be that." I scowled at Donner. "Any more conversations about groceries?"

"No." The General made no effort to hide his distaste.

"We're alert to trace calls. I stationed rapid response teams throughout England."

Despite myself, I giggled. "You'll swoop down on the greengrocer at the first mention of cabbage?"

"It's not funny, Mr. SecGen. You of all people should know that." His screen went dead.

"That wasn't necessary, Mr. Seafort." Jerence sounded annoyed. "He's frustrated beyond bearing."

I sighed. "I'll make it up to him. That's all for now."

"Be diplomatic with Saythor, would you?"

"I'm always diplomatic." I gave him no chance to respond. "Out, chair. To the living room."

Bishop Saythor sat placidly on my favorite sofa. Around him stood and sat three aides. Across the room, Bevin had assumed the at-ease stance.

"Hold, chair. Is this to be a private conversation?"

"Why ask me? My job is transport."

"Be silent, chair. I was speaking to the Elder." My back twinged.

"These gentlemen have my confidence." Saythor's tone was pious.

He'd demanded a private conference, and now this. I was in no mood for games. "As do Karen Burns and my cadet. And my wife. I'll call them."

"That won't be necessary. Your point is taken." He gestured, and his joeys moved to the door.

"Can I be of help, sir?" Bevin.

"Yes. Take a position outside the door. See we're not disturbed." See that Saythor's aides don't listen at the keyhole, but I couldn't say that. I ought not even think it, but a sore backbone shortened my temper.

The Elder regarded me skeptically.

I waited.

"I pray you're recovering from your dreadful injuries."

"Yes." He didn't give Lord God's damn whether I was well; of that I was certain.

"Mr. Seafort, what I have to say is difficult. You've been ill, and you're still not your old self."

True, but soon they would evaluate me for the Ghenili procedure. It was my lifeline.

"The bombing shook public confidence in all our institutions. Many influential citizens are upset at your policies."

My face was stony.

"Let me not beat around the bush. Mr. SecGen, I want you to resign."

"Very well."

"Very well, you'll resign?"

"Very well, you want me to resign."

"Will you?"

"No."

"Why not?"

A good question. He did, after all, represent the power and authority of Mother Church.

No, he did not. The Patriarchs did, in conclave.

"Well, Mr. Seafort?"

I hated to be pushed. If he weren't so arrogant, he'd know that. I leaned forward, clutching the armrests so as not to fall out of my chair. "Bishop Saythor, what in hell gave you the idea you could meddle in politics?"

He gasped.

I hurtled on. "You demand I resign, but surely you don't speak for the Church. The Patriarchs have every confidence in my Administration; I know so from your statement to *Holoworld*." He flushed. "But even if you gather your colleagues in conclave, you haven't the right to order me to resign."

"We represent Lord God's will!"

What in His name was I doing? I thought to rein myself in, but Saythor's sneer unraveled my intentions. "You may disavow me, excommunicate me if it comes to that. No more. The Assembly may dismiss me by a vote of no-confidence, or the electorate by voting for my opponent at a general election. That is how a government is removed."

"It comes to the same thing. If we declare we've lost confidence—"

"Do so. Reverse yourselves publicly. I'll have no quarrel."

"Then why be so obstinate?"

"Because, sir, you overstep yourself!" My eyes blazed. "The Eco Action League would crumble our Government, reduce our system to chaos. There are paths, legitimate ones, for them to express their views. They ignore the proper means, proclaim themselves with bombs. They thwart the will of Lord God, whose Government I head."

"But—"

"And you do likewise! Where does the U.N. Charter give an Elder the right to dismiss His Government? Where does Church doctrine allow the Patriarchs to ally themselves with a particular party?"

"Listen here—"

"No, sir, *you* listen." I spun the wheels of my chair, lurched forward. "I will do the work of Lord God, as He gives me to see that task. Ask the Assembly to dismiss me, if that is your mind. Perhaps they would." No doubt they would. Especially if they heard me speaking so to His representative on Earth.

Saythor rose, white of face. "You skirt blasphemy!"

"Then excommunication is your remedy." Obdurate, I faced his wrath. "Until you're prepared to use it, I'll hear no more apostasy."

"Apostasy?" He was nearly apoplectic.

"What else? You attempt to subvert our Charter and Church doctrine to bring down His Government!"

His eyes bulged.

"Out of love for His Church, sir, I will say nothing of what transpired here. Feel free to make any public statement you wish." I gestured to the door. "Anselm! MIDDY!"

The door crashed open. "Midshipman Anselm reporting—"

"Our conference is concluded. Show Bishop Saythor to his heli, if he will not partake of refreshments."

I waited, alone in the room, for my heart to steady, for my breath to calm. I leaned back. A stab of warning, from my spine. I groaned.

After a time, a knock.

"Now what?"

Danil Bevin shut the door behind him, marched across the carpet, came to attention, threw a parade-ground salute.

"Yes, Cadet?"

His eyes shone. "You were . . . magnificent, sir!"

I reared up, or tried to. "You spied? Despicable." I pounded the chair. "I'll have you caned. No, dismissed from Academy. If you haven't the honor—"

"You ordered me to stand outside the door!"

My mouth worked. How dare this insolent, impudent child defend anything so contemptible as eavesdropping? What effrontery. What—

I *had* told him to stand outside the door, to stop Saythor's aides from doing precisely what he'd done.

"Hmpff." It was all I could say.

"May I speak?" His tone was pleading. I nodded. "Sarge used to tell us stories about your days in Academy. How you and Admiral Thorne went on secret missions raiding the coolers. How later you stood up alone to the fish. Sir, I . . ." He squirmed. "Sometimes I didn't believe everything they—but today you were wonderful. The Elder was out of line, and you faced him down without a qualm. Now I see how it could all be true."

"Goofjuice. I've never heard such nonsense."

"Yes, sir. Thank you so much for assigning me. It's— I'm—"

"Yesterday you begged to go home."

It was as if I'd knocked the wind from his sails. He deflated. "Yes, sir. I'm . . ." He bit his lip. "Shit."

"Bevin!" I'd have said more, but his eyes were damp. "It's all right, boy. Come." I grasped his hand. "We'll say no more about it."

"Thank you, sir." It was barely a whisper.

"Help me awhile in my office." I rolled to the hall, basking in the gleam of his approval.

For two hours, Danil and I worked diligently, making significant inroads on my stack of paperwork. To my surprise, I found the cadet a willing and cheerful worker, toiling without complaint at whatever task I gave him. When he came upon the Boland report concerning the Volgograd gravitron works, he scanned it quickly, posed a series of acute questions that had me thinking. Yes, we needed its production, but was it absolutely necessary that it spew so many metallic by-products? I scrawled a series of queries.

Moira Tamarov arrived at midday. She'd brought the children by Hitrans train from New York, and by taxi from the station. The gate guards confirmed their authorization on their list, admitted them past the guardhouse. Why she hadn't come by heli, I didn't know. Certainly, with Alexi's pension, she could afford it. I made a note to ask.

Arlene greeted the Tamarovs while I extricated myself from my office. I joined the women in the kitchen, over tea. My wife perched on the counter, smiling down at Moira in the breakfast nook.

"Mr. Seafort." Moira came to her feet. Her dark hair was tied behind her neck. Her oriental eyes were dull and lifeless, much changed from the last time I'd seen her, a decade past.

"It's Nick, please." I rolled forward, gave her an awkward embrace. "I'm so sorry about Alexi."

"I know."

"I was sedated when they held his funeral." Perhaps I

might have begged his forgiveness. "Where are the children?"

"Outside, I think, with your middy." She seemed uneasy.

"Is there something wrong?" Of course there was, you idiot. Her husband had been blown to pieces a month before.

"I hope, while we're here . . . I warned them."

"Who?"

"Carla and Mikhael. They're . . . it's mostly him, but she goes along."

"With what?"

A commotion, at the door. "Excuse me, could we have—" Tad Anselm, two teeners in tow. He glanced among us. "Oops. I'm intruding."

"Nick, you've met our joeys, have you not?"

The girl was about twelve, awkward, with the promise of grace.

"This is Carla, and . . . Mikhael, don't hide in the hall. Come say hello."

"Good to meet . . ." I ground to a halt, sucked in breath. *"Alexi?"* It couldn't be so. The room spun. "But you're—" I covered my face.

"It's all right, Nick." Arlene slipped from the counter, hugged me from behind.

I wept.

The boy was his father, as I'd met him many years ago, on *Hibernia*. To the life. His face, his height, his slim form, his hair. Every aspect but the sullen look he wore.

"What's the matter with *him?*"

"Mikhael!" His mother was aghast.

I mumbled, "How old is he?"

"Fifteen, and don't talk past me."

I wiped my eyes. "Sorry. You gave me a start."

"Ask me if I give a fuck." Mikhael thrust through our stunned tableau to the hall. A moment later, the slam of the veranda door.

With a grimace, Anselm backed out of the room.

Moira's hands fluttered. "I'm so sorry. He's been wild and angry ever since Alexi left on *Melbourne*. Disobedient, and . . ." She seemed oblivious of Carla's contempt. "It's best we go, I think."

"Stop that." I tried to smile. "I'm glad you're here; we'll work it out."

Carla snorted.

I wheeled on her. "Are you angry too?"

"Not especially."

"Is your brother usually like this?"

"When there's reason."

"What's the cause?"

"If you don't know, there's no point discussing it."

Moira threw up her hands. "I can't deal with them, and they know it. We lost Alexi so suddenly, he's not there to reassure them, and . . ." Her eyes filled.

I rolled to the door.

"Nick, where are you going?" Arlene's voice was soft.

"To find Mikhael."

"Be . . . understanding."

"As always. I'll join you at dinner. Chair, outside, and this time don't scrape the wall."

"I didn't—"

"Be silent." I was in no mood for argument.

The sun beat down. I glanced up, debating. Should I carry a sunshield? I hadn't heard the day's ozone report. Well, I wouldn't be out long.

"To the gate." I beckoned the guard. "Have you seen the Tamarov boy?"

"No, sir."

"Chair, circle the house." Thank heaven the ground was dry; I could imagine the chair backing and filling its way out of soft mud. Well, I wouldn't wander the lawn often, and I wouldn't live in the chair long. Death was infinitely preferable.

We bounced over the lawn, to no avail. I tried the sheds, the helipad, the guardhouse at the rear wall.

I found Mikhael at the bungalow that once belonged to Adam and Jared Tenere. These days it was unoccupied, though occasionally, when the house was full, the cottage served to accommodate guests.

The boy was sprawled on a chaise lounge in the shaded patio, where Adam had liked to sit.

"May I join you?"

He gave no response; I took it for assent, rolled past the hedge.

"It's hot." No answer. I had to do better than that, and knew it. "Mikhael, why are you angry?"

He folded his arms, looked away.

"Is it about your father?"

"I didn't need him. I'm almost grown."

"I'm sorry you lost him."

"What's it to you?" His tone was scornful.

If I'd dared speak so to Father, Lord knew what . . . a strapping, at best. Where did this sullen joey find the gall to sneer at the Secretary-General of the U.N.?

"You done glaring?" He spat the words.

"Well, your dad wouldn't fault your courage."

"Don't speak of him!"

I owed Alexi the effort, but the boy was unreachable. Defeated, I resettled in the chair to ease my aching back.

Steps, behind me. "Oh. I didn't realize . . ."

I twisted. "Jared."

"I'll leave you." Philip's partner shifted awkwardly.

"No, stay."

With a look of distaste Mikhael uncoiled his lanky form, brushed past Jared to the path.

"Get back here!" I spoke without thought.

The boy turned, hands on hips.

"This instant!" If he ignored me, I was helpless.

Slowly, Mikhael returned to the patio.

"Plant yourself in that chair! How dare you walk off without excusing yourself!"

"You're not my—"

"Father? No, but I'm adult and you're a child. You'll show me courtesy, or . . ."

"Yes?"

"Try me." My tone was level. After a moment his eyes dropped. "You'll stay put until we're done." Still annoyed, I looked to Jared.

Tenere said hesitantly, "I didn't mean to intrude."

"Jared, this is Mikhael Tamarov, son of my old friend Alexi. Mikhael, take his hand or . . . take it!" I'd had enough.

Jared blushed. "If that's how you'd dealt with me when I was a boy, I'd . . ." His voice trailed off.

I studied him. He was what, now? Twenty-seven? Three years older than Philip. Had we ever spoken in depth, in the dozen years since he'd fled our compound? From time to time I'd met Jared in his guardian Rob Boland's company, and he'd murmured something polite. On my part, I'd had little desire to speak to him.

"You'd what?" I sounded testy.

"I'd have been better off." Again, he colored. "Perhaps I shouldn't bring it up."

"Why not?" I was barely civil. How could I extricate myself? I'd thoroughly alienated the boy I'd wanted to engage, and found myself in a conversation with a joey I wished to see as little as possible.

He glanced uneasily at Mikhael, plunged ahead. "Mr. Seafort, there's something I've wanted to say for years."

"Get it said, then." In a moment I'd order the chair inside. Somehow, we would all make it through the week.

"I was horrible as a teener. I see that now. I resent—I hated you." His gaze was almost defiant. "Because you gave P.T. what I never had."

"Love?" His father had literally died for him. If he didn't understand the depth of Adam's love, I had no sympathy.

"More. A sense of . . . order. Of P.T. knowing his place in the family, and your limits. Of knowing he had to behave."

I wasn't having it. "The difference is that he wanted to."

"Yes, sir." His glance was shy. "I used to sneer at P.T. for calling you 'sir.' "

From Mikhael, a snort of contempt.

"And now?"

Abruptly his composure wavered. "I wish I could undo so much! If Dad had thrown my puter out that window"—he jabbed at the bungalow—"and if you—that night you caught me on the roof . . ." He'd been spying on Rob Boland and his father, in our guest room. "If you had put an end to it . . ."

Had I possibly . . . I shied from the thought. Could it be that I'd misjudged him? "Adam wanted me to discipline you." My tone was gruff. "He didn't know how."

Abruptly, Jared seemed to change the subject. "You know, I love—"

"I'm going inside." Mikhael, truculent.

I turned, wheeled my chair to his seat. Deliberately, I slapped his face.

"God damn you!" He clawed at my eyes.

Somehow I caught his fingers, grasped his wrist, managed to twist his arm behind his back. Struggling, he fell across my chair. I raised his wrist ever higher between his shoulders, until he squealed.

"You'll sit until I tell you." No answer. "Right?"

"Okay!"

"Yes, sir!"

"I won't—stop twisting—*yes, sir!*"

I let go. Mikhael fell back, nursing his arm. Breathing heavily, I turned back to Jared, thankful for my incredible luck. The boy could easily have pulled me from my chair, left me flopping helpless on the ground.

"You were saying?"

"I love Philip." Perhaps my savagery had unnerved him; his tone held a challenge.

"I'm aware."

"He doesn't speak much of you. He doesn't want to hurt me, you see. He's dom, even though I'm older. He knows so much more, and . . ." Blessedly, he left it at that.

"What do you want of me?"

"I don't want you between us! Oh, God, that's not how I meant it. I know I was awful. Only Uncle Robbie saved me from prison. And Dad . . . what I did was terrible, but I love P.T. so, and we . . ." He broke off. "I want to crawl into that cottage, and be fifteen again, and come out right, not glitched like I've been. If only you knew how I dream of it."

A long silence, broken only by Mikhael's breathing.

My voice was soft. "I do, son." More than Jared knew.

"Mr. Seafort, could you possibly forgive me?"

Slowly, shyly, I offered my hand.

Minutes later I watched him go, warmed by I knew not what.

Time to cope with the disaster I'd caused. I turned to Mikhael, my face grim. How could I explain this fiasco to Moira? I had no more right to touch her son than . . . than . . . I rolled myself toward him.

He recoiled, flung up an arm to cover his cheek.

"I came to get you to stop hating me. Now I don't care. Hate me all you like." I glowered. "You're not to show it in my presence."

A subdued nod.

"Now, before we go in, I want . . . no, that's not fair. I'm asking you, not ordering. Would you please tell me why you're so angry at me? What did I do?"

"You know goddamn . . ." He swallowed.

"It's all right. Tell me in anger, if that's the only way."

He studied my face, to see if I meant it. Apparently reassured, he said bitterly, "You killed him."

"Nonsense."

"You might as well have. You dragged him to the U.N., knowing they'd already tried to assassinate you."

I cried, "Wild horses couldn't have stopped him!" He stared in surprise. "Son . . . Mikhael . . . you didn't know your father very well, did you?"

"Dad's last cruise to New China . . . it was a year and a half. I begged to go, but he and Mother decided I should stay in school. When he brought *Melbourne* home he arranged six months' extra leave, so we'd get to know each other again. Only, before he could . . ." His voice caught.

I spoke to the hedge. "Once upon a time, your dad was a middy with me, on *Hibernia*. He was . . . how can I make you see him? Conscientious, of course. Handsome, as you are. Poised. In fact, he looked so like you I thought I saw a ghost today."

I waited for his scorn, but none came.

"We lost several officers, so we were shorthanded. Captain Malstrom appointed him to defend a sailor at his courtmartial. No defense was possible, and the man was condemned to death."

"So?"

"I found Alexi on his bunk in the wardroom, crying." How could I make him understand? "The sailor set up a still to make and sell illegal drugs. He clubbed a petty officer. He deserved conviction, but your dad tried his best to save him. He was heartbroken he couldn't. That's the sort of man he was."

I stole a glance; Mikhael contemplated his fingers.

"I comforted him. I wasn't good at it, but I stroked him, tried to give him peace."

A sniffle.

"Of course he went with me to the Rotunda, son. I was to be dismissed by the Patriarchs that day, and he couldn't let me face it alone."

The boy's eyes rose, tormented.

My voice strained. "If you pray to Lord God that we switch places, he and I, I'll pray it with you."

We sat in silence.

"I'm going to give you a special present. If you don't want it, don't reject it in scorn. That's all I ask. Treat it with respect."

"What is it?"

"A surprise. After I have your promise."

A long while passed. "I promise."

"I promise, *sir.*"

A pause I thought would last forever. "I promise, sir."

9

Safe at last in the privacy of my study, I called my Rotunda office. "Where's Derek Carr?"

"In Singapore, arranging wheat contracts. He's due back Monday next."

I frowned; Derek lost no chance to subvert our colonial policy. Now he was bypassing the Import Bureau. "Put me through to him."

In ten minutes the caller buzzed. I said softly, "Derek, old friend, I need you. Will you come?"

"When?"

"As soon as you can."

"I've negotiations in progress . . ." A sigh. "I suppose I can move some of them to Washington, and do others by holo. Tomorrow morning. I'll wrap up a meeting tonight and catch a suborbital."

We rang off. Thank Lord God for Derek. Knowing I wouldn't summon him lightly, he didn't ask my cause. Fifty years of trust will do that.

I did my best to bring cheer to dinner, but nothing could salvage the day. There'd been too much emotion, and we were all tired. Afterward, I apologized to Moira for striking her son. To my astonishment, she threw her arms around me.

Late in the evening, I retreated to my study, where Midshipman Anselm found me.

He hemmed and hawed, before at last he came out with it. "I want a drink."

"I told you—"

"Yes, sir. I spent the afternoon thinking of going out. I could jump the wall, if I had to. But I don't; I found every kind of liquor in your cabinet."

"You sneaking little—two demerits! Four!"

"I didn't say I drank it." His shoulders slumped. "I was stupid to come here. I thought perhaps you'd help." It could have been contempt, and insolence. Or desperation.

I shifted, to ease my back. "Why me?"

"Who else, sir? You're my commanding officer."

Why did every bloody joey I knew toss his problems in my lap? I had too many of my own, and no more strength. "Very well, my order is rescinded. Drink all you want."

He blinked. His fists clenched, relaxed, clenched again.

"Anything else, Anselm?"

He sagged, as if defeated. "No, sir." He trudged to the door.

Let him sink or swim. He hadn't been born an alcoholic, he'd become one. He'd made his bed, now he could sleep in it.

It was always day somewhere. When the Americas were in moonlight, functionaries in other parts of the world were toiling at their desks. I took as many calls as I could, but in an hour I was yawning uncontrollably. Giving up, I rang Security, wheeled myself to the stairs. In a few moments, three burly guards gripped my chair.

I sighed. "Not yet." I wheeled myself to the living room. Anselm sat before the liquor cabinet, staring moodily.

"How much have you had?" My voice dripped scorn.

"None yet."

"Why not?"

"God, you're a cruel son of a bitch." He swallowed a sob. "I suppose you'll cashier me, but I don't think I care."

Lord Christ, what had I done? I maneuvered into the room, swung shut the door. "Anselm . . ."

He drew himself up. "I apologize, Mr. SecGen. On duty or not, I'm way out of line."

"Not when you tell the truth. I *am* cruel. I've never been able to help it." I patted the couch. "It's I who apologize. Come sit near." He did. "You're how old, seventeen?"

"Well . . . in two months."

"When did you start drinking?"

"Three years ago."

"Devon has ample opportunity." Half a dozen pubs within walking distance of the gate. Still, he'd have been only a cadet, then. Someone risked the law's wrath. I wondered why.

"It's zarky. They don't even ask ID; my uniform is enough."

"On your honor, Midshipman. Do you ever drink on duty?"

He bristled. "Never. Not once."

"But you report back to base soused?"

"Not exactly." A grin flickered. "Anyway, I wouldn't be the only one."

I didn't rise to the bait. Servicemen were the same, all over the world. "Do you get leave all that often?"

"Almost every week. Commandant Hazen is . . . kind?" He colored. "Generous is a better word."

"Foolish" was more apt. As Commandant, I'd allowed my middies occasional leave, but not so often as to make them sots.

"Too much leave," I mused aloud. "And you're on holiday even now. That was a mistake."

"You're sending me back." For some reason, he sounded crestfallen.

That would be putting the fox in the henhouse. He had little self-control, this lad, and to place him unsupervised among the brewhouses . . .

"No, Tad. I'll have orders cut. You'll be posted with us." Though Danil Bevin was willing and good-natured, it was too much to expect the cadet to cope alone with a cantankerous SecGen. I needed a middy, and Anselm might as well be he. I owed him something for my cruelty.

His expression was that of a boy who found an Arcvid console in his Christmas stocking. He gulped, unsure it was real. "Working for you, sir?" His voice was tremulous.

"You approve, Mr. Anselm?"

"Yes. Oh, yes."

I grunted, glad of my decision. "You've had all the leave you'll see for a while. No drinking, on or off duty. You're not to leave the grounds without permission from me or Mr. Branstead."

"Aye aye, sir. Anything else?"

"Yes. It's unthinkable to disobey a direct order, but if you do—that is, if you have so much as a sip of liquor, you're to put yourself on report immediately."

"Aye aye, sir."

"And, I might add, I'll have you caned within an inch of your life. Perhaps the threat will help."

He looked wistfully at the cabinet. "You'd trust me around all these bottles, and to tell you afterward?"

"I hope you understand honor, boy. Else the Navy has no place for you." It was no more than was asked of any middy: to log the strenuous exercise that worked off a demerit, for example. Nobody ever checked. To lie about such things was unimaginable.

"Yes, sir. What are my duties?"

"I'll try to keep you busy. Start by leading Bevin in his calisthenics each morning. I don't want you two getting soft."

I could have sworn I heard a snort of derision.

*   *   *

After breakfast, Philip caught me on the way to my office. "Why was Jared in tears last night?"

I stopped short. "I have no idea."

"You had a talk with him, did you not?"

"Rather the reverse. I don't recall being harsh." I hesitated. "Did you ask?"

"He wouldn't tell me, except he was glad to be home at last." Philip grimaced. "I hope it isn't mood swings. He'll be devastated if he needs more treatment."

I patted his arm. "You've always looked after him, haven't you?" At twelve, he'd followed Jared to the urban jungle of Lower New York in a frantic attempt to rescue him.

"I tried. Fath, we need to talk."

"In my study." I led the way.

"You look grim. Is something wrong?"

"No, it's . . ." I shook my head. "They called from Johns Hopkins. Charlie Witrek's transplants failed. They'll have to try again." I made an effort to put it behind me. "What is it, son?"

P.T. pulled up a hassock, sat at my knees, as he had as a boy. "In the old days, a man could ask the king a boon."

I snorted. "I'm no king."

"Merely an autocrat." He smiled, to take the sting from his words. "How difficult was your trip to England?"

"Terrible. Blood was everywhere. I called some of the families. And the water damage . . . The exhibits were ruined. They'll be ages cleaning—"

"I meant, how difficult for you to travel?"

I wanted no pity. "I'm fine. Well, obviously, I'm less mobile than before. Otherwise, have no concern." I ought not be so short with him. His motives were only the best.

"In that case, I ask a favor."

His formality startled me. I made a noncommittal sound.

"A few days of your time."

"I know I've been busy since you came home. I'll try to

do better." Lunch, just the two of us. And after dinner, I could squeeze—

"I want to take you on a trip."

"Where?"

"I'd rather show you."

"Son, I have a huge staff. The advance team, security . . . I can't just take off—"

Mischievously he raised an eyebrow. "What about London?"

"That was different."

"Please, sir. If there's anything you want in return, I'll do it." His tone was quiet, his manner calm, as if he'd found some inner peace.

"Give up your enviro politics?" I was only half joking.

A long pause. "If that's the cost."

After a moment I looked away. "I won't ask that." Not if I had a shred of decency.

"Fath, I need you. Will you come?"

My breath hissed. How could he know I'd summoned Derek with the exact words?

I had no idea into what marsh I was casting myself. "Yes, son. How soon?"

We negotiated, settled on five days hence. It would give me time to clear my schedule, and I wouldn't abandon the Tamarovs.

I sent my chair racing to the pad the moment I heard the drone of Derek's heli. Bevin sprinted desperately to keep up; we'd been in the study, working on Admiralty dispatches.

At the pad, we waited for the blades to slow. Danil panted, "That wasn't fair. You kept telling it to go faster."

"Only once."

"'Flank, chair, flank!'" He bent, hands on his knees.

"All right, twice. Ah, Derek. Thanks so much."

He took my hand. "No fire? No one's ill?"

"No, but I needed—"

"I could actually have had a night's sleep? Why is the cadet's face red?"

"He's out of shape. Danil, find Mikhael Tamarov, tell him I have his present. We'll be in my office."

Derek and I settled over iced drinks. I waved at a waiting stack of chips, all classified too highly to send over the nets. "It never ends."

"Delegate," he said.

"I try, but . . ." I slipped one into the holovid. "Here's an example. Admiral Dubrovik's been injured in a fall. The Board of Admiralty wants to appoint his aide Simovich as Acting. If the old man doesn't recover, he'll be named to the post. Should I—"

"What post?"

"Lunapolis Command. Should I involve myself, or let them do their job? Yes, phrasing it that way answers the question. But sometimes they appoint idiots, and it's hell removing them."

"Do you know Simovich?"

"No, but he can't be worse than Admiral Dubrovik." At *Galactic*'s dedication, to my embarrassment, he'd lauded me beyond reason.

The door swung open. "You wanted me?" Mikhael. His tone wasn't combative. Not quite. At breakfast his manner had wavered between belligerence and civility.

"This is my office. Knock before you enter."

We glared.

"Go out and do it properly. I'm waiting."

He didn't quite slam the door. After a long moment, a knock.

"Come in, Mikhael." I waved to a seat. "This is Mr. Carr, from Hope Nation. He served with your father on *Hibernia* and *Portia*. He's going to sit with you for an hour and tell you stories."

"This is why you called me from Singapore?" Derek's tone was plaintive.

"I'll explain later."

"*That's* your present?" The boy snorted.

"I have your promise, Mikhael: no scorn. Reject my gift if you wish, and I'll send Derek home with my apology." I waited, holding my breath. He was silent. "Go on, you two." I shepherded them out.

Nervous as a cat, I rolled from window to door and back. I'd never realized how much I needed to pace. In a chair it wasn't the same.

What in the Lord's name was I doing? I'd summoned Derek from work he deemed important—for which he'd endured the nine-month journey from his home—to help a sulky, spoiled joeykid who didn't esteem the gift of his company. And all for what? The boy wasn't mine to raise. If he were, I'd have long since wiped the petulance from his manner. Alexi had erred, leaving him home with Moira. A ship was a healthy environment: no drugs, no Arcvid, middies to set an example of discipline. And of course, Mikhael would have been under the stern eyes of his father.

I thumbed the caller, dialed Anselm. Another boy who couldn't be left alone for long. Perhaps I should mark my liquor bottles. "Middy? Report to my office." I rang off.

In a moment, the thunder of footsteps racing down the stairs. "Midshipman Anselm reporting!"

"As you were. Where's Danil?"

"Ms. Seafort offered him lunch."

"I suppose you're hungry too?"

"Not really." He made a face. "My stomach hurts."

"Withdrawal pains?"

"Sir, even if I'm an alcoholic like you say, it's not gone that far."

"Pray it hasn't. Help me file. Those chips on the desk are sorted by—now look what you've done!" With clumsy enthusiasm he'd knocked a dozen chips to the floor. "You're just begging for demerits, aren't you?"

His voice was small. "No, sir, I'm not." He gathered them up.

"No matter." I tried to hide my contrition. "It's my back-ache." And worry over Derek and Mikhael. "Put each in the holovid, check the header, file them—now what?"

My caller buzzed. The private line that few knew.

"Mr. Seafort? Jerence Branstead. I'm at the Assembly." He seemed grim. "The Territorials pulled a surprise vote to kill the Greenhouse Gases Act."

"Can't you stop them?"

"They're calling the roll."

Over fifteen hundred members to poll. An arduous process, but if the Terries had organized themselves and we hadn't, the result was inevitable. I'd planned to persuade our waverers, rally the doubtful. I said, "We'll reintroduce next session."

"It's not just the one bill. They'll claim they defeated us on a major package, that it's a vote of no-confidence."

"Goofjuice." The vote was a tactical surprise, and we'd had no opportunity to gather our forces. Assembly rules allowed no proxy votes, no call-ins or puter tallies. Members had to vote in person; the Terries must have worked hard to spring this on us. Why the sudden lunge for power?

"You and I think so, but that's not how the media will play it. Sir, we'll look hopelessly inept. The Government could even fall."

"That bad?" If I retired, I wanted to hand over my Government to a Supra, even a ditherer like Cisno Valera. Our opposition, the Territorials, were too heavy-handed, both with the colonies and our own joeys at home. It was they who'd sent U.N.A.F. heavy brigades into hapless transpop neighborhoods, they who had aimed Lunapolis's lasers at New York. I'd tried to strike a balance between the enviro fringe and legitimate business needs, but the Terries would sell home system for a short-term profit.

"There's no way to stop the vote?" My fingers ached, from gripping the chair arm.

"None. In three hours we're done."

Three hours. That was the key. "Jerence, get to the floor. Stall."

"How? Why?"

"Have our joeys switch their votes, call points of order. I'm on my way."

"You're what?"

"Meet me at the Assembly entrance. I'll be there in . . . two hours or so. As long as the vote's still in progress, we have a chance. In the meantime, stay on your caller; round up every Supra you can find, pressure the Indie caucus. We—"

"You can't be here in time. Mark has to secure the site—"

"Get to work." I spun my chair. "ANSELM!"

He jumped. "Jesus, I'm right here! You scared the life—"

"Find Derek, tell him we're borrowing his heli, meet me at the pad. Run!" I thumbed the caller. "Cadet, to the hallway, flank speed! Mark, report to the helipad. Chair, to the veranda." I flung open the door, cannoned into a pair of legs.

"Ow!"

"Get off of—sorry, Jared. Hold the outside door, will you? Bevin, where in blazes—ahh, there you are. Put down the sandwich, we're in a hurry."

"To where, sir?"

"New York. Chair, I could crawl faster than you—haie!" I clung desperately to the armrests. "Not *that* fast."

In moments we were at the pad. Anselm galloped to meet us. Jared Tenere followed, slowly at first, then breaking into a trot.

"Get me in there." I pointed to the fuselage. "Danil, Tad, lift me." I tried to help. "Where's Tilnitz?"

"Did he come back?" Bevin. "He went out the gate about an hour—"

"Jared, give a hand, will you? I'm too heavy for them." Damn. I was counting on Mark to drive the heli. "I don't suppose any of you can pilot? I would, but my legs . . ."

My three assistants flung me into the heli.

Anselm said tentatively, "I've had lessons, sir." Learning to pilot was one of the joys of Academy. Ironically, many of our cadets could fly long before they could drive a ground-car.

"How many? Did you qualify?"

"Only a few, but—"

Jared Tenere said with quiet confidence, "I have my license. I'll fly you there."

"Did Derek leave the keys? Good. Get us started. Put that chair in the back." With effort I hauled myself into a seat, brushed off my jacket. "Call Philip and tell him you won't be home for dinner."

In a moment, Jared had our blades turning. I jabbed at the caller. "Arlene, I'm off to the Rotunda. Tell Mark, when you see him. We'll be back tonight."

"Nick, be careful."

"Of course."

"Who's with you?"

"The boys and Jared."

"I mean, for security."

"The boys and Jared. I'll be all right." I devoutly hoped it was true.

"Fly northeast." I gave Jared the coordinates. "Let the autopilot handle it. Ignore the speed limit, I'm in a hurry."

We hurtled across the landscape. I called Branstead. "Clear a flight path. They're a bit trigger-happy at the Rotunda these days; make sure we're not shot down. Jared, what's our transponder?" I fed Branstead the code. "We'll set down in an hour and a half, if this youngster doesn't dawdle."

Abruptly the engine roared. Satisfied, I sat back.

*　　*　　*

We put down on the browning grass in front of the General Assembly, where no heli was allowed to land. Instantly my excited crew flung open the door, threw my chair to the ground, hauled me after. I glanced about; thank heaven, the only mediamen present had their view blocked by the heli. Else I could imagine the zines' lead: SecGen Seafort dragged protesting across the lawn.

They bundled me into my chair. I ordered it up the ramp. Branstead swung open the door. "Where's Mark? Get in, before someone takes a shot at you. They're almost through the roll. I couldn't slow them much. We'll be down a hundred eleven. I met with seven of the Indies—"

"Jerence, take a breath."

"—and they won't agree—"

"A deep breath. Now." I rolled along the marble corridor, toward the Assembly. "Call Perrel out, and Bosconi." I stopped. The SecGen never entered the Assembly chamber during a session; it just wasn't done. On the other hand, I knew of no rule that codified the custom. "Never mind. Straight ahead, chair. Boys, come with me."

"You're not—" Branstead seemed to read my mind.

"Watch me." A uniformed officer stood by the entry. "Mr. SecGen? There's a session in—" He flung open the door to save it from collision damage.

"Where's Assemblyman Perrel?" I peered at astonished faces. "Ahh. Make way." I rolled down the aisle. Perrel was a weak man. Venal, but weak. If I could break him, I'd make a start.

The President of the Assembly looked up. A flicker of surprise. She nodded to the clerk, who droned on.

"Jared, find Denlow; he's the fattest man here and has a walrus mustache. Bring him here." As the young man rushed off I swung to Perrel. "You're voting against us, Howard?"

Perrel had the grace to blush. "Sorry, but—"

"No time for reasons. You're ready to see a change of Government?"

"It doesn't have to come to that."

"Of course it does."

"If you'd given in on the mining bill . . ."

"Never mind. How many did you carry along?"

He shrugged. "A few."

"Thirty?"

"Thirty-seven, I figure." He sounded proud.

"Get busy. Reverse their votes."

"Why? You can't threaten me. I have an understanding with the Terries. Once you go down——"

"Minister of what? Resources?"

He flushed. "That's none of your concern."

"Resources?"

"Yes."

"Very well." I backed the chair, to turn. "Cadet, have Mr. Branstead round up the Indie caucus."

"What are you going to do?" Perrel.

"Hold a news conference, the moment the vote's done."

"To say what?"

I smiled. "Why, Howard, nothing but the truth. That you made a deal with the Terries, that you brought them thirty-seven votes in exchange for a ministry, that I find such sordid dealing despicable and wonder if the electorate will stomach it. That's all." I rolled a few paces, said over my shoulder, "The voters probably won't throw you out of office. But the Terries won't touch you with a ten-foot pole. Say good-bye to a ministry. And who'd trust you, after?"

He licked his lips.

"Bring back your thirty-seven votes, and I'll send Rob Boland to talk about the mining bill. No promises." I strained to see over a bulky figure. "Where are the Indies?"

With some I cajoled, with others, pleaded. As the President finished the roll, one by one, members of Perrel's cohort rose reluctantly to switch their votes. It all took time, which I badly needed. I promised the Indies support on education funding that I'd already intended to give. Sixteen votes; two refused to go along. I wheeled about the chamber, forcing down my gorge, buttonholing politicians. While Branstead snapped hushed orders into his caller, Jared Tenere raced from one aisle to another, summoning those I wished to browbeat.

They might not have liked me, but still I was SecGen; they came at my call.

As the vote narrowed, Branstead and his staff fanned out through the hall, luring others into the fold. With each vote we gained, the remainder became easier. And my chief of staff had made a heroic effort; absent Supras rushed into the chamber, recalled by suborbital from their far-flung destinations.

I careened around the Assembly chamber.

When it was done we'd won by three.

"Relieved?" Derek sat comfortably, legs crossed, nursing his evening drink.

"I suppose." I mused. "It's ironic; we nearly fell, over an enviro bill I don't really support. That's not how I'd care to go out of office."

"Why'd you—"

"We have to give the enviros something." The Greenhouse Gases Act was all I'd concede, though. It would play havoc with our economy, and I wasn't at all sure it was necessary. Yet a surprising number of Assemblymen supported it.

I hated the compromise of politics. Richard Boland, Rob's father, had tried to teach me his love of dealmaking, but I couldn't abide it.

Across the room, Moira Tamarov drowsed in the sofa. Carla played listlessly at a video. It reminded me of unfinished business. "How was your talk with Mikhael?"

"I reminisced. At first he was surly."

"And then?"

"He liked the part about Alexi and the Admiral. When I told him about *Portia,* he had to wipe his eyes. Nick, what's this about?"

"You'll see." I keyed the caller. "Mr. Anselm, join us downstairs, and bring Mikhael, if you would."

In a moment the boys appeared.

"Mr. Anselm, you were to begin exercises with the cadet. Did you?"

"Not yet, sir. This morning, we—"

"One demerit. You'll start tomorrow." I turned to Mikhael. "Did you like my present?"

"I guess." He perched on the arm of a chair.

"If that's all, go back upstairs."

He stayed put. "All right, I liked it."

"Very well." My tone was frosty. "You'll be here five more days. Every morning, Mr. Carr will tell you about your father." I paused. "An hour of stories for every hour you exercise with the middy and cadet."

"Forget it!"

"It's forgotten. Go to bed."

He stalked to the door. Footsteps pounded upstairs.

"Sorry, Derek." I made a face. "It didn't work."

"He's not an easy one. Unpleasant, snotty—"

"Like you, at his age."

Derek colored. "Yes, you knocked some sense into me. But he's a civilian; you have no authority over him."

"I have to try."

Derek said gently, "Nick, I had urgent business in Singapore. For you, I don't mind rearranging my schedule, though it's not as efficient. But for him . . ."

"Make allowances. He lost his father."

Derek's tone was sharp. "I lost mine." Randolph Carr had been killed in the explosion of *Hibernia's* launch. "It didn't turn me into a . . ." He paused, reflective. "Still, for months, I was in shock. If you hadn't befriended me . . ."

I sat moodily, drifting through old times.

"Nick, you have so much on your plate; why discommode yourself for him?"

"Not for him, for an old shipmate. I owe Alexi that."

"He was my first friend, after you." Derek stared into his glass. "In the wardroom, Vax Holser was . . . difficult. Alexi helped me through."

"Tell him. The boy."

"It's hard to speak of. But we were good friends. And later, after you left for *Challenger,* it was grim. I was afraid Alexi would get himself beached for his open contempt of the Admiral."

"He never told me."

"There's a lot he never told you." Derek was moody. "Ah, well. Days long past. Do you think you can salvage the boy?"

"Unlikely. You were his only chance."

"Why make me work?" Mikhael, from the doorway.

I said without turning, "Why, *sir.*"

"Why, sir?" He spat the words.

"Because you're spoiled and sullen, and I don't like you. Because you'll never see Mr. Carr after he goes home; you have a once in a lifetime opportunity you don't appreciate. Because . . ." I threw up my hands.

Derek asked, "Why me? You served with Alexi, too."

"He'll believe you. He'll never be sure I'm not lying."

"I never said that." Mikhael was petulant.

"You didn't have to."

"I don't want to exercise."

"Then don't, joey. Middy, what time will you start?"

"Eight-thirty, sir."

"Be there or not, as you choose. Say good night civilly, before you go."

Fuming, Mikhael did as I bade.

"Derek, if your negotiations suffer, I'll make it up to you.

We'll fiddle with the transport rates, or—" My caller chirped. With resignation, I keyed it. "Yes?"

"Branstead, here. What do you think?"

"Of the vote? About all we could have—"

"The message on your puter. Didn't you see it?"

"No."

"Read it. You pushed him too far. I'll talk to you after." He rang off.

"Chair, to my office." I was too weary to roll myself.

The message was on my opening screen.

> *Mr. SecGen Seafort:*
> *It is with regret that, for personal reasons, I resign as Director of Security for the Secretary-General. I wish you the best of fortune.*
> *Mark H. Tilnitz*

"Damn." My cavalier jaunt to New York had pushed him over the edge.

"Problems, sir?" Anselm, from the doorway.

I didn't know I'd spoken aloud. "No. Yes. Come in and be quiet." I keyed my night secretary, in New York. "Can you reach Tilnitz?"

"Just a moment, sir."

A click. Another. "Karen Burns."

"I asked for Mark."

"I understand he's left the detail." Her voice was cool. "And I believe he went on leave."

"Very well."

"I'll be in Washington in three hours. Do you travel tomorrow?"

"There's nothing planned."

"I knew that, Mr. SecGen."

So. Burns, too, was annoyed at my impetuosity. Perhaps it would mean mass resignations, but I wouldn't allow myself to be a prisoner of my security detail. In mutual hostility, we rang off. I punched in Branstead's code. "Can we get him back?"

"Will you accept protection?"

I debated. "Jerence, security drives me crazy."

"A short drive." It was little over a whisper.

I whirled. The middy studied the ceiling. "I heard that. Fifty push-ups."

"Aye aye, sir." He loosened his tie.

"What's going on?" Branstead.

"A minor mutiny." Was it my wheelchair? The relaxed atmosphere of home? Something in the air? Not only Anselm, but Bevin and, for that matter, Mikhael, felt free to say whatever came into their heads.

Intolerable. Why, then, did I feel like grinning? Why did I bear the midshipman no animosity? Why did it remind me of Philip's younger days? "Jerence, can you work a compromise with Mark?"

"So he'll only protect you from the waist up? Oh, I make jokes, but it's not funny. None of us want you killed."

The middy grunted, halfway through his labors.

"Mr. SecGen, I'll try, but I'm with Mark on this."

"I know, Jerence."

"By the way, you not only won the vote, you won the zines. 'SecGen Races to Save Administration.' 'Surprise Visit Turns Vote.' 'Seafort Saves Enviro Cause.'"

I snorted.

"I'm done, sir."

"Thirty more. Take off your jacket." Let the boy twit me if he must. He'd learn that all things came at a cost. Then, "Give yourself a rest if you need one." My tone was gruff.

"We have messages of support pouring in. It's not just Winstead's crowd. Suddenly everyone's behind the greenhouse bill. The Paki Prime Minister, the Filipinos. Tomorrow's *Calcutta Times* calls it the most important legislation of the decade. Andrus Bevin of the Enviro Council lauds your staunch leadership. You know, the Terries miscalculated badly."

"Hmpph." So had we, if I'd unleashed a new flood of enviro fervor.

"It's a groundswell," said Branstead, as if to irritate me further. "Mothers For a Sane Tomorrow, the Swedish Better Government League, the Small Business Council—"

"All *right*, Jerence." I threw up my hands. "Send me a summary."

"Will do, sir. Congratulations."

After we rang off, I had Anselm get himself a softie. "Have a seat. If you're as insolent as you are, no need to stand on formality."

He blushed. "You weren't supposed to hear that."

"Are you sure?"

His eyes danced. "Well . . . not quite, sir."

Abruptly, his mischief recalled Alexi, as a boy. Saddened, I asked, "Do you know what's wrong with Mikhael Tamarov?"

"Didn't he just lose his father?"

"Beyond that."

His tone was bleak. "Is there anything beyond that?"

I fell silent. I'd never seen the middy's file, never thought to ask. "Tell me."

"Three years ago. I was at Academy. The Berlin suborbital."

I winced. A corroded engine cowling; the shuttle had been based near the Volgograd plant. Some blamed pollution. Whatever the cause, the fiery crash had left three hundred dead. We were lucky at that; the craft was only half full. "I'm sorry."

"It's just . . ." He sought the last of his drink. "It doesn't matter."

I rolled myself close. "Tell me."

He shook his head. Just as I decided to let him be, the words spewed out. "He was on his way to visit me. My first leave. We were going . . . going to . . ." His shoulders shook in a silent spasm.

Lord Christ, why couldn't I have left well enough alone?

"Mr. Hazen called me in. He tried to be kind." A sniffle. "When I saw his face, a blade twisted in my gut. I started to cry before I heard a word."

Helpless, I squeezed his shoulder.

"My mother had died years before, all I had was a distant pair of aunts. I spent my two weeks' leave at Devon, in a daze." His smile was bitter. "Evenings, a middy took me out."

A window opened. "That's when you began to drink."

"We found a barkeep who didn't notice I wore gray."

"Oh, Tad."

"I'd been . . . I couldn't wait for Pa to arrive. My ratings, my reports were decent. More than that. He'd have glanced at them, smiled in that way he had, looked at me with such pride." His eyes were wet. "But that's not how it was."

I yearned to hug him, but I was stuck in a bloody chair, and it wouldn't be right. Not if I was SecGen and his C.O. to boot.

"And now, to whom do you show your ratings?"

A shrug. "No one. It doesn't matter." His tone was elaborately casual.

We'd both lost fathers at Academy. His had vanished in fire, mine simply strode away. Would he ever recover?

Would I?

"Come here, lad." I tugged him nearer the chair. To his astonishment, I pulled him to my chest.

After a time, my jacket was damp.

10

Two dreary days passed. Branstead toiled in New York with the aftershocks of the failed Territorial coup. I sought Mark Tilnitz, but he made himself unavailable. Meanwhile, the Victoria and Albert investigation made slow progress. We now knew a great deal more about the terrorist dead, their families, their friends, their work. But nothing about their living cohorts.

Seething, Mikhael Tamarov joined Anselm and the cadet at exercises. He stalked off after forty minutes; I gave him forty minutes with Derek.

The next day, he worked an hour and a half.

Outside my home, throngs gathered each day; tourists, the curious, the desperate. Word of my sojourn outside the hospital had spread. On a whim, I made Karen open the gate, let the seekers in a few at a time, while I sat in the courtyard.

In the afternoons I struggled through paperwork with Bevin and the middy. In three days' time I would leave with Philip for whatever mysterious journey he had in mind. I had to clear my desk.

I had an appointment with the neurologists; to keep peace I let Karen Burns arrange the outing. Arlene insisted on going as well. With reluctance, I acquiesced. If the news were bad, I wasn't sure I wanted her to hear. I'd have arrangements to make, preparatory to my end, that she might want to block.

I'd considered making a life of it in the chair. If that was what Lord God wanted for me . . .

But I'd defied Him so often it was becoming a habit. There was no way I could earn his Hell more than I already had. So I would kill myself, rather than struggle to hoist myself on the toilet, toil to dress myself, roll about my compound dependent on aides to lift me up the stairs.

Life wasn't so precious as that. Not when I'd sailed to the stars.

"May I come in, please?" Mikhael. His wiry hair was neatly brushed, his shirt pressed.

I gestured to a seat.

"I want more . . ." He reined himself in, started over. "There's just so much calisthenics I can handle. What if I want more time with Mr. Carr?"

"Cadets exercise two hours a day."

"I'm no frazzing cadet!"

"Certainly not; there's no way they'd have you."

"That's not fair."

I couldn't abide his sullenness. "Get out."

His running steps faded up the stairs.

I toyed with my holovid, furious at him. At myself. I wheeled out, to the foot of the stairs, opened my mouth to call him down.

A faint sound. Was it a sob?

Bevin and Anselm were nowhere in sight. Who would lift me? With a muttered epithet I hoisted myself to the bottom step, sat facing downward. One stair at a time, I dragged my lower body upward. Halfway up I stopped, worked my way out of my jacket so as not to roast. Then I labored on my way.

At the top I met Carla Tamarov. She'd been watching. "Go down, please. Find someone to help with my chair."

"You made him cry."

"Yes. I do that."

She trotted down the stairs. Sitting, I dragged myself toward Mikhael's room. I knocked, reached up, swung the door open.

"Get—" His eyes widened. Disheveled, perspiring, I was a sight.

I hauled myself toward his bed. "Alexi would give you comfort. I don't know how."

"I don't need you." His tone was scornful.

"You do." I was bitter. "There's no one else."

"To do what?"

"Help me up. I'll show you."

Puzzled, he helped hoist me onto the bed. I pulled my legs straight, paused for breath. I took his chin, held it so his eyes faced mine. "I'm sorry I chased you out. I loved your father. If I were dead, he'd have cared for my son too."

He jerked from my grasp, spun to the wall.

"Your mother is . . . overwhelmed."

"I know." His voice was muffled.

"Shall I ask her if you can stay awhile?" What was I saying? I hadn't time enough for my daily holochips, to say nothing of the middy, Arlene, P.T. . . .

"We wouldn't get along a minute."

He was right. Thank heavens one of us had sense to know it.

"Don't discredit what you were to me. And still are." Alexi, in my Lunapolis suite.

I considered.

Mikhael looked away. "You're scowling."

"If your father saw how you behaved in my house, what would he say?"

"I have no idea."

"Tell me!" I gripped his wrist.

He shrugged, but I held him tightly. "He'd . . . I don't—"

Suddenly his voice became Alexi's. "Straighten out, joey, and I mean *RIGHT NOW!*" He reddened.

I turned his face to mine. I said slowly, levelly, "Straighten out, joey, and I mean right now."

"What do . . . he's gone and you can't—"

"I did. I'll ask your mother."

"Ask me what?" Moira stood at the door, her daughter watching from behind.

"If Mikhael can stay a couple of months. He needs . . ." I wasn't sure what.

"It's up to him." Softly, she brushed a lock of hair from his eyes. "Or you can go with us to Kiev."

We waited.

"I'm spoiled and sullen, remember? And you don't like me."

"Can we be alone a moment?" I waited until the door shut. "You're all that I said, joey. And I despise your behavior."

He bridled.

"As Alexi would." I let go his chin. "You need kindness. More than I'm used to giving. But that's not all of it."

His voice was subdued. "I've been upset."

"Cry for Alexi. I'll respect that. But act to make him proud. And yourself." It was all I knew of life.

"I miss him so!" A cry from the heart.

"As do I. Are you staying?"

"I'll think about it."

"Decide now." My back throbbed abominably, I was near tears, and I needed an end to it.

"You'll be rough on me."

"When you deserve it."

"I'm almost grown. I don't need someone trying to be my father."

"Then leave with Moira. Or go off on your own." I raised my voice. "Moira, is my chair upstairs?"

He pounded a pillow. "All right, God damn it, I'll stay!"

"No dinner tonight," I shot back. "I won't tolerate blasphemy." Straining, I managed to reach the doorknob. Bevin and Arlene waited with my chair. "Roll it in, would you?"

"And if I say it again?"

"I'll have you strapped. On the other hand, two hours with Anselm tomorrow and you get as much with Mr. Carr. And more time with me. I'll try to think of stories he doesn't know. Cadets manage two hours. You can."

"I'm going to hate this." His wave took in the room, the house, me.

I smiled. "But it's good for you."

In the morning, when Bevin and I came in to work, a hand-scrawled note was propped on my holovid. *Sir, I'm placing myself on report as ordered. Midshipman Thadeus Anselm.*

I groaned. "Where's our middy?"

"In his room, I think."

"Get him."

Bevin glanced at the caller.

"Run upstairs and fetch him. I expect him here in the next minute." I was barely civil.

"Aye aye, sir!" He dashed out.

When they raced in Anselm was still thrusting his shirt into his pants. "Midshipman Anselm reporting!"

"Stand at attention. Danil, wait outside." Holding his note, I regarded him balefully. "You disobeyed?"

His eyes were locked front. "Yes, sir."

"Give me specifics."

"I had—" He took a deep breath. "Yesterday afternoon, sir, while you were with Mikhael, I went to your liquor cabinet, helped myself to some bourbon."

I roared, "You won't get away with it!" My fist crashed on the desk, sent the holovid flying.

He made no response.

"Well?" I knew that was unfair. I hadn't asked a question, and held at attention, he wasn't free to speak.

"Yes, sir, I won't get away with it. I knew that when I put myself on report." His forehead had a faint sheen.

"How much?"

"Bourbon? A few slugs."

Thanks to my dead legs I couldn't launch myself from my chair. I pounded the arm. "Contemptible. Disgraceful."

"Yes, sir, it is." His voice quavered.

I eyed him sourly. His stomach was sucked tight, hands pressed to his sides. Sighing, I reached for my official letterhead. It didn't take long to write my note.

"Finish dressing. Go at once to the Potomac Naval Station, give this to the duty officer. This time you'll be put across a real barrel."

"Aye aye, sir." He took the note.

"On your return, stop at a liquor store and replace my bottle of bourbon from your own funds."

"Aye aye, sir."

"Report to me afterward, Mr. Anselm. We'll talk. Dismissed."

With proper precision he saluted, wheeled, and marched out.

Whatever work we dealt with that morning, I barely knew. It was just before lunch when Anselm knocked dejectedly at my door.

"Midshipman Anselm reporting discipline, sir." He had no need to tell me. It was evident in his gait and the misery in his countenance.

"Very well. That's all for now, Danil. Tad, stand or sit, as you prefer."

Gingerly, Anselm put himself in a chair, twisted so he rested on his side.

"I wish it hadn't been necessary to cane you. I admire

your courage in placing yourself on report. You acted honorably."

"It was an order."

"So was not drinking."

"I couldn't . . ." His eyes misted. "I couldn't help that."

My tone was gentle. "Help me understand why."

"Must I?"

I relented. "No." I could punish his acts, but not invade his thoughts.

For a long time there was only the sound of his breathing. Then, "You ever have a dream that came back?"

"When I was younger." I would wake sweating, with the image of Father striding from Academy's gate. No doubt Father loved me, after his fashion, though he rarely showed it.

"I have one. It's . . . sir, I know I've no right to ask, especially today, but . . ." He swallowed. "Don't laugh at me. I couldn't stand it."

"I won't."

"I've had it about a dozen times. I'm in a train station, the HiTrans terminal, I think. I'm on the platform. I'm with my father, and a train is about to leave."

Silent, I rolled from behind the desk.

"We board the train. Only, he's inside, and I'm not. I don't know why. I try to get on, but the doors are shut. And then the—the . . . the . . ." He fought for control. "The train starts out of the station. Slowly at first. Pa is standing by the door, looking sadly through the glass. I'm running alongside, trying to get in, to go with him. The train moves faster, until I can't keep up. He's looking back at me through the glass as the train pulls out. Leaving me alone."

I didn't dare speak.

"And then I wake. Usually I'm crying."

"God in heaven."

"I dreamed it again yesterday."

"And so you had my bourbon."

"Yes, sir. I did."

"Very well. I know your rump smarts; take the afternoon off."

"Aye aye, sir. Thank you."

"If you drink again, you'll be caned again. It's that simple."

"Yes, sir."

I hesitated, decided to throw caution to the winds. "A standing order: if you have the dream again, you're to wake me immediately. Acknowledge."

"Orders received and understood, sir. If I have the dream again, I'm to wake you."

"Dismissed."

In a bright-lit examining room at Boland Memorial, I buttoned my shirt. "So?"

Dr. Knorr said brightly, "It's going as well as can be expected."

Arlene tapped her foot. "Which means?"

"The incision is healed, there's no infection."

"He has horrid stabbing pains. Sometimes, at night—"

I squirmed. It was my body, my decision whether to complain.

"It's a good sign, actually. The connections aren't entirely severed." Knorr's hands spread in an apologetic gesture. "And now you're using muscles you never used. Imagine an old house that's stood for years. You replace half the basement beams. It will creak a bit, as it settles."

"That's the silliest—"

"Nick." Her warning tone.

"Well, it is. Can't any of you speak plainly?"

"What do you want me to say, Mr. SecGen?"

I took a deep breath, and another. "The operation to restore my legs?"

"It looks promising, especially as you still have some feeling at groin level. I'll want you to see Ghenili."

"How soon can he be here?"

"You'll have to go to Lunapolis."

I bristled. "I'm paraplegic and I have work waiting. Call him here."

"That won't be possible." He raised a hand to forestall my objection. "All his diagnostic equipment is at his clinic. He can't relocate his practice for one patient."

I struggled from the table to my chair. "Good day."

"Nick, let him—"

"Out, chair. To the helipad." We lurched to the door.

My wife sighed, followed to the hall. Karen Burns and her detail fell into step.

Arlene asked, "What did that accomplish?"

"The arrogance of him. That snide, supercilious, pompous—"

"Hold, chair." Her tone was a command. Surprisingly, the machine obeyed. "What did you achieve, Nick? A call aloft, and Ghenili could refuse to see you."

"I'll break him. I'll call challenge. I'll have him—"

She bent to put both hands on the arms of my chair, faced me eye to eye. "Enough."

I swallowed. "Am I that out of line?"

"Yes."

"Arggh. It's just . . . I hate doctors." The image flashed of Dr. Uburu, on *Hibernia*, whose gentle decency succored me more than once. Of Dr. Bros on *Portia*, who'd delivered my first child. "Well, most of them."

She regarded me a moment, kissed me gravely on the nose.

"Arrange it for me, will you, hon? I don't want to speak to Knorr again."

"All right."

"Let's go home."

"In a bit. I've arranged a surprise."

"Karen doesn't like surprises." We'd achieved a truce, of a sort.

"She knows."

The heli lifted off as soon as we were strapped in. It set down, a few minutes later, on a rooftop. "Which tower—"

"Franjee Four." It was one of the many towers that had sprung out of the rubble of Lower New York, in the horrid ruin of the Transpop Rebellion. After the devastation of the lasers, it had been all I could do to preserve their culture. For every tower, I'd seen that blocks of neighborhood were rebuilt.

"Robbie Boland?"

She nodded. "Dinner."

Perhaps he wanted to toast our defeat of the Terries in the Assembly. I wouldn't begrudge his celebration.

We crowded into the elevator. As always, Karen sent security joeys ahead. Lord knew how many residents of the tower were barred from their lifts, so I could descend in safety.

Hands at their guns, Security took us to his apartment. I insisted they wait in the hall. Only Karen accompanied us within.

"Welcome, sir." Robbie stood aside.

In the living room two handsome young men waited to greet me. Jared Tenere, and my Philip.

"Hallo, boys." I held out a hand. Jared shook with me. P.T. hugged me. I patted his back.

We started with cocktails. "What did the doctors say, Fath?"

I grimaced. "Don't remind me."

"Are you well enough to travel?"

"If I don't have to dance." Why did my load seem lighter for P.T.'s presence?

How could I have let our estrangement drag on for years?

Over dinner and wine, we chatted amiably about politics, sport, the Navy. For almost the first time, I observed my son with Jared, outside my home. Now and then Jared rested a hand on his. I wondered if they would adopt, as Philip suggested. If he was omni, as he'd said, would I ever see grandchildren of my blood?

Moodily, I refilled my wineglass.

He was my only child. There was Nate, of course, long dead. And perhaps I could call sons the many youngsters who'd followed me to their doom. Even now, I held innocent lives in my hands. Danil Bevin, fearless in the passion of truth. Anselm, accepting even my harsh guidance to save himself. Young Mikhael, desperate for a father forever lost.

If only I could offer more. All I had was myself, flawed, choleric, helpless.

"Fath, why are you weeping?" Philip rose, hurried around the table.

"Because I'm becoming an old man. Because I'm drunk. Because I love you." I fell into his embrace.

Wisely, they gave me little more wine. Over time, my head cleared. After dessert, we adjourned to a huge room whose balcony and picture windows overlooked the reclaimed park, a view only the very wealthy could afford. When I'd been a young officer, I'd visited apartments such as these, and felt only contempt for the occupants.

They said time brings wisdom.

Our mood was mellow. I reminisced about my better days in the Navy. Karen sat quietly in the corner.

Jared perched cross-legged on the floor, near his guardian. "Have you seen *Galactic*, Uncle Rob?"

"Not yet. I keep meaning to go aloft." As Senator, and confidant of the SecGen, Boland would have no difficulty gaining entry.

"We could have toured her with Father, if we'd stayed at Earthport." Philip.

"And Mother." Arlene's tone was tart. "You always speak as if Nick was the only officer in the family."

"Oops. Sorry, ma'am." Philip smiled weakly. Even in the depths of his adolescence, he'd been unstinting in his courtesy. "You were aboard. Tell us what we missed."

"A floating palace. I'm not sure I approve."

"I'm appalled," I said. "Rob, how did we let the Navy go so wrong?"

"Admiralty has a mind of its own. We can't micro-manage every detail."

"The devil," Jared said, "is in the details."

I eyed him suspiciously, not sure whether he was blasphemous.

He blushed. "I read that somewhere."

Rob patted him absently. "Sir, have you met with the Board of Admiralty lately?"

"Not all of them," I said, "but I intend to."

"There's a clique of officers who aren't shy about expressing their views. Their politics are . . . outdated."

"I've met a few."

"They're a danger. We can't start a war to reclaim the colonies; anyone with sense knows that, but these joeys would devote our whole budget to Naval expansion. I'd like to know Admiralty has a grasp of the situation." Rob was blunt. "The sooner you weed them out, the better."

I waved it away. "A long cruise or two will settle them."

"Do it soon, then." Boland sounded uneasy. "What with the eco-terrorists, your disability, the hotheads in the Assembly—"

"Rob, don't be alarmist. I'll look into it." No matter what, we could count on the Navy. The Naval Service was our lifeline to the colonies; it carried the cargoes that nourished our world. And the Navy knew it. Her officers were steeped in honor and proud of their myriad responsibilities.

I drowsed on the ride back to Washington, glad for once that we flew in a huge jet instead of the clattering heli. I dialed my light low, stretched out in my seat, dozed contentedly.

Home at last, I got myself ready for bed, remembering just before I climbed out of the chair to say good night to Mikhael. He was half-asleep, and if he resented my intrusion, he gave no sign.

Gratefully, I dragged myself into bed. I snuggled next to Arlene, reveled in her warmth, fell into sleep.

The Venturas were stunning. Their bristling peaks dominated Hope Nation's uninhabited western continent. Derek sweated happily as we scrambled through scrub and brush to the far side of the valley. We caught glimpses of the icy pool that was our goal.

"Race you, sir?"

I was Captain and he a mere middy, but on our glorious furlough we'd relaxed the rules. "Don't be silly. What's that?" I pointed up the hill.

As soon as his head turned I charged ahead, branches whipping at my face.

"Hey! Wait!" He came crashing after.

I thundered down the slope, pulling my shirt from my pants, fumbling at the buttons. I risked a glance back. The middy was gaining.

My legs pumped. My chest heaved. God, it was fine to be young.

"Nick?"

I would just beat him. It would be close. I thudded through tall grasses, panting. A low-hanging branch loomed; I scrambled through the gap.

"Nicky?"

"Got you, Middy!" I could barely gasp the words. "Last one in is a—"

"Nick!"

I came awake, heart pounding.

"Hon, you were thrashing about. Was it a nightmare?"

No.

The nightmare was in waking. I clutched her like a drowning man a liferaft, my head pressed to her breast.

Wretched hours later, soothed at last by the soft steady stroke of her palm, I slept.

PART II

September, in the Year
of our Lord 2241

11

You'll behave?"

Mikhael looked uncomfortable. "Yes, sir."

"What do I expect?" I rolled from behind my desk.

He rolled his eyes. "You know I won't think of everything."

"I'll give you a start. Courtesy to Arlene, while I'm gone. Calisthenics with Mr. Anselm. A bath every day."

"Why are you down on me? I'm trying not to give you trouble."

"You've done well the past few days. I'm proud of you."

"When you get back, Mr. Carr will be gone."

"He has to go back to work. We'll see him again." Derek's ship wouldn't leave for a month.

"Why can't I go with you?"

"P.T. needs me alone. I don't know why. I'll call every day."

"Yeah."

I waited.

"Yes, sir." It still came hard. After each day of Derek's stories, Mikhael came farther out of his shell, made a greater effort to please me.

I'd asked Derek why. "Not all of my stories are of Alexi," was all he said. "Some are of you." Incomprehensible.

"Tell Philip I'm ready." I keyed the caller. "Danil?" In seconds, the cadet appeared with his duffel. He must have been waiting on the stair. "Where's my gear?"

"In the heli, sir." Bevin grinned from ear to ear, like a foolish puppy. As instructed, he was in civilian garb so as not to call attention to me.

"What's your problem?" I tried to sound severe.

"Nothing, sir. I'm just happy."

At the helipad, Karen Burns intercepted my chair. Her tone was cold. "Mr. SecGen, again I protest."

"Noted. I'll check in at least once a day, and I'll call in an emergency." As if that would be any use.

"We'll monitor your transponder."

"Very well."

P.T. and Jared Tenere strolled to the heli, carrying their gear. Arlene walked with Philip, arm in arm.

"Hon, do you know where they're taking me?"

"Don't ask."

"That means you do."

"Philip and I had a chat." She gave him a casual hug. "Take care of your father."

"I will, Mom." He busied himself helping Jared load the duffels.

"I didn't know what to bring." My tone had a hint of reproach.

Arlene was firm. "It's Philip's show."

I growled, "It's my heli."

"Look again, love." I did. The machine was smaller than my usual craft, and showed more wear.

P.T. said, "I rented it."

"Where'd you get the coin?" I doubted his work with the Enviro Council paid much; they were always strapped for funds.

"The money Grandma Sanders left me." He seemed untroubled. "I told you it was important, Fath."

We said our good-byes and lifted off.

Strapped into the front seat, my chair stowed between Jared and the cadet, I tried to let myself relax. P.T. was a competent pilot; I'd taught him myself.

I peered at the compass. "Now, will you tell me?"

"Soon, Fath." We were heading west. "I thought you'd end up taking her."

"Mom? Oh, you mean Karen." I shrugged. "You can't blame her for trying to do her job." I thought a moment. "That reminds me." I reached to the dash, keyed off the transponder.

P.T. raised an eyebrow.

"Otherwise they'll track us. I presume you want privacy." If Karen traced our transponder, next would come over-flights, then open surveillance.

"Why provoke them?"

"Adolescent rebellion." It made no sense, but it quieted him awhile.

In the back seat, Jared chatted animatedly with Danil, about puters, Arcvid, and nets. The cadet was polite at first, as he was required to be with civilians. Soon he warmed to Jared's enthusiasm, and the two were deep in discourse.

I dozed.

"Fath, we're here." The engine was silent.

"That was fast."

"You've been snoring three hours."

I peered about. "Where are we?"

"South of Lawrence, Kansas." He jumped out, came around, swung open my door. To Jared, "Help with the chair, love." The boys manhandled the machine to the dusty ground. Philip made me comfortable, gave me a reassuring pat. Did I seem that old, that doddering?

"Now what?"

He hauled out the sunshields, inserted an umbrella in the receptacle in my chair, handed the others around. "Take a look, Fath."

At what? The remains of a swaybacked farmhouse sagged

in tired defeat. Rusty barbed fencing still stood for most of its length, but behind them acreage was gone to weed. Past the house, the lower half of a silo jutted angrily at a lowering sky.

Philip had brought me here for a reason. It was my job to figure out why, but I could not. "Son, it's just an abandoned farm." The American countryside was littered with them.

"Let's sit on the porch." He strolled ahead. I was forced to follow, Bevin and Jared flanking my chair. P.T. perched on the floor under the splintered rail, his feet dangling. I rolled as far as the broken steps.

I shivered. "It's cold."

"The wind will be up soon. It's early afternoon. I'll have to get you under cover."

I glanced up at the sunshield. It would do. "I'm not afraid of a little wind."

He smiled, sat peaceably. Somewhat bored, I looked about, while the cadet scuffed his feet in the dust.

The house had once been painted soft green, faded now to gray. An animal skittered under the porch.

"The last owners were the Wattersons. Janice and Tom. They bought it from her father, in 2199."

Forty-two years ago. I shrugged. "So?"

"The place had been in her family for two and a half centuries, Fath."

"Philip, don't be cryptic. If you've something to—"

"When did you stop trusting me?" His voice was sharp.

Why had I agreed to this jaunt if I had no faith in my son? "I'm sorry."

"They grew sorghum, wheat, corn. Sometimes they'd put in beans. Janice's father was named Roland. Roland Kitner. His friends all called him Rollo. He farmed here with his own father. The high school he attended is three miles down that road." He pointed.

Dutifully, I peered, saw nothing.

"Janice died a few years ago. She was a widow by then. Jared, roll Fath's chair so he can see the barn."

I suppressed my annoyance, let the boy move me, scowled at the cowshed.

"She became a widow in 2212, when Tom Watterson blew his brains out in that barn. Their joeykids were seven and nine. The older girl—"

Enough. "Son, why are you telling me this?" Wind ruffled my hair.

"I'm personalizing, so you'll understand. With you, it's the only way."

I snarled, "Don't patronize me!"

"Be quiet and listen!"

I gawped.

"I've staked everything I have on this expedition! You owe me my chance."

"I'll pay for the heli."

"You will not!"

We glared in mutual fury.

Jared cleared his throat. "Please . . ." He looked from one to the other of us.

I said heavily, "Go on, Philip."

"First National Bank of Irvington held a crop mortgage, Farmer's Bank the second. Wheat prices were sky-high, but for some reason the Wattersons couldn't keep a crop. The first year—2208—was a fluke. Everyone said so."

"And they lost the farm. Get on with it."

"Not the first year. Not until July 2212, after they tried every damn crop they could plant, one after another!" Viciously, he tore a blade of grass that poked through the floor.

"I'm sorry for them, but that was twenty-nine years ago."

"Aye." It startled me to hear him use the old speech. It recalled Father, in Cardiff. "It wasn't just the Wattersons, sir. How many American farms went under in 2212?"

A gust swirled dirt in a small dust devil.

I said, "I've no idea."

"Six thousand two hundred twelve, according to census."

"How do you know all this?" My wave took in the house, the barn, the fields.

"I've studied." Philip sounded bitter. "How many were abandoned last year?"

"Ask my agri minister."

"Eleven hundred fourteen. Not many, except as a percentage. There are so few left to abandon. Did you know America was once the breadbasket of the world?"

Yes, I knew. But that was what our colonies were for. I glanced upward at the darkening sky. "Times have changed."

"Yes!" Abruptly, he stood. "We'd better get you in the heli." Without leave, he turned my chair, rolled me along the walk.

In a few moments I was glad he did. The wind had come up sharply. Clouds scudded overhead. Dust swirled.

"Help me cover the intakes!" Philip had to shout to be heard. Danil scrambled to help. Agile as a monkey, he climbed atop our craft, helped P.T. adjust tarps.

"Please, Lord." Jared spoke softly, almost in my ear. "No tornadoes. Not today." He rocked.

"Are you frightened, son?"

"No. Yes." His hand sought mine. "I'm supposed to avoid anxiety. It throws me out of balance."

"We'll be all right." My tone was gruff.

A sudden roar, as the door was yanked open. P.T. and Danil jumped into the heli. The cadet was panting happily. "What a zark!"

Jared smiled weakly.

"This would be a dust bowl," Philip shouted, "except for the daily rain." As if on cue, a few drops splattered the windshield. "Nothing but weeds would grow for Janice and Tom, you see. Any crop that grew high enough, the wind got. But rainfall was up by thirty-two inches a year. It washed out the seed. The fields were a sea of mud and weeds. If you'd like, in an hour I'll show you. I'll have to carry you, I think."

"We have to stay here an hour?"

"I can't fly in this, Fath." Around us, wind howled and battered at the windows. Our blades swung wildly, disengaged.

Jared moaned.

Outside, the drumming crash of hail.

I said harshly, "Let Danil sit in front with me." Startled, P.T. gave way, moved to the rear with Jared. I hoped it would help.

Late in the afternoon, the weather calm, we lifted off from a soggy field. Philip spoke loudly, over the engine's whine. "Notice the landscape, Fath. This was once the most productive land in the world." Obligingly, he tilted to provide a view of the lacerated land.

I hung tight.

"Now where?" It was getting late.

"I've booked us rooms in Florida."

"Zarky!" Bevin bounced in his seat.

"*Cadet!*"

He subsided. Grumbling, I tightened my strap.

"Where the hell have you been, Mr. SecGen?" Karen's voice was tight.

I grimaced at the caller. I'd intended to be apologetic, but her manner irked me. "Out," I said coolly.

"I have you at the Searest in Tampa." She was showing off.

"Very well, next time I won't call."

"If you're spotted . . ."

"There'll be a nuisance. Autograph seekers, who knows what." I made no effort to hide my sarcasm. We'd checked into the hotel without a problem. Of course, I'd sat in the heli while Philip made the arrangements.

"I see why Tilnitz resigned."

"That's quite enough." I broke the connection. I'd promised to call, not to put up with her presumption. Were they my detail, or I theirs?

Fuming, I punched in Arlene's code, waited. "Hi, hon."

"All's well. How goes it?"

"Lord knows what Philip hopes to accomplish. If he expects me to go mushy and tearful at a rotting farmhouse . . ."

Her tone was dry. "I think he knows you better than that."

"Hmpff." I changed the subject. "Is the middy behaving himself?"

"I suppose. I don't take inventory."

"I left him chores. See that he's kept busy, would you?"

"I'll have him to dinner tonight."

"No need to spoil him. How was Mikhael?"

"A bit sullen, after you left. I put him to work in the sheds."

"He didn't mind?"

"Yes, he rather did." Her tone was cool.

I grinned. An old salt like Arlene, used to handling middies shipboard, wouldn't take guff from a teenager. Mikhael would have to learn.

"Moira doesn't object?"

"She asked me to do the same with Carla. Nick, some joeys just shouldn't be parents."

"Don't bring that up." During the Kahn Administration, the licensing bill had almost wrecked the Terrie Party. It failed, but Arlene and I had differed sharply on its provisions.

"I almost wish P.T. were young again," she said wistfully. "He'd set Mikhael an example."

"He was a good lad," I said. Then, grudgingly, "Still is."

Her mind was still on Moira Tamarov. "It was no accident," she said. "We made him so."

We chatted a bit longer, and rang off.

In the morning, the boys and I had breakfast in the hotel restaurant. I ignored odd looks and whispers. One joey actually peered at me and told his wife, "He looks just like the SecGen." Of course, they knew it was out of the question for the head of Government to spend the night in such a seedy, run-down inn; my resemblance to the SecGen was mere co-incidence. I found I was actually enjoying myself.

On the way to the heli, Bevin picked up a handful of pebbles, skipped them one by one across the lot.

"Cadet . . ." It was a warning growl.

P.T. said, "Why not let him play?"

"Because . . ." I searched for a reason, gave it up. "Carry on, Danil." My own fault, dragooning a joeykid out of Academy. He hadn't even the maturity of a middy. I snorted. The maturity of a middy like Anselm. I asked Bevin suddenly, "Have you ever tasted liquor?"

Danil's eyes widened. "No, sir. It's illegal."

Our gear packed, we lifted off. Squinting into the unrelenting glare of the sun, I asked, "Where to?"

"A few miles south."

Below, an incomplete causeway stretched across a spacious bay. Philip slowed, banked to give me a view.

"All right, I've seen it. Where are we headed?"

"This is it." We swooped down. When the blades came to a stop he flung open the door.

The air was a soggy brick: hot, heavy, unyielding. I wore no tie, but I felt like whipping off my shirt. "People live in this climate?"

"It's worse than it used to be."

I rolled my eyes at the lecture I'd no doubt triggered. "Do tell."

"We're on the run-up to the Tampa Bay bridge. The causeway began as an American interstate connecting Tampa to St. Petersburg. Let's get you in the chair." Danil jumped out, tugged at my transport, tongue in his teeth.

"Easy, joey." Jared worked the other end. Between them, they lowered the machine to the ground. "Let me help you, sir." With surprising gentleness, Jared guided me to the chair. Abruptly he pulled a handkerchief, wiped my brow. "You'll need your umbrella." He raised it. P.T. looked on, a smile in his eyes.

I asked my son, "What do you want me to do?"

"Ride along the roadway."

"I'll be run down."

"That's not possible." He sounded sad. "It's been closed twenty years."

"Why?"

"Tell your chair to go south."

In for a pence . . . "South, chair. Along the roadway."

The concrete roadbed was cracked and broken. We veered around huge potholes, past piles of driftwood. Philip trotted to keep pace. "Tides, Fath. They're up . . ."

"Two point seven feet." The zines parroted the figure, over and again.

"No, sir, that's only the last four decades." He drew breath. "The bridge is a hundred seventy years old. Add another foot and a half."

"Slow, chair." If I weren't careful I'd give P.T. heatstroke. "Surely they built five feet over water level?"

"More than that; they weren't idiots in the twentieth. It's storm surges, Fath."

"Hold, chair." He leaned on the arm; I patted his hand to forestall his speech. "Get your breath. I'm sorry." I waited.

"A hundred years ago, high tides began to wash over the roadway. The road people repaired the damage."

"Get under my shade."

"Yes, sir. After a time, water again undercut the roadway. We rebuilt. That is, the old American Government; they were still independent then. Two billion of their dollars. Fifteen years later, water was again lapping over the road. No one knew tides would rise so fast. See over there? It was a fishing pier. Joeys would drive out to the bridge, park, fish any time of day or night."

"Why don't they still?"

He looked at me strangely. "Fath, they can't get here. The road's washed out in thirteen places."

"Oh." I felt a fool.

"Look at the bridge."

"I did."

"No, really look."

I studied the mighty span that soared into the distance. Elegant, slim supports soared to the clouds. The causeway ran many miles, hugging the waterline, until it reached the bridge. "It's beautiful."

"And horribly expensive."

I shrugged. "A pity." I wiped my face. At least the heli was air-conditioned.

"Care to see it up close?"

"Yes."

"We can't reach it. The bridge is isolated. I suppose in a stunt heli it might be possible to land between the pillars."

Huge cables, mighty pylons, a few gulls. Other than ourselves, not a soul was in sight.

"At its peak, this roadway served ninety million vehicles a year. SecGen Von Walthers authorized vast sums for dredging the bay. See those rocks? They were a breakwater."

"Are we done?"

"Fath, don't you care?"

"Yes, it was a stupid waste of resources. I don't think I've let money be spent so foolishly on my watch."

"Fath, ninety million vehicles. Even discounting multiples, that means millions of citizens who can't cross the bay."

"Isn't there a new bridge?"

"Yes, but the feeder routes . . ." He made a face.

The sun was broiling me. "Anything else, son?"

"I guess not." He sounded disconsolate. "We'll talk over lunch."

A few minutes later we lifted off. I basked in the blessed cool.

We headed north. Somewhere in the Carolinas, he set us down. The restaurant was pleasant enough. Philip fished in his pocket, gave Jared and Danil coin. "I need to speak with Father alone." The two settled at another table.

Philip waited for me to dig into soyburger and rice. "Fath, do you see a theme?"

"The world's going to hell." There was nothing I could do about it.

"Anything else?"

"You've been brainwashed by your lunatic friends."

His fingers tightened on his glass. "Is that all?"

"What do you want me to say?"

"Excuse me." A woman, tawdry in a purple jumpsuit and matching shades. "Are you by any chance the SecGen?"

I rolled my eyes. *"Of course."* My voice dripped with sarcasm.

"Well!" She went off in a huff.

Philip grinned. "You have the damnedest way of not lying."

"Don't blaspheme." But it had dissipated the strain between us. I took a fork of rice. "P.T., I'm not an idiot. You're showing me enviro disasters. I don't know why. Are you looking for a change of heart?"

"A change of policy. Radical, extreme, fundamental. We haven't much time."

"Before what?"

"Before we make the planet unsurvivable."

"The planet will survive." I made my tone light. "If it gets too rough, there's always emigration. We'll board a liferaft."

He gripped my arm with an iron hand. "Be serious. For once in your life, don't evade me on the issue."

I tried to twist loose, found I could hot. "Let go my wrist!" My voice was ice.

"Do as I ask!"

"Let *go!*" At last, I clawed free. "That's it, laddie. I'm going home." I spun my chair.

"You gave me three days."

I wheeled out of the restaurant. "Not anymore." He'd laid hand on me. Were I younger . . . no, were I not tied to this bloody God-cursed chair . . .

He caught me at the door. "I'm sorry."

"Out of my way!"

He stood aside. I barreled past. I'd find an air taxi, or call Karen Burns. I wasn't dependent on him. Not yet.

He found me in the lot. "Sir, I apologize. Truly." He dropped to one knee, to my level. "I'll never hold you again."

I was shaking. "If you were a boy I'd . . ."

"I'll let you beat me now, if you'll forgive me after."

It was like a splash of ice water. I closed my eyes, willed my heart to slow. "Oh, Philip."

"I'm going to rev in a moment. Hold me."

I did. I could feel him tremble.

When we were calm, I gave him an awkward pat.

"Fath, there's two more places I want to take you."

I sighed. "All right." I'd have to hold my temper.

"But if you respect me as much as I do you, you owe me an answer. Why do you reject enviro policies out of hand? Why won't you even discuss it?"

"Son, I—"

He held up a hand. "No. The truth or nothing."

I'd raised a formidable child.

In the sweltering parking lot, I sat and mused. Enviros were all fundamentally glitched, wanting to reverse Lord God's changes to our world. But there was something more. I wasn't sure why I was loath to discuss it; there was no cause for shame.

"Philip, do you believe in Him?"

"Yes, sir. Not quite the way you do."

I wasn't sure what that meant, but let it pass. "He is the center of my life, no matter how badly I act."

"I know."

"He made the world in seven days. I'm not sure how, or how long were the days. I also accept physics and geology." I smiled. "And paleontology." Father had taught me there was much we would not know. He accepted it, and therefore, so did I. "This is His world. I believe that with all my soul. But . . . soon or not, it will end."

"You speak of the Apocalypse?"

"What else? *For the Lord Himself shall descend from heaven with a shout, with the voice of the archangel.* Philip, don't you see how presumptuous it would be, to try to alter His world?"

"We've already altered it."

"But not as a deliberate act, for the purpose of change. It suggests we're here to stay, that His promise is false. That we have to safeguard the world for infinite generations."

"But we do!"

"That's His role, not ours. To say otherwise is impertinent."

"We're stewards of His—"

"No, we're inheritors and possessors. Lord God gave us this Earth to do with as we wished." My voice was hot. *"Ye shall inherit their land, and I will give it unto you to possess it, a land that floweth with milk and honey.* And that's what we've done."

He leaned over my chair. "Fath, you'd let the Earth go to hell for some half-baked *theology?*"

"I ought to slap your face." My voice was tight.

Philip nodded, unmoving.

I turned away, or tried to. "If you don't understand, I can't make you."

His voice was dull. "We'll go on as I planned. Perhaps . . ."

"Yes?"

"You asked if I believed. Tonight, I'll get on my knees, as we did when I was young. I'll pray for a miracle."

"Don't blaspheme." But my heart wasn't in it.

* * *

"Near Ravensburg."

I stretched, feeling every one of my years.

"A valley in southern Bavaria, below the Alps. Tourists used to come from all over the world."

"And now the tides—"

"Please don't joke. Those peaks"—he pointed past rolling hills—"they're over twelve thousand feet high." In the distant heights, lightning flashed.

Gloomy fields, brown grass, a lush fetid odor. A road, curving into a valley.

"That chairlift. It was for skiing. There's still snow occasionally, but not enough to make the business profitable."

"I know the climate's warmed; it's true everywhere. Hauling me around the world won't—"

"That's not why we're here. Do you smell it?"

"Yes, it's sort of a rich . . ." I sniffed. "Like a marsh."

"Rotting wood. Come." He turned my chair. "Jared, care to hike with us? You too, Danil. Bring the masks."

I asked, "What for?"

"It gets worse." We started down the road.

It was a pleasant afternoon, though the sights would be gloriously enhanced if the sun broke through the sullen clouds. We left the solar umbrellas behind. We wouldn't be out all that long, and the weather report said gamma counts were down.

The road had been paved, but hadn't seen traffic for years; eager stalks of grass sprang from cracks and fissures.

P.T. strode at my side. "This town was inhabited for two thousand years. The earliest tourists were Roman."

Danil squinted at the hills. "There's no trees."

"Very few."

I said, "Global warming doesn't kill trees."

"No, Fath. Acid rain does, and chemical pollutants."

"That's under control. We've reduced emissions by thirty—"

"No, we haven't. We've reduced their rate of increase. It's by no means the same. The trees started dying in earnest seventy years ago. Manfred Rolf was burgermeister then. He lived by the stream, in a . . . never mind, you'll see it in a moment."

The air was humid, but tolerable. Altitude had its advantages. I let myself relax, while Philip wheeled me along, past ancient dwellings with picturesque mansard roofs. No one was in sight. Was the town abandoned?

"Old Manfred was a difficult man. Big bushy eyebrows, a hot temper. His house belonged to his grandfather, and his grandfather's grandfather before him. It was built after the Last War."

"Did he shoot himself in the barn?"

"Please, Fath. I'm really begging you. No more."

"I'm sorry." Too late, I was contrite.

I jounced past scraggly bushes, sodden fields, the ruins of what might have been a store.

"He died in bed, as a man should. When he wasn't mayor, he was a puter technician. Quite good at it, for his day."

I held my peace. Philip would come to the point.

"Town business didn't take much of his time. The only industry was tourism, and that consisted merely of the hotels and restaurants that fanned out from the square."

Danil stooped to pick up pebbles. Ahead, the road turned.

"You can hear the stream. We'll see it in a moment. All these villages started out as mill towns. Water ground the grain."

Near the stream, the cement roadway gave way to gravel. A crude, temporary metal footbridge had been thrown over a brisk stream whose channel was lined with large rounded rocks. Beyond was the center of town. P.T. jounced and rocked my chair across. "There's Manfred's house."

"Where?"

"Those foundations. The flood of '99 was the highest in

memory. By then all the lower houses had gone; folk retreated to the hills."

I stared balefully at the jagged stones. Floods had been with us a long time. Ever since Noah.

The road curved sharply. P.T. strode at a brisk pace, pushing my chair.

We turned the bend. "The last burgermeister was Hermann Rolf. Manfred's grandson, as it happens. He lived with his wife—"

I caught my breath.

It was a scene of appalling devastation. Windows, doors, walls lay strewn about. Downed trees had been hurled this way and that.

"Hurricanes? Tornadoes?"

"No, Fath. Floods. You see, those hills used to be covered with trees. The pollutants killed them, and vegetation holds water. Each year, the floods get worse."

"So, one town—"

"It isn't one town, Fath. The wind blows from central Europe."

I stirred, for once on sure ground. "The Balkans are catching up at last. Finally their economies are strong enough to compete." Coal production was up, iron was being gouged from the earth at a prodigious rate. And manufactories like the state-of-the-art chip works at Dresden were a symbol of Europe's brave new times.

He said, "Lung cancer deaths are up thirty-seven percent. Despite anticars."

I protested, "That's worldwide." Aghast, I realized what I'd said. Rivulets of doubt trickled through the stones of my certainty.

As if understanding, P.T. patted my shoulder.

We picked our way through rubble. A few raindrops splashed.

"Hermann Rolf lived there, above the stream. He was

sixty when he married; she was nineteen. They were deeply in love."

"Brake, chair." I looked over my shoulder. "Son, how do you know these things?"

He knelt by my side. "That's what I do, Fath." His tone was sober. "It's my project, when I'm not analyzing Winstead's stats. I do research for the Enviro Council, to put a human face on the disaster. Some of their P.R. joeys make it up. All my stories are accurate."

He was so solemn I yearned to hug him. Of course they were accurate. This was P.T., the boy I cherished.

"I speak to survivors, to descendants. I find pictures, read old records. It's much more interesting than stat analysis."

"You can do anything you set your hand at."

The rain picked up. I wrapped my jacket tighter.

"Mostly." He was free of false modesty. "Her name—Frau Rolf—was Marlena. She played piano like an angel. Had taken lessons since she was five. No children, but they kept hoping, despite the difference in their age."

I steeled myself. "What happened to him?"

"They had six years together. The spring of 2219, Burgermeister Rolf attended a party conference in Berlin. It was a bad season for rain. Most of Europe was drenched." He glanced at the grim sky, the brooding peaks, above which ominous lightning flashed. "In fact, we should get going."

"Finish." After my derision, I owed him that.

"What's to say? A terrible storm swept the hills. The callers were out, he hurried home. Three days later when they dug out the house, they found Marlena wedged under the bed clutching a bisque doll. She'd drowned in mud."

"Lord Christ."

"Amen. It broke him. He's still alive, at a nursing home in Munich. I'll take you to see him if you like."

"No. Please, no."

Surreptitiously, Bevin ran a sleeve across his eyes. As if by chance, Jared's arm fell across his shoulder.

A slow roll of kettledrums in the distant hills.

"They didn't need a mayor after 2219. No one wanted to rebuild. Fath, it was the trees. Tall leafless stalks line those ridges mile upon mile, like ghostly sentries of His creation. Saplings struggle, and fall half-grown. When the wind is right . . ." His voice was ragged. "I wish I could show you. Today we don't need a mask."

"I believe you." I could barely hear myself.

"I collected cards, pictures, holos. I couldn't stop. Bavaria was so beautiful, Fath. This was Eden." He tried to speak, fell silent.

Jared took his arm, led him to a secluded pile of brush. I huddled within my coat, watching raindrops strike the gravel.

After a time Danil said, "*Do* something, Mr. SecGen."

"What, boy? Send cadets to replant the mountainside? Close the Dresden plants? Ruin Eastern Europe?"

"We already did that." His tone was bitter. "My father thinks the only way to save—"

"Don't start. I warn you."

"Sir, I— Aye aye, sir. May I speak my mind?"

"No." I could abide Philip's passion; he was my son. But not an enviroist lecture from the cadet. Not today.

Footsteps.

"Sorry, Fath." P.T.'s tone was brisk. "You're soaked. Let's get moving." He turned my chair. Danil, impatient, ran ahead.

My legs were sopping, but I couldn't feel them. I'd have to be careful to avoid colds. Any injury, for that matter. Without sensation, I risked—no, it wouldn't come to that. In two weeks' time I was to see Ghenili. Surgery would follow within days. If it went wrong, I'd make an end.

"The whole valley's abandoned?"

"Mostly. A few farmers eke out—"

Danil's shrill voice rose. "Hurry!" He dashed our way.

"Sir, the creek . . ." He skidded to a halt. "The water's much higher. Louder too. I don't like it."

"Shit!" P.T. pushed harder. "Jared, run ahead."

"I stay with you."

I snapped, "Are you all glitched? No one stays. Chair, faster. Across the bridge. Don't throw me out."

"I can't judge—"

"Stop if you hear me yell from the ditch."

"I'm not programmed to comply with distant commands. Only when you're sitting—"

We jounced over a rut. "Reprogram, then." All my life, puters had plagued me. I hated them.

Bevin had been right. The burble of the brook was definitely louder. We neared the metal bridge. Under it, torrents swirled and eddied. The rocky walls of the channel were submerged. White froth licked at the bridge supports.

"Holy Christ, it's moving!" Jared licked his lips.

"No." I ordered the chair to slow, approached cautiously. "Just vibrating. Help me across. This bucket of chips may miscalculate."

"My guidance systems—"

"Stow it, chair."

Water frothed and churned, barely a foot under the decking.

Philip was calm. "Fath, I'll run across and get the heli. I can reland here."

"No need. Boys, on three. One . . . two . . ." I spun my wheels.

They raced me onto the bridge. A wheel caught; my chair lurched. I pitched to the deck, struck my head.

Thunder rattled. I lay dazed. Water splashed my chin.

"It's moving!"

A plate shivered under my ear. The bridge lurched. I rolled, caught myself at the edge.

"Hold him!"

I clawed at the rail. Philip snagged one arm, Jared the other. They dragged me from the edge.

"I'm all right."

The bridge wasn't. Wavelets splashed on the flooring. "What's—"

"It's rained hard in the hills." Philip.

"Put me in the chair!"

"No time. Pull, Jared!" Together they half dragged, half carried me to the bank. Danil danced helpless around us.

I called, "Chair, roll! Now!" Without a passenger, the chair careened off the bridge, sank itself in mud. Bevin ran to dislodge it, worked it free. Water dripped in my eyes.

The bridge groaned.

"We need high ground!" P.T. spun, looked about.

"Put me down!" They still held me; I was helpless. I tried to wriggle myself free. As one, they let me go. I flopped in the mud, knocked my head yet again. "P.T., start the god— the heli. Did you hear me. *Move!* Jared, put me in the bloody chair!"

Philip sprinted.

"Cadet, I lost a shoe. Do you see it?"

To my horror, Danil darted onto the bridge, scooped it up. I was a fool. He raced to safety.

Grunting, Jared dragged me to the chair, heaved me in.

I flopped in my seat, squishing, mud-soaked. I wiped water from my forehead; my hand came away red.

Angry white swirls chewed the banks of the creek.

"Chair, to the heli!" We reeled down the road to the higher ground on which we'd landed the heli.

Philip jumped out, threw open the door. "You're injured?"

"No."

The chair said reproachfully, "If you'd let me guide myself, I wouldn't have overturned—"

"Shut the fuck *up!*" Philip gave it a mighty kick that dented a wheel.

I caught his hand. "I'm not hurt, son. Truly."

He stifled a sound.

They worked me into the heli, like a sodden sack. Danil pawed through my gear, emerged with fresh trousers. Minutes later, the engine running, I sat shivering before the heat vent, holding a handkerchief to the cut on my scalp.

Philip strapped himself in.

I muttered, "I could use a drink."

"So could I." Danil.

I raised an eyebrow. "You said you didn't."

"Today I'd start." His gaze was defiant.

When we lifted off, the bridge still stood, engulfed in turbulent eddies.

12

We've got them." General Donner sounded triumphant.

I stared at my caller, biting my lip. "How can you be sure?" I lay on my bed in a posh Munich hotel. A warm bath had done wonders, though getting myself out of the tub unaided had been a battle. Afterward, I'd flopped on the bathmat like a beached fish.

"We monitored every call every joey made, who had anything to do with the dead terrorists, or Booker's family. The puters watched for patterns."

I asked, "Only seven?"

"There have to be more. That's why we haven't picked them up."

"It's a risk."

"To a degree, Mr. SecGen. But they can't sneeze without our knowing. We've parabolic mikes, sensors above and beneath their flats, wires in their cars, agents following everywhere."

"One of your joeys will let himself be seen. They'll catch on."

"And we take them in custody. It's under control, Mr. SecGen."

"Have you found Booker?"

"Not yet. P and D will reveal his whereabouts. One of them has to know."

"And if not?"

He sounded patient. "We keep looking."

"Be careful, Donner. If they escape I'll . . ." No need to threaten. He knew. "Keep it under wraps."

"No one knows we found them but Ms. Burns from Naval Intelligence, and three of my own U.N. Security aides. I didn't even tell the jerries."

"Very well." We rang off.

I'd see that P and D was authorized for the lot of them. This time we had the evidence, and no rational judge could object. Our cadets would be avenged. And Alexi. I sat brooding, until the caller woke me from a doze.

"It's Mikhael. Ms. Seafort said I could call."

"How are you?"

"Let me go home." A silence, which I did nothing to break. "It's a mistake, staying with you."

"Your mother said two months."

"She won't mind."

"I will." The gash in my forehead throbbed. I would have a lump. Lord God knew what the mediamen would make of it.

"I hate it here. I'm calling Mom."

"Be silent!" I spoke as to a middy.

"She'll send a frazzing ticket. I'm out of here."

I choked the caller, wishing it were he. "For the moment I'm your guardian. You'll—"

"So?"

I roared, "Put Arlene on the line! Do it now!"

"All I said—"

"This instant!"

Long moments passed.

Her tone was cautious. "I hear you're on the warpath?"

"Give him calisthenics 'til his tongue hangs out. Put him

to work, and ground him to his room otherwise. I'll be back day after tomorrow. He's not to use the caller."

"He irked you?"

"I won't put up with—" Distant, impotent, I fumed. "I've caned middies for less!"

"No doubt."

I gathered the shreds of my calm. "He wanted to go home. Why?"

"He told a few tasteless jokes. I was a bit short with him."

"Such as?"

"What do you call a Hollander with a life vest? Bob. What's a Hollander doing in a boat? Camping out."

"Ugh."

"Nicky, those joeys have been through hell since the polders flooded. I wish you'd been here to greet them, that day you stayed at Academy. I wasn't that hard on him, after all he's an adolescent, but—"

"Alexi would be disgusted." I was sure of it. Once, he'd heard our middies make jokes about the transpops, and . . . I brought myself back to the present. "The jokes were obnoxious, but more important, Mikhael was rude to me. Deal with him, hon. You have a knack with joeykids."

"Easy for you to say, from across the globe." Her tone turned serious. "Love, I spoke with Philip. He's rather upset."

It took me aback. "Why?"

"He says he hurt you. And that you mock him."

"Hon, it's . . ." I couldn't explain; it was too complicated. "I'm all right. And I won't mock. Now, as to Mikhael—"

"I'll set him straight." Her tone was grim. Almost, I pitied the boy. Arlene was quite capable of enforcing her will. Even P.T. had learned that, in his teen years.

A knock. I rolled to the door.

Jared Tenere, shifting from foot to foot like an errant

schoolboy. "May I come in?" He squeezed past. "P.T. thinks I'm out for a walk."

"Why?"

He sat. "Mr. Seafort, I haven't known you long enough to . . . I mean, since our talk . . ."

"It's all right."

He studied the carpet. "I came to explain him."

I snorted. "There's no need."

"You're wrong." His quiet assurance startled me. "You think he's . . . impulsive, as he was as a boy."

I smiled. "You were more so."

"I was glitched." A calm acceptance, that earned my approval. "But he's planned this trip for months. Years."

I swallowed.

"My Philip . . ." He came off the chair, settled on the floor at my feet, crossed his legs. "He's the most passionate joey I ever met." A sudden blush. "I don't mean that way, though even there . . ." A shy smile. "He'd give his life for his beliefs. He's so intense he frightens me."

I said, "A fanatic."

"Not at all. He listens; fanatics don't. You can convince him he's wrong, but that's seldom."

"I wish I could."

"He wants desperately to persuade you, Mr. Seafort. I don't know what he'll do if he fails."

"There are other politicians."

"We've lived together . . . how long now, five years? I love him. But you're still the focus of his life. He reveres you. When he saw your blood . . . tonight I held him for over an hour. He couldn't stop revving. He held it off all afternoon; he couldn't let you see."

"Why not?"

"He was afraid you'd commit to help him, from pity."

Oh, Philip.

He whispered, "You've so much power to hurt him."

"That's not fair."

"It's not that you try." He groped for words. "But you won't truly listen. You won't open your heart to him. And you know, is it so terrible what he wants? To bring the world back from ruin?"

"It's not so simple."

"It is, if you do it." His hand darted to my knee, for a fleeting moment. "If you simply do it."

I sat silent a long while. "Rob Boland did a good job with you." My tone was gruff.

"Uncle Robbie saved my life." A tentative smile. "That's all I came to say."

I leaned forward, kissed him softly on the brow. "Take care of my son."

Just past midnight, the caller buzzed. Groggily, I switched it on. "Yes?"

"Mr. Seafort? Cisno Valera."

I tried to sit up, realized I'd have to haul my legs into position, gave it up. "Something's gone wrong?"

"I do wish you'd turn on visuals." My Deputy SecGen sounded peevish. "It's so much easier, seeing who you're talking to."

I hated visuals, and he knew it. Everyone knew, who'd ever called me. But no point alienating Cisno; I'd embarrassed him enough in my hospital press conference. I tried not to sigh aloud. "Just a moment."

With an effort, I dragged my legs into position, sat up, propped pillows behind my back, brushed back my hair. I flicked the visuals switch, waited for the intellilens to find me, lock in its focus.

"Yes?"

Valera's sallow face loomed. "Oh, sorry, I didn't realize you'd gone to bed. You're going too far, with the enviro bills. The natives are restless."

"What natives?"

"The Senate is up in arms." He spoke from his Rotunda

office. He was staying late. No, it wasn't that late in North America. "For one thing, why haven't you cracked down on the enviro fringe?"

I raised an eyebrow. "You demand my explanation?"

"Not I." His tone was unctuous. "The Senate does. We have to show those eco loonies we won't dream of caving in. Instead, you push enviro legislation, and let the Eco League go unpunished. You haven't—"

"We're searching for—"

"—a state of emergency would let us use P and D—"

"—any sign of them. And until—"

"—you've gone soft!"

His words rang in the sudden silence.

Valera cleared his throat, spoke with less vehemence. "Look, you can sway the Assembly with foolish enviro sentiment, but Senators tend to ally themselves with business interests, regardless of party. You know that's so."

"Cisno, what's the crisis that provoked your call?"

"The Senate won't go along with your Greenhouse Gases Act." Did I detect a hint of satisfaction? "I had word today from Rob Boland. Such a massive reduction in emissions—"

"Five percent is a pittance!" Now I sounded like Cadet Bevin, or worse, his father. Forgetting I had visuals, I rolled my eyes.

"Interstellar Ltd. doesn't think so, or Boeing Airbus, or—"

"Spare me the list." I rubbed my face. "You support the Administration on this?"

"I always support your Administration." His voice was silky.

"Mine, or ours?"

"You're the SecGen. It's *your* policy."

"And if we fail in the Senate . . ." The Government wouldn't fall; only an Assembly vote could unseat us. But a defeat on legislation that had so caught the public eye would bring calls for my resignation, some from my own party. Valera, of course, would be waiting quietly in the wings. I could almost sense his glee.

"So, now." I savored the moment. "How shall we handle this? Dissolve the Assembly and Senate and call new elections?"

"Mr. SecGen!" That would be the last solution he sought: my bringing the battle to them, on my own terms. The game of politics was truly dreadful. I quelled my distaste.

"Or perhaps I ought to reshuffle the Cabinet," I mused. "Give you that Colonial Affairs post you always wanted. Bring Robbie Boland in as Deputy SecGen."

I'd resign before I put Colonial Affairs in Valera's hands, but he needn't know that. He would be aghast at my proposal; what he'd hoped for was the colonial ministry in addition to his post as deputy, not in place of it.

As I expected, he launched a flurry of protest. I let him persuade me to leave things as they were.

Regardless, he'd heard my unspoken message; I considered him expendable, and would throw him overboard if I heard a hint of disloyalty. He'd still work against me, perhaps, but with much more caution.

One of these days, I would have to squeeze him out of Government. He had worked assiduously to cultivate the party, and many were beholden to him. But if I pitted my approval against his, he would lose.

For now.

Breakfast, in my suite, was a miserable affair. I hadn't slept an iota. In the small hours, I'd crawled out of bed, done my best to kneel, spent an hour in unanswered prayer.

Now, I was tired, irritable, and sore.

"Fath?" Philip's hand covered mine. "One more favor?"

"Whatever it is, all right."

He looked startled. "You mean it?"

"Yes." Did he doubt me?

"When we get in the heli, I want . . ." He looked uncomfortable. "I'd like you to sit on the floor."

I roared, "What?"

"So you won't see where we're going. It won't take long."

"Absolutely not! Out of the question." Was he twitting me? Of all the disrespect . . .

"Very well, sir." He said no more.

Bevin looked reproachful. Almost, I slapped him. "One demerit. Change your demeanor."

"Aye aye, sir." He threw down his napkin. "May I leave the table?"

"Make it two."

I gulped my lukewarm coffee, poured more. Maybe it would help.

While Philip loaded the heli, I called the desk, asked to pay our bill. Philip already had. I told them to change it to my name. They refused; he'd left instructions not to allow it. I slammed down the caller.

Danil held the doors for my chair. At the heli, I sat in the doorway, useless legs dangling, while they loaded my battered machine. Jared threw in the duffels.

I eyed him sourly. "Sit in front, with Philip."

"And you, Mr. Seafort?"

"Back here." I tried to make myself comfortable on the heli's deck. "Give me a cushion." Philip shot me a look of such gratitude it was almost worth the discomfort.

With the sun behind clouds, I had no clue as to our heading. The engine droned. I dozed. Bevin sat, arms folded, staring out the window. I debated canceling his demerits; if he'd looked at me even once, I would have.

An acrid odor woke me. I raised my voice over the motor. "How much longer?"

"Soon, Fath."

"I ache."

"This is our last stop." His voice was sad.

Home. A decent bed. Arlene's warm embrace.

A while later we swooped down. In moments the blades came to a halt. Wearily, I stretched. Danil threw open the door. A stench assaulted my nose, my throat. My eyes burned.

"We'll need these today." Philip handed out masks. I slipped mine on. After a moment my breathing eased. The heli's filters had done well; the pollution hadn't been a problem until we landed.

"Where are we, Volgograd?" The pollution from heavy metals outside the sprawling gravitron plant was infamous.

Philip made no answer. From the deck of the heli, all I could see was a roadway, barren dead trees beyond.

P.T. said, "Danil, help Jared with the chair." He climbed in, sat beside me. "Let me tell you about the joeys—"

"Don't personalize it. Not again." An effective tactic, until one grew weary.

"—who lived here last. Three generations." His voice was muffled in the mask. "Farmers, two of them. The son went off to the Service. Later, he brought his wife home, to stay. By then, the land was no longer farmed. They divorced. She lived on awhile, with her second husband. They sold out."

"No one died? No flood?" I'd promised not to mock, but the night had unraveled my intent.

"No, they just left. The neighbor who bought it hoped to add it to his farm. But that wasn't possible."

"Because of the smell. Show me what you came for. It must be exceptional, if you saved it for last."

He grasped me around the shoulders, slipped his hand under my arm. With strength I didn't know he had, he moved me to the doorway. Together, he and Jared lifted me to the chair.

"Behind us."

The heli blocked my view. For a moment, in our bulky masks, we were huge ungainly flies come to survey a windowsill.

"Chair, around the heli." Obediently, it rolled. "Philip, what am I looking for?" He couldn't hear me. I tore off the mask. "P.T.!" Sulphur gagged me. I coughed, spluttered, wheezed. Hastily I donned the mask.

I blinked to clear my streaming eyes. I'd rub them, but the mask interfered. Placidly, Philip rushed my chair along a walk, down a slope toward a dimly seen house.

"I don't need to see, son. You've made your point."

He squeezed my shoulder, turned, and walked away.

Danil took his place. "Sir, where are we?"

"Some godforsaken hellhole. No doubt he picked the worst place on the planet, to impress me." I blinked; my vision began to clear. Brown, unhealthy grass. A neglected fence. A few scraggly trees, struggling against impossible odds.

"It's just a farm," said Danil. "A ratty old place, if you ask me. Mr. Winstead could show you a thousand—"

A cry of despair.

He leaped, as if galvanized.

"No. Not here. NO!"

"Sir, what—"

"Take me away!" My fists beat a tattoo on the chair.

He drew back, stared at me in shock.

Father's farm, the home of my boyhood.

Cardiff.

The remains of blistered paint hung from sagging siding.

A quarter century, since I'd last been home. Not since my wife Annie . . . I'd left her here with Eddie Boss, and fled to the monastery. Eventually she divorced me. The farm was a last gift. I hadn't wanted to see it, see her, recall life's promise I'd squandered.

The gate I'd oft vowed to fix lay rotted across the walk.

The hill behind, down which I'd run, arms spread wide to catch the wind, was gray and dead.

In my mask, I began to weep.

Danil's hand flicked to my shoulder, darted away as if burned.

"Philip!" It was a plea.

"Yes, Fath." His breath rasped in his mask.

"Why?"

"I had to personalize it." His tone was gentle. "So you'd understand."

It undid me.

When he thought I could hear, he said, "Part of it is the reopened mills." He gestured toward Bridgend road, and Cardiff.

"We have pollution laws—"

"After the fish bombed us, the regs were waived. We needed every iota of production. But the worst of it isn't ours. It blows across from the continent."

"It's unspeakable!"

"I tried to tell you."

I clutched him. "Take me away."

"Not just yet, Fath. You mustn't forget." Then, softer, "We must none of us forget."

"What happened to . . . them?"

"Annie died, a few years ago. Eddie lives in Prague."

"Would he let me see him?" Why did I ask?

"I imagine so, sir."

"You said they sold it." My wave took in the house, the land, my past.

"To Garth." The neighbor, whose straying cows so maddened Father. "He gave it up."

"Who owns it now?"

"I do, sir." He met my gaze. "Uncle Rob lent me the money. I pay him each month."

I surveyed the abandoned house, the useless land. My tone was bitter. "It couldn't have been much."

"Enough."

I stared at the rotted gate. Abruptly I whipped off my mask, leaned over the side of the chair, retched.

"Easy, sir. You'll be all right."

"Oh, no. I'll never be that." I fumbled with the mask. "Forgive me."

Was it Philip, or Lord God, to whom I spoke?

Neither answered.

After a time I said, "Why did you buy it?"

"I hope to live here before I die."

A long time passed.

"You will." My grip on his arm was iron. "I swear so, Philip. You will."

We sat in the heli, drained. Jared produced a flask; eagerly I swallowed the stinging liquor. I handed it back; he drank deep, offered it again. I poured a small amount into a tiny cup, gave it to Danil. "None of you see me." SecGen or not, it could land me in gaol. The boy likewise.

Manfully he downed it, and spluttered until his face was red.

Philip started the engine. "The hotel?"

"Where is it?"

"I booked us in Devon." He tried to sound casual, knowing I'd be pleased.

"Not quite yet. Can you find the cemetery?"

"From the air."

Again we set down. I visited Father's grave. Those around it were untended and forlorn, but his plot was neatly mowed. A few flowers drooped. I raised an eyebrow within my mask.

Philip shrugged. "It doesn't cost much."

"Thank you." It was my task, unfulfilled. Forgive me, Father.

"Shall we go?"

"In a moment." I tried to wheel my chair up the hill. Breathing heavily through his mask, Danil came behind to push. "Over there, to the left. Two rows back." I could find the place in my sleep.

Oftentimes, I had.

"That granite marker. The brown one." We stopped. "Help me out of the chair." I hadn't knelt for Father, but I would here.

He lowered me to the ground. "Who is it, sir?"

"My best friend, Jason. He was just your age." As I had been, in the distant past.

I bowed my head. Presently, I became aware of a small form, kneeling at my side.

Somehow, it gave me solace.

A few minutes later, I struggled into my chair. "The demerits are canceled."

"Thank you."

"I'm sorry I'm cruel."

"I'm sorry I provoke you. I'll try to do it less." A wise young joey. He didn't promise the impossible.

13

"A complete reversal." Jerence Branstead looked stunned.

"I'll do what I can to help." I drummed my desktop. It was an immense relief to be home. Outside the complex, a crowd had once more gathered. Perhaps I ought to make time to see them, but shaking each outthrust hand could fill my day, if not my life. I sighed. With what I had planned, I'd probably not be in office long. Perhaps somehow they sensed that, and were saying their farewells.

"I'm not sure who'll stay faithful," he said. "It'll split the party."

"Yes." So be it. I'd spent a sleepless night debating my course. "Jerence . . ." Automatically, I looked about to make sure no one heard except Philip, sitting quietly in the corner. "About a third of the Terries are closet enviros. If we hold half our Supras, and pull in the Enviros and the Indies, we'll have just enough votes."

"Form a new coalition? Sir, on an issue this big, there's no going back. The parties will realign." He seemed awed.

"Perhaps that's for the best." The Terries and the Supras had traded Governments between them long enough.

"But . . . scrap the Greenhouse Gases Act, after we barely saved it?"

"I won't pretend that a five percent reduction is enough."

"Last week it was too much for you."

I closed my eyes, recalling our long deliberation at Devon. During the course of the evening P.T. had overwhelmed me with figures, with charts he called up on my puter, with frightening statistics. He gave me his word they were not exaggerated, and Philip's word was rock.

Why, during all my years, had I not seen?

I'd been occupied with the fish wars. Busy restoring our desperately injured economy. Busy halting the extermination of the transpops, the spoliation of our cities.

It was fundamentally wrong to interfere with His plan; nothing Philip showed me changed my belief. But we *had* interfered. Surely, Lord God couldn't have meant us to befoul Father's homestead. Or reduce Bavaria to a sodden ruin. Or devastate Volgograd, or Amsterdam, or Louisiana . . .

I'm sorry.

When You send me to Hell, You will hear me bleat, as always, "I'm sorry."

I said, "We need a full sixteen percent reduction."

"Unachievable, politically."

We'd see.

"That's only the start," I warned. "Of course we'll work on cleaning up the filth we spew—that goes without saying—but atmospheric warming is our biggest problem. Every time we burn a fossil fuel, we're releasing the energy of sunlight stored millions of years ago. That, in addition to our normal complement of sunlight today. We simply put out too much energy."

"I've seen the briefings."

"We can reduce the energy we expend, or the energy that reaches us. A top priority will be the Solar Umbrella." As I spoke, P.T. watched with approval that was almost parental.

Branstead folded his arms. "Not that wild scheme again."

"It's been around almost two hundred years. Set a shield between us and the sun—"

"It would be two thousand kilometers across! Mr. Sec-Gen, no matter what we make it of, we can't lift that much mass from our gravity well."

"We don't have to. We'll buy ore from the asteroid mines."

"The Navy won't be amused." The vast majority of asteroid production was earmarked for Naval hulls, years in advance.

"The Navy will do what it's told."

Jerence sighed. "Give me a few days to break it to our joeys." He shook his head. "A shake-up this big . . . You'll have to lead. Actively."

"Very well. I'll work the caller, and make speeches."

"Deals, also. Not every pol is a visionary."

I'd known it would be necessary. "That too." I smiled, thinly. "What shall we call ourselves?"

Philip cleared his throat. "The Born Again Ecos?"

My smile vanished. "That's not funny." We would birth a political party, not a religious revolution. To suggest otherwise, even in jest, skirted heresy.

"And then there's the Eco League." Branstead looked grim. "It'll look like you're caving in, no matter how we phrase it."

"Not after they're captured." Even Jerence didn't know the extent of Donner's surveillance.

Our meeting drew to a close. Jerence shook hands gravely, wandered off with P.T. to find Arlene. I rolled to the door. "Is our cadet up? Oh. You." I frowned.

Mikhael stood quickly. "May I see you?"

"Very well."

He shut the door, leaned against it. "I apologize. I won't do it again, sir. I'm here for two months and I won't give you any more goofjuice about it."

I regarded him. He was sweating. "Getting along with Arlene?" My tone held a gentle malice.

"She's—" Whatever he intended to say, he thought better of it.

"Not to be trifled with," I finished.

"No, sir."

"Take a seat." Promptly, he did so. Perhaps that was the solution to all my problems: pass them to Arlene. "Did she hit you?"

"No, she—" He swallowed. "Almost."

"Anything else she told you to say?"

He flushed deep red. "I'm to call you 'sir,' agree with you or keep my opinions to myself, and that it's decent of you to take me in."

"She went a bit too far." I permitted myself a wintry smile. "You're that afraid of her?"

"Not afraid, exactly. It's . . . sir, the next time you take a trip, could I come along?"

My smile widened. I'd have to ask her technique. On the other hand, perhaps I didn't want to know. "Easy, joey. I want you civilized, not terrorized."

"Thank you." He hesitated. "Would you tell her I spoke to you?"

"Ahh." I made a tent of my fingers. "What was her deadline?"

"One o'clock sir. Would she really . . ." He squirmed. "May I be excused?"

"Yes." As he stood, I said, "No, stay awhile." I liked the new Mikhael much better. On the other hand, fear wasn't respect; I still had to reach him. "I'll be going on a speaking tour. Would you like to come?"

"Yes, please." His response was instant. Then, "Does it have to do with your closed door meetings? All the calls?"

"It's none of your— Yes." I shouldn't tell him; he had no discretion. But he was Alexi's son, and in my care.

"We're planning a major change in policy," I said.

"Enviro policy."

If I could, I'd have bolted to my feet. "How'd you know?"

"I'm not stupid." Seeing my face, he added hastily, "Bevin, sir. The cadet's had a goofy smile on his face ever since you got home. He's enviro, isn't he? Told me his father worked for the Enviro League."

"Council. The Eco League is an entirely . . . the Enviro Council."

"Whatever. So, if it made him so happy . . ." Mikhael shrugged.

For an instant I hesitated, then thrust my future in his hands. "We're going all out for enviro restoration."

"Why?" It wasn't a challenge, just curiosity.

"Don't you think we need it?"

"Who cares what I think?" His tone was bitter.

"I do."

"I suppose. The sea levels are . . ." His face twisted. "I didn't mean anything by that Dutch joke, sir!"

"I know, Mikhael." My tone was gentle.

"She made me feel like I drowned them myself. It wasn't fair."

"We don't laugh at people in pain." I told him of the visit from the Dutch relief committee, described the appalling devastation of Bangladesh I'd seen on my overflights. "Arlene was with me. She cried."

Mikhael scuffed his foot. "I'm sorry."

"She'll be glad to know."

"But Holland is nothing new. What changed your mind?"

"Philip. Though it was there for me to see."

He studied me, as if weighing my answer.

I said, "In Academy nowadays, they don't let cadets outdoors when gamma radiation is high, and it happens more and more often. We've had spills, spews, horrid floods, fires, an upsurge in cancers for the first time in a century. Food production is in chaos; we're utterly dependent on the colonies. It's all eco-related."

"It's not your fault."

"I made myself blind!" I rested head in hands. "How many died while I was obstinate?"

"Dad told me, don't take on the cares of the world."

"Father taught me otherwise. The joey who shot at me . . . his family lost their fishing boat in the Pacific die-off. That sergeant who killed those cadets: his family died of toxic contamination. The Eco Action League is wrong, and irresponsible, but I ignored their pleas, goaded them until . . ." I cut it off, appalled.

"Yes?"

I couldn't say it.

No. Let it be part of my punishment.

I whispered, "You were right. I killed your father. If I'd seen reason, the Eco League wouldn't have set off the bomb."

"Oh, Mr. Seafort!" His eyes glistened. "I want so much to hate you." A long pause. "But Mr. Carr told me all about you and Dad. I know why he wanted to go to the Rotunda."

I swallowed. "I'm sorry, Mikhael."

"I miss him so damn much." He hugged himself. "But I won't blame it on you."

A silence, in which we found a sort of peace. Eventually, I cleared my throat. "Let's sit on the veranda. I'll pretend I'm Derek, and tell you stories."

"Yes, sir." He jumped to his feet, still anxious to show his good behavior.

I gestured to him to open the double doors.

It was one of those increasing rarities, a cool summer day. A few years ago I'd had alumalloy awnings installed to block the sun. Unconsciously, I now realized, I'd made my accommodations to the growing enviro calamity.

I patted a nearby seat. "I met Derek—I mean, Mr. Carr—when he was about your age."

"You enlisted him. He told me."

"As a cadet, first. I couldn't make him middy directly."

"My dad thought it was a stupid idea. He told Mr. Carr—I'm sorry!" Mikhael jumped to his feet. "Sir, I didn't mean that!"

This had gone far enough. "Sit." I waited for him to comply. "I'll tell Arlene you're my responsibility, except when you irritate *her*. I'll handle the rest."

"I feel like a fool." He stared at his shoes. "I'm being so careful, I stumble over my tongue."

"You need not be quite so afraid of me. Or her, for that matter. I'll allow you an occasional lapse. Now, go change your shirt, you've sweated through it. And then I'll tell you about your dad and Mr. Carr."

Three days passed, in relative calm.

As far as I knew, Anselm stayed out of my liquor. He helped me in the office, and during his off-hours coached Bevin at his studies. The fact that the cadet was off campus didn't excuse him from his learning. Or, for that matter, from physical labors. From time to time, of the mornings, I took a break and wheeled myself to the lawn, where the middy led two perspiring youngsters at calisthenics.

Bevin exercised without complaint, as was fitting. Cadets were worked hard, and thrived on it. Wistfully, I remembered my own Academy days, the slow filling out of my form, the gradual growth of pride and confidence.

Mikhael was another matter. Though trim and relatively fit, he hated the exercises with a passion, particularly in that Anselm led them. He decided to test me; I was adamant in refusing him reminiscences until he earned them with calisthenics. He responded with a volley of curses, and was made to spend a day in his room. Next time I'd be harder on him.

The next morning he joined Anselm and Bevin for their full two hours. I was lavish in my praise, and wracked my brain for tales of my youth.

Toward the end of the week I began to prepare my tour. For a major campaign I would rely heavily on my official staff; the sat-relays between Washington and the Rotunda crackled with our conferences.

We would announce our enviro proposals two days hence, at a session of the Assembly. I'd follow with a whirlwind of interviews and appearances. I busied myself dragooning local officials into joining me on bandstands. As more and more joeys were taken into our confidence, rumors began to swirl. I did my best to keep Cisno Valera in the dark, sure that he'd trumpet the news of our reversal if he saw advantage in it.

Nonetheless, my speech, which I wrote myself, was kept totally under wraps, except from Jerence Branstead. No speechwriter, no staffer, not even Karen Burns was allowed to see it.

At last the time came to pack. It would be many days before I was home. Eagerly, Mikhael readied his own gear, helped me with mine. He was crestfallen when he learned Arlene would accompany us, but made a manful effort to contain himself, no doubt fearful I'd tell her.

He was more disconcerted when she went through his suitcase, smoothing and repacking his dress clothes. That she did the same for Anselm mollified him to a degree. Though Mikhael and Bevin got along well, there was a rivalry between Tamarov and the middy that threatened to flare into something more contentious.

It was late in the evening; we were to leave in the morning. I sat in my office, reviewing chipnotes. Danil Bevin looked in.

"Yes?" I frowned.

"Sorry, sir." He turned to go. Then, "What will you tell them?"

"The Assembly?" A momentary annoyance, that a mere cadet had the gall even to ask. "That we're doing an about-face."

"Will they understand?" Unbidden, he took his customary workseat.

A wintry smile. "I certainly hope so."

"You ought to tell them about our trip."

"Don't be ridiculous." I'd marshaled my logic, worked endlessly to get the facts straight and in proper order.

"But the places he took you make it interesting. Poor Philip." He chewed a fingernail. "He must have been terrified he wouldn't convince you."

"Oh?"

Danil blushed. "Sorry, it's none of my . . . sir, I have to say it. Thank you so much."

I raised an eyebrow. "For?"

"For doing what you're about to. For taking me along so I could see how it happened. I think . . . I'm watching history in the making. I know our work's confidential, but do you know how much I want to call my father, make sure he'll be at the holovid?"

"Have no fear." My tone was sour. There'd been rumors aplenty; every enviro on the planet would be glued to the nets.

"I cried, that night."

"When?"

"In Munich, after the flood. The joeys in that town . . . lives, generations drowned in mud." His eyes glistened. "If Philip—Mr. Seafort—if he hadn't—"

"Easy, boy. You're overwrought."

He nodded, ran a hand over his eyes. "May I see your speech?"

"No."

A sigh. "I'm sorry."

"It's all right." Almost, I showed it to him, but there were limits. "Your father's enviro work is that important to you?"

"He's how I got interested, but . . . is it true you used to be able to go out whenever you wanted? Play ball in the sun?"

"You still can, if you're careful." I leaned back. "When Jason and I were joeykids . . ." No. I wouldn't follow that thought, or I'd become as emotional as he. "Someday,

Danil, when you're grown, it will be that way again. If we can get the ozone layer reseeded . . ." It was our biggest unsolved problem. "You deserve a time in the sun."

"Will they understand, Mr. Seafort?" A whisper.

I tapped a copy of my carefully reasoned speech. "We'll make them understand."

My staff, my family, and I left for New York in full panoply. The news zines covered our departure, having for days trumpeted the rumors, now grown to near certainty, that the Seafort Administration would either resign or turn itself inside out.

We took a suite for my family at the Skytel Sheraton, completely rebuilt after the invasion of the Transpop Rebellion. If the accommodations made Jared Tenere uncomfortable, he gave no sign. P.T. seemed troubled, and wheeled me to the stairwell that once we'd climbed to escape smoke and flames.

To ease his mind I asked, "Have you heard from Pook?" The young Mid transpop had been sent to an Uppie tower school.

"Not since Mr. Chang died. Fath, you're doing the right thing."

"I know." Day by day, I grew more comfortable with my conversion.

"They may crucify you for it."

"I hope not literally."

My humor failed in its goal. Philip slumped on a concrete stair. "It's vital that we cleanse the planet. But I don't want to sacrifice you to it." His fingers toyed with his shirt.

"Philip . . . no, look at me. Into my eyes. Do you recall that day in the launch?" We'd sailed almost into Earthport's lasers, to end the transpop war.

"Yes, sir." His voice quavered.

"We were prepared that day for a greater sacrifice. If I'm

made to retire, I'll still have you. We lost each other for a while. Now I have you back, little else matters."

Something in his eyes seemed to calm. Slowly, his fingers stilled.

I sat at the well of the Rotunda, resplendent in my best clothes. I'd instructed my chair to wheel itself in, and then, in full view of holocams and the Assembly, had Philip and Mikhael transfer me to an armless chair. I wanted no mechanical curiosity to distract from my theme. Poor Mikhael, in his best crisply ironed jumpsuit and neckerchief, was so nervous he almost dropped me, but I didn't think anyone noticed. It was important that he understand the extent of my trust.

I stared at the expectant Assembly. In the front row, Arlene and Philip glowed with pride. The boys had retreated upstairs, in the galleries. Seats below were unavailable. Branstead had heard they were being resold, at scalpers' prices. Many wanted to witness the fall of the perpetual Seafort Administration. Row after row was filled with prosperous politicians, their hair perfectly coifed, their suits the latest style.

At various levels of the hall, holocams pulsed. No address since my fervent plea to the world during the Transpop Rebellion, a dozen years prior, had been beamed to so wide an audience. My words would be simultaneously translated into more than fifty languages.

The hall quieted. I cleared my throat, looked down at the expectant faces.

"I have come to confess my error. An error you share." My hands lay still in my lap. "For years—for decades—our gaze has been turned outward. To the produce of our colonies, to the exploits of our magnificent Navy, to warding off, and then repairing, the depredations of the fish."

My voice was flinty. "And now we must pay the price. One which would have been lower, had we acted sooner.

One which will strain our purse, but which can and must be paid."

An uneasy stir.

And then I laid before them my grand strategy. A massive reestablishment of agriculture, corresponding cutbacks in industry. An end to the filth that poured into our air, and to the particles that devastated our ozone layer.

All the wild-eyed schemes for which I'd belittled the Enviro Council over the years.

As I spoke, my tone was serene, but I saw I was losing my audience. There was that look of calculation, while Assemblymen contemplated which industries in their districts might falter, which wealthy contributors would shut off the tap of their munificence.

I had to persuade the fifteen hundred men and women in the room, else my aspirations would miscarry. The joeys in the fine leather chairs before me were the world's only hope.

My speech slowed.

No. It wasn't so.

They were only the delegates of my true audience. It was the joeys of the world I dared not lose, not these self-satisfied politicos stuffed into their well-padded seats.

I would have to sell the world my ideas. Or failing that, sell myself. Above all, the people trusted me. For years I'd scorned them for it. Now I would call upon that trust.

But, how to reach them?

Danil Bevin's earnest face floated before me. *You ought to tell them about our trip . . .*

I abandoned my memorized text.

"Perhaps some of you, in your cities, your villages, your towns, saw how I traveled tonight, to reach this Assembly. A heli from my compound, a jet from Potomac Shuttleport to New York, a fleet of helis to carry my staff to the Rotunda."

Mediamen held up tiny recorders, aghast that I'd departed from the speech Branstead had just distributed. Now they'd actually have to think.

"I don't always travel that way. Sometimes I jounce around in a motorized chair, a cumbersome contraption with a mind of its own." As I'd hoped, titters loosened the mood of the hall.

"And then there's the trip my security joeys hope I won't reveal. A few days ago, I hopped into a heli—well, *hop* isn't quite the right word." I grinned.

Chuckles, that broadened into guffaws.

"It was an old battered heli, a rental. I won't tell you which company supplied it." Laughter. "And once we were aloft, I switched off my transponder. No doubt I had U.N. Security climbing the walls."

I had them now, every ear.

"And we went on a holiday of sorts, my son and I, and two aides. The joeys who saw us dismissed out of hand my resemblance to the SecGen. After all, even Seafort wouldn't be such a fool as to travel alone."

A roar of mirth.

I told them of the woman who'd accosted me at the Carolina restaurant. My evasion evoked gales of laughter. I spoke of the Kansas hail, the Bavarian floods, the bisque doll in the drowned hausfrau's hand. Of the broken highway in Florida that symbolized America's dream.

Casually, I mentioned every town we'd overflown, every motel at which we'd slept, every restaurant in which we'd eaten. I strove to make my audience see me not as a remote authority, but a fellow voyager roaming the same world as they. I told them how Philip dented the chair that had the effrontery to fling me to the mud.

My tone was gentle, cheerful, in fact, very much like the manner in which I'd spoken to Mikhael about Alexi, after his daily exercises. Just old friends, enjoying a quiet chat.

I told them what I'd seen on my journey, and the horror it evoked, and my resolve that while I remained in office, I would not allow it to continue. I laid out our plans that would reverse the worst of our depredations in a very few years. Moving so fast would cause greater turmoil, I said, but it had the incomparable advantage of producing results quickly enough to persuade citizens that their sacrifices were not in vain.

I spoke of the vast combination of interests that would oppose our design, that included many of the joeys in this very chamber.

An uneasy rustle.

"It is up to you," I said. "All of you across the world, who hear me today. We cannot allow politics to prevail. We cannot let economic self-interest threaten the continuance of our very race."

I paused, gazed solemnly into the holocams. "If the Assembly and Senate of the United Nations support us, well and good. But those members who don't, I ask you to remove. If our bills are amended without my consent, I will dissolve the Senate and Assembly—"

A murmur of protest. But from more than a few, willing applause.

"—and call new elections. Fellow citizens, we have edged our way to imminent disaster. It is time to reverse course. The need is great, the goal achievable, and the reward infinite. For yourselves, your children, and the honor of Lord God, I ask your support and your trust. Thank you, and may He bless us all."

At first, silence. My face impassive, I stared back at them, daring their hostility.

The applause began slowly, uncertainly. Then, like swelling thunder heralding an approaching storm, it rolled in great waves across the hall. Whistles. Calls. The gallery rose in enthusiastic ovation, followed, shortly, by much of the Assembly itself. But there were those few, Terries and Supras among them, who remained seated, arms folded.

Through it all, engulfed in adulation, I sat unmoving, trembling beneath my calm.

It was the greatest performance of my life, and the most

dishonest. I'd spoken to the holocams as to a friend. I'd offered a version of myself I knew to be untrue: a friendly, cheerful soul revealing himself to the public for the first time. An Everyman, a neighborhood joey who happened to hold a special office, a . . .

Enough. What I'd done was for Philip, and for Father. Over many years I'd done worse, and for less.

I would abide the cost.

14

Interviews with *Holoworld, Newsnet,* and *Holoweek,* from the Skytel Sheraton. A much publicized visit to the New York Seawall, where I scowled at the Hudson estuary lapping at its massive algae-stained blocks. Then a suborbital to Brazil, and a tour of the wasteland of worked-out farms that generations ago had been rain forest.

Vehement speeches in Rio, São Paulo, and Brasilia. Then on to Buenos Aires and La Plata. Montevideo. Mexico City.

Our days fell into a wearisome routine. Mikhael, Tad Anselm, and Bevin helped me get in and out of my chair, ran errands, took charge of our gear. When there was time, I let them out to explore.

Arlene reviewed drafts of my speeches, amending them to keep me on point and lucid.

Jerence Branstead orchestrated quiet meetings with local leaders, in which I tried to win them to our program. I soon became adept at emphasizing the new manufactories that our enviro crusade would call forth.

Still, persistent questions dogged us. Why had I submitted to Eco League extortion? Would a covey of anonymous terrorists dictate enviro policy? I tried my best to keep my temper.

Over dinner, Arlene soothed me. "It's part of the process. Every political leader has gone through it."

"Genghis Khan didn't."

Anselm snorted. Mikhael repressed a grin.

"Be patient, Nick. You're succeeding." The polls showed us holding our support. Our foes in the Assembly would take note. Few dared oppose us openly; I'd crafted a weighty coalition. Instead, they would kill our plans with hearings, with studies, with helpful amendments.

I called Cisno Valera. "Tell them it won't work. The package goes to the floor in three weeks, or I dissolve the Assembly."

"They can't move so fast."

"They'd better." I would make the issue their political survival.

"Mr. Seafort . . ." He sounded uncomfortable. "As Deputy SecGen I can't support what amounts to a coup against the legislative process."

"Is this a parting of the ways, Cisno?"

He backpedaled. "The Senate has rules, procedures, customs . . ."

"Hurry them along. Three weeks." I was too tired to be diplomatic.

The next morning we were in Ireland. I spoke at the Naval training station, near the site of the Belfast nuke. "There are those who would counsel delay. Perhaps they mean well. Meanwhile the tides rise two inches a year. We can afford no caution. We need action, strength, and resolve."

That night Anselm failed to come home to the hotel. Karen Burns woke me at three: he'd been arrested in a drunken brawl at a Navy bar. Did I want him released?

"No." I went back to sleep.

In the morning, groggy and disgusted, I reversed myself, sent an aide to arrange bail. When the middy appeared, I sent him for a caning, with instructions not to go easy. Mikhael saw his demeanor afterward, and laughed outright.

Trouble, but no time to deal with it; we were on to South Africa. Forty-seven U.N. Senators announced they would block my legislation after the Assembly was through with it. Jerence Branstead scrambled for a key to their conversion.

Finally, after fifteen exhausting days, we flew home. A conference with the Patriarchs awaited.

Anselm sat next to me on the suborbital. I'd barely spoken to him in the days since his lapse. "I've decided to send you back to Devon."

He flinched. "Yes, sir." Then, "You don't know why I was fight—"

"I don't care."

"They called you a traitor to the Navy!"

"Who?"

"Lieutenants and middies, on leave from *Seville*. They said—"

"I don't want to hear it."

"That you sold out. That you went over to the ecos!"

"Bah. Idle talk, by drunken louts. And you were one of them."

He flushed. "I—yes."

"Why'd you drink? The dream again?"

"No." He squared his shoulders. "I was feeling sorry for myself."

"You imagine you did me honor, standing up for me? I despise it."

His voice was tremulous. "So do I, now I'm sober. But when I heard them—"

"Perhaps you'll do better in your next posting."

"Yes, sir." His tone was forlorn. A last appeal. "I don't think I'll do it again."

"Too late."

"I'm ready to swear—"

"You already swore to obey all lawful orders. Your word is worthless." Brutal, but I no longer cared. The Senators were inflexible. I had too many burdens, and a miscreant middy was more than I could deal with.

He cried, "Help me rather than ruin me!"

"Tad, you're not the center of my life."

He put his head in his hands.

After a moment I asked gruffly, "How?"

A glance, as if hoping against hope. "Keep me busy. Give me extra duties. Those letters you wanted, to the Norwegian legislators. I'll draft them. You said you'd like to have Charlie Witrek visit. I'll arrange it. Anything you say, I'll do. Just let me talk . . ." He blushed furiously. "Let me talk with you and Ms. Seafort sometimes. I get so lonely."

On base, or aboard ship, middies were among their own kind. They had the wardroom, their mates, for companionship and solace.

While I mused, he fidgeted. "Sir, I won't drink. I can't stand it anymore."

"Being drunk?"

"The caning. You don't know what it's like."

"Of course I do."

"I'm seventeen next week. That's supposed to be too old for—I'm sorry, no criticism, sir. But I'm not a joeykid. To be bent across a barrel, and have some lieutenant beat me, his knowing that I disgraced myself, that I was slobbering drunk . . ." He bit back a sob. "It hurts so. And then to come home to Mikhael's laughter, and your contempt, that's the worst part." His eyes were damp. "Sir, it won't—I don't know how I'll stop myself, but I will."

If I didn't send him home to Devon, I'd be responsible for the consequences. And yet . . . "A caning every time you drink: that won't change."

"Yes, sir."

"And if you fail to inform me, you're dismissed from the Service." Honor was everything.

"I know, sir."

"Tell Mr. Branstead you're to help with my appointments

list. Evenings, you can help Warren sort my mail." I rarely spoke with my puter in the Rotunda, preferring to let him handle routine inquiries. He sounded more like me than I did myself.

"Sir, I thank you with all my heart." An old-fashioned phrase, that moved me unduly.

We broke out of the clouds, into the smog of the Northeast.

"Most unwise." Bishop Saythor glowered. His colleagues seemed to agree; their expressions were unfavorable, some downright unfriendly. All the Patriarchs save one were assembled in Council, at the magnificent, soaring Reunification Cathedral in Chicago. I sat alone, facing them, nervously tapping the arms of my chair.

I said, "It must be done."

"Just as our economy was starting to rebound—"

"Sir, is this about wealth?"

The President of the Latter-day Saints wagged a finger. "Not wealth, but what it represents. The power of Lord God made manifest, His embodiment on Earth—"

I was still jet-lagged, and resented being summoned so abruptly. "Was Jesus not that?"

The Bishop of Rome bristled. "You dare argue theology with us?"

"No, sir, I apologize. I was wrong." Inwardly, I cursed my folly. Theirs was to speak on matters ecclesiastical, mine to obey.

"By shattering the wealth of nations, you threaten Mother Church herself." Saythor was stern. "It's vital that we advance the good name of the Church at home and in the colonies."

"What would you have me do?"

"Scale back your ambitions. Accomplish what you may without wreaking havoc."

"You wouldn't have me forsake enviroism altogether?"

"You spoke publicly, for the Government. You mustn't be seen to reverse yourself." But I *had* reversed myself, in my speech to the Assembly. Abruptly I'd revoked a decades-old policy of benign neglect. What the Patriarchs meant was that my proposals had gained too much popular support to be abandoned utterly.

Bishop Saythor said, "As much as we dislike the thought, the Church must be run as a business. Destabilizing change, one that leaves our parishioners in poverty, impacts inevitably on Church finances and on its work."

I watched curiously. Would Lord God strike him dead? Surely He would not allow such thoughts to be uttered in the name of His Church.

But He was silent.

So was I.

"Well, Mr. SecGen?"

"I'll think on it." Why did I temporize?

"We need more than that."

"We've had this conversation before, sir." I held his gaze.

He flushed. "Yes, we can disavow you. We've discussed it."

"And?"

"The time isn't opportune." They'd read the polls. *I'm sorry, Lord. I apologize for Your vicars.*

Later, I called Arlene. "I still hold office."

"Shall I say it's a relief?"

"Not for you, I know." My tone was gentle. "It won't be long now. I have a sense."

"Before I forget, Mark Tilnitz called. He's most anxious to see you."

"What about?"

"He wouldn't say. Nicky, something's wrong; I think he's gone glitched. Be careful. Talk to him by caller."

"I'm not afraid of Mark. If he wants his job back I'd be delight—"

"Twice he asked me who else was on the line. Security's a horrible job; the pressure may have been too much—"

"Mark's as stable as they come." I shrugged, forgetting Arlene couldn't see. "Call him back, have him to the house tonight." A few hours wouldn't matter.

On the way to Daley Shuttleport a priority call from General Donner. "We have a lead on Booker!"

"Praise God." The murderer of my cadets would be brought to justice. "How? When?"

"Our phone taps. He finally called the cousin. He's in Barcelona."

"We've waited long enough. Round them up."

"I concur. This evening, in a coordinated sweep."

In the plane, I was exultant. The terrorists were broken. I called in Karen Burns, shared a toast. "They'll hang, every one of them."

"Naturally."

"P and D will tell the whole story." I wondered why we'd waited. Still, better safe than sorry.

"Congratulations, sir."

I exulted, "Now, the enviro bills will sail through the Assembly. A lot of the Terries hesitated because they feared I was giving in to blackmail."

"It must be a great relief." She'd been present, I recalled, at the Rotunda bombing. To have her principal injured on her watch must be a nightmare.

I poured more champagne. "Mark wants to see me. Does he want back on the detail?"

"I wouldn't know." She sounded cool. "You haven't spoken to him?"

"This evening. He's coming to the compound."

Home at last, I let them help me from the heli to the chair. Karen excused herself to make some calls. I summoned Danil. During my long trip, a mountain of paperwork had accumulated.

The cadet slipped into my office.

"Start with the summaries of the zines. File them by—good heavens, let me see that."

Reluctantly, he came close. A mouse, under his right eye. "How'd that happen?"

He shuffled his feet. "I, uh, ran into something, sir." It served me right, asking him to criticize a superior. He'd never betray his midshipman, not if he wanted my respect.

Unlike middies, cadets were considered children, subject to the discipline of their betters. But I'd never allowed a middy to punish a cadet, not once in my career. It too easily led to abuse. The gall of Anselm, after my own leniency. "Why did he do it?"

Danil shuffled his feet. "We had a fight."

I went off like a skyrocket. "ANSELM, GET DOWN HERE!" I slammed down the caller. "Get some ice, boy."

"Sir, he—"

"Don't argue! Put ice on that bruise, this very moment."

"Aye aye, sir." He rushed off.

"Midshipman Anselm reporting, sir!"

"Take that jacket off! Fifty push-ups. Move!"

"Aye aye, sir!" He dropped to the ground.

I fumed, rolling my chair from side to side, as if to pace. "Faster! If you think you can get away with—"

"Is this good enough, sir?" Bevin, with a cloth full of ice. He held it to his cheek.

"Why'd he hit you? None of that guff about not telling me. I won't—"

"Sir, I—"

"Middy, be silent. Thirty more push-ups. Well, Cadet?"

"It wasn't Mr. Anselm, sir. I tried to tell you!"

At my feet, Anselm labored. His breath came hard.

"Who, then?"

"Mr. Tamarov, sir."

I gaped. Then, at last. "As you were, Anselm."

Gratefully, the middy let himself sag.

"I'm, er, sorry." I grimaced at the panting boy. "How many demerits have you accumulated?"

"Three, sir."

"One is canceled." It was the least I could do.

"Thank you." Anselm hesitated. "Could I do eighty more for another?" Amazingly, his eye held a twinkle.

"No. And don't twit me or—" Well, I couldn't always be an ogre. "Yes, you may."

With delight, he dropped to the floor. Canceling a demerit normally required two full hours of calisthenics.

"Danil, did you strike Mikhael first?"

"No, sir." Firm, no hesitation.

"Very well, file those zines; you know where they go. Chair, out." I found Mikhael in the den, watching a holo. "You. Come along." I led him to the office. "Apologize to Mr. Bevin."

"Mister? He's a frazzing cadet!"

"Fair warning, Mikhael. You've gone too far." If he retracted his horns now, I'd let him be.

Fists bunched, he took a step toward Anselm. "Don't smirk, you fucking grode!"

"Danil, Tad, excuse us." My tone was low, ominous. I whirled on Mikhael. "You have a foul mouth."

"Who cares?"

What possessed a joeykid to speak so to an adult? Did he think we still lived in the Rebellious Ages? "Fetch a bar of soap."

"You're out of your mind! Nobody's going to—"

"You'll do it yourself."

"The fuck I will!"

With great effort, I wheeled from behind the desk, skidded to the door, turned my chair. "That's it, Mikhael." I fumbled at my belt.

"You're not touching me."

I rolled toward him. He darted behind my desk. Laboriously, I rolled after.

Mikhael threw open the veranda doors, bolted into the dusk.

Cursing under my breath, I retraced my path, opened my door. "Come in, boys." I indicated chairs. "What was this about?" They exchanged glances. "None of that! Speak."

Bevin looked uncomfortable. "He was ragging Mr. Anselm again."

"And?"

"Instead of decking him, Mr. Anselm walked off. I told Mikhael what I thought of him." A sheepish grin. "And he smacked me."

"I would have too," I said sharply. Since when did a cadet berate a civilian, no matter what his age?

"It's my fault, sir." Anselm. "Danil should know better." As middy, he was in charge.

"Most certainly. Whatever is the matter between you? I won't tolerate it. Go to your rooms."

"Sir, I'm—"

"Now."

They departed. I rolled from door to desk, muttering epithets.

The caller buzzed. "Wilkins, at the gate. Mark Tilnitz is here, sir. He's no longer on the list."

"Let him in. Call Karen to escort him; she'll want to bring him up-to-date." I wiped my brow, resettled myself. It would be a difficult interview. I liked Mark, but I would no longer let security dictate my day. I'd go where I wished, speak with—

The door flew open. Karen Burns, her laser drawn.

"What the devil—" I stared.

She hauled me out of my chair, clubbed me in the temple. Dazed, I tried to drag myself to safety.

"Come here, you prick." She whipped off my belt, lashed my hands behind my back, yanked off my tie, used it for a gag. She threw open a closet, dragged me inside. "I'll be back. Then we'll go for a ride." Locking my hall door, she dashed to the veranda.

In the dark, I flopped about, to no avail. My hands were firmly bound.

Frantically, I chewed at my tie. I couldn't tear it, but I managed at last to thrust it to one side. "Hehp! Shecuhity!" My voice was muffled. "Ansem! Ahhene!"

Nothing. I couldn't be heard.

"HIDDY!" My voice held a note of terror.

I rolled from side to side in desperate frenzy. "Ahhene!" My mouth ached. I could barely articulate.

Lord God knew what madness possessed Karen. Arlene was in the house, as was my son. If Karen . . . a chill shivered my spine.

Karen had to be stopped. I struggled to free my hands.

I was helpless.

Not quite. "Chaih, coe heah!"

The hum of a motor.

"Chaih, ahsweh he!"

"I'm here."

"Get hehp!"

"Reference not understood."

"Get hehp, you vucking hucket ah chifs!"

"I'm assigned to Nicholas E. Seafort, U.N. SecGen. Outside commands not recognized."

"I'h no outsaideh, I'h Sehavoht!" I tore at my belt, but couldn't free my wrists. "Nicholas Sehavoht!"

"Please speak clearly. Commands must be entered in—"

"He sileht!" I was beside myself. "I cah't talk. I heed you to caw foh hehp."

"First, I need positive identification."

"Nicholas Sheavoht. Hod damhh it, ghaph hy voice! Neveh hind the wohds!" I held my breath, hoping it would understand.

"Voiceprint graphed. Tentative ID as Nicholas Seafort."

"Fihd Ahhene, do you uhdehshand?"

"Command interpreted as 'Find Arlene, do you understand.'"

"Thah's iht."

"I'm not programmed to comply with distant commands. I may respond only when you're sitting in my seat."

"In Vavaria I tohd you to rephogham."

"Response modified. I may obey a distant command."

"Chaih, cahn you heave the ofvhice?"

"The door is shut."

"Ham it. Dhive thew it!"

"And then?" The chair sounded dubious.

"Fihd Ahhene. Tehh huh I said dangeh. Kahen Vuhrns has a laseh. Tehh huh I an tied in hy ofvice closet. Confihm cowwand!"

"You want me to tell Arlene you said danger. Kahen Vuhrns has a laser. Tell her you are tied in your office closet."

It would do. "Huhhy, chaih!"

"You command me to destroy property, an office door?"

"Yesh."

"This door belongs to you?"

"Yesh!"

The whir of a motor. A crash. Another. Splintering wood. The motor, coming closer. A pause. A tremendous smash. Silence.

From the yard, shouts. A desperate shriek, that faded into a ghastly moan. Running feet. Silence.

I waited, in an agony of suspense.

"Nick, where are you?"

"Ih heah!"

The door rattled. "The bitch took the key!" The whine of a laser. A crackle. Burning wood. A kick. The door gave way. Arlene, pistol in hand.

She clawed at my gag. At last, my mouth was free.

"Never mind me, get Philip to safety!"

She flopped me on my stomach, worked loose the belt.

"Did you hear? Find P.T.!"

"I will. Chair, where the hell are you?"

"Here." It rolled through the door.

Grunting with effort, she dragged me toward the chair. I helped her haul me into it. "Nick, where's your pistol?"

"In my desk." She threw open the drawer, checked the charge. "Watch for Karen. I'll roll you—"

"Back me to that wall; I can watch both doors. Save Philip."

A peck on my cheek. She shoved my chair toward the wall, peered cautiously out the door, dashed down the hallway.

I sat sweating. My arm trembled; the pistol wavered.

On the lawn, pounding feet. I took aim with both hands.

The doors crashed open. Karen gaped at the sight of me. I fired. My bolt singed her hair as she dived outside, to safety.

"Seafort, put down the gun. Else I'll kill you."

I waited, my hands steady now.

She flung herself past the doorway, firing. A bolt sizzled my desk, between us. I returned fire, but she was gone.

Shouts. She muttered something foul. Running steps, fading. The distant whine of a laser. A cry of pain.

"Chair." It was almost a whisper. "To the veranda door."

Instantly the machine began to roll.

I braced myself with one hand, aimed. My legs would emerge first; there was no help for it. If she fired into them, at least I wouldn't feel it.

"Through the door, fast right turn."

We did. Nobody was there.

I lowered the gun. "Back inside."

"Nick, what in hell are you doing?" Arlene hauled my chair backward. "You lunatic."

"Where's P.T.?"

"With Jared, in their room. Anselm's guarding the stairs."

"With what?"

"I gave him a rifle."

"We don't have a rifle."

"The guard won't be needing it. P.T. wanted to fight. I wouldn't let him."

"Good."

"He's furious."

"Mr. SecGen?" A voice, from the yard. As one, we raised our pistols.

"Who goes?"

"Wilkins. Come out where I can see you."

"No." Arlene. "Drop your pistol and show yourself with your hands raised."

"I can't. How do I know you're not a prisoner?"

"I'm not." No longer.

"I'm coming in. I'll have my weapon."

"I'll kill anyone who enters this room armed." Arlene, with a note of finality.

"Enough, you two." I rolled to the door. "We can't have a standoff." I peered outside. Wilkins was alone. About twenty paces behind him, a guard knelt, covering him with his rifle. "Where's Karen Burns?"

"She escaped. Tilnitz is dead."

"Oh, no!"

"It was his scream you heard." Wilkins waved to the other guard. "The SecGen's all right."

Slowly, we sorted ourselves out.

If Karen was an enemy, who could I trust? Had Tilnitz been her accomplice? Why in Lord God's name did she assault me?

We had no answers. I called the Potomac Naval Station, had the duty officer rouse his commander. "Send me two squads of Marines, well armed, flank. They'll guard the perimeter."

We were groundside; I should have called U.N.A.F. instead of Navy. To hell with the niceties.

I rolled across the lawn, halted at Mark's body.

The laser had caught him at close range, burned an arm entirely off. I tried not to retch.

Two gate guards were dead, one burned.

I rang Jerence Branstead in New York. Two hours later, he was on his way, with a company of reliable troops. General Donner was half an hour behind.

Anselm, flushed with tension, reluctantly surrendered his rifle. Bevin put down the bat with which he'd guarded the top of the stairwell. Jared and P.T. emerged. Philip was white-faced. "It was wrong, Mom. Dead wrong."

I left them to argue.

Mikhael Tamarov was nowhere to be found. I was frantic; after Alexi, his son's death would be unendurable. Someone thought to check the gate log. Mikhael had signed out just after he'd run from my office. Destination left blank. It was one vexation too many. I cursed long and fluently, felt slightly better.

Branstead landed on the pad, in a huge military craft filled with soldiers. "You're all right? Thank God." Fervently, he embraced me.

"We have to untangle ourselves. What in God's name—"

"Mark called me on his way to you, distraught. He thought Karen was one of them."

"Of whom?"

"The Eco League!"

"Why the hell didn't you call? He died, two gate guards—"

"You don't think I tried? Your callers were down. Even your personal line was jammed."

"But . . ." I spluttered to a halt.

"I went half out of my mind, sir. No one could reach you."

"Why tonight, Jerence? What was she up to?" Then it hit me. "Lord God, I'm responsible." I pounded my insensate knee.

"How?"

"I told her, on the plane. That we'd caught the Eco League

and were rounding them up tonight. She knew she was out of time. I broke security and killed Mark."

"*She* killed Mark." His voice was firm.

"It was my stupidity."

"Ours. We all share the blame. Donner, me, you . . . at least we know who planted the Rotunda bomb."

"Who?" I puzzled it out. "Good Christ. Karen?"

"Opportunity, motive . . ."

Donner's craft landed. An hour later we met in the kitchen, a council of four. Arlene handed around coffee, sat grimly. "They invaded my home."

"We'll get her, Ms. Seafort."

"My home!" She smashed the table. "She was one of yours!"

I said, "That's not quite fair, hon. She—"

"From now on, I personally approve every security file." Arlene's tone brooked no refusal.

"Done." The General seemed glad to comply. "We grabbed the suspects. Karen made a flurry of calls, no doubt to them, but your personal lines can't be traced. Four of the eco bastards were throwing clothes in their kit, one was out the door."

"You have them all?"

"All we know of, except Karen. And Booker."

I swore. "You said you had him."

"I think we do. They're combing the streets. He called his cousin from the Barcelona Ramblas; they're watching—"

I shook my head. The one I wanted most had escaped. Perhaps I should invoke martial law after all.

Jerence asked, "What shall we tell the mediamen?"

"The truth. We were attacked, and have three dead."

"And about the Eco League?"

"That we have them in custody. Put Booker's picture on the holonets. Ten thousand Unies as reward. Twenty."

"Very well." We adjourned.

Late in the night, a call. Bishop Saythor, aghast. He offered me his sympathy, his prayers. He seemed sincere.

At last, holding Arlene, I slept.

In the morning the street was swarming with mediamen, their holocams surveying the gate. To General Donner's dismay, I ordered them invited in, allowed them to photograph the lawn, gave a terse statement.

I awaited the poly and drug examiners' report.

At noon, a call. "Sir, Edgar Tolliver here." My onetime aide, later a Captain, now retired and settled in Philadelphia.

"Edgar! Good of you to call. We're, um, having a bad day."

"I imagine." His tone was dry. "I have the Tamarov boy."

"Good heavens. Why you?"

"His father and I were friends. Mikhael says he fled your compound and your custody. Shall I deliver him? I'm off to Lunapolis tomorrow night. Vacation."

"Is he willing?"

"Not particularly. His attitude lacks a certain, ah, suavity. Do you want him?"

"Not unless he agrees." Not even then, but I owed it to Alexi to do what I could.

"You'll of course soothe and coddle him when he returns?"

"Tolliver!"

"Just asking." I could hear his grin. He'd always taken pleasure in tweaking me, and for years I'd let him. "Mikhael's floundering, sir. He wants me to talk him into going back, but he's wary of your, ah, renowned kindness."

"Don't bother."

"Why, Mr. SecGen, it's no trouble at all." Abruptly, he turned serious. "My condolences on the attack, sir. Is there anything I can do?"

"No, but thanks."

"My best to Ms. Seafort."

"Take care, Edgar." We rang off.

Another terse conference with Branstead and Donner. "Cousin Sara implicated two more joeys, but they'd flown the coop. We'll catch them."

"What in God's name," Jerence asked, "possessed them to go on a killing spree? All those attacks . . ."

Donner grimaced. "I'm not sure if they're political fanatics, or a form of cult. Death didn't matter, they said, because our enviro neglect already killed so many."

Satan worked in mysterious and subtle ways. I shivered.

Jerence said, "Karen Burns and that Booker joey are still loose. Mr. SecGen"—he tapped my appointment book—"you have to stay under guard. At least until they're caught."

"Why, if my own guards are—"

"Karen must have meant to kidnap you, else she'd have burned you down. She may still—"

"How do you know?"

"She said she'd take you on a ride, right?"

"But where?"

He shrugged. "Your guess is as good as mine."

"But why, damn it?" Silently, a small prayer of contrition.

"The E.A.L. was desperate to alter your policies, despite your speech. They wanted even more change."

"Was I supposed to shut down our entire economy?"

"Apparently."

I shrugged. Lunatics. Like all glitched enviros, they—no, I'd switched sides. I must remember that.

"Guard Arlene and Philip," I said. "I won't take a company of soldiers to the head to relieve myself."

Branstead and the General exchanged glances. "Now your speaking tour is wound down, we feel—"

"We?"

"Donner and I talked it over. Sir, you travel too much. Until we catch those bastards, stay here or at the Rotunda. There's no guarding you when you go gallivanting about."

"I will not be their prisoner!" I slammed the table.

"Sir, it's only for a little—"

"No! I have appointments. Dr. Ghenili has me scheduled in four days: should I cancel? My future depends on it."

"There are committed terrorists roaming—"

I shouted, "I don't care!"

Arlene poked her head into my office. "Bellow more softly, love."

I waved her in. "These joeys want me to lock myself in the compound. Cancel all travel. Did you ever hear such goofjuice?"

"That reminds me, Donner," she said. "I want a laser license for P.T."

He frowned. "I can swing it, but public policy . . ." Few were allowed to carry a laser pistol. I was licensed, of course, and Arlene.

"He shoots well; I taught him myself. And he has sense."

"Very well, I'll see to it. But if you stay under wraps . . ." Donner looked hopeful.

"How well do you know my Nick?" Arlene's tone was sardonic. "He won't agree, no matter the cost." She looked thoughtful. "On the other hand, I could disable his chair."

"On the other hand, I could crawl." I didn't see the humor. Yet, my stubbornness risked whoever traveled with me. And I'd have a hard time forcing P.T. and Arlene to stay at home, if I left the compound. "Look, what if . . ." I puzzled it through. "Jerence, what if I traveled in secret? Why announce that I'm going to Lunapolis to see Ghenili?"

"The media watch your jet, your official heli."

"Smuggle me aloft in a military shuttle. Dock at the Naval wing in Earthport, transfer me to a private craft."

"Word will get out."

"Branstead, you're a born plotter. Look how you smuggled goofjuice onto *Victoria*. I have faith in you."

"You're bigger than a vial of—"

"We'll use this trip as a test. If it works, fine. Else we'll try something else. In the meantime, catch Karen and

Sergeant Booker. I'll expect to see their holos every hour on the news. See to it."

"The nets don't always—"

"See to it."

Midafternoon. I took a break from a series of dreary political calls, sat on the veranda. Thadeus Anselm leaned in the doorway, hands in pockets. "May I join you?"

"If you'd like." I sounded ungracious, at best. I made an effort. "Sit. Get yourself a softie."

Shyly, he relaxed into a lounge chair.

I recalled he'd told me he was lonely. Awkwardly, I sought a topic of conversation. "What's between you and Mikhael, boy?"

"I don't know, sir. Maybe it's the exercise."

"Are you hard on him?"

"I can't be; I have no authority. I tell Bevin what to do, and Mikhael does it or not as he chooses. I've never complained."

"What, then?"

For a moment he looked troubled. "I guess I'm not that likable."

"You had friends, at Devon?"

"A few. Cadet Santini, but she . . ."

"Was murdered. I'm sorry." I cleared my throat. "When you're not drinking, I find you likable."

"Thanks." He brooded. "Danil was crying last night."

"During the . . . commotion?"

"After."

"Understandable." I should have found the boy, comforted him. He was but fourteen. "Look after him, Tad."

"Aye aye, sir." It would be good practice, for when he was first middy.

The caller rang. Senator Uzuki, stubborn as ever about our enviro package. Reluctantly, I went back to work.

By evening, alone in my office, I dared hope I was making progress. Using every pressure I knew, I'd gotten seven Senators to reconsider their opposition. Not much, but it was a start. I was confident I could carry the Assembly, but if the Senate dug in, our legislation was dead in the water.

A knock. Mikhael Tamarov, his jumpsuit rumpled, his hair awry. He eyed me uncertainly.

"You're here for your clothes?" My face was impassive.

"And to talk to you."

"That's not necessary."

Unbidden, he flopped into the chair across my desk. "I'm messed up, Mr. Seafort."

"I'm aware." My tone was flinty.

"I think I'm glitched, sometimes. I was waiting to talk to Dad. He understands these . . . understood." His fists clenched. "Understood."

He looked so much like Alexi, my heart ached. "And now he's gone. You'll never again have a talk with him. Never have his caring, the rest of your life." Brutal, but I saw no choice. "You're on your own."

"Am I?" His cheeks were wet.

"You sure are, joey." I took up my caller. "Shall I send the cadet to help you pack?"

He wept openly.

I waited him out.

"Where should I go?"

"Kiev, I suppose." I let the silence lengthen. "Unless you ask me to take you back."

"Would you?" It was a whisper.

"This time, only with a judge's custody order." With his consent and his mother's, it could be arranged.

"Why?"

How to make him understand? "We're a family. Arlene and I, P.T. . . . we treat each other a special way."

"I'm not part of it."

"You are, when you live with us."

Footsteps in the hall. Philip peered in. "Am I interrupting?"

"Yes, we're—no, wait. You can help." I waved him to a seat, wheeled myself from behind my desk to join them. "Remember when you were sixteen, and we had that talk?"

He flushed. "Vividly."

"Mikhael needs to understand. Would you tell him?"

"If I must." Philip crossed his legs, pursed his lips in thought. "I was giving Fath a hard time that year. We fought, and he rarely let me have my way."

I opened my mouth to protest the unfairness of it, but subsided. I'd asked him to speak.

"Partly it's that I was certain I was right, which made courtesy unnecessary. I worked myself into a decision to leave. If you won't bother to look at me, why should I talk to you?"

Mikhael jumped as if shot. "I'm sorry. I didn't mean . . ." He crossed his arms, hugged himself. "Go on." From time to time he threw Philip an anxious glance.

"Where was I? . . . I was ready to leave. I dared Fath to call the jerries. He said he wouldn't. I called him . . ." P.T. swallowed. "I called him a liar, told him he wouldn't really let me go.

"'I'll help you pack,' Fath told me. 'I'll give you food for your dinner, and escort you to the gate. Then you're on your own.'"

The room was hushed.

"He sat me down—right where you're sitting, in fact—and told me Mom and I were his reason for living. We had a bond, a family bond, that was sacred to him. There was absolutely nothing I could do—nothing—that would make him throw me out. I could spit at him, steal his heli, scream curses at him all day long. I was still his son and I would share his home. He would endure any behavior at all because of our bond.

"But, Fath added, he would respond to that behavior. With

discipline. And if I chose to break that bond by walking out, he would not take me back, ever. And, Mikhael . . . he meant it."

I said quietly, "Thank you, son."

Mikhael licked his lips. "What happened . . . after?"

"I got a strapping, for the second time in my life. And then we made up."

"He's not ever going to hit me."

"All right. Anything else, Fath?"

"Did Mom talk to you about a pistol?"

"Yes, sir. It's a good idea." He stood, stretched. "Good night."

When we were alone, I busied myself with papers. "Make your decision, and be quick about it."

"Mr. Seafort?"

I put down my holovid, tried not to sound impatient. "Yes?"

"What would Dad want me to do?"

I pondered. Alexi loved Moira, of that I had no doubt. Had he known she was a weak parent? Did it matter? "I'm not sure. If I'd died and Arlene couldn't raise P.T., I'd hope Alexi would. Or Derek."

"Why them?"

"They knew who I was, and what I wanted for my son."

"I won't let you hit me." His tone was stubborn.

"Good, the decision's made. Get your clothes."

Instead, he sat hunched forward on his arms, staring at a scuffed shoe. Minutes stretched into a quarter hour.

I fussed at holochips, battling not to give in.

A sigh of resignation. "What do I have to do, sir?" His voice was subdued.

"I warn you, any more of yesterday's curses and I'll wash out your mouth. As for your conduct, it's been unacceptable. Bend over the desk."

He made as if to speak, chose not to. With a grimace, he bent himself across the desk, rested head in hands.

I tugged off my belt, the same one Karen had tied me with. Carefully, I maneuvered my chair. I gripped the side rail, raised my arm high, cracked the leather across his rump.

"Straighten out, joey," I said. "And I mean *right now.*"

15

At our Devon guest quarters, I peered into the mirror. "Smooth your hair, Anselm. It's a matter of respect."

"Yes, sir."

"It's 'aye aye, sir.' Have you forgotten everything? Mikhael, we'll be back soon. Danil, are you ready?"

The cadet bounded into the room, his gray uniform neat and crisp. "Yes, sir!"

It was a memorial service for the five slain cadets. I'd put off Hazen's suggestion of a service until the capture of the ecos; somehow it seemed obscene to memorialize our joeys while their murderers ran free.

For the solemn ceremony, he'd assembled the entire Academy at Devon, even calling down his cadets stationed at Farside Base.

We met in the dining hall, the only Academy chamber large enough to hold the whole company. Soberly, Hazen eulogized our dead, whose blood-soaked bodies I'd found in the grass, that awful July day.

If I be bereaved of my children, I am bereaved.

When Hazen was done, I wheeled to the front of the hall to speak. I spoke of the hopes unfulfilled, the lives cut short, the friendships shattered.

"I have come out of respect for your fellows who died,

but also out of respect for you, and to address the wrong we did you." I forced myself to look into their eyes.

"The Service is honor and trust, and no more. You have the right, the absolute right, to trust your fellow cadets, the midshipmen, your instructors, your officers. As they have the right and obligation to trust you."

Throughout the hall, not a sound.

"When the joeys of Krane Barracks passed through the suiting room, they were entitled, each and every one of them, to the certainty that no person in God's Navy would wish them ill. That no one, regardless of his politics, would betray the trust that binds our lives together. We each of us, as we sail the stars, depend on our mates for our very lives. At Devon Academy, that trust was shaken. I hope and pray that you will allow it to be rebuilt.

"On behalf of the United Nations, of the Government of Lord God, I humbly apologize to you all."

I took a long slow breath.

"Dismissed."

In his office, Hazen swirled the ice in his glass. "Well said. It's what we strive to teach them."

"Thank you." I noticed that he, or a predecessor, had replaced much of the furniture I'd removed as Commandant. I'd found it impossible to pace without barking a shin.

"I wish everyone felt that way." He spoke lightly, but with an undercurrent of tension.

There was something he wanted to tell me. "Who doesn't?"

"You've been around longer than I, sir. Has the Navy always been so political?"

I thought of Admiral Duhaney, in my youth, and his machinations with the Senate. "From time to time."

"These days there's a certain . . . vehemence." Hazen hesitated. "That damned *Galactic* is a symbol. All my cadets want her. Three middies have put in for transfers."

"How is that political?"

"I've had half a dozen calls from officers aghast at your—excuse me, *our* new enviro policy. They're afraid it will scuttle *Olympiad* and the three unbuilt sister ships. Do I have any influence with you, et cetera."

My eyes narrowed. "Who called?"

"You spoke, sir, of trust?"

I closed my eyes. Infuriating. If I ordered him outright, he'd likely tell me, but then he'd despise me. I should be grateful he was concerned enough to hint at all. I made another note to confer with Admiralty as soon as our bills passed the Senate. What with our vote-seeking and the savage attack on my home, that resolve had gotten lost in the shuffle.

"I think," he said, choosing his words carefully, "the Navy needs to hear that our emphasis on ecology won't disrupt shipbuilding, or ultimately weaken the Service."

And that was precisely what I couldn't promise. Our enviro measures would do so, beyond a doubt. Should I tell him so? I hesitated, unsure of his divided loyalty.

Outside the window, cadets drilled at precision march in the fading light. I suspected he'd arranged the show for my benefit. "You'll send the Farside lot back aloft?"

"Soon. I may grant leave while they're groundside." At Farside Base, on the far side of the moon, our joeys were cut off from even routine contact with Earth. There were no public callers, no sat-relays except those operated by the Navy.

Parents would be grateful for the unscheduled leave. I pictured Bevin preparing eagerly for his father's visit, and sighed. "I suppose I should collect my joeys and move on."

"You've found the Bevin boy satisfactory?"

"Quite." Now that I'd become an enviro—a shift that still left me dizzy—I could hardly object to his politics.

"And Anselm?"

Should I tell him his middy was a souse? No, it would

put a black mark on his record, one that I wasn't yet ready to chisel in stone. "A pity about his father."

"Eh? Oh, that. Yes." He stood. "I'll see you to your heli."

Two U.N.A.F. commandos accompanied us, on a rugged military heli. My trip to Devon had been unannounced, as was our return. Bevin and Anselm chattered above the whine of the engine. Near me, where I could keep an eye on him, was Mikhael. From time to time, miserable, he wiped his mouth with a handkerchief.

I frowned, crossed my arms. The boy was impossible. When we'd returned to guest quarters for our gear, he'd accosted me, laden with petulance.

"Why couldn't I go?"

I'd tucked my coat into my duffel. "It was a private memorial, for Naval officers." The cadets deserved my apology, but it was unthinkable to wash the Navy's dirty linen in public. No one outside the Service, even family, ought to be present.

Mikhael had muttered something, turned away.

Outraged, I caught his arm. "What was that?"

He shrugged.

"I heard, 'Fucking nonsense.'"

He said nothing, but his stare was defiant.

"Into the head." I pointed to the lavatory.

"Why?"

"Move!" I followed him, half pushing.

I grabbed the soap from the sink. "Use it."

"You can't make me!"

"Two days ago, you promised me a new start." In my office, after his chastisement, a tearful reconciliation, pledges of good behavior.

"I tried."

"I won't have your foul language. '*Whoso curseth his father and mother, his lamp shall be put out in obscure darkness.'"* Eyes blazing, I thrust out the soap. "Do as I say!"

Now, in the heli, grimacing, he spit a foul taste into his handkerchief. Perhaps he'd learn. There was ample soap, and I'd reached the end of my tolerance. My surprise was that his defiance had crumbled, that he'd meekly washed out his own mouth. Perhaps he sought a father after all. Certainly the Alexi I knew wouldn't have borne the boy's behavior. Not for a moment.

Casually, as if unaware, I threw an arm across his shoulder.

"We'll win in the Assembly. We've lost the Senate." Branstead looked glum.

"Robbie?" I turned to Senator Boland, down from New York for the day.

"He's right. I can't swing enough votes."

"Our campaign, my speeches . . ."

"It's helped. North American mail is running three to one in our favor, European mail two to one. But only a third of the Senate faces election next year, and—"

"What can we offer we haven't already?" They stared. I could hardly blame them. For years I'd eschewed the give-and-take of compromise. "The emigration bill? Banking reform?"

"We'd gain ten, at best," Robbie said. "We're still nineteen short. I've scratched my head over and again, asking what tricks my father would have used. If there's a way, I can't find it."

We were undone. Short of martial law, there was no way to override a veto by the United Nations Senate. "We can't persuade them?"

"Sir, they're insulated from their constituencies by longer terms, and they resent the pressure you put on the Assembly. I've run out of arguments. Frankly, if the Sec-

Gen were anyone else, I myself might be on the other side."

I said gently, "You'd vote for me, not the enviro package?"

"I trust you, sir. Despite your disclaimer at the Von Walthers banquet, your moral compass is truer than mine." We'd parted company over the transpops, years back, and he'd come to regret his failure of conscience.

"If somehow the Patriarchs would climb aboard . . ." Jerence eyed me hopefully.

"That's out." I wouldn't encourage them to meddle in politics, and in any event their sympathies lay with the opposition.

"What, then?"

"I don't know. Play it out." Sometimes, on ship, it was all I'd known to do. At times, it had worked. But under the circumstances, that was unlikely. How, if we failed, could I face Philip? "Does Valera have a hand in—"

"Excuse me." Anselm was at the door. "May I join you?"

Had he no sense? "Senator Boland is the majority whip, Jerence is my chief of staff, our enviro package is failing, and you'd barge in for a chat?"

"I'm sorry."

"Out!"

He swung shut the door.

Boland and Branstead exchanged glances.

"ANSELM!"

He reappeared.

I beckoned him in. "Sit." To Robbie, "Is Valera undercutting us?"

"Not actively, but you're destabilizing the party. He wants to hold the Supras together; he's heir apparent."

Idly, I toyed with my puter, keyed up an Arcvid simulation, turned the screen to the boy. He gaped. "Go on, show me your stuff."

He grasped the controls, braced himself, took a deep breath.

Boland asked, "Did you and Cisno have words? He's, ah, more cautious than usual."

My smile was bleak. "I didn't want him to bolt us."

"I'm glad I'm not in his shoes." A glance at his watch. "By the way, I'm taking Jared to dinner. Care to come along?"

"Thanks, no. You ought to have time to yourselves."

"Oh, I see him often enough. Join us. It's a new Ukrainian restaurant. Real meat."

I hesitated, reluctant to abandon Arlene. On the other hand, it would give her time alone with Philip. And if Ghenili accepted me as a patient, who knew how long I'd be away. Charlie Witrek was scheduled after dinner; a therapist from Johns Hopkins would drop him off at the compound. Still, I would enjoy a good meal out. "All right." Security would go ballistic, but that was their problem.

Later, when Robbie had gone to change clothes, I asked Anselm, "What was that about?"

"I was bored, and wandering the house." He shrugged. "I found myself in the living room, staring at your liquor cabinet."

"So you came to me?"

"I shouldn't have interrupted, sir."

True, but I'd kept him on staff, knowing his disabilities. I said, "All remaining demerits are canceled. Well done, Mr. Anselm."

He broke into a pleased grin. "Thank you."

"Inspection tomorrow morning. Have your gear ready."

"Aye aye, sir, but Ms. Seafort told me."

I raised an eyebrow. "Told you what?"

"About Lunapolis. What time do we leave?"

So much for secrets. "And you, of course, told Bevin." Who no doubt told a guard, who told *Newsnet*, who would tell the entire world.

He drew himself up. "I did not."

"Hmpff. The shuttle lifts at nine in the morning."

"I'll be ready. She said you're taking us all."

"Bevin may be useful. And it's not fair to leave Mikhael behind. He's my foster son." The court had approved our petition. Jerence Branstead, as usual, had worked with smooth efficiency.

"Five of us, counting Ms. Seafort."

"You have some objection?"

"Of course not. It's just . . . sir, Danil is no difficulty. But if you're in the clinic, who's to look after Mr. Tamarov?"

"Arlene."

"Won't she be with you?"

"Most of the time." It would be a problem. I added, "I think I have a solution."

We raced through blocked streets in an armor-plated groundcar, pulled up directly to the restaurant. As quickly as they could manage, my guards hustled me inside. Thanks to my speaking tour, my chair and I were instantly recognized. I had time for a quick wave at a blur of astonished faces before I was rushed to a private room. Jared Tenere and Robbie were already seated. Security checked the room, waited just outside.

We fussed over wine, ordered dishes of genuine meats off the lavish menu.

Jared raised his glass. "Thank you, sir. You're making Philip very happy."

"It's still only words. The Senate . . ."

Boland nodded glumly. "They're a problem." He brightened, patting Jared's knee. "My boy tells me you saw my . . . ah, investment."

I puzzled it out. "Cardiff, you mean? I'm embarrassed P.T. came to you for the mortgage."

"It was my idea," said Jared modestly. "I knew Uncle

Robbie would understand. And P.T. . . . once he saw the place, he had to have it."

I said without thinking, "You truly see yourselves living there?"

"When the air's breathable. In the meantime we could hermetically seal the house, but . . ."

I nodded agreement. Quite impractical. "Why outside Cardiff, of all places?"

His voice was quiet. "It's a good place to raise a child."

My wine spilled, and I dabbed ineffectually at the cloth until the waiter came.

"I'm sorry. Shouldn't I have said that?"

"No, it's just . . ." I gave it up. "You startled me." P.T. and Jared were more serious than I'd known. I tried not to imagine myself as a grandparent. How could it be so? I'd barely finished raising my son.

Jared smiled. "P.T. will make a good father."

I said something polite.

Later in the meal Robbie Boland leaned close. "A word, if I might." To Jared, "This is private. You won't repeat it to anyone."

"Of course not, Uncle Rob."

I waited.

Boland kept his voice low. "That Burns woman. Are you sure she was the only bad apple on your staff?"

A stab of alarm. "We rechecked everyone. As far as we know . . ."

"Sir, make absolutely sure."

He had my full attention. "Rob, what do you know?"

"Nothing." A grimace. "That's what's so frustrating. But I've rarely seen politics so unsettled. If the enviro bills go through, joeys stand to make fortunes, others to lose them. Someone else might have a go at you."

"There's not much I can do. Besides, it all comes back to the Senate. We're losing them."

"Yes." A frown.

Jared said softly, "I'm not in politics, but growing up around you and Uncle Rob . . ."

"Yes?" I hoped my voice didn't show my irritation.

"Why don't you just announce you have the votes?"

I stared.

He licked his lips. "I mean, you know how politicians are about getting on a bandwagon. Declare you have pledges from enough Senators to pass the bill. It'll bring others on board."

I said coldly, "That would be lying."

"Oh, goofjuice."

"Jared!" Robbie's eyes were sharp. "He's the SecGen."

"Yes, I'm sorry, but it's not lying, it's a ruse of war." His tone was defiant.

"I'm not at war, Jared."

"Of course you are. A war for their hearts and souls. A war to save the Earth from itself. And don't tell me it isn't done; candidates always claim polls show them ahead, even when they're behind."

"I never did."

Rob Boland's mouth twitched in a smile. "You never had to."

"And I wouldn't have. I'll speak truth, no matter what the cost."

"Well . . ." Jared toyed with his bread. "Would it be a lie, if you make it true?"

"I'm sorry." Charlie clutched my shoulder as I rolled to the sofa. "I don't know the living room as well. In the office, I could find the chair blindfol—as I am." He felt for the upholstered armrest. "Ah. I have it now." Cautiously, he sat. "I don't mean to inconven—"

"Don't." It was a plea. "Charlie, don't apologize. We did this to you."

"No you didn't." His voice was cheerful. "Those fucking eco bastards did. Oops. Sorry for the language."

"Nonsense." I waved it away, forgetting he couldn't see. "Just one thing I beg of you. Catch them."

"We have most of them, and we'll get the others." I spoke with confidence I didn't feel. I poured him a softie from the waiting tray, placed it in his hand. "So. The doctors will try again?"

"In a week or two, they say." His fingers brushed through his hair. "This time it had better work."

"I feel responsible. If there's anything I can do . . ."

"You're doing it." A wry smile. "I was thirsty." He made a show of tasting his drink.

"Charlie . . ."

"I know." His voice was quiet. "It's ghastly, isn't it? Do you have scars?" His hand flitted to his ravaged face.

"No, son."

"They'll repair mine. They're waiting to know whether the eyes will be real, or cosmetic. But . . ." A long silence.

"Yes?"

"Even if the transplants take, I won't see well enough for the active list. I won't get a ship." A smile, that seemed forced. "If I see at all. Most likely, I'll be the youngest middy on the retired list."

I raised my head, to the heavens. Lord, if You have any mercy, any decency . . .

"What will you do?"

"I wonder that, sometimes, at night." A laugh. His voice was bright. "There's a lot of night nowadays."

My luxurious dinner sat congealed in my stomach. "Oh, Charlie." I wheeled myself to his side.

"Don't feel pity, Mr. SecGen." He shied away. "These things happen. You're by far the worse off. I'm so sorry for what they did to you."

"I'm managing." For now. Until Ghenili healed me, or I ended matters.

We sat quietly.

"Funny thing," he said at last. "When you have no eyes, you can't cry."

Late in the evening I sat in my living room, staring at my unexpected visitor. "Are you out of your mind?"

"I don't believe so." Derek Carr's tone was cool.

"You already lost a week's negotiations when I called you for Mikhael. I'll be fine; even if Ghenili accepts me, he may not operate immediately."

"I'll set up holoconferences, and fly groundside next week for final negotiations. I'm going with you."

Mikhael watched the byplay, as did Arlene.

"Isn't that for me to say?"

"Only if you close all of Lunapolis." Derek folded his arms.

"I appreciate . . ." I swallowed a lump in my throat. "Truly, it's not necessary."

"Say then that I'm going in Alexi's place."

"He wouldn't have—"

"The hell he wouldn't!" For a moment, Derek's gaze was fierce. "I'll have no more of it. You insult me."

I stole a glance at Mikhael. His eyes were riveted on Derek.

"I suppose," I grumbled, "we can make a place for one more."

The boy's mouth relaxed into a goofy smile.

"I don't suppose you have any more stories?"

"A few."

"Not a one, if you hear anything from his mouth not fit for a nunnery."

Derek's eyebrow shot up. "Mikhael, have you been giving him trouble?"

"No, sir. Not—I mean, not lately."

"Come along, joey. Let's take a walk." He uncoiled his lanky frame from the couch. "Did I ever tell you about the time Alexi got caned?"

* * *

That night, slowly, carefully, Arlene and I made love. We'd been sixteen, our first time, middies on our first leave. Then, I'd been ignorant, unsure, and she'd helped me along. She did so now. It was hell, having legs that wouldn't go where you sent them, muscles that failed to respond, nerves that sent only erratic sensations from my groin.

Afterward, content in the fullness of satiation, we lay drowsing.

"Nick, you know I've had eggs frozen."

"What?" I snapped awake.

"We're not too old. Having Mikhael . . . seems to make you whole."

"I'm doing it for Alexi."

"And for yourself. You take joeykids under your wing. Look at Danil and Tad."

"What are you saying?"

"That it's not too late to have another child."

"When he was grown I'd be . . ." I was scandalized. "In my seventies!"

"So? If you'd start enzyme treatments . . ."

"I'd look younger, and still be seventy. It's not natural."

"Neither are tooth implants. You've had your share of those."

"That's different."

"Or new lungs."

I propped myself on an arm. "Hon, do *you* want a child?"

A long while passed. "I'm not sure." She nuzzled my chest. "But if so, it would have to be yours."

I tried not to cry. "God, I love you."

Her hand crept lower. Presently, I murmured, "Quiet, love. We'll frighten the horses."

* * *

They sneaked us out of the house in Branstead's heli, and in Derek's, just past dawn. We all of us were giddy as children, giggling at the subterfuge. Arlene and I sat together, entwined, on the deck of Derek's machine. The boys rode with Jerence. From time to time Arlene jabbed me, like cadets when Sarge wasn't looking. I tickled her beneath the neck, one of her few vulnerable spots.

Derek tolerantly kept his eyes on the instruments, ignoring the guffaws from the back seat.

"I've decided," she said, "that I do."

I blinked. "Do what?"

"Don't claim senility on me, you old fool." She hushed my indignant protest with a kiss.

"You want a child?" My voice soared, almost to a squeak. "You're serious?"

She nodded.

Bemused, I lay silent, cuddling her all the way to the shuttleport.

Potomac Naval Station had its own hangars, part of the shuttleport complex. To get to Lunapolis we had to transfer at Earthport Orbiting Station. Most shuttles to Earthport were run by U.N.A.F., but the Navy jealously guarded its prerogative to maintain its own.

If I had to trust one unit over the other to maintain secrecy, I'd choose the Navy every time. My own prior service would help ensure their loyalty, but even more, the Navy's long tradition of honor was something the more prosaic U.N.A.F. lacked. For further security, only two people at Earthport had been told I would be aboard, and one of them was Admiral McKay.

We boarded the shuttle in a closed hangar, for secrecy. Jerence had gone directly to the shuttleport's commander, who sent a lieutenant to direct operations. At the sight of him, Anselm fidgeted, blushing. I raised an eyebrow. "He's the one who caned me," he whispered.

The lieutenant introduced the Station medico. "Mr. Sec-

Gen, it's not often we send a paraplegic aloft. Understand, the seats are not designed to accommodate—"

I groaned. "Get on with it. I'll be all right."

"And in zero gravity, once the shuttle breaks free of Earth . . ."

"Arlene, tell him I'm no greenie."

"Hush, love."

I bore his anxious instructions with what grace I could muster. Afterward, I craned my head to Mikhael. "You've been aloft?"

"Dad took me. I'm used to it."

At last, liftoff. Strapped securely in my seat, I practiced relaxation, as Sarge had taught his eager cadets. I could still hear his chuckle. "Relax your chest muscles, Seafort. Feel it press you. Just like a woman lay atop you, but I guess you wouldn't know about that." At the time, I hadn't.

After an endless roar and interminable pressure, the red receded from the corners of my eyes. I sucked in air, loosened my straps, floated off the chair.

Behind me, Anselm happily undid his straps. Mikhael gulped, his face green.

I roared, "Don't even think about it! Sit up straight! Behave yourself!"

It worked. He was too startled to remember he felt sick.

More gently, I said, "Take deep, slow breaths, son. You'll be fine. If not, there's the bag."

"Yessir." He clutched it like a security blanket.

"Danil, see if you and Mikhael can spot Earthport." Greenies tended to lose their breakfast in zero gee. A diversion would help.

Derek winked.

"How are you feeling, love?" Arlene floated overhead.

"Fine." My ribs were sore, but no need to mention them.

The cockpit door opened; the copilot swam back, from handhold to handhold. "Mr. SecGen, a priority message from your chief of staff."

"Very well." I took the scrawled note. *"Admiral McKay killed in depressurization accident at Earthport. Whom do you want as replacement? Otherwise, Admiralty will appoint Hoi of BuPers."*

Without thinking, I hauled myself upright. In zero gee, I realized, I had again the freedom for which I yearned. "I need to speak to Branstead. Have you a secure caller?"

"Of course, sir. In the cockpit."

He and the pilot would overhear my end of the conversation, but it couldn't be helped. "If you please."

"Nick?" Arlene looked between us.

"Trouble at Earthport. I'll be right back." Hand by hand, I hauled myself forward, my useless legs trailing.

I punched in codes. "Jerence?"

"That was fast." Branstead's voice crackled.

"How did it happen?"

"A freak accident. Exterior maintenance. Someone lost control of a tool carrier, and it smashed a porthole."

I swore. A tool carrier was halfway between a giant thrustersuit and a tiny gig. Just large enough to be ungainly, too big for fine control. I hated them, never used them on ship.

"You're sure it was an accident?"

"There'll be an inquiry, of course. But I imagine a seaman's attention wandered. McKay's dead, in any case."

"Right. What do we know about Hoi?"

"You met him on Earthport, didn't you?"

"Ah, yes." At Admiral McKay's conference, the one at which they'd lectured me about *Galactic.* A smallish joey, dapper, concerned about the Navy's colonial role. "Do we have a preferred candidate? Someone you recommend?" Jerence deserved a say in our appointments; pay couldn't adequately reimburse his loyalty.

"No one in particular. I could check the list, but Admiralty's collective nose would be bent out of joint."

"Then go with their man. And summon the Board of Admiralty to a conference, as soon as I'm back groundside. Reserve a whole day." I would warn them off of politics, and break the news about canceling *Olympiad* and her sisters. "And send the usual condolences to McKay's family." I hadn't known the man well.

"Done. Promise you'll call when you've seen Ghenili."

"I will."

"The very best of luck, sir." He rang off.

I maneuvered myself back to my seat. Mikhael seemed better, and was talking earnestly with Derek. As I buckled myself in, Bevin pulled himself alongside. "Are you busy, sir?"

"Speak."

"I've been—Mr. Seafort told me details about our enviro bills. Your bills, I mean."

For a moment I was puzzled, until I realized he'd referred to Philip. "And?"

His face lit. "They're wonderful, sir. You should be proud."

"You're grading my policy, at fourteen?"

"Yes, sir, I'm out of line. But it's still wonderful."

"Hmpff. Don't get your hopes up. The Senate is against us."

"You'll find a way. Like you did with the Assembly." He spoke with the misplaced confidence of youth.

"I doubt it. Besides, they were Philip's ideas, not mine."

"No, sir, if you'll pardon me. It was his idea, but your doing."

Arlene, swinging back to her seat, ruffled his hair in passing; Danil grinned like a foolish puppy. Appalling. Next she'd have him on her lap. How were we supposed to train cadets to manhood, if she coddled them constantly? Sometimes Arlene had no sense.

As Earthport neared I squinted out the porthole, hoping to spot signs of the damage that had killed Admiral McKay. But I knew I wouldn't; Earthport was so vast that the accident site would be invisible. A shame he'd been in that particular compartment at the moment; one chance in ten thousand. But if it hadn't been he, it might have been someone else. Space travel was as safe as we could make it, which meant it was still dangerous. There was risk, albeit small, in bringing Mikhael aloft. As his guardian it was my job to fret about such things.

Arlene's suggestion that we have another child astounded me. Despite my own upbringing—I'd never seen my host mother—my wife and I were both rather old-fashioned about parenting. Could we count on being around and in good health long enough to raise him, or her?

I wasn't, truth be told, all that old for current times. There were Captains on the active list well past eighty; old Hoskins couldn't even walk without aid. Despite the overwrought popular holodramas, command was exercised by cool decisions from an experienced master, not by a wild-eyed young hero sporting matching platinum lasers.

Did I want another son? For that matter, should we choose the sex? Could I raise a daughter? Would I strangle the first young middy who eyed her?

I sat musing while we neared the Station. Our docking berth was on Level 7, amid the Naval cargo bays.

It was unusual, though not unheard of, to seal entry to a bay before unloading; some cargoes were military and classified. We emerged into a deserted bay, and were whisked directly to a lunar shuttle. Mikhael was bitterly disappointed; he'd hoped to go exploring. Derek took him aside and spoke rather sharply, before I could erupt. A fine father I'd be: I had no patience. Lord God only knew how P.T. had turned out so well.

A few hours later we were in Lunapolis.

Dr. Ghenili's clinic was near the terminus of a clean but seedy warren, three levels belowground. Half my face covered with a disguising bandage, we wheeled past indifferent throngs, past emergency corridor seals and the occasional shop, to the entry hatch.

The clinic installed me in a modest room. I'd have preferred a hotel, but it was out of the question if secrecy was to be maintained. Even if I bunked in a Naval warren, word would sooner or later escape. The clinic was better schooled in protecting the privacy of its patients. As it turned out, Ghenili himself was an avid enviro; he was delighted to accommodate me.

Arlene and Derek fussed to make me comfortable. I lacked only my motorized chair; it would have been a prodigious waste of fuel to haul it aloft, and to what purpose?

The three boys wandered my room, bored, touching everything, picking up instruments, sensors, my gear. I called them together. "Mr. Anselm, you and Danil may go on leave." A momentary twinge of doubt. "Not a drop, Tad. Agreed?"

"I will not drink." A formal resolve that startled me.

"Visit me daily, and the moment you feel the urge. Don't hesitate. Keep an eye on Danil, and report to the Hilton by midnight."

"Aye aye, sir."

"What about me?" Mikhael.

"Watch holodramas at the hotel." It devastated him, as I knew it would. Before his protest burst forth I said, "Or you may go out with Mr. Anselm."

He shot the middy a dubious look.

"Under his supervision."

"No!" Pure dismay.

"You're fifteen, and I know Lunapolis too well. You won't go out alone." The lowermost lunar warrens were famous for entertainments that would make a sailor blush.

"He's only a year—"

"But Mr. Anselm is a gentleman and an adult, by act of the General Assembly." It was so for all officers, even if they were but sixteen. "Middy, you're in charge. Treat him civilly, but don't take any guff. He's a minor and I place him in your custody."

"Aye aye, sir." Anselm's tone was cool.

Mikhael said angrily, "I'll stay in the room."

"Boys, outside a moment." I held Mikhael back. "I know you don't like it, but it's good practice. You have to learn to control yourself. Any cadet would—"

"I'm no cadet."

"You interrupted me." My tone was cold.

He gulped. "Sorry, sir."

"Good lad. Mikhael, your father joined the Navy at thirteen. He learned the very discipline I'm trying to teach you. Give it a try for him, if not for me."

"I hate Anselm. I won't call him 'sir.'"

"It's not necessary. Be polite, and do what he tells you." He folded his arms. I added softly, "Please?"

After a moment he nodded his surrender. "Yes, sir."

Not knowing what else to do, I ruffled his hair.

"Yes."

My heart leaped.

"There's no guarantee of success," Ghenili added. "In fact, you have only about a forty percent—"

"That's good enough."

"You understand there's a certain possibility you won't survive the—"

"I know. Get on with it."

"Listen, love." Arlene squeezed my hand.

For two days they'd poked and prodded, probed and palpitated me until I was on the ragged edge of frustration.

"How soon?" This very moment, if it was possible.

"Friday."

Three days. It would suffice.

"Then at least a week before we can get you out of bed. You'll be immobilized."

"I know." They'd told me, over and again.

Time slowed to a relentless crawl. Hours became weeks. I climbed into an unmotored chair, rolled around the room, and into the hall beyond.

Arlene spent as much time with me as possible; from time to time we had to separate to save our marriage. Perhaps I was difficult.

When he wasn't making business calls from his hotel room, Derek spent hours stretched out on my bed, while I groused in the chair. At times he brought Mikhael, and together we gave the boy a double dose of reminiscences.

Anselm and Bevin reported daily. They seemed to be enjoying themselves. Well, a young middy could certainly expand his horizons in lower Lunapolis. I hoped he was leaving Danil behind.

I watched holos, tuned in the news. The enviro battle dominated the newsnets; Senators and Assemblymen pontificated before the holocams as they maneuvered.

Branstead called me, using the best security circuits we could devise. He wanted to claim we had enough votes in both houses.

"This is your idea?" I favored him with a scowl.

"Well . . . no. Rob Boland thought of it, actually."

I suppressed a smile. "Did he, now?"

"I suppose you'll call it lying. Think of it as subterfuge." His voice grew somber. "We don't have many other options."

"I'll think on it." Decades past, I had spewed forth lies that sent innocent boys and girls to their death. Perhaps it was necessary, but nothing in Lord God's firmament would get me to do it again. I'd see the Earth crumble first. It was all that kept me sane.

"I'll make the announcement, sir. You don't have to say a word."

I wasn't custodian of Branstead's morals, was I? Still, it left me uneasy. "Wait. I'll let you know."

Admiral McKay's funeral made the news, as did the strange death of a U.N.A.F. officer who'd been posted to Lunapolis, but was found in an abandoned New Jersey warehouse. I wouldn't have noticed, except that she reminded me of Karen Burns.

Burns eluded our net. Our investigation was leading nowhere; we hadn't even found out where she'd have taken me, or why. Sergeant Booker, too, remained at large. Donner should have blockaded Barcelona, the moment Booker's call came through. If I'd been properly prepared, declared martial law on the instant . . .

I sighed. Von Rourke had begun his infamy before the Final War by declaring martial law; perhaps Hitler had as well. Booker would no doubt be caught. If so, I'd attend his execution, to rejoice. Thank Lord God executions were public.

Jerence urged me to speak anew in favor of our program, in the hope of persuading a few Senators. He'd evolved a wild scheme to beam my broadcast home on a private sat-relay, and issue it from my compound as if I were speaking from there. He'd even have our puter Warren replace the white-walled background of the clinic with the familiar paneling of my office.

I refused, of course. Not only was it too close to lying outright, though the point was debatable, but I doubted one more speech would turn the tide.

"Hello, Fath." P.T. and Jared stood grinning in the clinic doorway.

"What's this? Where'd you boys come from?"

"We caught a shuttle." Philip brandished a small holo-cam. "Before and after. This is the before." He aimed.

"No!" I threw my covers over my torso. "Not while I'm wearing this . . . this . . ."

"All right, I'll stop." But he didn't. "Mom says you've been charming, as usual."

"She can bring her complaints to me."

"To our autocrat?" At last, he stopped filming, bent close to kiss the top of my head. "Winstead asks after you. I didn't tell him you're here."

"Give him my"—it hurt to say it—"best."

"Andrus Bevin just learned you have his son on staff. He's ecstatic."

"I can imagine." A mole for the enviros, placed in—no, I was enviro too. I sighed. A year past, I couldn't have imagined being allied with the fanatics of the Enviro Council. "Jared, don't block the doorway; that nurse wants through."

"Sorry."

I bared my arm for the usual punctures. "Ms. Gow, the joey with the holocam is Philip Seafort, and the one fidgeting by the door is Jared, my son-in-law." It wasn't quite correct; they were paired, not married, but . . .

Jared broke into a pleased smile. Was it possible I'd never publicly acknowledged our relationship? Well, it was long since time. Gruffly, I patted the bed. "Sit awhile."

At least one day of my vigil passed quickly.

Friday, I sent last-minute messages to Rob Boland, and notes begging support from a pair of recalcitrant Senators who no doubt assumed I was safe in my compound.

Before the relaxants left me too groggy to concentrate, a final good-bye to Jerence Branstead. He rang off abruptly, almost in mid-word, just as I was telling how well I thought of him. A grave hug from Philip, another, to my infinite surprise, from Jared.

Derek's hand flitted across my brow. "I'll be here, sir, when you wake."

"I know." How could I deserve him?

He snorted. "Feel free to take me for granted."

"You were a fine boy. I was proud to . . ."

"Was?"

"Am. Will be, if I come out of this. If not . . ."

"Damn." He blinked rapidly, disappeared from view.

I drifted in soft mist.

Mikhael's face loomed over my bed. "Sir—Mr. Seafort . . ." He was dressed in his best, and immaculately groomed.

"Can't call me that. Have to find something else." His father couldn't be a "mister."

"Yessir. I just wanted to say—" His glance shot back, to Arlene. "Get well. Thank you for everything. I mean it. Get well, sir." To Arlene, a look of appeal. She nodded.

"Very good, Middy." Why did he seem puzzled? He'd been promoted . . . when? Where was he posted? I'd recall in a moment. Right now it was too . . . too . . .

Black.

An endless expanse of white scrolled overhead. A bump; a sickening wave of pain.

Oblivion.

I drifted in and out, visiting with Father, chewed out Mikhael for his belligerence, watched P.T. grow. One day I could lift him on my shoulders, the next . . .

Hot. So hot.

Sleep.

"—fection is taking hold. I increased the antibi—"

"Nick? Squeeze my hand."

The bed jounced. Red waves of torment.

My mouth was dry and cracked.

"—been three days and he's not responding. If his kidneys shut down—"

White haze. Pain.

"Sir?" Derek. "Hold on, sir. Please."

"Farewell." I tried to clear my throat. "Old friend."

"God damn you!" Arlene's voice was a nail on slate. "Don't die on me, you son of a bitch!"

"It's . . . time."

"The hell it is!"

I drifted toward sleep.

"Breathe, Nick. Breathe deep." Fingers squeezed my shoulder. "Stay with me, sir." Derek's voice was tight.

I tried.

Red faded to white. My breathing eased. The world faded.

I blinked. Derek, grizzled and gray, hunched in the corner.

"What time is it?" A voice from an ancient grave.

He jumped. "Lord Christ!"

"Don't blaspheme."

"Thank God." He ran to the bed, fell on his knees. "Oh, thank God."

"Don't weep."

"I thought I'd lose you."

"Where's your dignity? You're head of Government."

"You're . . ." Resolutely, he raised his head. ". . . my head of Government."

I drifted off.

When I woke, Arlene and the three boys were keeping vigil. I was ravenously hungry. They fed me pablum from a spoon.

"Give me real food."

"Dr. Ghenili says—"

"Where is he?"

"Right here." From the doorway. "Welcome back, Mr. SecGen."

"I was . . . lost." Perhaps it was always so. I tried to wiggle my foot, could not. "It failed?"

"You're in a full body cast. Don't try to move."

"It itches."

"Does it, now?" He regarded me gravely.

After a puzzled moment I cried out in joy. "I can feel!" Despite his warning I wiggled my toes frantically. Bevin danced from foot to foot. Anselm's eyes glistened.

I looked to Arlene. "Where's Derek?"

"He's drunk. Mikhael's looking after him."

"Good Lord. Doctor, how long will I be laid up?"

"Three more days, even with the growth stimulator. You have to heal. Then restricted movement for a month. After that, you should be well."

My eyes slid to Arlene. "Long enough to raise a child?" Her smile warmed my soul.

16

If time passed slowly before my surgery, afterward it stopped entirely. I was even more helpless than before, serviced by tubes snaking under my sheets. If I used the caller, the time lag from Lunapolis to New York and back would give away my location, so I could do no politicking on behalf of our enviro bills.

I spoke to Branstead, who sounded glum. There was no hope in the Senate. He and Robbie were determined to claim victory, stake all on a last throw of the dice. I acquiesced.

Philip and Jared sat with me when Arlene was out.

The second night, Tad Anselm didn't return to their hotel. Mikhael told Arlene, perhaps out of spite. She went back to sleep, informed me the next day.

I was saddened, more than anything else. Despite intimations I should have heeded, I'd come to expect better of Anselm.

Derek came to visit, sat awhile. "I'm going groundside to wrap up my trade talks . . . Sometimes you have to be in the room, and watch their eyes."

I smiled. "To learn what?"

"The last Unidollar they'll go. Nick, the grain tonnage we'll be sending . . ." He shook his head. "It's huge, and your delegates have no choice but to buy. Only the Navy's outlandish freight charges keep a semblance of a trade balance."

"Enjoy it while you can. In a few years our production—"

"You've said that before. I hope this time it's true."

"Why? You've got us where you want us."

"Ultimately, our interest coincides with yours. Most of us know that." He glanced at his watch.

"When do you leave?"

"This evening."

There was no reason to feel betrayed. None at all. "Very well." We'd had little enough time together over the years. "Mikhael will be sad."

"Nick, may I give you advice?"

"Of course."

"You gave him a terrible scare."

"Me? What are you talking about?" I'd punished him, true, but he was hardly terrorized.

"He lost Alexi. You reached through his misery and made him trust you. Then you threatened to abandon him."

"It was he who ran away, not—"

"Nick, the way Alexi left him."

I was silent. "I mean that much to him?"

"He's moping about the hotel, fragile and weepy."

"He needs rebalancing."

"He needs you."

"I'm no psych. These things are—"

"Midshipman Anselm reporting, sir." Thadeus, from the doorway. His tone was belligerent, his uniform disheveled and stained.

"How dare you show your face!"

"Shall I go to the hotel?"

"Where were you?" Not that it mattered. He'd broken one rule too many.

"The lower warrens, mostly."

"Get out of my sight. I'll decide what to do with you."

"Aye aye, sir." He was gone.

I asked Derek, "How would you handle him?"

He shrugged. "I never made it past middy."

"Still."

"He's not much different from Mikhael, really. Young, lonely, and in pain."

"We're all in pain, Derek. And he's not my son."

"Why did you take him on?"

I fell silent.

"In the old days, you saved them. Us."

"I've nothing left to give."

"You'll cashier him?"

"I don't see how to avoid it."

"Damn it, Nick, the Navy is more than calisthenics and canings." Derek was immensely proud of his five-year enlistment. "What about mercy?"

"They shouldn't have graduated Anselm. He's not ready."

"Don't destroy his life."

"He did that."

Derek had no reply.

I watched Jerence Branstead on *Newsnet*. He sounded utterly convincing. We'd won the Assembly, had six votes to spare in the Senate. Would that it were true.

They cut me out of my body cast. I could move, slowly, carefully, only in the moon's one-sixth gravity. Earth's one gee could shatter my healing spine.

Mikhael came to see me. "Don't dismiss him. Please."

"You made sure Arlene knew he was missing."

"Yeah." He slouched.

"Sorry you did?"

"Yeah." He stirred. "Mr. Carr talked to me."

"Why do you hate him so?"

"Because you like him so!" He scuffed the deck. "Whatever I do isn't good enough." His tone was bitter. "See, I'm not one of your frazzing cadets. I don't wear a godda—a uniform and stand stiff at attention. I don't shout 'aye aye, sir' and jump at your every command. But Anselm does, so you respect him."

Because I like him so. I tasted the idea. Anselm disappointed me, infuriated me. A seasoned middy, he knew better than to fail to report to barracks. And it wasn't his first offense.

Yet . . .

I liked him so.

"Mikhael, I don't expect a middy's behavior from you. And I'm sorry I was so ill."

"What does that have . . ." He ground to a halt, blinking tears.

"Come take my hand." We sat awhile, peaceably. Then, "I like who you're becoming, Mikhael."

"You're all over me. Sit up. Get that tone out of your voice. Behave."

"Know how to make your children like themselves?"

He shook his head.

"Make them likable."

"Is that what you're doing, Mr. Seafort?"

"I'm trying. And I told you not to call me that." I'd asked for custody. This is what came of it.

"What should I call you? I have a dad."

"Pa. Father. Sir."

"You really take this seriously, don't you?"

I said wonderingly, "You don't?"

He sat for a moment. "May I tell the truth?" I nodded. "Yeah, I do. I'm lost, sometimes. Dad is gone, and I'm glad to have someone who understands. I'll call you anything you want, but not 'Dad.' Not ever. He'll always be that."

"I wouldn't have it any other way." I was proud of him.

"I'll try 'Pa,' but it's embarrassing. And, about the middy . . . he was nice to me, when you had him in charge."

"It's my decision. I'll think on it."

"Yes, sir. Pa."

*   *   *

Arlene thought I should cashier Anselm. As always, she stated her opinion, but didn't try to impose it, aware I followed her advice more often than not. "He knew better," she said. "And did it anyway. What if he were on ship?"

"He wasn't." Restlessly, I wheeled myself about the clinic cubicle.

"It makes no difference."

Still, I was reluctant to do as I ought.

Derek was coming in the afternoon, to say good-bye. P.T. and Jared would be in tonight. I summoned the midshipman, to get our confrontation out of the way.

Anselm came to my clinic room, deep circles under his eyes.

I released him from attention. "You drank, of course?"

"I went from one bar to another. The warrens are full of them."

"I'm disgusted with—"

"But I didn't have a single drink."

"Nonetheless, you—"

"Not one."

I shouted, "Stop interrupting!"

"That's why I went. To drink myself unconscious."

"Are you glitched?" A Captain ought to be as God to a middy: august, remote, uninterruptible. And as SecGen I was so far above a Captain . . . yet he overrode me at will.

"Yes, I think I am." His eyes met mine. "I didn't forget your orders. Midnight, you said. I chose to ignore them."

"You leave me little choice."

"I know, sir." He sounded regretful. "Get it over with."

"Very well, you're—" Cashiered, I was about to say. "Why didn't you drink?"

"I wanted to know I could stop myself. Just this once. At first I didn't intend to stay out all night. I wanted scotch, and it made me so bloody angry I couldn't have it, nothing else mattered." He was bitter. "I'll have plenty of time for liquor, after."

My tone was gentle. "Anselm, I can't risk leaving you in command of cadets, or a squad of sailors. You're not fit. As Commander in Chief of U.N. military forces, I withdraw your commission."

"I'm cashiered."

"No, you're back to cadet."

His jaw dropped.

It was the only alternative I saw. To let him off with any lesser rebuke would be an insult to his comrades. And he knew it. Yet I wasn't ready to wash my hands of him.

"You can do that?"

"I just did. And of course a caning. Report to the Naval quartermaster and indent for a set of grays. Then see Arlene for your punishment."

"Ms. Seafort?" He blanched.

"I'd send you to the Lunapolis duty officer, but it would call attention to my presence. This way, I doubt you'll try this stunt again." Arlene would see to that. She'd been first lieutenant in *Wellington*, and had little tolerance for middies' nonsense. "Pull in your horns, Anselm. A cadet is treated as a child. You'll call everything that moves 'sir' or 'ma'am.' I won't hesitate to enforce cadet discipline."

"Yes, sir!"

"This misbehavior is about missing your father?"

"I don't know." His eyes were tormented.

"You wanted to show him your ratings, eh? Very well, we'll do that. Write him a letter."

"What?"

"You heard me. A letter explaining what's happened since his death. Address it to him. Tell him how you act, how you feel about it. Mention everything."

"You can't make me do that."

The caller buzzed, but I ignored it. Unsteadily, using the

two sturdy alumalloy canes they'd provided, I hoisted myself from the bed. "I can't, Cadet?" Lightly, I cuffed him.

It was a reminder of his status, and had the desired effect. He crumpled. "Aye aye, sir." A defeated whisper.

"Dismissed. Get your grays."

Derek stood aside for him in the hatchway. "Very interesting."

"How long were you listening?"

"Awhile. I assumed if you wanted privacy you'd shut the door." He shifted. "Nick, my shuttle leaves at eight. Two hours."

"I'll see you again?"

"I doubt it. My ship sails in a week, and I'm way behind in my negotiations."

"I'll miss you."

"And I you. Will you get to Hope Nation again?"

"Unlikely," I said. "I'm getting no younger."

Our eyes locked. "Is this really farewell?" His voice held a note of wonder.

"Oh, Derek."

The caller buzzed again.

"It's been . . ." He couldn't finish.

Ms. Gow, the nurse, hurried into the room. "A Mr. Branstead says he's desperate to reach you. Are you ignoring your caller?"

"Wait a moment, Derek. Hello?"

"Turn on the news!" Branstead's voice was panicky.

I fumbled with the holovid, keyed in *Newsnet*.

"*—missing and presumed dead in his Washington home, where he was recovering from injuries in the Rotunda bombing.*"

I tried to sit bolt upright, gasped with pain.

"*Rescue workers say due to the intensity of the laser attack there's no chance of finding bodies in the smoking ruins. SecGen Seafort was best known as the implacable enemy of the alien race known as the fish. Born in Cardiff, Wales, in—*"

"Lord Jesus Christ!"

A helicam floated over a mass of rubble. A few pieces of the outer wall remained. Of the house, nothing.

"Amen," said Branstead.

"Who? Why?"

"Lasers, from aloft. Defense puters say Earthport or *Galactic*. At the moment they're so close together—"

"Who's in charge on the Station?"

"Admiral Hoi. There's more, sir. Admiralty in London took a radio intercept. Just over an hour ago *Galactic* sent a launch full of sailors to Earthport. They stormed the civilian command center."

"Lord in heaven."

Iron fingers gripped my arm. "Where's your pistol?"

"Not now, Derek. What about the Naval Station?"

"WHERE IS IT?"

"In the drawer. Has Earthport Naval Command responded?"

"I can't get through to Admiral Hoi."

Derek crossed to the hatch, slapped it open, took up position outside, my laser charged and blinking. The safety was off.

The hatch slid closed.

Branstead said, "Captain Stanger is apparently leading the coup. He beamed an ultimatum to the Rotunda, the Senate and Assembly, and U.N.A.F. Command. We're to abandon the enviro legislation at once. SecGen Valera's to meet him on *Galactic* no later than Wednesday, or their lasers will target as many cities as it takes to end resistance. He wants an answer in six hours. The first target is the Rotunda."

I asked, "What about Dubrovik in Lunapolis?" The Admiral ran our lunar Naval base, at the opposite end of the city from the clinic.

"He's on sick leave, you'll recall. Injured. Captain Simovich is Acting Commander. I can't reach him either."

I said heavily, "Full-scale mutiny."

"If we're lucky, sir."

I exploded. "Lucky? What else would you call it?"

"Revolution."

The room spun. I marshaled my thoughts. "What ships have we?"

The few seconds lag was just enough to madden me. Finally Branstead's voice crackled. "In home system, nothing to speak of. *Melbourne*'s gone to Titan, with a full load of tourists. *New Orleans* is docked at Earthport awaiting a refit. You know the problem." These days, virtually all of home fleet had been pressed into service between colonies and the homeworld. We desperately needed more ships.

Captain Stanger's point exactly. The irony was that the ships he demanded, I'd use against him.

"You can't get through to Hoi?" I grasped at straws. "Is it possible he's still loyal?"

"McKay was killed. Probably to put Hoi in place."

I groaned. I'd had warning, and ignored it. Warning too of the Navy's dismay at our policies. I'd ignored that. Warning that our officers were becoming politicized. I'd ignored that as well.

My follies had destroyed us.

"Sir, now what?"

"You're at the Rotunda? Get out, before they level it."

"I have time yet. Will you fight?"

The hatch opened.

I laughed, a hawking, bitter sound. "With what? We've no ships, no command, and a gun to our heads."

Arlene strode in, Bevin in tow. "U.N.A.F. has ground defense lasers." Her mouth was grim. "Use them. Blast *Galactic* out of home system."

"You heard?"

"Their ultimatum is on the vids."

Jerence overheard. His voice was strained in the caller. "Mr. SecGen, be aware that *Galactic* was boarding passengers all this week. There's two thousand civilians already aboard."

Arlene grated, "Destroy his ship. He's mutinied." Never in history had the Navy faltered. Now, two hundred years of honor were forfeit.

I said, "It's mass murder."

"I don't care."

"We can't do it."

Hands on hips, she glared down at me. "What, then? Surrender?"

I didn't know. "Jerence, who's with us?"

"I can't tell yet. It all happened so fast . . ." He took a long slow breath. "U.N.A.F. Command, most likely, once they hear you're alive. The Board of Admiralty, I hope. But they endorsed the changes in command that put Simovich and Hoi in position. It's dicey."

"What's public opinion?"

"The public thinks you're dead. The news zines are running retrospectives. *De mortuis nil nisi bonum.*"

"We'll have the colonials, the transpops, the enviros."

"Right. No one with guns. They'll have the Senate, half the Assembly, and the Navy. The worst—"

"They do not!"

"They've got the Naval forces that count: Lunapolis and Earthport bases, and *Galactic*, the only major ship near Earth. They've got absolute laser superiority. Sir, we have to rally public support. Tell them you're in Lunapolis, taking charge; that will firm up U.N.A.F."

"How? From a hospital bed?"

"We don't say you're at the clinic." A pause. "You went aloft for a conference, and you've assumed personal control."

"Lies."

"Mr. SecGen, this is war."

I cried, "No, it's not!" We couldn't do battle with our own Navy. It was abominable. My spine throbbed. "Let Valera handle it."

"You're not serious. He'd go over to them in a minute. He's an Earth Firster at heart."

I said, "Then we'll talk to Stanger."

Arlene shook her head. "If you let him know you're alive, he'll launch a massive manhunt or, worse, a laser strike."

"Wait." Jerence. "I'm getting something on the U.N. public info circuit." A long pause. "Valera explained Stanger's ultimatum. He says he's giving in, to save the U.N. complex." A pause. "To save lives. Misguided enviro policies—"

"The son of a bitch!"

"Regrettable death of the SecGen, et cetera . . . you bastard!" Branstead's voice shook with rage. "As Acting Sec-Gen he's ordering U.N.A.F. and Admiralty to offer no resistance until the situation is clarified."

"Clarified!"

A long string of oaths from Jerence. "Valera's been in touch with Stanger. *Galactic* will hold off blasting the Rotunda. He's calling a joint session of the Senate and Assembly at seventeen hundred hours to vote down the enviro package. He'll make a public statement just prior."

I swung out of bed, ignoring a warning stab. "Arlene, my clothes. Bevin, find a video caller in the clinic office. Set it up against a white wall; I don't want any clues where we are from the background. Move! Jerence, take over the nets for an emergency announcement."

"On whose authority? Valera will—"

"Special Rule three eighteen, you know the drill. In this confusion no one is likely to stop you, even if they think it's Valera's call to make."

"For what time?"

"Sixteen thirty Eastern." I checked my watch. Two hours. "We'll feed to you. Rebroadcast from there." Perhaps that would conceal the origin of my transmission.

"What are you—"

"I'll speak to the world. They will *not* take over my Government. They will *not* scuttle my legislation!" Feverishly, I threw on a fresh shirt. "From now on, go armed, Jerence. If we lose contact, call through Jeff Thorne in London. He'll be with us no matter what."

"Yes, sir."

I rang off.

"Why are you out of bed?" Dr. Ghenili, from the doorway, peering past Derek.

"Leave us alone." My voice was tight.

"I told you, fifteen minutes a day. Any more and you'll injure yourself."

"We have a crisis."

"I don't care. You're due for a session with the growth stimulator. The orderlies will take you—"

"Out!" It was a snarl. "This instant!"

He retreated, shock and hurt mingling.

"Bevin, shut the door!" I worked my pants over my leg, as the hatch slid shut in my savior's face.

In a medical conference room, framed by a white drape, I rubbed my knee, glad of its familiar ache.

What in God's own Hell was keeping them? The circuit should be established by now. "Jerence?"

No answer. I rubbed my sweating palms.

Galactic. I tried to wipe its image from my mind. Our magnificent new ship, opulent corridors sparkling, passengers settling into their elegant staterooms. The vigilant purser and his mates, smoothing every concern. Courteous young middies, hurrying to their duties in that stride just short of a run that would earn them demerits. Laser turrets, bristling from the hull.

And on the gleaming bridge, a cancer had metastasized and was coursing through my beloved Navy.

And the worst of it was that I'd had warning. Robbie

Boland tried to tell me the Navy had gone awry. Hazen, too. Even Derek. Smug in my authority as SecGen, I'd ignored them all.

Under my nose, they'd replaced loyal Admirals with their own men. Dubrovik, injured and shunted aside. McKay. Idly, I'd even asked Branstead if it was an accident. But I hadn't investigated.

Unwilling to deal with distasteful politics, I hadn't even confronted Admiralty. Not about politicized officers, or the folly of *Galactic*, or cancellation of the new fleet.

I'd left them to their anxieties and fears.

My smug blindness had fomented rebellion.

If I abandoned the clinic, I risked lifelong paralysis. In no event could I return to Earth, direct my Government's response.

No matter; even were I mobile, what could I do?

Resign. Accept the consequences of my folly.

No. Not yet.

I would play it out.

I had no time to write a speech. I would speak off the cuff. I would ask the world's help, ask time to resolve the crisis. Ask their patience. It was all I could do.

Sixteen hundred thirty hours. A silent circuit, to the Rotunda.

Across the conference room, out of holocam view, Arlene, Derek, Mikhael, two solemn boys in gray. Anselm was back from Lunapolis Base, properly dressed. If he resented his forced return to childhood, he gave no sign. Perhaps the coup had driven it from his mind. He said that indenting for his grays at the Naval base, he'd noticed nothing out of the ordinary. Interesting.

I glared at the holocam. I was one of the few in public life who hated visuals, and rarely used them.

Where in Lord God's name was Branstead? It was sixteen forty-five. If we waited much longer, Valera would be on the nets.

"Are you there, Mr. SecGen?"

I jumped. "Yes."

"Sorry, but the situation is . . . strained. Valera's men . . . they demanded your office. I've been stalling. I don't see you. All we have is audio."

"Derek!"

He fiddled with the holocam.

"Here, let me, sir." Bevin, eager. Derek stood aside. The boy tapped the keys. In a moment we had full visuals.

"Sir, Valera's on the air!" Jerence.

"Can we cut in?"

"I doubt the nets would let us."

I fumed. "The moment he's done!"

"Right."

Valera spoke solemnly of the tragedy of my death, and further tragedy to be averted. Of my misguided idealism.

He praised the patriotism of the Navy. I muttered curses without end, until Arlene reached across, took my hand.

The Senate and Assembly were in session even as Valera spoke. In moments, they would, by voice vote, permanently table the enviro bills. Afterward, he would speak again.

He'd left me no time. Before I could rally public opinion, the issue would be lost.

The screen went blank.

The whole purpose of my speech was confounded.

"Now, Mr. SecGen. You're on in three . . . two . . ."

I smoothed my hair, straightened my tie.

"One . . . go!"

"I am Secretary-General Seafort. I was not injured in the cowardly attack that destroyed my home. I speak to you today from an undisclosed location, where I rally loyal U.N. forces to suppress the rebellion led by Captain Ulysses Stanger of *Galactic*."

It wasn't enough, and I knew it. In moments, by repudiating our legislation, the Senate and Assembly would endorse Stanger's coup.

There was left only the unthinkable.

So be it.

"By authority of the Charter of the United Nations, by the grace of Lord God, I now declare martial law. The U.N. Charter is suspended throughout Earth, Lunapolis, Earthport Station, and all home system's colonies, ships, and stations."

My words rang out in the hushed clinic.

"The Senate and General Assembly of the United Nations are dissolved. All their edicts, proclamations, acts, and decrees issued henceforth, I declare void. Now do I, Nicholas Ewing Seafort, assume personal government of the worlds."

There was left only the unthinkable.

So be it.

"By authority of the Charter of the United Nations, by the grace of Lord God, I now declare martial law. The U.N. Charter is suspended throughout Earth, Lunapolis, Earthport Station, and all home system's colonies, ships, and stations."

My words rang out in the hushed cabin.

"The Senate and General Assembly of the United Nations are dissolved. All their edicts, proclamations, acts, and decrees issued henceforth, I declare void. Now do I, Nicholas Ewing Seafort, assume personal government of the worlds."

PART III

October, in the Year
of our Lord 2241

17

Cisno Valera was unreachable.

Derek took charge of the clinic. On the considerable authority of his steely personality, he had the administrator postpone or cancel appointments. The staff that didn't know of my presence—most of them—was sent home. He stationed Bevin and Anselm at the clinic's outer hatch, with my precious laser, one of our only two weapons. Arlene had the other.

It was a stopgap measure. I'd have to find secure quarters. More important, I had to find allies. Despite my brave words, I didn't dare show myself, and had no forces under my command.

Branstead reestablished contact an hour after my broadcast. "Sir, it's . . . difficult. Squads of U.N.A.F. roam the halls. No one's sure whom to trust. Or who's in command."

"Where's Valera?" Seconds passed, while my words flew to Earth, and his sped back.

"At the Assembly. They've set up a headquarters."

"He's gone over?" I'd hoped my declaration would steady him.

"I don't know. Probably. When can you come ground-side?"

Not for weeks, according to Ghenili. If I subjected myself to a full one gee, I might lie on my back the rest of my life.

"Not yet, Jerence." I massaged my spine. The pain was worse. "Set up a relay to Stanger." I had still to hide my whereabouts, and communicating through the Rotunda would produce the expected lag.

"Very well, sir. Visuals?"

"No. Well, yes." I needed to see Stanger, to appraise his state.

In an hour, the Rotunda puter was ready. We made contact with *Galactic*.

"Mr. SecGen." Stanger was haggard. He spoke from his bridge. "We need an end to this."

"I agree."

"Despite your speech, we still hold the cards. I don't want to cause deaths. Will you cooperate?"

"What, exactly, do you want?"

"Drop your enviro package. That includes the five percent greenhouse gas reduction you proposed earlier. Use the funds to speed construction of *Olympiad* and her sister hulls. A public pledge to expand the Navy to its full pre-war complement."

"How do you know I'd follow through?"

He said simply, "You'll give me your word."

"It's better than your oath?"

He flushed. "You left us no choice. I don't know how you corralled enough Senators to pass your insane enviro fantasies. We were sure they'd stand firm. Your plan would gut the Navy."

"Not so. It would slow the growth—"

"Sir, ships are vital. The colonies are restless. We can't afford another Hope Nation."

In the side of my vision, Derek frowned.

"So you mutinied."

"Against what, sir? The Government is of Lord God. We have His support."

"Presumptuous of you."

"Don't you believe the Patriarchs represent Him?"

"They've taken no stand." I spoke with an assurance I didn't feel.

"Not in public." He glanced aside. "Later, Mr. Speke." To me, "Sir, I've tried to show good faith. We could have blasted the Rotunda to ashes while you spoke. We didn't. Do you want me to open fire?"

"No."

"Then you haven't much choice. If a single groundside laser targets *Galactic*, we'll return fire with everything we have. So will Earthport and Lunapolis. Give us our ships, and put a halt to this enviro madness."

"Why, damn it? Why?"

"We need ships to hold the colonies, the colonies to safeguard our supply of grain and ores. Earth will remain strong, Mr. SecGen, despite your glitched enviro cohorts."

"And if I give you my word?" At that, Bevin grimaced in dismay.

"You'll put it in writing, of course. A treaty, or memorandum between the Government and the Navy. Then you're free to go."

"Go?"

"I want you aloft, aboard *Galactic*. No political aides, no troops, no Marines. Just you. We'll cement our understanding."

"When?"

"Day after tomorrow, at the latest." Wednesday. "Sir, Admiral Hoi has an eye on incoming shuttles from Earth and Lunapolis, but I'll want your word you won't try anything. Don't try to storm *Galactic*. We've innocent civilians aboard, and besides, you don't want to damage the most powerful ship in your arsenal."

"*MY* arsenal?"

"It was, and will be again, sir." Stanger's voice wavered. "I hate what you're making us do. I want to be loyal." He glanced away, at an officer off-camera. "Let me know in three hours, else we'll be forced to show our power."

"How?"

"From Earthport, Lunapolis Base, and *Galactic,* we have our choice of targets. I want this over with, so we'll go for maximum effect. Major cities. Paris, Madrid, Sydney. Caracas. The civilian warrens of Lunapolis. Don't look so shocked that we're as ruthless as you." His blue eyes met mine, unflinching.

"You'll kill thousands. Millions."

"If you make it necessary."

"Very well. Three hours." Fuming, I cut the connection. "Branstead!"

"Here, sir."

"Cut orders for U.N.A.F. installations with a clear line of fire."

"They may not comply."

"But some will." If I was forced to give the order.

"I want to consult Robbie Boland and Senator McGhan."

"You'll do no such thing." I glared, but he couldn't see me; I'd rolled away from the intellilens. "They're removed from office with the rest of the Senate." I rang off.

"Well?" Derek raised an eyebrow. "How will you fight?"

"Do we know who's with us?" My question wasn't clear. "Has Lunapolis Base truly gone over to the rebels?"

"Captain Simovich is—"

"Yes, but what about his sailors? If I go to the warren, will they let me assume command?"

"You can't take the risk." Arlene.

"It's my job."

"If they capture you, who'd rally the Government? Valera? Kahn?"

Tad Anselm stirred. "I could go—"

"Be silent." She didn't even look at him.

I needed all the help I could get. "Go on, Tad."

"I could go back to the Naval warrens, wander around. Pretend I was delivering a message. See what the talk is."

"They'd tell you nothing. You're just a cadet."

He flushed. I hadn't meant it as criticism.

"No cadets are stationed at Lunapolis," I added gently. "You'd stand out like a sore thumb. And they just saw you dressed in middy blues. If I go, perhaps I can rally the Naval base."

"And start a civil war," said Arlene. "Simovich is their commander."

"If we get control of their lasers—"

"We can target *Galactic*. And she can target us. How many would die?"

In my mind, alarms shrieked. Airlock doors slammed shut, crushing the unlucky. Warrens crumbled in thick clouds of dust. Smoke, screams, the crush of rock. And then there was *Galactic*, its immense cost wasted. Hundreds writhing in the merciless laser light. For a fortunate few, vacuum.

The vision faded. "No," I agreed. "We won't provoke war."

Yet if we gave in, I'd foment enviro disaster. And the Naval dictatorship would inevitably grow, not wither.

I was helpless. I could call no Army, no Navy, no political allies.

There was nothing but resignation and disgrace.

"Nick." Derek rested his hands on my shoulders. "There's nothing between war and surrender."

I thought a very long while. My heart beat faster. "Isn't there?"

I set down the caller, Commandant Hazen's questions ringing in my ears. I'd finally snarled an acid remark about obeying orders, or giving over Academy to someone prepared to set a better example. Unfair. I'd only called him because I was almost certain of his loyalty.

By now he should be on his way.

I waited impatiently for Branstead's call. Finally it came. "Well?"

"Lincroft, Andersen, Polluck . . ." And four other Naval officers, all members of the Board of Admiralty.

"That's all?"

"Bondell and Petrov refused. 'Personal reasons.' The rest are out of touch." Branstead sounded ironic.

Seven out of fifteen. I would convene a rump board.

"Dismiss Bondell and Petrov," I said. "Give the rest two hours to answer your call, then do the same. What have you told the seven?"

"That they're to meet in London this evening. Admiral Thorne's been summoned back to duty. He'll pass along your orders."

I could rely on Jeff Thorne. For anything. "The shuttle's ready?"

"Yes, sir. You're sure? It complicates matters."

"It has to be face-to-face, and I can't go to them."

"Reconsider, sir. Let me come aloft too."

"No." Branstead was a civilian, and no longer young. I wanted him out of harm's way.

A sigh. "What's left to do?"

"Leave the Rotunda. Lie low." I cleared my throat. "Jerence, when this is done . . ."

"Don't say it."

"Don't say what?"

"That you may not be coming back. This is another of your harebrained schemes, isn't it?"

"Nonsense." My tone was gruff.

"You forget, sir, I was with you on *Trafalgar.* And I saw you nuke Orbit Station. Whatever you have in mind, let someone younger, more agile, do it. Someone—"

"That's quite enough, Jerence." I had no one to carry out my hapless plan, and besides, I might be called on to make some small measure of atonement.

His tone was somber. "You'll call me?"

"Before dawn, Eastern."

"I'll be up. Godspeed."

When I rang off, Arlene massaged my shoulders. It helped. "Nicky, you're going to tell me."

"Yes."

"Now."

"No." She might still try to stop me. I temporized. "It's almost time to call Stanger." The slightest miscalculation on my part, and my slim hopes were dashed. With great difficulty, I persuaded her to go to the hotel to retrieve P.T. and Jared. If Stanger contemplated bombing Lunapolis, I wanted our party together.

I waited for the connection, reminding myself Stanger still thought I was on Earth. I would have to insert a small pause before each reply.

"Stanger."

"I'll come to *Galactic*." Idly, I rubbed my aching knee.

A sigh, that might have been relief. "Very well."

"You want me there Wednesday?"

"The longer we wait, the more chance some hothead will open fire."

"I agree. I'll make shuttle arrangements. You have my oath that I'll be on *Galactic* Wednesday next."

"No tricks. No weapons, no military forces. Just you."

"Captain Stanger, I swear to you by Lord God that I will come to *Galactic* alone and unarmed, that I will bring aboard no Marines, U.N.A.F. troops, or Naval officers. Or sailors, for that matter. Not even a London jerry."

A chuckle.

I asked, "Will you be prepared to negotiate?"

"Only to draft the memorandum we spoke of. No changes."

"I may try to persuade you otherwise." My tone was sardonic. "Anything else?" I held my breath.

"You swear all this without reservation? You will put nobody armed onto *Galactic*, including yourself?"

"Yes. My solemn oath. Alone, unarmed, Wednesday."

"As an act of good faith, tell me your whereabouts."

"No."

"Why not?"

"There are others with me you might harm."

"You son of . . ." He left it unfinished.

"Stanger, how many of your crew are aware of what you've done?" He controlled his comm room; it was possible no one aboard *Galactic* save a few officers knew of his perfidy.

"I've told those who need to know. They'll be sailing with me. We're off to Constantine, you know, when we take on our remaining passengers. We're loading our last supplies even now."

The gall of the man. A minor mutiny, an overthrow of government, and then a routine cruise. I found myself trembling. "Good day, sir."

"Really, son, I'm fine now. There's no need for you to stay."

"Fath, why are you so grim?"

"I've a lot on my mind."

Philip regarded me. "Jared, please wait outside." In a moment, we were alone in my clinic room. "Sir, shall I start lying to you?"

"No."

"Then don't lie to me." He made himself comfortable in the side chair, as if prepared for a long chat.

"It wasn't a lie."

"Don't quibble. Between us, truth is more than a technicality."

He was right. "There's something I don't want you to know. Get some rest. In the morning, I'll—it will be clearer."

"You're agitated. You're trying to send us off. All right, there's a crisis. What's your scheme? Why are you evasive? Why is Derek furious with you?"

"Is he?"

"He's sitting with the cadets, like death incarnate. I wouldn't want to cross him."

"He's a tad miffed because I won't tell him." I sighed. "You're making it harder. You both are."

"Shall I call him, so we hear it together?"

I threw up my hands. "If you must."

I wheeled about the room, in a forlorn attempt to pace.

"Fath, you can't do it. There are courts, laws, the machinery of government. Let *them* bring Stanger to justice."

At that, even Derek shook his head.

I said, "When he spoke of loyalty, I almost laughed in his face. Power is seductive." I glanced from Derek to my son. "Believe me, I ought to know. You see . . ." I wheeled from wall to wall. "If we submit—if U.N.A.F. and the Assembly go along—it'll only get worse. They'll want a higher Naval budget, more ships, guaranteed autonomy, control of the colonies. One demand will lead to another. I know we risk innocent lives, but I see no choice."

Derek asked simply, "When do we go?"

"You don't. Only the cadets."

"Why them?"

"They're available, they're trained, they're military and have accepted the risk."

"I'm available, trained, and accept the risk."

"You're not even a citizen. What matter to you if my Government falls?"

"It's more personal than that."

"Sorry, Derek, but no."

His eyes blazed. "Listen well, Nick. I was a boy when you refused me passage on *Challenger*. Never again. I choose to go. Don't shake your head; refuse me and I'll tell Stanger what you plan."

"You wouldn't."

"I swear to Lord God I will." He held my gaze until I had to turn away. "I won't abandon you twice."

I sagged, defeated. "Three of you, then."

"Four." Philip.

"I go with P.T." Jared.

"Then none of us go." Beyond words, I flung my cane across the room. It bounced off the hatch, just as it opened. "I won't have it."

"Hey," said Mikhael. He stooped for my cane. "Weren't you teaching me to hold my temper?"

"No lip from you!" I hobbled across the room, snatched the cane from his hands.

"Why's the middy wearing gray, Pa?"

"He's been demoted. Where's Arlene?"

"Here." She studied Derek, her son, then me. "Who won?"

My back throbbed. "It's a standoff."

"Your husband," said Derek icily, "is acting an ass."

A sharp intake of breath, from Jared.

I debated hurling the cane at my old friend's head, restrained myself.

"It wouldn't be the first time," Arlene said sweetly. Smoldering, I contemplated a new target.

"Father's not the enemy," P.T. said quietly. "Stanger is."

"Thank you." By brute force, I quenched my ire. "Only the cadets go with me."

"Go where, sir?" Bevin, from the hatch. Anselm peered over his shoulder.

I surveyed the small room, suddenly so crowded.

"Yes, where?" Dr. Ghenili, behind them all.

"I'm checking out."

"You mustn't leave." Ghenili stood on tiptoe, to look over

the crowd. "Nerves knit slowly. If the ganglia fail to heal . . ." He thrust Bevin aside, crossed to my bed.

"I know."

"Mr. SecGen, God knows what damage you may do yourself. Paralysis, this time permanent. Or worse."

I disengaged his hand. "I understand." If that was the cost, I'd pay it. I owed my people much. Perhaps I could atone to the countless millions whom my neglect, my stupidity, had betrayed.

Walking in my cumbersome suit was more difficult than I'd hoped. The throbbing in my spine had become a persistent ache, then a glowing ember. Perhaps it was the twisting, when I climbed into the suit. Regardless of the pain, the helmet hid my face, for which I was immensely grateful. I'd sweated through my clothes during the long trudge through the warrens, but I'd remained unnoticed. Perhaps the three boisterous youngsters running about and whooping, as I'd bade them, had distracted unwanted attention. I'd have to commend them, when all was done.

Most shuttles were operated by U.N.A.F. or the Navy. We didn't dare show ourselves in an area under their control.

There were only a few public airlocks from the upper warrens. One, of course, led to the famous light show. At this hour, nominal night, the show was closed though we were in the long dark.

We dutifully signed out as a private party, in rented suits. Idiots were allowed to kill themselves on the surface, if they really cared to. No watchmen were posted, except when the light show was scheduled.

We cycled through the lock.

Rope guides led toward the nearby crater where the show was held. Breath rasping in my suit, I practiced the peculiar Lunar gait groundsiders found so hard to master: half jump, half tread.

Ahead, Bevin and Anselm played at long running leaps,

landing in slow motion in sprays of Lunar dust. The last time they'd been on the Lunar surface, it had been across the globe at Farside, under the strict tutelage of their sergeants.

Mikhael clutched Arlene's hand as he took small, careful steps. No stranger to a pressure suit, he was nonetheless cautious and unsure. A healthy attitude.

Derek, an old hand, walked nonchalantly. P.T. and Jared were less acclimated, but managed well enough. I shook my head, marveling that I'd been weak enough to allow them all on my odyssey. On the other hand, I couldn't leave them at Lunapolis to face Simovich's wrath. I'd have to find some way to detach Arlene and P.T., at the very least. And Mikhael; he was too young to risk himself.

My foster son was older than Bevin.

Still. I owed him parental protection.

P.T. touched helmets. "Now where, Fath?"

"A kilometer northeast of the crater."

It was a long walk, even in Lunar gravity. It was made longer by my reliance on two canes. In a pinch, I could just manage with one, but after a few steps it was too painful, and my steps were wobbly and unsteady.

After a time I found Arlene's arm under mine, gently supporting my weight. Casually, Derek took up station on the other side.

The ember grew to a blowtorch. I grunted with each step.

"I need a rest." Derek.

"Don't patronize me." I spoke through gritted teeth.

"All right. You need a rest."

"It can't be much farther." I checked my readout. Two A.M. local. "Anytime now. Watch the horizon." Unlike the portrayals in holodramas, shuttles glided in at an angle, rather than straight down. Until final descent, that is. Then they braked and landed as any other VTOL. I peered through my visor.

"I see it!" Mikhael's shrill scream nearly burst my

eardrums. Too late, I dialed down my volume. He jumped up and down, in high, slow-motion leaps. "Over there!"

The tiny shuttle's engine glowed as braking propellant spewed. Slowly, it settled, a good half kilometer distant.

I sighed, took hesitant steps.

At long last we were climbing the shuttle's ramp.

A suited figure met us at the lock. "Good morning, sir. I'm Pilot Van Peer."

The hatch closed; we cycled through. I checked the air gauge, unscrewed my helmet. "We haven't met in years," I said. "Not since *Portia*."

His jaw dropped. "But you're . . . you're—Mr. SecGen?"

"The very same." The Commandant had followed orders to the letter; his pilot had been told to pick up a party beyond the crater, but not whom to expect. Well, the only way to keep the secret any longer would be to wear my sweltering suit all the way to Farside, and I wasn't in the mood. I wiped my damp forehead.

"Sir, it's . . . I'm amazed." Van Peer had been quite a young man when I'd had UNS *Portia*. Casual, irrepressible, as interested in chess as I was. He'd aged gracefully, like Derek.

"Shall we?" I indicated the cockpit.

"Aye aye, sir." Van Peer made preparations for takeoff.

As we strapped in, Mikhael took in every fixture, the oxy bottles secured to the bulkheads, the thirty-one seats normally occupied by cadets. "Care to sign up, son?" My tone was as jovial as my aching back permitted.

"No way." He bent forward to get a better look at the cockpit. "What's he doing?"

"Preflight check." If the bloody puter would cooperate. I'd found shuttle puters notoriously stubborn.

I tried to find a tolerable position. We would be hours on board the tiny craft, and I was in considerable pain.

I was afraid liftoff would be a problem.

It wasn't. I passed out.

* * *

"Careful. Lift him gently."

"I'm all right." I thrust away helpful hands. "I'll walk."

"Let me help." Mikhael's voice was subdued. He offered a shoulder on which to lean.

"You've been crying?" I eased to my feet. Thank Lord God for the low gravity; Hazen had been told to turn the gravitrons down.

"No." Mikhael wiped reddened eyes.

Bevin made a word without sound. "Liar." I pretended not to notice, leaned more heavily on Mikhael than I might have.

A burly figure came to attention just past the lock. "Commandant Hazen reporting as ordered, sir."

"Very good. Stand easy." The corridor was deserted, as I'd expected. I looked about. "Your staff?"

"Most are groundside, with the cadets. The rest are—"

"You've no cadets aloft?" I'd forgotten; he'd sent them all to Devon for the memorial. My plans were wrecked.

Seafort, you fool. All my schemes assumed I'd have use of his cadets.

Now what?

"I'll get a chair." He disappeared. In a moment I found myself sitting, taking deep breaths of relief.

"I've a barracks ready if you'd care to rest."

"Yes." My head swam.

Arlene said, "Call your med tech."

I said, "Don't be ridiculous."

"At least he can block the pain. Commandant, call him. Nicky, it's an isolated base, and almost deserted. No one but the med tech will know you're here. Don't glower."

At times, Arlene had to have her way. I nodded. At snail's pace, I tottered to the dormitory.

"I put you in Thomas Keene," the Commandant said. "The new barracks." Fifteen years old, and still they called it new. It was named after the brave boy I'd killed, one heartless afternoon in the training boats.

"Who knows we're here?"

"No one. They're aware I have special guests, of course." That couldn't be helped. In a small base such as Farside, the Commandant's mysterious preparations couldn't go unnoticed.

"When is Admiralty due?"

He checked his watch. "Six hours. Van Peer will meet them as arranged. Sir, it's all been done. You're pale as a ghost. Please, get off your feet."

"All right." I was too spent to argue.

I warned the med tech not to give me anything that would cloud my mind. Perhaps as a result, my back throbbed unbearably.

I woke to the murmur of the boys' voices. "I'd like another softie." An expectant pause.

"All right, Mr. Tamarov." Anselm. He crossed the dormitory to an improvised refreshment table, returned with a cold drink.

I opened one eye. Mikhael sat cross-legged on a bunk.

"You trained here, huh? Were you in this dorm?"

"No, sir." Anselm's tone was level.

"It must be for the smart ones."

"I don't know, sir."

"That's enough, Mikhael." Anselm, like all cadets, had routinely endured hazing far more intense than my foster son could mete out, but it wasn't for Mikhael to dispense. Carefully, I shifted. Nothing broke, but a wave of fire swept my spine.

"I wasn't doing anything, Pa."

"Come here." I gave him my sternest eye. "Twenty pushups. Right this moment."

He gulped, but complied. In the weak gravity, it wasn't hard.

"Put that chair at the foot of the bed. Stand on it. You heard me. Now, what's the capital of Ireland?"

"Dublin."

"Argentina."

"Brasilia?"

"Wrong. Don't you ever study? Are you an idiot?"

"Pa, I—"

"Ten push-ups. Quick!"

He jumped off the chair. When he was done, I patted the bed. *"That's* hazing, son. Leave it to the experts."

"Yessir." Casually, he wiped an eye.

"And you aren't an idiot." My tone was gruff. Then, "Anselm, come here." I regarded him. "Take this joey outside, and settle it between you. I don't care how."

"Aye aye, sir." With a polite gesture to Mikhael, he indicated the hatch.

I hadn't slept well in ages. I dozed anew.

I woke to a dull haze of pain, and the blare of a zine. Idly, Danil played with the holovid receiver.

"—declared SecGen Seafort's claim illegal. Valera will command from—"

"Admiral Hoi pledged loyalty to the Valera-Stanger government as—"

"—imprisoned pending charges of treason. Branstead was chief of staff to former SecGen—"

"—tomorrow's editions."

"LEAVE IT!" I struggled to sit.

"What, sir?"

"Put it back!"

"Jerence Branstead, a Hope Nation colonial, served despite the objection of traditionalists who felt only a citizen should be chief of staff. His capture by a U.N.A.F. patrol outside the Rotunda—"

"Oh, God." I hadn't heeded the warnings, and now this.

And a trial for treason . . . they would execute him, out of sheer vindictiveness.

I stirred. I could move, but barely. Even if Hazen's cadets weren't groundside, I might not be able to carry out my forlorn plan. Without them, I faced almost certain failure, and death.

I thought a long while.

Very well. I deserved no less.

The hatch slid open. Jared Tenere.

I beckoned. "Talk with me." He took a chair. "Jared, if Philip goes with me he'll be in considerable risk. Dissuade him."

His smile was a touch sad. "How might I do that, Mr. Seafort? His mind's made up."

"You said he listens to reason."

"When he's wrong. Is he?"

"Of course. He may get himself killed."

Jared asked, "Would you allow him to go off and risk his life alone?"

"Of course not. I'm his father."

"He feels the same. He's your son." A pause. "I don't know what you plan, but I have to go too."

"I don't want that."

"Because I'm fragile?"

"Partly."

"I'm no wallflower, you know." Jared's tone was almost conversational. "I killed joeys in the trannie war. I can do it again. Especially to protect P.T."

A chill rolled down my spine. For a moment, there was something fierce about him, that I'd not previously seen.

"I don't want you to kill."

"I won't let Philip die." It was final, unarguable.

Derek peered in, saw I was awake. "Nick, the shuttle's here."

At last. "Tell Mr. Hazen we'll use his office." I struggled out of bed.

*   *   *

"Pa—"

I was shaken by my long, grueling meeting, and had no patience. "You'll stay here." I'd have Hazen look after him. "Don't argue."

"But why?"

I was blunt. "You could get killed."

Mikhael said, "Let me do something brave. Dad would have. It's time I learned. There's more to me than whining and running away." His eyes beseeched mine. "Please, Pa."

I pulled him into an embrace. "Not yet, son. But I'm proud of you."

He stamped his foot. "I came to live with you like you asked. I'm doing what you tell me. I call you 'Pa' like you want. I let you punish me like I'm your joey. Now, when it counts . . ." His lip quivered.

Derek took me aside. "Are you *trying* to drive him to a re-balancing ward? You offered him a home. You can't abandon him now."

"Our home is blasted to rubble."

"*You're* his home!"

We were almost out of time. I struggled with my thruster-suit. To Anselm and Bevin, "You're sure you understand?"

"Yes, sir." Danil looked for reassurance to the older cadet.

"Sir?" Pilot Van Peer, from the hatchway. "If you want to make your deadline . . ."

As casually as I could, I said, "Arlene, keep an eye on Mikhael. P.T., I'll see you in a day or two. Derek, I won't need—"

"You've been SecGen too long," Derek remarked. "You think the whole world follows your orders."

I rounded on him. "Don't start!"

He tightened his suit seals. "Accept the inevitable. I'm part of it."

"I order—"

Arlene kissed my lips to quiet me. "Hush, you foolish man. You don't decide our lives!"

"And Mikhael?"

"I agree, he stays."

"Ma'am, no!" Mikhael was so earnest, I could barely abide it. "Let me go as far as I can. On the shuttle, at least. If I have to say good-bye . . ." He hugged himself.

Derek said, "The shuttle itself won't be in danger. Van Peer can drop him at Earthport if we . . ." He grimaced. "If he has to go to Kiev."

"Very well." It was a minor mercy, one of the few I could bestow. We trudged to the shuttle lock.

"Your extra tanks?"

"Full." I peered past Derek, trying to spot Earthport Station against the backdrop of stars.

Derek cleared his throat. "Mr. Seafort—"

"I'm no longer 'Nick'?"

"Not at the moment." His tone was grave. "Sir, God-speed."

"And to you." Awkwardly, dangling my alumalloy canes, I embraced him.

I turned to the others. "No weapons. For all of us, I gave my word."

"Agreed." Arlene looked cross. From the rest, nods.

"Good-bye, Mikhael. I'll see you soon." But I wouldn't. He'd come to grips with his loss. He had Alexi in him.

I had to pry his fingers loose.

"All right, Pilot."

Van Peer took up the caller. "Academy Shuttle T-455 to Earthport Approach Control."

The speaker crackled. "Go ahead."

"We'll be docking at a Naval bay. We have a middy aboard whom Mr. Hazen wants drilled. Permission to maneuver before docking. I'd guess fifteen minutes."

"Outside two-kilometer docking zone, shuttle."

"Naturally. Changing course to 025, 36, 198."

I cycled the lock. "No radio. Nothing."

"Understood, sir." Van Peer's eyes never left his controls.

I switched off my radionics, stepped into the lock.

When the chamber was pumped to vacuum, I grasped a handhold, pulled myself out of the shuttle. The lock was nearly in zero gee, which helped immensely. If I could somehow live between planets, my spine would ache not at all.

I waited, searching among the uncaring stars until I saw the blazing lights of *Galactic*.

There would come a moment in Van Peer's maneuvers when he was at rest relative to the great starship. In about fifteen minutes, if all went according to plan. I had merely to let go my handhold, drift far enough to be out of range of his maneuvering thrusters. I locked my gaze on the ship.

When the time came I let go, floated dreamily into space. In a shuttle porthole, Arlene's anxious face. I waved, but she watched me recede, unblinking, as if to etch my form into her memory.

After a time, the shuttle was gone.

Carefully, so carefully, I nudged my thrusters.

The trick was to move hardly at all.

Galactic, like Earthport itself, had numerous external sensors. But, especially near an orbiting station, space was filled with abandoned tanks, lost tools, waste packets, and other slow-moving debris that drifted endlessly, until sucked into Earth's gravitational well. If I floated ever so slowly toward the starship, I wouldn't register.

At any rate, that was my hope.

My rate of speed was so slow it would take me eight hours.

I'd reach *Galactic* at seventeen hundred.

On Tuesday. I'd promised Stanger I would be in *Galactic* on Wednesday.

I would be.

I meant to kill Stanger, if I could. That went without saying. I owed Lord God a life, Stanger's or mine.

Drifting, I struggled to stay awake. Sleep was deadly; I'd have to adjust my course with the most minute of corrections, rather than change direction when I was close to *Galactic*. The last thing I wanted was some alert middy noticing debris homing on his ship in a great arc.

From time to time I prayed. For Mikhael, for poor Anselm, for Jared. For those I'd misjudged.

After a time my boyhood friend Jason drifted with me in companionable silence. Then Vax Holser, my great enemy, then my friend. Vax was among the first I murdered.

I snapped awake. Watch your tank, Seafort. Still green, but you'll have to change it soon.

Where was I?

Nearer to *Galactic*, but still a good way off. I contemplated a quick burst from my thrusters. But I might as well activate a beacon. Or blast an announcement of my presence across all frequencies. I sighed.

Where was Van Peer's shuttle? His instructions had been to finish maneuvers, dock for four hours, then, on Wednesday, separate from the Station.

Again, I reviewed my plan. It had one overwhelming advantage: I need not survive to win. As long as Stanger was thwarted . . .

Arlene had spoken of having another child. A pity. Perhaps she'd use my stored DNA to build one. I'd be a better posthumous father than a living one. For years I'd alienated P.T., thanks to my stubborn refusal to countenance his enviro pleas. And I'd beaten Mikhael, brutalized him. If he weren't so desperate for a model he wouldn't have allowed it.

My death was no great loss.

Laboriously, I made ready to switch tanks. It was an awkward maneuver, but not impossible. For a brief time I'd be dependent on the air in my suit, but that would last minutes, and the switch would take seconds. I unclamped the old tank, moved the nozzle to the new, secured the clamp. There.

When had I last changed tanks Outside? I must have been Anselm's age, a middy. Poor Tad . . . a cadet again, at sixteen? In all Academy's history I knew of no similar demotion. A midshipman made his bed, and was expected to sleep in it. If he couldn't cope with middy life, he washed out. Though . . . I had to smile. Anselm had lost his legal majority. As a cadet he couldn't buy liquor. Perhaps I'd done him a favor after all.

Ahead, the hull loomed. Would I need a correction?

No.

My feet would hit first. That wouldn't do; if I jarred my spine I'd probably pass out. At the last moment I'd touch the rear thruster just so . . .

Closer. I braced myself.

Switch on your hand magnets, you idiot! Do you want to bounce?

Now nudge the thruster.

Softly, gently, contact.

I clung to the huge hull, a barnacle on a whale. Where was I? Outside a disk, but which one? I was too close to tell; why hadn't I paid attention? Only the Level 1 or Level 2 lock would do.

Don't panic. It'll be labeled. You wouldn't be the first sailor to go Outside and become disoriented.

Avoiding mounted sensors, I clambered from handhold to handhold. The hull stretched into the distance. It was longer than three football fields, and I had to pull myself along a vast section of it, my canes hanging from my back.

Normally, a sailor in a thrustersuit would jet off from the hull, propel himself to his goal, and reattach. But I was most anxious not to trigger any external sensors.

Only zero gee made my labors possible.

A good hour later, I clung to a handhold near the Level 2 airlock. Carefully, I pulled myself onto the hull, clumped step by step to the sensor mounted just above the lock. I took from my pouch the one tool I'd brought: a wrench. Careful not to float into the sensor's view, I unbolted the sensor's housing and yanked loose the data cable.

Now, the hardest part. Waiting for some poor joey to come fix the sensor.

Just above the airlock, I hooked my arm through a handhold, and began my vigil. I might use all my air and asphyxiate before my plan came to fruition.

Seconds dragged into minutes, then into an hour. Two. I contemplated my last bottle of oxy. I'd have to change while my old one was well in the green, so my attention wouldn't be diverted at a critical moment.

Three hours.

What if I disconnected another sensor? Would it make them suspicious, or—

The outer lock indicator began to blink.

I opened my pouch.

I didn't dare crouch down to peer through the airlock porthole. I'd have to hope there were no more than two sailors.

The lock pumped to vacuum. The outer hatch slid open. A suited figure emerged, clinging to the handhold. I pressed myself against the hull, making myself smaller.

Spanner in hand, he hoisted himself over the lock, toward the sensor by which I crouched. I waited for his mate. No one emerged.

Could there possibly be only one?

He was almost on me. No more time. Clutching the handhold against recoil, I raised my wrench high over my head, smashed it into the helmet as hard as I could.

A puff of air. No time even for a scream. The figure jerked, clawed at a shattered helmet, twitched.

Forgive me, Lord. He was one of Your innocents. I call it duty, but in truth it's murder.

His suit was standard ship's issue, not a thrustersuit like my own. Thrustersuits were white, mag suits gray. That meant . . . I grabbed his already-stiffening arm, climbed down the handholds into the lock, trailing him like an ungainly balloon.

Hurry, before some bored rating peeks into the porthole. I slapped shut the outer hatch, re-aired the lock. First my own suit, a piece at a time. The helmet. The thruster pack. The torso and legs. It was harder now, under the influence of *Galactic*'s gravitrons. A lance of pain; I'd twisted in the wrong direction.

Crouching below porthole level, I pulled the sailor's smashed helmet. A gasp. My own. Soft brown hair, unseeing eyes, a woman's face.

Gritting my teeth, I stripped off the rest of her suit. Would it have made a difference? Could I have killed a woman in cold blood?

I already had, in my foul past.

Thrusting the thought to some dark recess of my mind, I began to don her suit. I had trouble working my legs into the opening; the effort sent warning twinges down my spine. The exertion left my clothes drenched, but finally I was ensconced in the mag suit. Thank heaven helmets were interchangeable. But that was to be expected; if each fit only its own suit, in a crisis, disaster could result by snatching the wrong helmet.

I cycled to vacuum, dragged the body to the outer lock. When the hatch slid open, I shoved out the sailor's corpse, watched her tumble toward Earthport Station. In a moment my thrustersuit followed, not before I'd secured my alumalloy canes.

Close the outer hatch. Recycle. Open the inner hatch. Hopefully, if someone on the bridge noticed the lock cycling, they'd simply assume the woman repairing the sensor had forgotten a tool. Perhaps they were calling her now. No, in that case I'd hear. I was wearing her suit.

I'd chosen Level 2 for several reasons. First, it wasn't Level 1; I'd be less likely to meet an officer before I wanted to. Second, Stanger kept only Levels 1 and 2 at reduced gravity. I'd be unable to walk if I emerged belowdecks. Last, according to Admiralty's specs, the berth of the master-at-arms was on Level 2.

Letting my canes support most of my weight, ungainly in my ill-fitting suit, I clumped down the carpeted corridor past curious passengers, past two ratings on cleanup detail. Where was the master-at-arms? To my right, a passenger lounge. Helpful plates above the hatch identified each compartment. An exercise room. Purser's storage.

Sweat ran down my spine. At any moment I might be stopped, my subterfuge unveiled, as I strolled halfway around an opulent circumference corridor the length of a bloody jogging track. In a stolen suit a size too small, supported by a cripple's canes. If they caught me, would they take me to the cells or to a psych?

At last, the compartment I sought.

I slapped open the hatch, hobbled in.

In any Naval ship the master-at-arms was a petty officer, and wore a sailor's blues. Short, muscular, swarthy, he put aside his holovid, turned from his console, rolled back his leather chair. "What do you want, Sailor?"

"Just a moment." Balancing on one cane, I unclamped my helmet, took a welcome breath of ship's air. "Would you help with this, please?" I unclasped the front of my thruster-suit.

A frown of annoyance as he helped peel off my suit.

He froze, gaping. Perhaps it was the Admiral's dress whites I wore beneath.

18

"Y ou are . . . ?"

"Admiral Seafort. Stand at attention."

Military discipline is automatic. He stiffened. I fished a chipcase from my pocket, slipped the chip Admiralty had given me into his console.

"United Nations Board of Admiralty to Nicholas Ewing Seafort, United Nations Naval Service," I read aloud. "Effective October 4, 2241, you are reinstated into the Naval Service with the rank of Admiral. You shall command a squadron consisting of UNS *Galactic*, a vessel moored alongside Earthport Station, and all other ships and boats now or hereafter sailing within home system. You are to direct the said squadron in the performance of its duties as may be determined by you, until relieved of your command . . ."

When done, I flipped the holovid for his inspection.

"Yes, sir?"

"Stand at ease. Your name?"

"Master-at-arms Yvgeni Tobrok."

"I trust you're familiar with Naval regs?" While most sailors relied on their officers' assumption of authority, a ship's jerry would know more of the law.

"Yes, sir."

"Listen carefully, Mr. Tobrok. First, I hereby take command of this squadron. Second, I relieve Ulysses Stanger as Captain of this vessel, and place him on the inactive list. Third, I appoint myself in his place. Do you question either my identity or my authority?"

Beads of sweat lined his forehead. "No, sir."

"Acknowledge my command, please. I caution you that if you err in this matter you will in all likelihood be hanged." No doubt he already knew. An officer—or any sailor—owed unquestioned obedience to his lawful Captain. To relieve a Captain without authority was a hanging offense, and the penalty was almost always carried out.

To his credit, Tobrok hesitated. "Let me see the holovid again, please." He read it carefully. When he was done his uniform was almost as damp as mine. "Sir, I acknowledge your authority. By your declaration, you're Captain of this vessel. But we have to tell Captain Stanger."

"Do we, now?" I took his chair, grateful to be off my feet.

It was a convoluted maneuver I'd performed.

A ship could have but one Captain, else its lines of authority would be muddled. By Naval regs, when two or more members of a ship's company held similar rank, seniority prevailed. The most senior was deemed of higher rank. I knew the provision well; I'd used it to steal a vessel to put an end to the Transpop Rebellion.

Captain Stanger, a seasoned hand, had far more seniority than I'd accumulated in my relatively brief Naval career. If I'd had Admiralty appoint me a mere Captain instead of Admiral, I'd have lacked authority to relieve him, were he to resist.

As Admiral, I couldn't command directly, but I could dismiss Stanger. I could then appoint myself to the vacant Captaincy, as I had.

Why did I bother, instead of relying on the vast powers I'd assumed under martial law?

Because of the very threat of hanging, of which I'd

warned Master-at-arms Tobrok. Officers wouldn't chance my vague claim of authority against their Captain's, unless I dismissed him in proper Naval fashion.

They still might not. But now at least I had a chance.

"What weapons have you, Mr. Tobrok?"

"Sir, we have to log your change of command."

"We will."

"I can't go against Mr. Stanger merely on your word, sir."

"You acknowledged my command, did you not?" Unarmed, I had to secure this man's weapons, but he could physically overpower me with ease. It was vital he accept my authority.

"Yes, sir. But"—a sheen of sweat—"I shouldn't have. Mr. Stanger has to be informed, and your relieving him recorded in the Log."

Tobrok was right: assumption of command must be logged, but the problem was, my doing so would alert Stanger. The Captain would hardly allow me to take over his ship; he'd already committed mutiny, a hanging offense. What matter that he defied Admiralty as well?

I cursed under my breath. All had been going so well, until I came upon this sea lawyer. No, that wasn't fair. A conscientious petty officer, trying to do his duty.

"In due time, Mr. Tobrok. The ship's safety—"

"Regs require it."

"I override the regs."

"Aye aye, sir. I insist your override be in writing and logged."

I regarded him. "Are you changing sides?"

"There are no sides." He sounded desperate. "There's *Galactic*, and the Naval Regulations and Code of Conduct."

Time was wasting, that I could ill afford. "If I find authority in the regs for not logging my assumption of command, will you be satisfied?"

"I'd have to be, sir." Almost, I felt sympathy. He was trying at all costs to avoid the threat of hanging.

"Very well. Let me think." As a youngster, in hazing such as Mikhael had toyed with at Farside, the middies had set me on a chair in the wardroom to make me recite regs. I'd uncovered an unexpected talent in memorizing them, that had served me well over the years.

"Section 135, General Provisions. Any ship's officer may rely upon the apparent authority of a superior, in carrying out—no." That supported Stanger's apparent authority as Captain, not my own as interloper. "Disregard that."

He waited, while I wracked my brain.

"During General Quarters routine ship's functions may be disregarded or delayed. Section 50 something."

"Only the Captain can pipe General Quarters, sir. Are you Captain if you haven't logged it?"

"I bloody well am." But my mere assertion wouldn't convince him. "Somewhere in Section 12. Any lawful order is valid, written or otherwise."

"Sir, no disrespect, but the question is whether your order is lawful." He shifted from foot to foot, like a joeykid needing to use the head.

I'd run out of regs. "Your console. Can you access the ship's puter?"

"Yes, sir, but only the Captain—"

"What's his name?"

"Baron, sir."

I sniffed. "Pretentious." Puters thought they ran the Navy. "Call him up."

"How may I help you?" A slight note of impatience in the puter's tone.

I fed in my Admiralty chip, and my own new ID code. "Acknowledge."

"Receipt of Admiralty orders acknowledged. Identity of Admiral SecGen Seafort confirmed through ID and voicerec."

"Very well." For Baron, I ran through the rigmarole I'd

conducted for Tobrok: I took command of my squadron, relieved the Captain, appointed myself.

"Assumption of authority acknowledged."

"Puter, can you make a copy of the Log?"

"Of course."

"Duplicate the Log as it existed prior to my assuming command."

A millisecond's pause. "Done."

"Very well. Freeze the second copy of the Log in its current state. Provide that copy in response to any request from the bridge. Acknowledge."

"Orders received and acknowledged, Captain."

I wiped my brow. "Now, Baron. Enter my orders relieving Captain Stanger and appointing myself Captain only in the original Log. Deem the original copy the official, current Log. Provide it upon request by Admiralty, or me."

"Noted. Captain, this is a most unusual—"

"Do you claim it's a violation of your programming?"

A most distinct hesitation. "No."

I glowered at Tobrok. "Satisfied?"

"Yes, sir, that should do it." He saluted. "Master-at-arms Yvgeni Tobrok reporting, Captain."

Thank Lord God.

"What weapons do you have?"

"Two stunners, sir."

My face showed my dismay. "That's all?"

"Mr. Stanger keeps the rest locked in the armory."

"On Level 1?"

"Yes, sir." He gave me an odd look. Armories were always on Level 1.

"What arms does he keep on the bridge?" Immediately, I knew it was a foolish question.

"I have no idea, sir." Stanger would have no reason to inform his master-at-arms of his weapons. No doubt he kept a laser pistol, if not more, in the bridge safe.

"Let's have the stunners."

Reluctantly, he parted with them. I shoved one in my pants, the other in my jacket.

"Who has the engine room?"

"Chief McAndrews."

"Have him—you're joking!" The stolid, reliable Chief Engineer of *Hibernia*, here on *Galactic*?

"I'm not, sir." Tobrok seemed puzzled.

"He'd be eighty, if he's a day."

"Oh, no, sir. Forty at most." A different man. My heart crept down to its usual place.

"His father was in the Navy too, I think."

An eager thump. "Let's go—no, I can't. Call him here."

"He's my superior, sir. I can't order him."

"Find an excuse. Get him here flank, but don't mention, uh, our doings."

"Aye aye, sir." Tobrok paused in thought. He keyed the caller. "Engine Room, master-at-arms."

"Go ahead." The voice seemed almost familiar.

"Chief, I collared one of your joeys rummaging through a passenger's cabin. She's willing not to press charges. I thought perhaps you—"

"I'll be right there." A click.

"Excellent, Mr. Tobrok. You're to be commended."

He flushed with pleasure.

After a time, the pounding of footsteps. The hatch was flung open. "Where is he?" A broad-shouldered man, with the physique of a village blacksmith. He ignored my braid.

Helplessly, Tobrok looked to me.

I put the Chief at attention, identified myself, ordered him to read the Log.

When he was done I said, "Well?"

"Well what, sir?"

"Do you acknowledge my authority?"

His brow knitted in puzzlement. "Of course."

Tobrok reddened.

"I believe I knew your father."

The Chief's ruddy face broke into a slow grin. "Aye, sir. I grew up on tales of the old days. I've always hoped to meet you."

"Is he alive?"

"As of last mail. He retired to Vega. Has a new wife."

"Marvelous." We'd passed many evenings over the fumes of his antique smoking apparatus.

"Sir, this is about the enviros?"

"No, it's about treason." Too late, I regretted my harsh tone. "What do you mean, the enviros?"

"The Captain told us the Navy was called in to put down an enviro insurrection. That you made your speech dissolving the Assembly because you were captive to a fanatic cult."

"You believed him?"

"Are you glitched? Of course not, after Pop's stories." A grin. "But I couldn't very well tell him so."

"Chief, Stanger has the bridge and I'm not sure how to dislodge him. Whatever happens, I don't want him to be able to Fuse, and we may need to cut power to the lasers."

"Fusion is no problem. I simply won't do it. Laser power is another matter. I'd have to reroute buses from the mains. He'd know, of course. There's no way to disconnect the safeties."

I pondered. "We have to lure him from the bridge." I glanced at my watch. "We only have an hour."

"What happens then, sir?" Tobrok.

Could I trust him? I hesitated. How could I not, after what he'd put me through? And Tobrok had summoned the Chief with a clever ruse. As for McAndrews, he was his father's son, and that would do.

"Reinforcements."

Tobrok's eyes widened. "Marines?"

"Unfortunately, no." I'd sworn not to put anyone armed on the ship. I'd deliberately broken one oath in my life. It was a matter that haunted me yet. Nothing in Lord God's creation could make me do it again.

"We need the comm room."

"I could call the comm room duty officer." Tobrok sounded dubious. "But he can't leave his post."

"What Level?"

"Three, sir."

Off-limits, unless I wanted to crawl; I couldn't walk in high gravity. "I can't manage it." A sudden thought. "Chief, you have the gravitrons?"

"Not the units themselves; each is at the center of its own vortex. But the controls, yes." He frowned. "Well, I have them, but can't adjust them unless the safeties are disconnected at the bridge console."

"Very well. Chief, back to your engine room. Stand by for my orders. Seal your corridor hatches."

His expression tightened. "Aye aye, sir."

"I don't suppose you keep weapons."

McAndrews paused in the hatchway. "Why, no, sir."

"Then we'll need cutting tools to breach the armory."

"No problem. I'll send a pair of my more reliable joeys." A salute, and he was gone.

I turned to Tobrok. "How many of your detail can you trust?"

"In this, sir? Let me . . . Two or three, at best. The others may, uh, waver."

"Call them. Have them wait for us outside the comm room." When he was done I asked, "I don't suppose there's a wheelchair about?"

"In sickbay, I imagine."

"Get it."

Waiting, I toyed at the console. With a chair, I'd risk Level 3. If we took the comm room, we had a chance. The hatch slid open. "Did you find—"

"Who are you?" A sailor, rather unkempt.

"Stand to!"

"You're not from the ship."

A desperate lunge that toppled me from the chair. On the way down I touched him with the tip of the stunner. He collapsed.

White jagged lightning, that threatened to cleave me asunder. I lay groaning.

"I have the wheel—good Christ!" Tobrok knelt. "What happened?"

"I fell."

"Did he—?" A glance at the sailor. If he'd touched me unbidden, it was a hanging offense. No crewman was allowed to touch the Captain.

"No." I held out a hand, an invitation. "Can you . . ."

Gently, he helped me to the wheelchair. "Now where, sir?"

"Brig him. Then the comm room, and hurry." I clutched my canes, heavy, alumalloy, useless objects. Tobrok dragged the unconscious sailor through the inner hatchway, to the brig.

Uneasy, glancing both ways, I followed him to the lift halfway around the corridor. Its hatch slid open. Two passengers made way, incurious, preoccupied with their conversation. I suspected they were unable to decipher one rank from another.

On the way below to Level 3 our weight altered. Even braced in the chair, I felt it as unbearable pressure. My face went pale and pasty.

With effort, I wheeled myself along in Tobrok's footsteps. The plush carpet eased my journey, but I held on to the armrests as if my life depended on it.

Two grim-looking joeys with billy clubs waited outside the comm room. Tobrok introduced them, quickly told them the situation. He rapped on the comm-room hatch. "Attention!" His bellow had the watch instantly on their feet.

With the ship in a state of undeclared war, I expected to find the comm room fully manned, and it was. Five ratings at their blinking consoles monitored Station traffic, watched the ship's many sensors.

"Mr. Tobrok, give them the news." Concisely, he did so. I had all three of them call up the revised Log, to verify our entries. "Who's in charge?"

Silence.

"Mr. Tobrok, throw the senior watch officer in the brig. The charge is insubordination."

"I guess I am, sir. Sorry." A beady-eyed joey, fingers clenching and unclenching. "Comm Specialist Panner."

"Very well. Hold, Mr. Tobrok. Mr. Panner, ignore all further communication from the bridge. Acknowledge."

"Orders received and acknowledged, sir. Ignore the bridge." He was sweating. "What if the Captain—"

"The former Captain."

"Yes, sir." He fell silent.

"Disconnect the bridge. I don't want them to have access to Earthport Station or Earth."

"Aye aye, sir, I can't." He licked greasy lips. "The bridge can't be cut off. The Captain can call out, or overhear anything sent from this compartment."

"What about other ship's stations?" I was afraid I already knew the answer.

"The bridge and the engine room can call anywhere. Maybe in complete powerdown they'd be cut off, but I doubt it."

"Very well. Put incoming communications on your speaker."

He tapped a few keys. The hiss of carriers, and an occasional bored instruction from Earthport's traffic control.

We waited. It was twenty-three fifty. Minutes passed at a glacial pace.

Twenty minutes later, a voice I knew. "*Galactic*, this is SecGen Seafort's shuttle." It *was* my shuttle. Had been.

Captain Stanger, his voice cold. "Identify yourself."

"Pilot Walter Van Peer, of Naval Academy Shuttle T-455."

"So that's where the son of a bitch was hiding. Who's with you?"

Van Peer's tone was laconic. "Sir, there's nobody else aboard. You have my oath."

Good. He'd said it exactly as we'd rehearsed.

"Very well, approach the Level 4 lock. He can swing across." Stanger was playing it safe. Forward of the Level 2 lock I'd used was a cargo bay, with capture latches for mating airlocks. But the Captain wanted no suspicious vessel moored to his starship.

We watched the sensor screens as Van Peer maneuvered the shuttle close.

Tobrok whispered, "How many does he have aboard?"

"None. He gave his oath on my behalf."

The master-at-arms gave me a fixed stare.

Van Peer brought the shuttle to rest a few meters from the airlock.

"Send Seafort through the Level 4 lock. Be warned, we have you targeted. Laser Room, prepare to fire."

Why had I taken over the comm room instead of laser control? I felt clammy inside my unfamiliar uniform.

The speaker crackled. "Mr. Tobrok, call the bridge."

We exchanged glances. I nodded.

He keyed the caller. "Master-at-arms Tobrok reporting, sir."

"Take a squad to the Level 4 lock. If Seafort is alone, let him in. Otherwise, defend the lock and report to me by caller."

I nodded.

He said, "Aye aye, sir."

I stirred. "Mr. Panner, seal your hatch, open only for me or the master-at-arms. Tobrok, get me to the Level 4 lock. Bring your joeys."

He slapped open the hatch. Outside, a midshipman stood

poised to knock. His gaze flickered past Tobrok. "The Sec-Gen, here?" His tone was unbelieving.

"Grab him!"

He spun and bolted. One of Tobrok's men gave chase, but it was hopeless.

"Run!" Canes in my lap, I flailed at my wheels. "Level 4! Hurry!"

We tore down the corridor past a gaggle of startled passengers.

The lift was a quarter turn beyond the stairwell. Too far. "Carry me! No time!" Only Tobrok dared touch me, at first. "Pick me up, damn you. Down the stairs! You, carry the chair. CHRIST JESUS, DON'T JOUNCE!" Sorry, Lord, but that was a bad one.

Alarms shrieked. Stanger, on shipwide circuit. *"Repel boarders, Level 4 airlock! All passengers, to your cabins!"*

At the foot of the ladder they threw me into the chair. We raced toward the lock. Tobrok panted, "Why, sir? Who's coming aboard?"

"My reinforcements." Just six, but Lord God willing, it might be enough. I'd gained the comm room and the engine room, stopped Stanger from Fusing. And I had the master-at-arms.

"If they're not on the shuttle, how . . . ?"

On a cable, tethered a hundred meters abaft the shuttle. Far enough so the gentle spurts of the shuttle's thrusters wouldn't roast them. Near enough to haul themselves in quickly. Van Peer's delicate touch had brought the shuttle to rest without swinging them into the hull.

Behind the shuttle. Not aboard it. I'd told truth.

No time to explain. "Trust me."

"Attention, ship's company!" Stanger's voice rasped in the corridor speakers. *"The master-at-arms is aiding the boarders. Apprehend him. Mr. Tobrok is relieved from his post. Speke, Wilkins, Tarnier, to the armory, flank!"*

Stanger had reacted with commendable speed. From the

middy's skimpy report, he'd pieced together enough to mobilize his defenses.

We skidded to a stop at the airlock, the first to arrive. I peered through the porthole, saw two suited figures. Then a third. The outer hatch gaped wide, held open by an alumalloy bar.

Hurry. I hammered at my armrest.

"Sir, the override!"

I glanced at the panel; the bridge override was flashing. Damn Stanger to hell. My party wouldn't be able to open the inner hatch. Neither would we, from the corridor. How could— "What's in there?"

"A suit locker, sir."

No help. I churned my brain. Aha. "Tobrok, the Chief left a cutting assembly in your berth. Get it, flank."

"Force the airlock?" He was incredulous. No sailor could easily contemplate damaging his ship.

"MOVE!"

I had both the stunners. I handed one to each of his joeys. "Give me the frazzing billy!" The startled sailor dropped the club in my lap. It wouldn't do much good, but it was better than nothing.

"There!" Down the corridor, a handful of *Galactic*'s sailors pointed at us, gathered their nerve for an attack.

"Charge them!" I prodded my crew.

Tobrok's two men took off, stunners aimed two-handed, stretched in front as they ran. They pounded along the carpet. The opposing sailors wavered. One turned, bolted. Abruptly, they all fled.

"Come back! Quick, to the lock!" Somehow, my joeys heard me above the rush of their adrenaline. They loped back.

The airlock was filling. Four figures. Five. I caught sight of Derek. Who was missing? Where the hell was Tobrok with the torch?

Running steps. The master-at-arms trotted round the

bend, lugging a heavy cutting assembly. His face was red from exertion; I should have sent two men.

I snapped, "Check the far ladder. Yell warning if they attack." Not that it would do much good. And they could come at us by the elevator as well.

Tobrok dropped the torch at my feet, leaned against the lock, chest heaving.

"Quick, get it set up!" He and his mate scrambled to put together the assembly. A click. Another, and we had flame.

Around the corridor bend, voices. I shoved my billy club at Tobrok. "Take your men, hold them off." I peered down the corridor. "Use those fire hoses!" Stanger could cut off the pressure, but it would gain us time. Especially if he first relayed his command through the engine room, where the ship's water was controlled. I snatched up the torch.

I pounded the airlock porthole. For Lord God's sake, hurry. There were six in the lock. Then, strangely, seven. Derek kicked free the bar. The outer hatch slid shut. He secured it, slammed down the pressure lever.

As the lock pressurized I began to cut. I needed to shear the bolts that held the hatch shut; the airlock control panel was disabled from the bridge. The bolts were at midlevel of the hatch. From my chair, I worked at a spot of the alumalloy, the torch assembly heavy on my lap. My canes were in the way; I tossed them to the deck.

Shouts of rage from the east. Tobrok's high pressure fire hose had found a target. A pity about the fine new carpet. I bent to my task. The alumalloy glowed, sagged. I jerked my feet away from the flow.

"Hurry, Captain!"

I grunted. To the west, Tobrok's man had pocketed his stunner and wrestled with a second fire hose. Clever. He could down more joeys with the icy water than the stunner, which had to be close enough to touch.

I had cut half through one of the two bolts. Stanger would have the water off any moment.

A scream. I glanced up. The corridor bulkhead smoked from a distant laser bolt. Lord help us. Fire hoses were no match for lasers. Tobrok retreated farther around the bend, toward me.

The first bolt was severed. I started the second. Was the bloody torch on full? Why hadn't I brought a torch of my own? Lasers? Or a nuke?

In excruciating slow motion, the second bolt glowed and began to separate.

"Now, sir! Hurry!" Tobrok was almost upon me, retreating from the laser. The fire hose was stretched tight. Only the curve of the corridor protected him, and he could retreat no farther. One good shot, and he'd be a blistered corpse.

Half the bolt cut. Two-thirds.

I held the torch steady, risked a glance to each side. To the west, Tobrok's man stood waiting with another hose. To the east, soggy carpet, a steady torrent of water slapping the bulkhead.

At the corridor curve a middy appeared, uniform immaculate and dry. Coolly, he aimed his laser pistol. I flinched. With a cry of rage Tobrok bounded forward, hose in hand. A bolt sizzled the bulkhead to his right. He charged the middy, dragging his hose. The middy aimed anew. Tobrok's burst caught him full in the chest, hurled him against the bulkhead. The laser went flying. The middy scrambled for it.

Pounding, on the hatch. I looked up. Christ, Seafort, you idiot. The bolt was cut, and still I played the flame at it. I twisted off the torch, slapped the panel just as someone in the lock did the same.

The smoking hatch slid open, grating against its pocket. Half-suited figures poured out the lock. Arlene. Philip. Bevin. Others still in helmets.

I threw down the torch, grabbed my canes. "Tobrok! You men!" I beckoned frantically.

The master-at-arms abandoned his hose. It flopped

wildly, like a beached fish. He raced down the corridor toward us.

"This way!" I pointed west, away from the armed party with the laser.

Someone grabbed my chair handles. I lurched along the corridor, hanging on as best I could.

Pounding feet, the rasp of breath. We thudded down the corridor. Jared tore off his heavy helmet.

Behind us, shouts.

"Faster!" I tried to spin the wheels. Where in God's own Hell was the ladder?

Three men lunged out of a cabin, brandishing billies. Derek ducked under one. Jared, with all his strength, swung his helmet in a vicious arc. It caught his attacker in the forehead, dropped him like a stone. We raced on.

Ahead, the ladder. As we neared, a dozen sailors charged down the steps from Level 3.

We were trapped. Someone hauled my chair backward. I pitched forward; a hand clutched my collar, hauled me into my seat as we retreated.

"This way!" Tobrok ran back the way we had come. "Fast!" That way lay the laser pistol, and death. "Hurry, sir!"

We had no choice. As one, we followed.

Twenty paces from the stairs, Tobrok dived to a hatch in the bulkhead. The lift.

He pounded the call button.

The hatch slid open. We piled in. We were too many. I grabbed someone onto my lap. Bevin. Derek, Anselm, and Jared swarmed into the packed lift like demented students in an electricar.

"Where?"

I gasped, "Two!" I had to get out of full gravity, no matter the cost.

"There they are!" Our pursuers charged the lift.

Someone slapped the hatch panel. The door slid. A billy

flashed; Derek cried out. I waited for the inevitable laser bolt that would end us all. None came.

The hatch closed. We started up.

"Bevin, hold still." My back was breaking. "Tobrok, where to?"

"My berth."

"They know you've gone over to us."

"The dining hall, then. West." It had several entrances, I recalled, and was as good a goal as any.

My load lightened. We were passing into the vortex of the bow gravitron.

The hatch slid open. I braced for the thud of clubs, the flash of lasers.

Nothing.

"Send the lift back down to six." It might throw them off.

"Quick!" Tobrok led us along the corridor past lounges, exercise rooms, cabins. At last, the dining-hall entry.

We dashed in.

Within, a deserted island of calm. Elegant crystalware. Plush seats.

"The galley, sir. It has hatches to the corridor."

"Go."

In a moment we were there. Well past midnight, it was deserted. Tobrok flicked off the light. By the glow of the emergency bulbs, we huddled behind a row of freezers, taking stock.

"Anyone hurt?"

"No, sir." Bevin.

"Not I." Anselm.

I looked about. "Good, everyone's—Lord God damn it, what are *you* doing here?"

Mikhael squirmed.

"I brought him." Derek's voice was calm.

"Why?"

"Because he's your son."

"I told you—"

"He's your son. Is he not?"

"Yes." That was why I wanted him in safety.

"You allowed Philip."

I had to. At twenty-four, he was beyond my control. Mikhael would never grasp the distinction.

I said deliberately, "You're right. Mikhael, I apologize. It was wrong to forbid you." His eyes glistened.

"Nick, we need guns." Arlene paced, a tigress on the prowl.

"I couldn't get to them." I felt a fool. "All we have is two stunners."

"And knives." Derek fingered the kitchenware.

"Fire axes, if it comes to that." Philip.

"Sir, they're my mates," said Tobrok. "I'll defend you, but don't ask me to take down my sailors with a fire ax."

"I understand." I'd already asked more of the man than was decent.

While they caught their breath, I brought my allies up-to-date. Questions; I did my best to answer.

Philip said little. When we were done he knelt by my chair. "The engine room has a tool shop. We can arm ourselves."

"No time to fabricate weapons."

"They'd have torches. Metal for clubs. Acid. Oil for fire-bombs." His voice was so calm, it belied the bloodthirsty implication of his words.

"Son, we're not looking for a bloodbath." I wanted to take the ship, not slaughter the crew.

"If we had lasers, we'd use them."

"True."

With great caution, I rose from my chair, grateful for the light gravity. My spine twinged, but I had full feeling, and my legs moved. With my canes, I paced. What we needed was to break into the bridge. Or the armory, if Stanger had left any arms.

"Stanger's our goal. Capture him and resistance will collapse."

"Not necessarily, sir. Anyone who supported him faces hanging. They'll be desperate."

"Only if they know I've relieved him."

"Make a shipwide announcement." Arlene. "Put them all on notice, drive a wedge into his forces."

Derek said, "For that we need the comm room."

"No. Just a caller." I looked about. "The comm room can switch us to shipwide circuit."

"Hold, sir." Tobrok. "If we call, the comm techs will know where we are."

Yes, but they'd acknowledged my command of *Galactic*. Would their loyalty revert to Stanger? Philip's and Arlene's lives were at stake. And Mikhael's.

Philip's voice was sharp. "Where's Jared?"

"He was here a minute ago." Anselm looked about.

"Find him." Philip strode to the serving doors to the eating room.

I snapped. "Stay in the galley." I cane-walked across the deck. "If one of them looks in—"

"I've got to find him."

"Do as you're told." My voice was ice.

"Fath—"

"This minute!"

"But I—" He sagged. "Yes, sir."

Jared was expendable. Any of us were. "Mr. Tobrok, send a man—"

"Seafort, this is the Captain." His voice was hard. *"We destroyed your shuttle. You have no way off the ship. Put down your arms and surrender."*

Arlene snorted. "What arms?"

"Shush."

"If we must, we'll seek you out compartment by compartment, and my men will shoot to kill. Call the bridge to give yourselves up."

I waited, but there was no more. "Now what?" I looked about.

"Make your announcement," said Arlene. "Before he rallies the crew against us."

"Tobrok, send a man to the comm room with a stunner. If we keep an eye on them, they won't betray—"

Outside, the murmur of voices. I put my finger to my lips. "The stunner!" It was barely a whisper. Arlene took up position by the door.

We'd barely come aboard, and already it was over. A futile, token resistance, and we'd be overwhelmed. I eased out of my chair, balanced on one cane, gripped my billy club.

Come on, you bastards.

"Move, God damn you!" A midshipman stumbled through the door, hands in air, his mouth set in a sneer. Behind him, a sailor. Another. To the rear, Jared, brandishing a laser. "Watch them, sir." Gingerly, he handed the laser to Derek.

Philip bounded across the galley. He slapped Jared hard, swept him into a fierce hug. "You idiot. You fool."

Derek smiled at the sailors. "Breathe funny. Try it." They stood perfectly still.

I found my voice. "Jared, how in God's name did you—"

His words were muffled, from P.T.'s shoulder. "You needed guns."

"Where—why—"

"I slipped out the side entrance."

"They might have killed you."

"I realized . . ." He raised his head, pulled clear of my son's embrace. "How many passengers have been ferried up? Two thousand? And they just boarded. Nobody would know me. So I was a frightened passenger looking for help. They're near my cabin, sir, come quick. The number? I don't know, but it's over—" His hand swept out, as if knocking a weapon from someone's grasp. "I didn't know what else to do, so I brought them here."

I turned to the middy. "You!" We'd met before.

"Edwin Speke."

"What Level were you on? What were your orders?"

"Edwin Speke, Midshipman. ID 76L542—"

"Answer!"

"Edwin Speke." His voice shook with hatred. "That grode asked for help! We were helping him when he attacked!" The unfairness overwhelmed him. "You goddamn frazzing—"

I raised a warning finger. There were limits.

He folded his arms. "That's all you'll get."

"I'm Nick Seafort. I've relieved your Captain, and appointed myself."

"I don't care."

What kind of middies was Academy sending us these days? "Care, boy. Your life depends on it."

"You'd shoot me?" His contempt dripped.

"Admiralty will hang you. I'm Captain of *Galactic*; you're subject to my orders."

"Prove it."

I glanced about, saw no console, said lamely, "It's in the Log."

"Show it to—"

"Sir, time's wasting." Derek.

"Tobrok, take your men and try to reach the comm room. Leave one of them to make sure they don't tell Stanger our location. Call here." I would broadcast my assumption of command to the ship.

"Aye aye, sir. And these two?" He indicated the sailors.

A problem. I couldn't brig more than a few of them; there was no room. That's assuming we could reach the brig, and that Stanger's forces didn't release them the moment we left.

The ship was simply too big, and with a crew of eight hundred, there were more on his side than on ours. I tried to puzzle it out.

"Arlene." My face was impassive. With the stunner, she touched one of them in the ribs. His eyes rolled upward as he fell. She whirled to his companion, dropped him before he could protest.

"You bastards!" The middy's fists clenched.

"Two demerits. Four."

"You can't issue me—"

"Five."

He fell silent.

I said, "We need to break into the armory, unless Stanger's emptied it." But the armory, like the bridge, was built as a fortress. Cutting through its reinforced plates would be a major undertaking. "I left the torch at the airlock."

"Stanger's territory, by now."

"No doubt." I needed help. Balefully, I eyed the middy. "Joey, where's the nearest console?"

"I don't have to tell you. The Captain—"

"Derek, shoot him. I've had enough."

"No!" A cry of genuine fear.

Obligingly, Derek aimed between his eyes. I wondered if the boy saw the safety was still on.

"Please, sir!"

"You'll do as I say?"

"Yes!" Reflexively, the middy ran fingers through his hair. His hand trembled.

"Go to the brig. It's a few hatchways past the bend. Sit at the console and call up the bloody Log!"

"Nick, he'll run to Stanger." Arlene.

"No, he won't. Not until he looks. Decide who's Captain, Mr. Speke. If it's me, enter your demerits. Hurry back." I glared. "Well?"

"Aye aye, sir."

"Don't let him go! We're all at risk."

"It's all right, hon." Though he might not know it, the

middy had acknowledged me when he lapsed silent at the threat of my demerits.

The boy slunk out.

Stanger had been quiet a long while. What was he up to? Would he turn his wrath on a world held hostage? "We need the laser room."

Derek checked his pistol. "Probably enough charge to burn through the hatch. But if they're waiting inside . . ." A shootout, with Lord knew how many killed.

"We need more guns."

P.T. said, "I'll go out as Jared did. Have Mom and Derek hide in a cabin, and I'll lead sailors into an ambush."

"You're too well known." As my son, his face had at times been in the holos.

"Not so well—"

"I'll go." Mikhael.

"Out of the question."

"Who else can you send? The cadets' uniforms would give them away. Jared's already been out. Mr. Carr? He's in the holozines too. And I'm just a joeykid, who'd be afraid of me?"

"Mikhael—" If I faced Alexi before Lord God, and had to explain I'd sent his son to slaughter . . .

"Please, Pa. Watch!" Mikhael jumped up and down excitedly. "Joeys with guns and stunners!" He pointed. "I was coming out of the lounge, and—"

I looked to Arlene.

She shrugged. "It might work."

"I don't want him hurt."

"Please! Let me be brave!"

While I hesitated Arlene said, "Tell them you're in cabin two sixteen. Lead them past the exercise room, that's where we'll be. Now, we have only one pistol. I can take four, perhaps five, with surprise. Don't lead a troop of fifteen to us."

"No, ma'am."

"If they're too many, walk up to them and ask if it's all

right to be out of your cabin. They'll tell you to get lost. Derek, let's go. Nick, make your announcement. You know where we'll be."

Knowing it was dangerous folly, I let them depart.

Waiting helplessly, I tried to plan. First, my announcement. Then the laser room. Somehow I'd disable *Galactic*'s lasers, if I had to burn their consoles into smoking puddles. If I could secure the ship, Stanger could have the bridge. He wasn't taking *Galactic* anywhere; Chief McAndrews wouldn't let him. I'd starve him out if necessary.

Hobbling, I paced. "Tobrok should have called by now."

P.T. said, "If he ran into a patrol . . ."

"Shall I risk calling the comm room?"

"No. Wait."

I should have taken the master-at-arms to the laser room as soon as I'd boarded. With that disabled, I'd have had time to figure out the rest. But he'd disputed my authority, and there was the comm room to secure, and we had to cut through the lock, and . . . I sighed.

Distant shouts. A scream.

I sat. After a time, my nerves were stretched tight.

Footsteps, in the dining hall.

P.T. pulled out his stunner, took position just inside the double door. He crouched. Anselm had a knife, Bevin an iron cooking pan with a long handle. They planted themselves in front of my chair.

"Nicky, it's us." Arlene. I let out a breath I hadn't known I was holding.

The door swung open. She dropped her booty on a counter: three pistols, an ugly laser rifle, even more accurate than a pistol. Derek, behind her, put his weapon on safety.

My voice was hoarse. "Where's Mikhael?"

"Outside. You'd better go to him."

Oh, Lord God. He was hurt. I leaned hard on my canes, practically launched myself in the light gravity.

I passed through the serving doors into the sumptuous dining hall.

Mikhael, his back to me, sagged against a pillar, sobbing. "What is it, son?"

His shoulders shook in a silent spasm. I put aside a cane, laid an arm across his shoulder. "Tell me."

"Look what I did." Scarlet with mortification, he faced me, revealing his damp pants. "Like a . . . like a . . ." He wept. "I wanted to be brave like Dad, and now this."

Relief swept through me. "Is that all?" I buried his head in my chest. "You must have been terrified."

"That middy, Speke. He saw me, and I thought he'd tell them, and then Ms. Seafort, she—"

It would have been grim, at close range.

"I can't go in. I can't let them see."

"I'll tell you a secret." I raised his chin. "It happened to me, once." An alien form skittered through the wreck of *Telstar*, close enough to touch. *Fuse, Vax. Fuse the ship.* I shuddered.

"You're just saying that." Misery permeated his features. "I want to die."

"It's true. I wet myself. What makes you think you're immune to fear?"

"You and Mr. Carr, you're so brave. Nothing frightens—"

"Oh, son. Courage isn't living without fear. It's in what you do despite your fear."

It seemed, after a time, to calm him. Clinging to me like a bashful toddler, he allowed me to guide him to the galley.

I was desperate. We'd apparently lost Tobrok and his men. The middy Speke hadn't returned. Stanger would come for us at any moment. I dared not call the comm room; it would give away our position. The laser room was on Level 1. We had the firepower to force its hatch, but the Captain almost certainly guarded the ladder wells. Even if, by some miracle, neither Speke nor Tobrok had told him our whereabouts, he'd certainly know his Level 2 patrols weren't disappearing by accident.

"I'm coming in." A voice from the darkened dining hall.

"Lord Jesus!" I tried to surge to my feet, and recoiled from a white-hot lance of pain.

"Don't shoot." Midshipman Speke poked his head into the galley.

Arlene grabbed him by the collar, slammed him against a cooler. "Where'd you go?" A shake, that rattled his teeth. "Answer!"

"Easy, hon."

"Don't 'easy' me." She drew her pistol. "If you betrayed us . . ."

"Ma'am—Captain, sir, I didn't!" He looked to me for succor. "I read the Log, and you're the lawful . . . You needed lasers, so I went to the bridge. Mr. Stanger—"

"Don't, Arlene!"

"I told Stanger I'd lost mine in a firefight, that you were on Level 4, could I indent for another, and he said—" The boy blushed furiously. "If I lose another pistol he'll have me caned. I'm supposed to lead CPO Fahren's squad. They're assembled on Level 5. I have lasers and billies and stunners."

"Where?"

"Just inside the corridor hatch." I peered into the dining hall, saw weapons piled on a powered cart.

I glowered. "How many demerits have you?"

"Eight, sir. Including your five." He blushed furiously. "Midshipman Edwin Speke reporting for duty, sir."

"Very well." His exploits deserved more. I cleared my throat. "Well done, Middy." I forced my thoughts to the problems we faced. We had arms, but needed more men. How . . . Ah. "Mr. Speke, find CPO Fahren's squad. Bring them here."

"But . . . aye aye, sir."

"If you run into opposition, I trust you can talk your way out of it?"

He looked sheepish. "Probably."

He'd be in little danger. Our party was concealed in the mess hall, and to the enemy, Speke would appear to be carrying out Stanger's orders.

Ten minutes later, I surveyed my new command. Fahren's squad consisted of twenty-two sailors under the chief petty officer. Speke had assured them with calm confidence that I was the lawful Captain, and seemed to be carrying the day. CPO Fahren nervously pledged his support.

Time to sally forth. The only reason we hadn't been discovered was that the dining hall was such an unlikely, useless place for us to hide.

Galactic was larger than any other vessel I'd known, but its structure was like all the Navy's starships: two stairwells crossed each level, east and west. If we held both ladders, we could defend Level 2. Oops, I'd forgotten the lift. Both stairs and the elevator.

"No."

Derek and P.T. looked at me strangely; I hadn't realized I'd spoken aloud. We didn't want to defend Level 2; we needed to seize Level 1. Officers' quarters, the laser room, the bridge.

"Mr. Speke, reconnoiter the east ladder."

In a few moments he was back. "Guards at the foot, sir. Probably also at Level 1, but I couldn't get close enough to see."

"Try the west." He did. It was the same.

"Midshipman, assemble your squad in the corridor. I want to mount a charge to the east stairs. You've how many lasers, ten? Laser carriers in front. Pick men who know how—"

"Nicky, let me lead."

"You're a civilian, hon." I frowned at Arlene. "They can't follow your orders, even if they had a mind—"

"Enlist me."

"What?" I wanted to say more, but I was speechless.

"You heard me. Appoint me lieutenant."

P.T. watched, solemn.

"Hon, this is no time to . . ." I sought a valid argument. "Enlistment is for five years." I added hurriedly, "Of course there's always remission." As Admiral, I could remit the enlistment of any officer. We'd done so for the passengers I'd impressed on *Challenger*.

A ridiculous notion, hers. A wife a subordinate officer, subject to her husband's commands, yet equal within their cabin? True, there were officers who had married, but none had been Captain.

Yet, why had I consented to her joining my mission, if I wouldn't use her skills? I temporized. "Hon, if you enlist, whatever orders I give—"

"For Christ's sake, Nicky. I know."

"Very well." Twenty-five years after her discharge, she'd be a lieutenant once more. "Raise your right hand. I do—"

"I, Arlene Sanders Seafort, do swear upon my immortal soul to preserve and protect the Charter of the General Assembly of the United Nations, to give loyalty and obedience for the term of my enlistment to the Naval Service of the United Nations and to obey all its lawful orders and regulations, so help me Lord God Almighty." She spoke without hesitation.

With a tug at my jacket, a quick smoothing of my tie, I snapped her a formal salute. Crisply, she replied.

Lord God, I loved her. "Go to it, Lieutenant."

"Aye aye, sir."

"You joeys heard: she's Navy now. Follow orders. Middy, detach three men from their squad, take my two cadets as well. Guard the rear of Fahren's squad. Take position between the dining hall and the west stairs."

Not to be outdone, Speke snapped an Academy salute. "Aye aye, sir." He strode off, Bevin and Anselm in tow.

"What about us?" Jared.

"You and P.T. will help me up the ladder, the moment it's safe." My tone was gruff. "Mikhael, the boys will need your help."

"Yes, sir." His gratitude was pathetic.

P.T. stirred. "Get in the chair, Fath."

"I don't need it." Now that we were in light gravity, I'd be able to walk. I hoisted myself on my canes. In fact, if I was careful, I could do with just one.

P.T. said, "Jar, check the corridor near the stairs. We need to know when Mom attacks."

Jared gave him a quick hug, left on his errand.

"Thanks, Fath."

"For what?"

"Not sending him into danger."

"He's very protective of you."

"Odd, isn't it? It's I who should be protecting him."

We waited.

Derek was pensive. "Mr. Seafort, you might give me men to command."

"Not you too. The same objection applies."

"That I'm civilian? You know the remedy."

"You're too old for midshipman." He was graying.

"But not for lieutenant."

I waved it away. "Next you'll have me enlisting Mikhael. Or Jared."

"Very well, sir." His tone was frosty. He turned to stare at the hatch.

I muttered something.

"What?"

"I said, 'Prima donnas.' "

A long moment, in which the temperature hovered around that of interstellar space.

I growled, "Raise your right hand."

19

"Ms. Seafort says five minutes." Jared was breathless. "She wants a diversion at the west ladder."

I grimaced. "She needs more men."

"I suppose I just stand here, sir?" Derek's tone was dry.

"You're my reserve." I came to a sudden decision. "Did you see a caller in the exercise room?"

"It was rather bloody in there. I didn't notice."

"Go check. If you find one, call the comm room. Get an idea whose side they're on." If my war party had to retreat to the galley, no point in alerting Stanger to our location by calling from it. "Hurry."

"Aye aye, sir." He strode out. Amazing how easily one reverted to the formalities of Naval life. I wondered if I could do the same, were I truly to return as Captain. I dismissed the fancy.

Jared returned to his post, behind the attackers.

In a few moments Derek was back. "No answer, sir."

"Impossible. The comm room's always manned."

"You heard me." His tone was tart. "I rang, and they didn't respond. Or wouldn't."

"Find Arlene. Help her."

He left. I wished I hadn't given all the lasers to our war party. We had nothing but a billy among us.

P.T. said, "Maybe the comm tech's playing it safe. If he—"

Jared burst in. "Now, Mr. Seafort!"

I hobbled to the dining-hall exit. P.T. hesitated, ran back for the chair. "Will you for God's sake get in?"

"I don't—" I gave it up, handed him my canes, settled myself. Jared ran ahead to hold hatches; P.T. and Mikhael raced me to the corridor and the east ladder.

Mikhael skidded to a stop. "Ukk."

The carpet was stained and sticky. Bodies lay where they had fallen. A horrid stench of charred meat pervaded the corridor.

I lurched out of the wheelchair. P.T. and Jared each grabbed one of my arms, helped me up the ladder. Mikhael scrambled up with the chair.

On Level 1, Arlene loped around the distant corridor bend. Her jumpsuit was splashed with blood. She cupped her hands to her mouth. "The laser room's in section nine!" She spun, ran back the way she'd come.

I tried to orient myself. This level was sparse, utilitarian, like the ships I knew. But so large . . . The bridge was west, the laser room east. Of course, ultimately it didn't matter; the circumference corridor was circular. But on a ship with disks so large, one didn't want to go the wrong way.

I hurried down the corridor on my canes. Where was the armory? We'd need that too.

"Attention. This is Captain Stanger."

I froze.

"There's been some confusion."

"Hurry, Fath."

"Listen." I limped on.

"In an act of desperation, former SecGen Seafort forced his way onto Galactic *with an armed party of attackers, violating his oath. He's murdered some of our sailors, and is roaming Levels 1 and 2. He's made a false claim to be Cap-*

tain of Galactic. *He is not, but even if he were so, I relieve him on the grounds that he is insane."*

"The bastard."

"Quiet, I said."

"Crew to Battle Stations, flank. Corridor hatches will seal in one minute. If you encounter the invaders, contact the bridge immediately. Passengers, do not, repeat, do not venture into the corridors."

I dropped into the chair. "Move me!" Once the emergency corridor hatches sealed, only authorized codes or a signal from the bridge could open them. Piping Battle Stations was a move I'd expected Stanger to make, sooner or later. By dividing the ship into isolated segments, he denied us the freedom of movement we needed.

We raced to the end of section seven. Through to eight. At a cabin, an officer emerged. He stopped dead in his tracks. We flashed by. He tugged at something black in his belt. The skin of my spine crawled as I waited for the shot.

"PA, IT'S CLOSING!" Mikhael scampered ahead.

P.T. thundered down the corridor, pushing my chair. Hatches flew past in a blur.

Corridor hatches were designed for decompression. When they shut, they shut fast. Philip raced toward the hatch, but too late. Abruptly realizing we were trapped, he let go my chair, spun back the way we'd come. I rolled onward, helpless against the momentum he'd achieved. Mikhael grabbed the handles, braced himself to slow me. The speeding chair yanked him off his feet; he fell with a thump.

Slowed, I crashed into the solid hatch. The impact almost threw me from my seat. Half-dazed, I wrenched the wheel.

Philip galloped down the corridor. Jared followed, legs pumping madly. The officer we'd passed stood waiting, stunner aimed.

With a shout Philip launched himself. He struck the officer full in the chest, fell slack to the deck, rolled over twice.

Jared hurtled down the corridor. The officer aimed anew as Jared hit him. They went down, flailing.

Jared sprang to his feet. He kicked the officer's limp form once, twice, three times, ran to Philip, knelt.

Slowly, aching, I wheeled myself toward them. Mikhael, shamefaced, came alongside and helped push.

Jared cradled P.T.'s head.

I patted his shoulder. "It's just a stunner. He'll be all right in an hour."

Jared's eyes were sorrowful. "He didn't warn me . . ."

"I know son." I looked about. "We can't stay here." Any moment we'd be found.

"Where—?"

We were locked in our section, until I devised a way out. "There." I picked a compartment at random. Anything was better than the middle of the corridor.

"I'll drag him." Jared got his arms under P.T.'s shoulders.

"Use the chair." I struggled to my feet, balanced on my canes. Any second now, someone would come. My back prickled.

Jared and Mikhael hauled my son into the chair. Insensate, he looked far younger than his twenty-four years. I swallowed, hobbled faster.

At the unlabeled compartment I slapped open the hatch. "In here." We hustled the chair inside, closed the hatch. I looked around.

Six bunk beds, four abandoned in haste. Built-in dressers. An inner room, with more beds.

The midshipmen's wardroom.

"Now what?" Jared.

"You and Mikhael put on middies' clothes."

His eyes widened. "You're enlisting us?"

"No, but you're too conspicuous in civvies." Was it possible Mikhael's look was disappointment?

"What about P.T.?"

"Yourselves first. Deal with him when he wakes."

Mikhael pawed through a drawer, found middy blues and a shirt. With obvious relief he stripped off his damp pants.

Jared would have more trouble; he'd filled out as an adult.

"Mikhael, can you manage the tie?" Bloody anachronism; at times I wondered why the Navy bothered. On the other hand, tradition was everything.

"No, sir." He sounded subdued.

"Come here." I made a clumsy knot. Good for a demerit, but tonight it would do. "You look handsome." Heartbreakingly like Alexi.

"Thanks, Pa. Here, Jared, try these, they're bigger."

We were fit to venture out, but to what purpose? "Where's the caller? Ahh." I hobbled to it. I'd try the comm room, or—

"All armed sailors on Level 1, to the laser room! Call the bridge to have corridor hatches opened. Lieutenant Perez, take charge outside the laser room."

"There's our chance." They stared, so I elaborated. "We go to the section nine hatch, call the bridge. In the confusion we'll get through." Lord God willing. "Leave P.T. here. We'll—"

The hatch slid open. A middy ran in. "What are you joeys—hey, you're not—"

As one, without my prompting, Jared and Mikhael tackled him. They rolled on the deck; Mikhael swarmed onto his chest. I managed to skirt the fracas, reach the hatch control, slap it shut.

The middy bucked and heaved. I prodded him with my cane. "That will do!"

At the sight of my uniform, momentary confusion. "You're . . . SecGen Seafort."

"Yes. Mikhael, is he armed? No? Let him up."

"He'll—"

"This instant!" I was used to obedience from joeys in middy blues.

Face flushed, *Galactic*'s middy scrambled to his feet. "What are you doing here?"

"Come to attention."

He hesitated. "How should I know whom to obey? Captain Stanger says you're relieved."

"By Admiralty directive, I relieved your Captain first. He's been placed inactive and has no authority to relieve me. And in any event I'm still SecGen."

"He says—" Whatever it was, he thought better of it. After a moment he drew himself up. Watching from the bulkhead, where he thought I couldn't see, Mikhael sucked in his chest, put his arms to his sides, tried to stiffen. A passable imitation, for a civilian.

To the middy, "Why are you here?"

"For a permalight. The Captain's going to—" His lips tightened.

"Go on."

"I won't betray my shipmates."

"Betray? Have you any idea what he's done?"

"He's saving the Navy."

My face grew red. "*Galactic*'s at Battle Stations, so insubordination is punishable by death. Summary proceedings. What's Stanger up to?"

"I'm not sure."

"Do you acknowledge my authority?"

A long moment. "I guess so . . . yes, sir. Midshipman Pyle reporting. I'll work for you, but don't ask me to tell you what they're doing. It isn't right."

I hesitated. It was as good as I'd get, and his position had merit. "Very well. Mikhael, who's in the corridor?"

He slid open the hatch. "A few sailors. No officers that I—oh, there's one." He ducked back inside. "They'll know we're not from the ship, right?"

"The officers will." Our fraudulent middies' uniforms might pass muster with the crew—*Galactic* was a new ship, and a huge one—but lieutenants would know their own mid-shipmen.

I had to use Pyle to pass through the corridor hatch, to reach the laser room in section nine. "Mr. Pyle, where were you expected to go?"

"Below to Level 4."

"Which stairs?"

"He didn't say, but . . ."

The east ladder was far closer, and it was the wrong way; to get to it Pyle should pass through to section seven, not nine. On the other hand, Stanger had a lot on his mind, and might not notice. "We'll try it."

Cautiously, I peered into the corridor. No officer in sight. "Lift Philip to that bunk. Let's go."

"Let me stay with him." Jared.

"No. He's as safe here as anywhere, and we need you."

He frowned, but gave a reluctant nod. "Your chair?"

"It's too obvious." As if my Admiral's uniform wasn't, or my pair of canes. I tried standing without them; it was just possible. If we were seen, I'd thrust them aside, hope some-how to brazen it out. Not a great plan, but from the start my attempt to seize *Galactic* had been an act of desperation, with little chance of success.

We went out to the corridor.

Pyle's eye searched for Mikhael's length of service pins, found none. "What ship?"

"*Melbourne.*" Mikhael blushed. It had been his father's. Now *Melbourne* was off to Titan, on one of the tourist cruises that so annoyed interstellar Captains. Though this cruise, with the holo star Anton Bourse aboard, would be something special.

I hobbled to the sealed section hatch. At the panel, a caller waited. "Pyle, tell him—"

"Now hear this. Seafort, this is for you."

A voice tinged with fear. *"Mr. Seafort? Cadet Bevin re-*

porting. They say they'll execute us for piracy unless you—"
The speaker clicked off.

"Pick up the caller, Seafort. Do it now."

I shoved Pyle. "Get us past the bloody hatch!"

He keyed the bridge. "Midshipman Pyle, sir. Please open the section nine hatch so I can go below." He listened. "Thank you."

The hatch slid open.

I growled, "Where's the laser room?"

"At the far end of the section." Just past the corridor bend. "Sir, who's with us? How many Marines do you—"

Pyle had helped us; I saw no reason to distrust him. "None."

He gaped. "But they attacked with lasers. Whom did you bring?"

My smile was grim. "A few friends." In his ill-fitting middy uniform, Jared flushed with pride.

"Two minutes, Seafort."

"Pyle, run ahead to the laser room. Report back."

"Aye aye, sir." He dashed off.

If we held the laser room, we had a chance. With the engine room to power the lasers, we could counteract the threat from Earthport and Lunapolis. As much as I dreaded civil war, I wouldn't allow civilians on Earth to be bombed.

In a moment Pyle was back. "We—I mean Captain Stanger—has the laser room blockaded. Lieutenant Garrow is in charge. There's no sign of your joeys. Are they inside?"

They must be, if Stanger had the compartment under siege.

I spotted a caller by a hatch panel, keyed it to the laser room.

A cool voice. "Lieutenant Sanders."

"Hon?"

"Nick! I mean, Captain."

"Sanders?" It was no time to ask, but I wondered why she'd used her unmarried name.

"It's how I was known in the Service." Calm, but with a bite. She must think me glitched, for bringing it up at this juncture.

"Very well. Your situation?"

"Fifteen of us. We burned through the hatch. I had Fahren reseal the door by laser-welding it. It won't hold long."

"The laser techs?"

"Bound and under watch, sir."

"The rest of your squad?"

"Three killed. The others went with Bevin and Anselm as a rear guard."

"*One minute left, Seafort. I have every right to execute them, and I will.*"

"And Derek?"

She said, "He's with us."

"Target Earthport Naval Station and the Naval warrens in Lunapolis. Open fire if you don't hear from me within an hour." My words came fast. "Defend the laser room, but surrender before you're killed."

"Aye aye, sir." A hesitation. "I believe that decision belongs to the commander on the scene."

"Obey orders, Lieutenant." I wouldn't let her sacrifice herself for naught.

"Aye aye, sir."

"Pyle, take these middies back to the wardroom, flank. Stay there until I call or come for you."

"But, sir—"

"Four demerits!" I was out of time. Deflated, Pyle led Jared and Mikhael back to the wardroom. As they ran off I keyed the caller. "Captain Seafort to bridge."

A voice I didn't know. "Just a moment, sir, for the Captain."

Stanger. "Ah, there you are. Your cadet was a tad worried."

"You are relieved."

"Goofjuice. I have the support of the Senate, of SecGen Valera, of the Patriarchy."

"I am head of Lord God's Government."

"It's debatable. Valera's nullified your proclamation. U.N.A.F.'s falling in line. You'll be impeached in a few hours. Just a moment. *Mr. Garrow, Seafort's at the section eight corridor hatch. Seize him.*"

"Take warning! Harm my cadet and I'll hang you myself. I swear to Lord God!" I slammed down the caller.

No time. No place to run. The hatch behind me was closed. I blundered to the nearest compartment. It was locked. The next.

It was the lift. I hammered at the call button. A light blinked.

Around the bend, voices. Garrow's patrol was coming for me.

Slowly, the hatch slid open. I staggered in, slapped the hatch panel.

The hatch began to slide. A shower of sparks, a searing burst of heat as someone fired a laser. Screaming, I lurched aside, slammed the first Level indicator I saw. The smoking hatch shut. The lift dropped.

Level 2. We plummeted downward. My eyes bulged. Level 3. Desperately, I hung on to my canes, as the full weight of Terra descended onto me.

Level 6. Somehow, I was still standing. Inch by inch, I dragged myself along the corridor. The pain was beyond belief. My legs were virtually useless; I doubted I could stand unaided.

The engine room was at the end of section nine. I'd blocked the lift hatch with my jacket, all I could manage. Stanger's crew would have to use the ladder in section seven. It gained me a few moments.

I dragged myself toward the engine room.

The corridor speaker came to life. *"Please, Mr. Seafort!*

Oh, God, please answer!" Danil Bevin, near tears. *"I'm begging you!"*

I tried not to retch. Minutes passed into hours, into days. I felt a sickly pallor. Sweating, faint, I moved at a snail's pace.

The engine-room hatch was ajar. I worked my way through. Two ratings stood by their panels.

"STAND AT ATTENTION!" I'd intended my tone to be harsh, but the haze of agony made it something more. They leaped to their feet. "Where's Chief McAndrews?"

"In the brig, sir." One of the sailors broke position to wipe his brow. I didn't blame him; I wanted to do the same, but didn't dare let go of a cane.

"Where are the gravitron controls?"

"In the electronics compartment, sir."

"Show me."

Nervously, he led the way.

Three series of boxes, with cables snaking from one to another. Chief McAndrews had said he couldn't adjust the controls.

Very well.

"A torch! Move, damn you!" I made an effort to control my voice, but my spine wouldn't have it. The rating ran to a locker, returned with a cutting unit. "That panel. Melt through the lid."

"Sir, I can't damage a gravitron, the Captain will—"

I shrieked, "I'll hang you! Do it this very second! I'm in command!"

It was too much for him. He aimed the torch. In a moment, the panel glowed. Alarms wailed. Lights blinked urgently. At last, the cover melted through. I had him play the flame on the circuitry within. A shower of sparks. He flinched, but they subsided harmlessly.

"Now the next." One by one, I had him melt through the panels. The alarms redoubled.

Suddenly, the pressure on my spine lessened. In a moment, it was gone. I pushed down on my canes, floated off the deck. Thank You, Lord. I couldn't have lasted much longer.

A horrid mess I'd left the Chief, but it could be repaired. If I'd damaged the gravitrons themselves, a lifetime of pay wouldn't reimburse the cost.

The engine-room console caught my eye. I pushed off from a bulkhead, snagged it. Wrapping an arm around the chair, I keyed in my ID code. "Baron!"

"Puter responding. Voicerec of Captain Seafort."

"Erase the frozen copy of the Log I told you to show the bridge. Substitute the real Log." Stanger knew I was aboard, and what I was up to. No need to hide it. "And while you're at it, disable bridge communication with—"

"There he is!" I glanced to the corridor. Hatches were open for as far as I could see. A squad of angry sailors worked their way from handhold to handhold toward the engine room.

"Bridge communication cannot be disabled. I'm hard-wired to allow—"

I pushed off with my canes toward the hatch. I made it through, ricocheted from bulkhead to deck to overhead, until I got the hang of it. Then I moved with surprising speed.

Zero gee narrowed the odds. Now all I had to contend with was Stanger's vast numbers, against my one.

Section ten. I caromed off a bulkhead, straightened my course. The canes were actually rather an advantage; I didn't have to be close to a surface to make headway.

Section eleven.

One sailor was more adept at zero gee than the rest. Slowly he gained on me, brandishing a stunner.

Section twelve. The west ladder. Like a mutant spider, I kicked and clawed my way. The sailor was breathing down my back.

He launched himself from a handhold. I stabbed with the cane, just touched a bulkhead, floated aside. As he passed I elbowed him viciously in the face. He bounced off the bulkhead, floated unmoving. I tugged the stunner from his unresisting hand, set the safety, shoved it in my belt.

Pulling myself up the ladder rail, I worked my way up to Level 5. Passengers blocked the top of the stairs, drifting helplessly, calling for help. Why the devil weren't they in their cabins? Even Stanger had ordered them out of the way.

Ignoring their pleas, their questions, I shoved them aside in growing fury. When the way was clear I swam upward to Level 4.

Half a dozen sailors with billies clung to the top of the rail. I tucked my canes under my arm, launched myself at them, leading with my stunner. Two came at me; the rest scattered.

I caught one in the forehead. A galvanized flop, and he floated past, inert. I'd killed him. Stunners were meant for the body, not the brain.

The second joey swung his club in a whistling arc. Lack of gravity weakened the blow. The recoil drove him upward with the same force it drove me down.

It was enough to numb my shoulder. I flipped the stunner to my left hand, kicked off the bulkhead. In midair, he was unable to escape. I left him twitching.

My way was clear. Upward, to three. The pain was returning, despite zero gee. I tried not to use my feet to propel myself, but it made the going slower.

The rasp of breath, over the speakers. "*Lieutenant Sanders to Captain Seafort. We've broken out.*"

Bless you, love. You saw a chance, and took it. The ship must be in chaos. Sailors were given zero-gee drills, but not that many. On the other hand, lasers fired just as well regardless of gees. Clever of you to announce your move over the speaker. No doubt Stanger already knew you'd fought free, so you used the opportunity to tell me as well.

Where would she head?

The galley. Level 2. Just what I had in mind.

*   *   *

The dining hall was brightly lit. I kicked off with my canes, floated through the hatch.

"Get him!" Figures moved. I was pinned in a crossfire, if they chose to shoot.

"BELAY THAT!" Arlene's voice was a scream. "Hold!" She showed herself from behind a pillar. "Captain!"

For her sake, I couldn't say what I yearned to. "Lieutenant." I tried to make my nod casual. "How many left?"

"Eleven, sir." Her eyes never left mine.

"Did you disable the lasers?"

"No, I thought you might need them against Earthport Naval Base."

A terrible error, but no time to say so. "Send a squad to force the brig. It's around the corridor bend. They'll have it guarded. Free Chief McAndrews."

"Aye aye, sir." No questions. Just an officer, doing her duty. "You, Tyrol. Bennett. Peng. Fall in." They couldn't do it literally, in zero gee, but they pushed forward, toward the hatch. All were armed with lasers.

She took them outside. "We'll go handhold by handhold to that cabin." She pointed. "Then we'll launch across the corridor to the far bulkhead. We'll have a view of the brig. Fire when you have a target. No sounds."

"Aye aye, ma'am."

Within the dining hall, we waited.

Shrieks, from the corridor. The crackle of lasers. Minutes later, Arlene kicked through the hatch. "Lieutenant Sanders reporting, sir. Two down." She sounded shaken. "We took the brig. They only had four guarding it. They're dead."

Behind her, the bulky form of the Chief. His face was battered. "Sorry, sir. The engine room has too many hatches." He'd been overwhelmed.

"Arlene, you took three men."

"Peng is coming." Four sailors appeared in the hatch. One

was Peng, his laser aimed. "These joeys say they're with you, sir."

"Mr. Tobrok." My face lit. Two ratings trailed the master-at-arms.

"We never had a chance. They were waiting at the comm room with lasers."

"I understand." For Comm Specialist Panner, there'd be a reckoning. To Arlene, "Can we hold either the engine room or the laser room?"

"Not the laser room. The hatch is useless."

"Pardon, sir." McAndrews. "In my stores I have plates to reinforce the hatch, and all the tools you'd need. But I doubt we could get to them."

"Why not?"

His bruised face brightened. "You took out the gravitrons, didn't you? Stanger will want them on-line, flank. Lord knows how many joeys he's got working down there."

"He won't get them on-line from the engine room."

"That bad?"

I nodded.

"He'll bypass the controls, then. Activate the direct power lines. Still, I imagine he'll post guards at my hatches so we can't make more trouble."

"Arlene—Lieutenant Sanders can take them out."

"Not forever, sir." She looked glum. "I lose men each time, and we don't have many."

"Sir." Derek Carr.

I turned to him. "You're alive."

"More or less." His knee was soaked with blood. "May I ask the plan?"

I closed my eyes, savoring the sour taste of defeat. "Evacuation." Stanger was too strong, too organized.

"How?"

"We'll seize a launch." One of the four launch bays was reached from Level 1, where Jared, Philip, and Mikhael hid in the wardroom.

"Just a moment."

I bridled. Chief McAndrews knew better than to talk to a Captain so, even in a crisis. Especially in a crisis.

"You'll let him steal the ship?" He rubbed his swollen face. "And take my engine room?"

I said, "Have we a choice?"

"What's changed since you came aboard?"

Derek said quietly, "It was hopeless from the start. Why give up now?"

"Be silent, Lieutenant." A gallant, futile charge was a noble idea, but I wouldn't see Philip killed to no purpose. Or my wife.

"Sir, may I speak?" Arlene.

"Yes."

"*Galactic* is the key. It's the only ship taking part in the rebellion. Her lasers can devastate North America and Europe, or they could—"

"I know that."

"Pardon, please let me finish. Or they could be turned on Earthport and quell the mutiny. If we lose *Galactic*, we lose our U.N. Government. Stanger's ilk will take over. If they do, the enviro cause is finished. There'll be a Naval dictatorship, in fact if not in name. The Patriarchs will eliminate the last freedom of relig—"

"So?"

"Would you die to prevent it?"

I said, "Yes."

She took a deep breath. "So would I."

One can't pace in zero gee. I flailed at nothing, until I drifted up to the overhead, and deflected myself. "I'd give my life to defeat Stanger. But I don't want to die in a useless gesture. I'm out of ideas."

"Get me into my engine room." McAndrews. "I'll find you torches to cut through the bridge hatch. The big ones, with the power cables."

"Four Levels down, then we'd have to fight our way back

up. And Stanger won't sit idly while we burn our way into the bridge."

Arlene glowered. "Damn it, sir, it's better than nothing!"

"That's quite enough, Lieutenant Sanders!" She fell silent. At that moment, I didn't think either of us remembered she was my wife.

Master-at-arms Tobrok said, "Captain, there's a way to— look out!" He hurled me aside. I sailed across the dining hall. So did he, the opposite direction. I fetched up against the far bulkhead.

"Thank God I found you." It was a hoarse whisper. Midshipman Edwin Speke. "May I come in?" He pushed off from a bulkhead, snagged a chair, wrapped his legs around it.

"Where the hell have you been?" I was past niceties.

"Hiding." He blushed beet red. "It happened so fast. Outside the laser room they came on us from the rear, and took the cadets and Jensen. Hickley was shot, and the other joey. I ducked into the purser's cabin before they saw me. They had lasers and I didn't." He took breath. "Then you were gone from the galley. I was afraid Captain Stanger knew I'd gone over to you, so I couldn't . . ." A look of mute appeal. "I'm sorry."

"Very well, you're back. Any weapons?"

"Just the billy club."

Before we raided the brig Arlene had eleven men, but she'd lost two. I'd joined her, and now the middy. And we had Tobrok's squad. Philip, Jared, and Mikhael made eighteen, if we could reach them. Nineteen, with Midshipman Pyle.

"Very well. The wardroom, to get P.T. and Jared, then we'll attack the engine room. Get organized."

"Sir?"

"Not now, Derek." A foray onto Level 1 would be risky. Should I send the whole party, or only a few. If—

"Sir!" Hands on hips, he floated just off the deck. His

blazing eyes scorched any humor from the situation. "You *will* listen!"

"What, then?" I'd deal with his insubordination later.

"Doesn't the wardroom have a caller?"

I opened my mouth to reply, found nothing to say. I gawped like a fish. "Well. Yes. Um." My ears burned. "Arlene, give them a call. Have whatshisname, the real middy . . . Pyle. Have him check the corridor. If it's safe, send them down. Meet them at the ladder."

"The real middy?"

"It's a long story. Go."

She kicked off to the galley caller.

The east ladder was unguarded. Stanger couldn't think of everything.

Finally, we were together again. I embraced Philip, then Mikhael. Jared seemed a natural third. I drew the line at Pyle.

The middy looked about. "Pardon, sir, is this all of us?"

"Yes."

He gazed from one to the other. "You attacked *Galactic*, half wrecked her, with . . . civilians?" He shook his head in wonder.

We girded ourselves to assault the engine room.

Arlene distributed our remaining lasers among us. We had few recharge packs, just those we'd salvaged from the enemy. Cautiously, we made our way along deserted corridors. The emergency corridor hatches were open; apparently zero gee and closed hatches were too difficult a combination for Stanger's untrained crew.

Galactic had a crew of eight hundred; where the devil were they hiding? Not at the east ladder. We pulled ourselves down. I worked mostly with my canes, that had become admirable zero-gee tools.

At Level 4 we met resistance. Tobrok and Derek took aim

with their lasers. They missed, but abruptly the stairwell was deserted. We hurried past the landing.

We worked our way down to Level 6. The engine room was in section nine. We advanced. Section seven. Then eight. Mikhael had the most trouble moving in zero gee; I stayed near, gave him a hand when I could.

We were in the midst of eight, propelling ourselves to nine, when abruptly the hatches closed. The long-silent speakers came to life. *"We have them trapped on Level 6, section eight! All sailors who've been issued arms, assemble outside the engine room!"*

Instantly Arlene snatched a laser from Speke's hand, slapped it in mine.

"What are you—"

Gripping the handhold, she gave me a mighty shove toward the section seven hatch. She launched herself after. I braked myself with my canes, nearly tearing out my arm sockets. Arlene seized a handhold, aimed her pistol at the hatch seal from close range. Mikhael, in his stolen midshipman's uniform, hauled himself laboriously toward us. The rest of us dived into cabins, behind whatever cover they found handy. Philip shoved Jared behind him, aimed coolly at the hatch to section nine. He waited for the enemy to appear.

The section eight hatch seal smoked and sputtered in the relentless beam of Arlene's laser. "Come on, God damn you!"

I muttered, "Don't blaspheme." It was unthinking. She paid no heed.

The seal gave way. Grunting with effort, she forced the hatch panels apart. "Move, Nick!" She blocked a panel with a foot, used her freed hand to shove me through. With a cry of alarm, Mikhael thrust himself after.

"What will you—"

"Save yourself, Captain! I love you." She glanced at her

laser; it still had a charge. She kicked off to defend the entry to nine. Unimpeded, the corridor hatch slammed shut.

Mikhael clung to me. "Get us out of here!"

I shook him off. "Steady, son."

"Hurry!"

I was hurrying, but to where? My voice was dull. "The laser room." As a last gesture, I would disable the lasers. I pulled myself along the handholds. "Mikhael, it's over. I'll put you in a cabin. When things quiet down, surrender. They won't harm you." I devoutly hoped it was true.

"I'm staying with you."

My heart was leaden. "No." Arlene was likely dead, and Philip. I would join them. But not by my own hand. I might, with great fortune, surprise the laser-room guards. And the hatch couldn't be defended.

We took the ladder to five. No one stopped us. I hammered on the first cabin hatch I came to. No response. I remembered the corridor panel, slapped the hatch open. "Mikhael, inside." I pushed him through. "Don't make a sound. Wait until—"

A wiry form swarmed atop him, flailed with fists and feet. A blow caught Mikhael in the forehead. Fingers clawed at his eyes. "Out of my cabin! Out!" The frantic passenger caromed off a bulkhead, launched himself anew. "You frazzing—" He slammed Mikhael into the bulkhead. "Get—"

I drew my pistol, fired, caught him square in the chest. A bubbling sound. Clots of blood spewed forth. I grabbed Mikhael by the scruff of the neck, threw him into the corridor. I slapped the hatch shut, and drifted, shaking from adrenaline.

Mikhael kicked desperately at the far bulkhead, shot back across the corridor. With a squeal of terror he wrapped himself around me. I tried to pull free. One of my canes went sailing off. I wrenched at his fingers. "Mikhael . . ." No use. He was a straitjacket. I bellowed, "LET GO THIS IN-STANT! BEHAVE YOURSELF!"

"I'm scared, Pa!"

"STOP THAT SNIVELING!"

It shocked him into letting go. He recoiled. I snatched his arm before he could drift off. "Easy, son. I'll take care of you."

"Oh, God!"

"Fetch my cane." Carefully, I shoved him in the right direction. He snatched it as he sailed past, bounced off a bulkhead. With the cane as an oar, he managed to propel himself back to me. His face was ashen.

There was no time. But if nothing mattered, everything did. "Do you need a hug?"

"Yessir."

I swept him into an embrace, squeezed as if to crush the life from him. After a long while, the tension oozed from his body. He rested a hand on my shoulder, buried his head under my chin. A sound, that might have been a sob.

After a time I held him away. "You all right now?"

Unable to meet my eyes, he nodded.

"Good lad. Let's go." I pushed off, a firm grip on his arm. We worked our way upward toward the laser room.

"Seafort, it's over." Captain Stanger. *"We have a few of your survivors. There's no one loose except you. Turn yourself in."*

"I'll see you in Hell." Had I spoken aloud? I wasn't sure. We labored up the ladder to Level 3.

"Pa?"

"Yes, son?"

"I'm so scared I can't think."

"We all are."

In the corridor, near the stairs, three sailors maneuvered a cart with electronic gear. I brandished my laser. They fled. Their abandoned cart drifted idly in midair.

Level 2.

"I want—" Mikhael's breath shuddered. "I want to say this while I can." He helped me around the landing. "I know you're not really my father. But . . ." He squirmed with embarrassment. "I wish you were."

"Don't ever say that." Alexi's reproachful face floated beyond the bulkhead.

"I'm sorry for all the stupid things I did. I know I'd never mean to you what P.T. does, but that's all right." He clutched my arm. "That's what I wanted to say. It's all right."

I should reproach him, but I couldn't. Not after he'd unwrapped his soul. "Thank you." It was a whisper.

"You're going away." It was more statement than question.

"I'm going to die now, yes." Strangely, I felt peace.

"How can I—"

"There he is!"

I whipped up my laser, fired without aim. A yelp, a shower of sparks. With one cane I launched myself up the ladder. A shadow. I fired.

"Get him, Middy!"

They let off a shot that wasn't even close. The bulkhead blistered. I grasped the rail, hurled myself upward with a vigorous shove. I rocketed past the landing, firing as I slammed into the overhead. A screech. More shots.

Silence.

I'd lost most of my momentum. Helpless in midair, I waited for inertia, in slow motion, to carry me to a bulkhead.

Mikhael kicked off, caught me, transferring his inertia. Together we sailed into the stairwell landing. I snatched a handhold, propelled myself to the ladder.

One more Level.

"How can I help, Pa?"

"You can't. I want to save you."

"No." His voice was tremulous. "I'll help."

Years past, I'd offered P.T. his death. Gladly he'd joined me in the launch to brave the lasers of Earthport.

It was my fate to annihilate the youngsters who laid their trust at my feet.

"You're sure, son?"

"Yes, sir." He looked down at his pants, and blushed.

Level 1. Here, the corridor hatches were sealed. Voices. Instinctively, I thrust Mikhael down the ladder.

"Got him!" A laser rifle, aimed unwaveringly at my chest. "No, you frazzin' grode, push yourself up. Let go the laser!"

I'd be dead before I could raise my pistol. Bleakly, I did as he told. Three of them, all armed. But only one laser; the other joeys had stunners and billies.

"Stand at attention, all of you!" The voice was ice. A very young middy launched himself from the ladder.

One tried to stiffen, realized he couldn't in zero gee. The others gawked. "Who are you, sir?"

"Midshipman Tamarov. I'm new." The voice was proud. "You caught him? Wonderful. I'll take him to the Captain." He held out his hand. "Hand over the rifle."

"Sir, I'd better—"

"That was an order."

Discipline was a reflex. "Aye aye, sir." Edging away from me, the sailor handed Tamarov his rifle.

"Come here, you." The middy hauled me closer. "You joeys, Lieutenant Garrow needs help in the galley. Give him a hand."

"If this one gets away . . ."

"I'll be the one gets the caning."

It brought nervous smiles. "Aye aye, sir." They retreated down the ladder.

When they were gone, Mikhael thrust the rifle into my arms. "I think I'll be sick!"

"No, you won't." Casually, I squeezed his shoulder, gave him a reassuring pat, as if his courage were no more than I expected. "The laser room's in section nine. Let's go."

At the corridor hatch to eight, I aimed the rifle, fired into the seals. Alarms screamed. I fired again, higher. Mikhael forced open the panels. We squeezed through.

"Fast as you can!" One section to go. I shouldered the

rifle. Using my canes as ski poles, I bounced off bulkheads and deck.

The rifle still had charge. I raised it, began firing many meters from the section hatch. The seals smoked, melted. A panel buckled. Mikhael dived to grab it.

"Careful, the metal's hot."

Cautiously, he forced open the corridor hatch. I pushed through, firing as I went. A face ducked behind a cabin hatch. Passenger or sailor? No matter; I couldn't take the chance. I fired into the bulkhead. From behind, a moan.

I strained to reach a handhold, worked my way onward with desperate haste. Alarms shrieked. Stanger knew exactly where I was.

Outside the laser room, three guards. Only one faced my way. At the same instant, we fired. Heat kissed my boot; the deck under me smoked and sizzled. The guard dissolved in a burst of blood and flame. I yelped, kicked away from the heat. A warning beep. I fired again, caught a bulkhead. Fiery droplets splashed a sailor's face. He bounced screaming from bulkhead to deck. The third guard fled.

My rifle glowed empty. With a savage curse I hurled it along the corridor, pulled out my pistol. Thrusting Mikhael into a supply compartment, I launched myself at the ruined laser-room hatch.

Inside, frozen with fear, three techs.

I pushed off, sailed to a chair bolted to the deck. "GET OUT!"

They clawed at each other in their haste to reach the corridor.

Two rows of laser consoles, each with its simulscreen and radionics. In battle, every chair would be manned.

No time for subtlety. Steadying myself with my canes, I took aim at the first console, pressed the trigger. The console glowed, burst into flame. Alarms wailed.

The second. I would need a recharge, to disable them all.

The third.

"Move and I'll kill you." A low voice, deadly. One I knew.

Slowly, I turned my head. It couldn't be. But it was.

Karen Burns.

I meant to swing my laser. I wanted to. Instead, turned to a pillar of salt, I gaped, uncomprehending.

"Don't even twitch, Seafort." Her pistol was aimed and ready, the charge light green and unwavering.

"What are—how did—my God!"

"Eloquent." Her pistol moved, in a suggestion. "Put the laser down."

"Why are you on ship?"

"You never had a clue, did you?" A harsh chuckle. "Bet you thought I was one of those Eco League loonies."

"Aren't you?"

"Stanger's rather annoyed; you led us a merry chase. Set down the pistol, or I'll blow your arm off. I'd just as soon kill you, but the Captain wants a public execution."

"Shoot." My laser remained at my side. I would have answers. "The Eco League was against supporting the Navy. If you're not with them, what were you doing?" My knuckles tightened on my canes.

"The ecos were too timid. They needed prodding; I was glad to help. The Rotunda bomb got things moving. It was a win-win situation. Either you'd be dead, and we'd have Valera's support for the Navy, or you'd survive, and you'd have no choice but to crack down on the enviros." A frown. "Only you didn't. Somehow, you kept the lid on. Damned if I know how, but you were doing it. We had to escalate."

"By kidnapping me? Why?"

"You were rounding up sweet Sara and her joeys. They didn't know my name, but they'd seen me. I was out of time, so we went after you. If I'd gotten you out of the compound, we had a groundcar waiting, and eventually a shuttle. We'd have brought you here. If I succeeded, we'd have the power of your proclamations at our disposal. How the *hell* did you get out of that closet? You can't walk."

"I teleported. Why, Karen? What was the point?"

"Ultimately, to restore the Navy. You knew that. For a time, we even hoped you'd join us. Keep your hand quite still."

I did. "So why bomb my compound?"

"Even you can figure that out. You wouldn't work with us, and you were in the way."

They'd won. Utterly, completely, with finality. The United Nations would be no more. The Navy, in its arrogance, would rule the worlds.

"And Booker?"

"Dead. A weakling. Such pangs of remorse. He'd have given us all away."

"Barcelona?"

"The call? Faked."

We'd been gulled, down the line. I steeled myself. There was nothing left. Only useless revenge. The safety was off; I had only to let go the cane, whirl, fire. If I took her with me ... To distract her, I asked, "How did you get here?"

"I found a woman who looked like me and borrowed her ID. She was U.N.A.F., but it got me to Earthport." Her smile was cruel. "And then I called Stanger."

Numbly, I reached for an ancient rite. *Hail Mary, full of grace* ...

Karen's eyes narrowed. Her pistol steady as a rock, she reached for a chair to steady herself.

Abruptly I felt it too. Slowly, the deck came up to meet me. Reflexively, I threw out my canes, caught myself. My laser skittered along the deck.

I began to grow heavy.

I was too far from a console to reach it. In seconds we were at a full gee, Terran standard, as the bow gravitrons came on-line. Beads of sweat popped from my skin. Desperately, I clung to my canes. Somehow, balanced, I remained on my feet, but white fire clawed at my spine. I breathed in shallow gasps.

"Why, Mr. Seafort." Her voice was a purr. "You have difficulty standing? You've been to Dr. Ghenili?"

I gritted my teeth.

"All crew to the Level 2 dining hall. Machinist's mates, report only when you've restored midship and aft gravitrons." Stanger.

Karen made as if to push me. I flinched, expecting to break in half.

A lithe form hurtled from the corridor. It leaped onto her back. She staggered. Fighting to stay erect, I could do no more than watch. Mikhael snaked a forearm around her throat, squeezed with all his might.

With a convulsive lunge, she threw him off. A paralyzing chop to the shoulder. A kick to his stomach; he squealed and clutched himself.

Coolly, Karen glanced to me, saw I was no threat. She hauled Mikhael to his feet. Methodically, brutally, she began to beat him. Panting with exertion, she drove blows into his ribs, stomach, chest. Her fists hammered his face.

"Stop it!" My voice was hoarse.

A vicious blow to the gut; Mikhael's spittle flew. His face was deathly green.

I tried to take a step. Lightning surged along my spine. I gasped.

Mikhael sagged, semiconscious.

"Don't, I beg you! Let him be. I'll do whatever you want!"

"He jumped me." With a grip of iron she held him against the bulkhead, slamming her fist into his side, his stomach, his groin. "I don't like that."

"Karen, for God's sake—"

Blows to the face. A backhand across his mouth that was a rifle shot. Another.

At last, she let go. Mikhael slid senseless to the deck. His blood oozed.

She sucked air into her lungs, until her breathing eased. "Now, where were we?"

I dared say nothing. Only white-hot rage held off the all-consuming pain. If I opened my mouth it might all come rushing out, and engulf the laser room. With tremendous effort, I held myself erect.

She reached to a console, keyed the caller. "Bridge, Lieutenant Burns reporting. I've got him, Captain. He's helpless; he can't walk in gravity. Where do you want him?"

A pause. Idly, she turned her back, covered one ear. Ignoring what passed beyond agony, I eased more weight onto my left foot.

"Aye aye, sir. He's in bad shape; I might have to carry him. It'll be a few minutes."

She replaced the caller. "He'll let you witness the exec—"

I flipped my right-hand cane, caught it by the toe. As I fell, I whipped it around in a vicious arc. The handgrip slammed into her temple.

She toppled to the deck. I crashed nearby. Something wrenched. My legs drummed convulsively. I clenched my teeth, desperate not to bite off my tongue. The pain was beyond horrid.

A ghastly sound. Mine.

Silence.

To my dismay, Karen struggled slowly to her knees; I hadn't hit her hard enough. I'd never get another chance. "You . . . fucking . . . son of a bitch." Her words were slurred. She groped for her pistol.

The safety was on. She clawed at it, shook her head, froze as if listening. A moan. She clutched her temples, rocked back and forth. Tormented eyes met mine. Her hand came away from her ear, red and dripping. Slowly, as if in a dream, she pitched forward onto her face. Blood poured from both ears. Massive cerebral hemorrhage. A pity.

I tried to retreat from the spreading pool. A lance of fire. Somehow, I hunched onto my elbows, waited for the red haze to dissipate. I dragged myself toward the hatch. Mikhael slumped against the bulkhead, as if asleep. His breath was shallow and ragged. His face was pasty.

I inched toward Karen's pistol. There were consoles to burn. I clasped it in a deathly grip.

The speaker crackled. *"Lieutenant Burns, bring him to the dining hall. We're waiting."*

Why the dining hall? Executions were held in the engine room, were they not? Or was it just the way I'd done it as Captain? I lay dreaming.

I'm sorry, Lord God. You pushed me too far. I can do no more, and I don't think I care. I hate them. Stanger, Admiral Hoi, Karen. No, she's dead. Still I hate her. Perhaps I hate You.

A sob. I bit it back. Slowly, shuddering with each motion, I raised myself to my knees. Trying not to scream, I reached back, dragged one leg forward. Then the other.

I couldn't do this.

Crooning mindlessly, I hunched my way to the bulkhead, leaned against it. Try again. It was easier, marginally, if I gave some of my weight to its panels. Pistol tucked into my belt, my shoulder rubbing the alumalloy, I worked my way on my knees to the hatch. My legs wouldn't lift; dragging one cane, I had to raise them by hand.

Outside. Along the deserted corridor.

It took forever.

We have sinned, we have sinned grievously, we are a sinner, we repent our sins . . . You don't listen. Perhaps You never did. Why, then, do I do this? Duty? Oh, Jesus, that hurt. Breathe. Hold a moment. What is duty without You? Well, perhaps You listen, now and then. But why don't You ever *answer*?

I'm sorry, I think. To tell truth, I'm not sure.

A head poked out of a cabin. A passenger. Her eyes fastened on mine, ducked away. The hatch slammed closed.

I inched past an exercise room. Scorched carpet, a stench that made me gag. Foot by endless foot, I crawled, the bulkhead my constant friend. My hand ached from the effort of dragging my useless legs.

The brig. Tobrok was there, was he not? No, he was dead, with Arlene and Philip. Or awaiting execution. I'd bullied him into a fight that was not his.

On my endless journey, I crawled past the master-at-arms' hatch.

Wait, Seafort. You're forgetting something.

Yes, you're forgetting it's hopeless. You've lost. You're crawling to see Arlene's purple tongue, your son's final twitch.

No. Something else.

Reaching cautiously with the cane, I punched the hatch panel, over my head. I didn't know what I sought. Inside, the console, where I'd met Tobrok. Beyond, cells. A chair. No more.

On my way again.

Wait. The chair. Unlike those at the laser consoles, it rolled.

This will hurt, Lord. Will You— No. You won't. I clutched the console with one hand, took a few breaths, let go the deck with the other. Hanging from the console, I raised myself slowly, as if trying to kneel.

I learned what Hell would be, so very soon. No worse than now.

Sweating from every pore, I inched toward the chair. My biceps strained. I drew myself up, bent over the console as if for a caning. My vision blurred.

Carefully, so cautiously, I inched backward. I wouldn't be able to do this more than once. In fact, I wasn't sure that even once—

The chair, at the edge of my slacks. Another inch. Another.

I hummed to myself, eyes squeezed shut. The brig was unbearably hot. After a time I blinked, tried to focus.

My shirt was soaked through.

But I sat in the chair.

With care, I reached down, grappled for my cane. If I pushed against the deck . . . no, from that angle, so. And again.

Like a deranged lover in an ancient canoe, I paddled my way down the corridor.

The carpet made it slow going.

"—to death for piracy and murder. The sentence will now be carried out."

Paddle, Seafort. Don't get your feet wet. Lord God won't like it. In a tippy canoe, with Saythor too . . .

I snapped awake. I was almost to the dining-hall hatch. A final lunge, that made me cough bile. I couldn't do that often.

I was in the hatchway. The dining-hall aisle was blocked by rows of sailors, lined in the at-ease position, hands clasped smartly behind their backs.

Before them, Arlene stood dazed, blood matting her auburn hair. Derek lay slumped over a starched linen tablecloth. Their hands were tied behind, their mouths taped.

A middy, the young one who'd taken my demerits. A sailor, one of Tobrok's. All bound.

Tad Anselm, his cadet gray stained a dull maroon, swayed as if asleep on his feet. His eyes were dull, unfocused.

I was sitting on my pistol. I tugged at it, fought a wave of torment.

Two sailors held Jared Tenere, standing, on a sturdy table. A noose was tight around his neck, secured to an overhead panel. He kicked, twisted against his ropes, struggled frantically to escape. I yanked at the pistol; my weight held it in my belt.

Jared squealed through the skintape. I could hear it across the hall. He wrapped a leg around the sailor's, worked the bonds tying his hands. Blood dripped from his torn wrists.

Below, two burly sailors grappled with Philip. Gagged by skintape, he kicked and lunged in a desperate frenzy to reach Jared. His pleading eyes were fastened on his friend.

I wrenched loose the laser, keyed off the safety. At Stanger's nod, the sailors shoved Jared from the table. He dropped like a stone.

I fired, downing a crewman. Another, who held P.T.'s arms. His blood gushed. Dangling, Jared convulsed and was still. Sailors dived to the deck. Screams and shouted commands. Stanger's eyes met mine. I aimed. He ducked behind a pillar. I sprayed a wide arc where he'd stood.

Someone, braver than the rest, lunged at my chair. A mighty kick missed me but sent the chair hurtling out the hatch. The hatch slammed shut.

I fetched up against the far bulkhead. My back arched in a spasm. I whipped the laser in front of my face. Two-handed, I fired without cease. The hatch smoked and sizzled. A beep. I was out of charge.

In blind fury, I lunged with my cane, rolled myself east. I'd find another laser. I paddled past a section hatch.

"This is the Captain! Lieutenant Garrow, shut all corridor hatches. I'll use my override codes. Watch for me; I'll direct from the bridge. We'll execute the rebels when that maniac is dead."

Behind me, the hiss of a hatch. I turned. The dining hall. A sailor emerged, braver than most, or maddened by the carnage. He brandished a laser. His wild eyes found mine. The corridor hatch slid shut. He dived through, almost losing his legs. He scrambled to his feet.

My tone was like ice. "Drop it, joey." I aimed my empty laser at his face.

His eyes darted to his pistol, at his side.

"Do it and you'll die. Let it go." My voice had a ragged edge that frightened even me.

He swallowed. The laser fell to the deck.

"Turn around." He did. Laser in my lap, I paddled myself across the corridor. "Kneel, pick up the laser by the barrel, hand it behind you." I'd never be able to bend without passing out.

I fingered the second laser, turned off the safety.

"Will you kill me?" His voice quavered.

"I think so."

Kneeling, he crossed himself, bowed his head.

I came to my senses. I took my discharged laser, rapped him sharply behind the ear. He slumped to the carpet.

Section hatches were all shut. Even if I burned the seals, I had no strength to force them open.

I rolled past the airlock I'd torched foolish years ago, to help my marauders aboard. Stanger's crew hadn't had time to repair it; warning tape plastered the entry.

In a moment Stanger would reach the bridge to organize his manhunt. The crew would fan out, with merciless intent.

I had one goal left in life.

It was a long way to the end of section seven. How to force the Christ-damned corridor hatch? Meters away, I stared at it balefully.

No. There was another way.

Ignoring a blaze of pain, I paddled back the way I came.

To the damaged airlock. Only the outer hatch stood vigil against decompression.

Past it, to the suit locker alongside. I aimed my laser, burst the flimsy latch. Straining, I hauled down a suit from a hook above my head.

Now for the impossible part. I wrestled with the torso. Arms would be no problem, but my legs . . . ?

Gritting my teeth, I bent forward, worked the stiff suit leg over my own. I had to stop, lean against the cool alumalloy of the locker, wait for the pain to recede to a throb that threatened to suck the life from me.

Why hadn't they opened the corridor hatch to get at me? Were they waiting for Stanger to reach the safety of the bridge? For sailors to work their way around, attack me from both sides at once?

One leg. Now the other. When I was done, I would somehow have to stand, to seal the suit.

I mumbled curses under my breath, snatches of old songs, remnants of lessons Father had taught me years ago, over the worn Bible and the steaming pot of tea.

"Damn You, God, I can't do this alone."

The legs were on. I stretched into the torso. The helmet would wait, until I'd sealed the rest.

"Come up unto me, and help me, that we may smite Gibeon!"

What was I muttering? I no longer knew.

I paddled to the lock, keyed my pistol, fired into the porthole of the ruined inner hatch. The porthole dissolved. I took several breaths to steady myself. I hooked my arm through the opening, clenched my teeth, hauled myself up by sheer willpower. Oh, God. No. I can't stand it.

With my free hand I clawed desperately at the suit seals, clasped them tight.

Done, I eased myself back into the chair, tried not to black out. No time, Seafort. They're coming for you.

Back to the locker. Lift the helmet. Screw it on. The oxy bottle. Never mind its pouch; set it in your lap. Reach behind, tighten the clamps. Back to the lock.

I reached through the porthole, found the lever. My cutting torch had utterly destroyed the inner hatch; it slid easily. I rolled inside.

The outer hatch wouldn't open against air pressure, no matter what I did. And I had no way to seal the inner hatch. For a moment I hesitated, knowing of the passengers' lives that would be lost. But Stanger must be stopped, else his coterie would foment a dictatorship, crush the colonies, and imprison the billions trapped on Earth.

I aimed my laser at the porthole. It glowed, dripped. Alarms shrieked. Abruptly the porthole vanished. I bowed my head against the roar of escaping air.

All was silent, in the vacuum of the ship. Only my section was decompressed; Stanger had sealed all corridor hatches. Should I pray for the passengers I'd chosen to kill? No. It would be blasphemous.

There were few cabins near the dining hall. Perhaps their occupants had fled. Perhaps Stanger had relocated them, away from the danger of the lock. Perhaps . . .

I'd never know.

My breath rasped in my suit. I slapped open the outer hatch. With my cane, I pushed the chair far enough forward to grip a handhold. I launched myself outward.

The alloy hull negated the field of the gravitron; abruptly I was weightless. The pain in my spine diminished to a sullen volcano.

I switched on my hand magnets. My legs floating behind, I worked my way along the hull toward the bow. A hand at a time, trailing my cane, I inched forward.

Lord God knew what Stanger assumed at this point, or planned. I was trying to escape; that much he'd figured. Would he pursue me? Would he be glad to see the last of me?

I didn't know.

I no longer cared.

20

Slowly, laboriously, I passed from one huge disk to another. Alongside the Level 1 disk was one of *Galactic*'s giant launch bays. Hand by hand, I crawled toward it.

A lifetime later, I floated in front of a vast hatch that opened the bay to its launch. There was no way I could breach it.

But I had no need to. Alongside was a service hatch, for crewmen working on the bay.

I slapped the panel.

The hatch slid open.

Stanger hadn't thought of securing the bridge override. But then, why should he? For safety's sake, locks were left openable from Outside. What crewman would venture on a repair detail otherwise? To be abandoned in space, unable to gain entry . . . despite my misery, I shuddered.

I knew enough to crawl into the hatch in a prone position. Immediately, gravity pinned me to the deck. I reached up with my cane, slapped shut the hatch, waited for the lock to cycle. Panel lights flashed, at the lock and on the bridge.

Now Stanger knows you're here. I jabbed at the inner hatch. It slid open, just as the override light began to flash.

Stifling a moan, I forced myself to crawl through.

My helmet was fogged. With a curse, I tore it off. My laser was in my pouch. I clawed it free.

Crawl, Seafort. Let it hurt. It won't be for long.

The launch bay was immense, but I was near the safety lock that led to the Level 1 corridor. I squirmed my way across the deck, pulling my legs with my hands.

I passed to a realm beyond hurt. It helped me crawl faster. If I remembered, I would save one charge to blast myself to Hell. Satan could inflict no worse than I now endured.

Behind me, the launch sat gleaming and silent. They would assume I intended to steal it.

As I expected, the airlock sensor between the bay and Level 1 began to flash. I lay on the launch bay deck, waiting, my beam set to high. The inner hatch slid open. I sprayed the lock. Screams, muffled by suits. My laser beeped. One charge left. I clicked the safety.

"This is the Captain. He's in the launch bay. Panner, Gosset, assemble a squad of twenty and meet me in section seven; we'll end this. If you see him first, shoot to kill."

I crawled on, toward the lock. Into it.

Over a smoking body.

I jabbed the inner hatch. Both sides were pressurized; no need to cycle. The hatch opened.

The corridor.

I was near the bridge; that much I knew. But which direction was it?

West. It had to be west. I had no strength to be wrong.

The corridor was empty. That was to be expected; the crew had been sent to the dining hall. But someone would man the bridge. Garrow, Stanger had said. A lieutenant.

I used the tried and true bulkhead method, lifting one leg at a time with my hand. Admiral SecGen Seafort, practicing his distinguished crawl. Singing to himself. Reeking of the sweat of torment.

A lump on the decking ahead. No time to look. Move, Seafort. You're about played out.

I flopped the last few meters to the bridge.

Trembling, I lay on the deck plates, facing the sealed hatch.

To my right, a body, horribly burned. I could barely discern that the charred uniform was gray.

Sightless eyes, an unmarked face contorted in agony.

I made a sound.

My hand crept out, clasped the limp hand of my Danil Bevin.

Together, we lay in the corridor outside the bridge. From time to time I checked the safety of my laser, rechecked the charge.

I failed you so. I failed You. You were only a boy. I snatched you from Academy. I mocked You. I'm sorry, Danil. Or is it Lord? I'm very tired. Both of you.

You left him in my charge, and I destroyed him, as I destroy them all. Why didn't You stop me?

I patted Danil's cold wrist. All will be well. I'll get you a fresh set of grays. Tad will brush off the char.

Lord God, I hate You for not stopping me. Always, You could. You turned Your face from me, but why from him? He was one of Yours.

The corridor was silent and still.

My chin on the deck, I drowsed, a meter from the thick alloy bridge hatch. My pistol, in my right hand, aimed straight ahead. From time to time I toyed with the idea of turning it to my face, and joining Danil and Jason. If they'd have me.

Danil's voice piped. "Do you think—if I do well, could I be posted to *Galactic* when I make middy?"

The nerve of him. Well, I'd shown him. I'd granted his wish. He'd never be posted anywhere else.

Some of us are Satan's instruments.

Cast forth lightning, and scatter them: shoot out thine arrows, and destroy them.

One shot left. My finger tightened.

Hot knives twisted in my spine.

Danil slid to his knees at Jason's grave, his small form brushing mine. Have you met, you two? Will you speak of me? Will you revile me, as you should?

Reassuringly, I squeezed Danil's hand. I would resist the temptation to live. Slowly, the barrel of the pistol turned. It crept toward my eager mouth.

The bridge hatch slid open.

A pair of gleaming boots.

My wrist turned. I squeezed the trigger. The boots dissolved in a flash of fire.

A thud. Captain Stanger's cheek hit the deck. His eyes bulged. He shrieked. Flopping on the deck, over and again, he shrieked.

Someone slapped the panel. The hatch slid closed.

I lay on the throbbing deck, caressing Danil's hand.

"Captain Seafort?"

I made no answer.

"Sir, hold your fire. Please, sir."

I couldn't move. The torment in my back had passed to another state. I was mercifully numb.

"I read the Log, sir, when I entered the Captain's death. I want to come out. I'm unarmed. That is, I'll leave my pistol on the console. Do you hear me?"

I lay silent, my cheek on the cool deck. He could come out if he wished. My laser was discharged. All I could do was bite his toe.

The hatch slid open. I was eye to eye with Ulysses Stanger. His were dull, unmoving. Mine flinched.

From around the hatch, a head peeked. "Sir? Don't— Lieutenant Avram Garrow reporting for duty." The bulk of his body was shielded by the bulkhead.

Something stirred, calling me back from a great distance. "You knew."

"Knew what, sir?"

"What Stanger was up to." My laser sought him.

"We all—not really. He was Captain. What could we do?"

The ready excuse the Navy—all of us—wore as a protective garment. *Satan, get thee behind me.*

"Take responsibility. Relieve him."

"He had Admiralty's blessing, didn't he? They'd have hanged—"

"He had no such thing."

"May I come out? I saw the exchanges myself, sir. He was in touch with Admiralty in London."

Admiralty, or what was left of it, awaited my report at Farside Base. Stanger and his cohorts must have rounded up the members who refused my summons. Perhaps even a majority. "Send all sailors to their bunks. All officers to their cabins. Release my people."

"Aye aye, sir. Excuse me, I'll just go . . ." He backed toward the console, trod in blood. "Oh, Jesus Christ." He leaped aside, wiped his feet. He glanced to the console. "Just the caller, sir. Not the laser."

"Very well." Garrow snatched the caller, issued a disordered jumble of commands.

Throughout *Galactic*, the rumble of corridor hatches sliding into their sockets.

"Sir, may I help you up?"

I shook my head. I might come apart.

"You'd better know . . ." He licked his lips. "I called Earthport, sir. After Mr. Stanger died. To tell them."

"That you'd take charge?"

"Only for the moment. They said they'd send someone. And . . ." He swallowed. "Before that, the Captain told them you blasted your way on board. Admiral Hoi offered to send Marines, but Stanger said they would only add to the confusion. That he could flush you out." It was as if Garrow was under compulsion to confess.

"Bring me the caller."

I keyed it to shipwide frequency. "Attention all crew and

passengers." My voice was a croak. "By order of the Board of Admiralty of the United Nations, I, Nicholas E. Seafort, hereby take command of UNS *Galactic*." There, it was done. A few lives late. "All officers and crew are to approach the bridge, as directed by their superiors, to acknowledge my command."

Behind me, in the corridor, footsteps pounded. Arlene, with Derek not far behind.

"Oh, Lord God. You there, get a stretcher. Get him to sickbay."

"No." My voice was muffled.

"Call the Ship's Doctor. Hurry!" Gently, she lifted my head.

"Take your hands off me!" My tone was glacial. "I am Captain!"

"Nick—"

"'*Sir!*'" If I let her beseech me, I'd be unable to resist.

Her eyes were wet. "Sir, let me help you."

"I've got work to do." Admiral Hoi still controlled Earthport; Simovich held Lunapolis Base. Their banks of lasers targeted our planet. My mind wandered; I forced myself back. "Philip?"

"Alive."

Thank Lord God.

"Where?"

"Sickbay. He's . . ."

I nodded. He would be, with Jared dead. "Send someone to the laser room. Mikhael's hurt."

"Aye aye, sir."

An officer raced down the corridor. "Who's injured? My God, the Captain!" Aghast, he brushed past me, stared down at the remains of Stanger.

With a growl Arlene spun the Doctor around, forced him to his knees before me. "Help him!"

"What do you need, sir?"

"He's had spinal surgery. He's badly injured."

"Get me to a motorized chair."

The Doctor looked from one to the other of us.

"I'm Captain. Do it!"

They had to pry my fingers from Danil's.

Ten minutes later, I sat ashen in a wheelchair from sickbay, tight against the Captain's console. "Pain blocker. Give me one. Now." I specialized in short sentences. And desperate screams, if I opened my mouth farther.

"Aye aye, sir."

I caught my reflection in the screen. My eyes had a glassy sheen. My tie was undone, my shirt a filthy mess, my jacket gone. Meet Admiral Seafort, commanding the *Galactic* squadron.

By twos and threes the ship's officers presented themselves to the bridge, came to attention, acknowledged me as their commander. Then the crew, a squad at a time. I sat as one carved in stone, my knuckles white on the armrests. The pain blocker wasn't working.

Tad Anselm was brought to the bridge. Dully, he saluted. His face was slack.

I bade him sit, in a watch officer's chair. "You were with Danil?"

"Yes, sir." A voice from a distant galaxy.

I looked to Arlene, to Derek. "Leave the bridge." From the console, I slapped shut the hatch. I studied the boy a long while. "What happened?"

"I want to resign. To go home."

"Tell me," I said softly, "what you're afraid I'll hear."

Without warning, he began to weep. Then, after a time, "They brought us to the bridge. Me and Danil." He wiped his nose on a grimy gray sleeve. "Stanger told Danil to call you, to make you surrender. He showed Danil his laser, said he'd shoot him if you didn't give up."

I put my head in my hands.

"Danil cried. Stanger slapped him, thrust the caller in his face. Danil made the call. You didn't surrender." His face was bleak. "Stanger waited, opened the hatch. He took Danil to the corridor. Stanger had to drag him. Danil was beside himself. He gibbered and begged. Stanger put the pistol to his chest and fired. He left him there. A warning, he said, if you reached the bridge."

I bent to the side, vomited bile.

"And what I felt . . ." Tears coursed down Anselm's face. "In Washington, you told me to look after him. But I was so . . . so . . . so g-g-lad, sir. That it wasn't me. I wanted it to be Danil." He was alone with his anguish. "I'm going home. I've got to."

"Oh, son." I tried to gather him into my arms, but he was a leaden weight.

"Where is he? Where did they take him?"

"The sickbay has coolers."

"That's where I'll be." No salute, no wait for dismissal. He wandered to the hatch, slapped it open. He vanished into the corridor.

I called Arlene in. "Is the laser room manned?"

"I don't know, sir."

"See to it. Three consoles are down, but the rest . . ." By redistributing the laser cannon among available consoles, we'd restore our firepower.

"Aye aye, sir."

"Get yourself a uniform. And Derek." I keyed the engine room. "Mr. McAndrews. Have we power?"

"Yes, sir."

"Fusion drives?"

"Unharmed."

"The gravitrons?"

"You made a mess of them. We'll work on it."

"Give me power to the thrusters." I keyed the caller. "Comm Room."

Arlene watched impassively, standing at ease.

"Tech Specialist Panner reporting, sir."

"You!" My lip curled. "Report to the brig; tell Tobrok

you're under arrest." He had surrendered the comm room to Stanger, the moment we'd left.

"Sir—aye aye, sir, but Mr. Tobrok's dead. The Captain hanged him."

I flinched. "Report to whoever's in charge. Put your replacement on the line." I waited. Then, "Set up a transmission on all available frequencies, Naval and civilian. Half an hour."

Now, for what must be done. I could wait no longer. I closed the hatch, looked up at Lieutenant Sanders. "We're off duty."

"Are we?"

"Yes." I waited, hoping against hope.

Her hand brushed my shoulder.

I seized it, pressed it to my lips. "Could you forgive me?"

"There's nothing to forgive. You're Captain. I accepted that when I took the oath. No, Nick, I mean it. Don't you know me at all?" She knelt. "I love you. Don't cry, I can't stand it."

Her lips were soft, and sweet.

"Let me get you to sickbay."

"After." There'd be plenty of time. "I'd like to see Philip."

"He won't speak."

"Bring him. Hon, find me a shirt and jacket. Insignia. I have to make a broadcast from the bridge. Perhaps you'd help me dress."

"Are we on duty again?"

"In a moment."

Quickly, she bent and kissed me. "Don't be too stubborn," she said as she strode to the hatch. "Preserve yourself."

For what?

"Attention, UNS *Galactic*. Admiral Johanson aboard Earthport local shuttle Zebra 12. I'm come to take command by Admiralty authority. We'll mate at your Level 2 bay."

"Shall I refuse him, sir?" Lieutenant Garrow. Another of his persistent efforts to be helpful.

"By no means. He's welcome."

"*Galactic*, confirm please. Be advised that we'll enter armed and ready."

"Confirm, Lieutenant. Ask how many. Get IDs."

He did. Nine. Three lieutenants, a handful of Marine sergeants, Deputy SecGen Valera's chief civilian aide.

"Mr. Carr to the bridge, flank!" Waiting, I drummed the console. What I was about to do was vile.

Derek Carr hurried in, distinguished in his crisp Naval uniform. A pity he'd let his enlistment run out, those many years ago. "Lieutenant Carr reporting, sir."

"These are the orders I ask you to volunteer to carry out. If you refuse, I won't hold it against you."

Silent, he waited.

"Have the master-at-arms' men evacuate Level 2, section five. You'll have to move fast, but be certain to miss none of the passengers. Don a thrustersuit. Put a spanner and a fully charged laser in the pouch. Understood?"

"Aye aye, sir." His face showed nothing.

"In your suit, greet Admiral Johanson's party at the section five lock on behalf of Captain Garrow. Treat him with courtesy and respect. Show him the suit lockers near the lock. Explain that you were on your way Outside to repair another faulty sensor. *Galactic*'s been plagued by them. When his party has desuited, call the bridge and ask Mr. Garrow where the middy is who was to escort them. Then enter the lock."

"Aye aye, sir."

"Cycle. When the outer hatch opens, block it with the spanner. Then take your laser from the pouch and burn through the inner lock porthole."

"Sir!"

I waited, impassive.

"Mr. Seafort, that will . . ." He swallowed.

"They're guilty of treason, Derek. They're armed. They'd kill or arrest me on sight."

"But . . ." He held up a hand, to forestall any further explanation. He perused the deck for several moments. Then, "Orders acknowledged and understood, sir. Will there be anything else?"

"As His representative aboard ship, I absolve you, now and after." It was but one of many abominations I'd committed in His name.

"Thank you, sir. That won't be necessary."

In fresh clothes, braced with a double dose of pain blockers, I faced the simulscreen. Its holocam transmitted my haggard face, my grim visage around the world, and throughout home system. Offscreen, by the bulkhead, Arlene held Philip's hand.

Belowdecks, a machinist's detail worked to replace the section five porthole. When they were done section five would be re-aired.

"This is Admiral and Secretary-General Seafort, acting under authority of martial law. UNS *Galactic* is again in Government hands. All forces, U.N.A.F. and Naval, are to return to barracks and await instructions. The commandants of Earthport Naval Station and Lunapolis Base shall place themselves under arrest."

I glowered. "Cisno Valera is removed as Deputy Secretary-General of the United Nations. He is summarily tried in absentia, found guilty of treason, and sentenced to death. The sentence is commuted provided that he surrenders himself to Potomac Naval Station forthwith. Beginning in four hours"—I checked my watch—"noon Eastern Standard Time, any Government officer, civil or military, who encounters Mr. Valera outside Potomac Naval Station is to carry out the sentence of death."

I looked sternly into the camera. "Those Senators who convened in defiance of authority are unseated from office, and are barred from elective office for the remainder of their lives. I shall tolerate no act of rebellion, no disregard of edicts while this crisis continues.

"Other matters. Jerence Branstead is to be released forthwith, and to resume his duties as chief of staff.

"The enviro package of bills, as submitted by my Administration, is deemed enacted as first submitted, the effective date one week from today. They will be known as the Jared Tenere Enviro Acts." Jared was no enviro fanatic, but Philip would be pleased, when he was again among us.

"That is all." I keyed off the simulscreen.

I leaned back, savoring an exquisite torment in my spine.

"Nick. Captain." Arlene's voice was soft.

I turned. P.T.'s hands scrabbled at his shirt, at each other. His fingers were red and raw. He stared unseeing past the console.

I rolled my chair as far as I could. "Philip."

Nothing. His lips moved whispering silent numbers.

"Son." I held his hands in mine. "We love you. You're all right. Try not to rev."

His hands jerked away. He made fists of them, thrust them beneath his arms. "Base twelve works. Leave me alone."

I cried, "I couldn't pull the pistol loose. It wouldn't budge."

Dully, he looked from me to his mother, and back.

"I'm so sorry, Philip!" Stupidity. Incompetence. Worse. I'd held Jared's life in my hands, and thrown it away.

"He was terrified." P.T.'s tone was conversational, as if discussing the weather. "We all die. He would too."

"Son, I—"

"But no one should die like that. No one." He hugged himself.

"I could have rolled faster. I should have had the laser—"

"I couldn't save him. I was there, and couldn't help. Couldn't comfort him. Even at the end, he looked to me."

No more. God, take me now. *NO MORE.*

"Sir." Lieutenant Garrow. "An urgent call."

"Later."

His voice was awed. "It's Bishop Saythor. The Patriarch."

"You understand, Fath? *I couldn't help!*"

I drew Philip to me.

He thrust me away. "Take your call."

"It doesn't—"

"I'll be here. Take it."

From my console, I stared into the simulscreen, with sunken eyes.

The Elder's pudgy face glowered. "This is Bishop Saythor, on behalf of the Patriarchy."

"Very well."

"Retract, this instant. Valera is not condemned. It wasn't an insurrection; the Senate has authorized—"

"No." Francis Saythor headed my Church. Our Church. The only true Church.

"The enviro legislation is madness. Cancel it before—"

"No!" He spoke for Lord God, in all matters ecclesiastic.

"Seafort, this isn't your Washington study. This time I speak from the Cathedral, for the Patriarchs of His Reunification Church. Your Government is in error and mortal sin. I order you—"

"NO!" My voice trembled. He was Lord God's representative on Earth.

"Else we'll disavow you this very day. A public statement, on the steps of the Cathedral. A drastic step, one we've rarely taken. Be warned, unless—"

I reared back in my seat, ignoring a blazing comet of pain. "Beware, lest I disavow *you!*"

His eyes narrowed, as if perplexed.

"Disavow you, Saythor!" My eyes were wild. "And your Patriarchy!" I felt something snap in my soul, as it had in my spine. My bond with Him was severed, utterly and irredeemably.

"You'll be burned. Heresy—"

"And disavow Mother Church!" Tears streamed down my face. "The Church, do you hear, Saythor? Will it be treason, if I declare my doubt that you could possibly be His instrument? If I wonder how we surrendered our conscience, our moral certitude, to an intolerant Church concerned of its prosperity more than our survival?"

"How dare you!"

"Likewise must the deacons be grave, not double-tongued, not given to much wine, not greedy of filthy lucre. What are my polls, Elder? Which of us will joeys follow, when they read the zines? Think it's worth the risk?"

He and I sat appalled.

I was excommunicate. I had threatened Lord God Himself, and spat upon His Church. Whether the Patriarch declared me so or not, I was barred forever from His community.

"Shall I disavow you, Bishop?" My unsteady hand hovered over the caller. "Shall I tell the world my mind?"

"You wouldn't besmirch—"

"By all that is holy, I swear that I will tell only truth. I'll speak of our meeting at the Rotunda, of your visit to my home. Of this call, which will be your last. Lift a finger to interfere, and it will come to pass." My voice could scratch glass. "As long as we live, Bishop, never speak to me again!" My fist slammed down on the keys, cutting the circuit.

I sat shaking, in awe of my ultimate folly.

Yet thou shalt be brought down to Hell, to the sides of the pit.

I dared not pray. Not ever again, lest I be blasted from the Earth.

Yet how could I live without prayer?

How could I live?

There were only Arlene and Philip. Mikhael. And duty.

From her quiet corner, Arlene gazed at me with awe.

P.T. picked ceaselessly at his shirt.

"Son, come to me." I held out my hands, pleading.

His eyes met mine, alone, tormented, sealed.

"I am bereft of Lord God, and have nothing save you!" My voice broke. "I beg you, as you have mercy!" I could say no more, from weeping.

Slowly at first, as an automaton, he rose from his chair, padded across the deck. A gentle hug. He fell into my arms, onto my lap as a small child. Our tears merged, mine for myself, his for his forever-lost Jared.

"U.N.A.F. Washington command to UNS *Galactic*."

I jerked awake. I'd been sleeping; I hoped the lieutenant sharing my watch hadn't noticed.

I took up the caller. Unusual, for the Captain to answer directly, but I still didn't fully trust any of Stanger's officers. I'd issued standing orders to the comm room that all communications be routed to the bridge. "*Galactic*, go ahead."

"General Donner reporting. I may not have much time. Sir, U.N.A.F. is going to sit it out."

"What?"

"The ranking generals conferred over the net. They won't respond to either side. They'll wait for a winner. We're supposed to be shut down for off-planet calls, but I know a colonel in communications."

The fools. Neither side would trust them, after. "It's treason, Donner."

"Technically. More realistically, caution."

I grunted my disgust. "Valera?"

"No sign of him, sir. I'd better make myself scarce after this call. Any orders?"

"Fly to London. Find Thorne." He knew Jeff; they'd worked together when Thorne had served as chief of staff. "Have him call *Galactic* by sat-relay from Devon Academy. Tell him Farside is reliable, if he finds the other nets locked out."

"Yes, sir."

"And thank you." Lord God knew what he risked by alerting me.

I brought my ship to General Quarters, started the repair of the many damaged corridor hatch seals. I'd prefer going to Battle Stations, but if I put the crew at a high state of alert after a night of chaos, they'd soon be asleep on their feet.

I dared not leave the bridge for long, and of my lieutenants, I trusted only Derek and Arlene. That meant I couldn't share a watch with them, else they'd be too fatigued to stand their own. I shared instead with men and women of whom I knew nothing, except that they'd failed to relieve Stanger, when their oaths demanded it.

Reeling with exhaustion, I had Midshipman Speke wheel me to the sickbay.

Mikhael's face was puffy. He lay listlessly in a bunk. The Ship's Doctor recited his injuries. Among them, three broken ribs, a bruised spleen, swollen testicles. "The bone growth stimulator will reknit the ribs in a few days. But the lassitude . . . the beating took something out of him."

I wheeled to his bed. "Mikhael . . ." I was at a loss. His eyes went elsewhere. "I'm sorry, Pa."

"For what? You were magnificent."

"I thought I could stop her. Knock her down. But she—" His face contorted.

"You're fifteen. You can't expect—"

"Captain to the bridge!" Alarms shrieked. *"Battle Stations!"*

"Lord Christ." I wheeled. "Middy! Speke!" We raced to the bridge.

Derek and Midshipman Pyle jumped to their feet. "Sir, incoming lasers. Target acquisition mode."

"The Station?" For the moment, Earth loomed between us and Lunapolis. Admiral Hoi would have done better to wait for his ally.

"Yes, sir." Derek looked grim.

"What's our heading?" I peered at the simulscreen. At Earthport, defense lasers bristled from every aperture, a legacy of our defense against the marauding fish. "Acquire targets! Aim only at their lasers." The destruction of Earthport would be a catastrophe; we'd have no way to transship the vast quantities of cargo that filled her warehouses. Perhaps Admiral Hoi counted on that fact.

What skill had Stanger drilled into his laser techs? No time to check his records.

"Laser Room, stand by to fire. Pilot to the bridge, flank. Chief McAndrews!"

"Yes, sir?"

"Stand by to Fuse. Coordinates follow. Full power to the thrusters."

"Aye aye, sir. Captain, we haven't achieved Fusion safety." If we Fused too close to a large mass, we'd destroy ourselves.

"Not yet. Derek, calculate Fusion coordinates."

"To where, sir?"

"Pilot Jasper Oren reporting." He sounded breathless.

"Anywhere nearby. Ceres. Pilot, how far to Fusion safety?"

"Just a moment, sir." He took in our coordinates. "Two and a half hours, more or le—"

"Bloody hell." I savored the language. Admiralty wouldn't beach me, and the Patriarchs would be silent.

We faced the Station almost head-on. Our vast cargo bays at the bow offered extra shielding against incoming fire, but few of our own lasers would bear.

Fight, or flee?

"Pilot, bring the ship about. Port side to the Station, broadside to the Naval wing. One-half kilometer distance."

"One-half?" Oren's tone was unbelieving.

At that range their powerful lasers would blast us to shreds, but our own fire would severely damage the Station.

"Now!"

"Aye aye, sir." His fingers flew at the thruster console.

Ponderously, we came about. It was a matter of inertia. *Galactic* had huge mass, many times that of a typical vessel. Our thrusters would move her, but we required an equal expenditure of propellant to halt our swing. Thank heaven we had a Pilot aboard. Turning a behemoth like *Galactic* was an exercise in nerve and patience.

"*Galactic* to Earthport Naval Station. Put on Admiral Hoi."

It took barely a moment. Hoi must have been glued to his console, as was I. His pinched face loomed in my simulscreen. "Turn away, Seafort. If I have to wreck you, I will."

"Our lasers are trained on the Naval wing. You'll die."

"I'm not in the Naval wing."

"Very well, we'll retarget." It would be mass murder, of civilians, and I couldn't do it.

He smiled. "We know you, Seafort. You'll do no such thing."

Inwardly, I cursed. "You know me not at all." I poised my finger on the console. "Activating fire controls. Laser Room, stand by."

"We have more firepower, Seafort! You'll be destroyed."

I shrugged. "I don't really care." That much was true.

"Why not?"

"My body is ravaged, my Government a shambles, my Navy disgraced." My covenant with Lord God shattered beyond repair.

"Put on Johanson!"

"Why?"

"He'll negotiate us out of a standoff."

"Not from my ship."

"Send him here."

My tone was casual. "If you wish."

"You'll speak to him after?"

"If he calls."

"A truce until then?"

"Six hours, no more."

"Very well." He broke contact.

"Derek, go to sickbay. Have them load Johanson and the rest onto their launch."

"You wouldn't."

"I beg your pardon, Mr. Carr?"

"You heard me. Isn't that a touch macabre?"

"Do it." I'd be damned if I'd give a traitor like Johanson a formal funeral. I keyed off, had Lieutenant Garrow assign a sailor to pilot the launch.

Six hours of truce. More than enough to reach Fusion safety. I could escape Earthport's lasers, but to where? I snorted; *Galactic* was set to cruise to Constantine. Her crew was functional, her stores nearly complete. We could repair our damage en route. It would serve them all right if I fled the madness into which we'd descended.

With a sigh, I put aside my fantasies.

How to retake Earthport? No troopship could run the gauntlet of the Station's powerful lasers. And in any event, what troops would respond to my call? Perhaps some isolated U.N.A.F. base would ignore the perfidy of its leaders and stand by the Government, but how would they board a shuttle unnoticed? And what would persuade Earthport to let it dock?

In the meantime, my hundreds of passengers had to be tended. Perhaps Hoi would allow me to off-load them; their presence foreclosed the option of battle. But he knew that; why would he let me?

I pondered. The two middies, Speke and Pyle, fidgeted under my gaze.

Lunapolis Base was also a factor. It had free access to the Station; their commanders were allied. And its lasers were a devastating threat, both to me and Earth.

If I attacked Lunapolis from aloft, I might kill thousands. Certainly there was no way to subdue it by ground attack. Any troops I sent would have to be transshipped through Earthport, which was impossible until Admiral Hoi was ousted. Worse, Earthport guarded Lunapolis, and Lunapolis Earthport, unless I could somehow time an assault for the hours when they were out of each other's sight.

I knew of but one way, and the risk was enormous.

Failure was death. Not so unwelcome.

Midshipman Speke blurted out, "What did I do?"

I raised an eyebrow.

"You—I thought you were angry. You were glaring like—"

"Two demerits." How dare he interrupt a Captain's thoughts?

A look of dismay. "Sir, that makes ten."

I drummed the console. "Very well. One. Go work it off."

"Aye aye, sir." He made his escape.

Anthony Pyle stared carefully at his console.

A crackle, from the speaker. "Admiral Thorne to *Galactic*."

I snatched the caller. "Jeff!"

A few seconds' pause. "Hello, sir."

"I need you."

A hesitation. "How?"

"You have doubts?" Better to face them now, though I was disappointed. I'd rallied Jeff from cynicism years past, and I'd hoped to count on his loyalty.

A pause. "Sir, it's the lag. I'm calling London to Devon to Farside to you."

"Ahh."

"The joey at Devon Academy didn't want to put me through. I had to drop names."

"Whose?" I waited out the lag.

"Every Admiral I could think of. You. The Commandant."

Midshipman Pyle smiled, until he saw my scowl.

"Jeff, may I recall you to duty?" Under martial law I had

the authority, even without his consent. But this was my mentor, my oldest living friend.

"Of course." He knew I wouldn't ask, if the need weren't desperate.

I said, "There's risk."

"There's always risk. What are your orders?"

I told him.

Pyle's eyes widened.

21

U.N.A.F. Security Command to *Galactic*. Mr. Seafort, if you're there, for God's sake answer!"

I wheeled onto the bridge, breathing hard. General Donner's saturnine face filled the simulscreen. "Go ahead."

"Valera's marching on the Rotunda. He's got the Thirteenth Armored, the Fifty-first Airbo—"

"U.N.A.F. would sit it out, you said."

"I was wrong." His voice had a touch of asperity. "Ibiera and Taubeck always were hotheads. It's only a few units, sir, but we have hardly anything to stop them. I've rounded up what I could. A few guard units. There's a store of old projectile rifles in storage; I outfitted the U.N. Military Band. They—"

"Ridiculous."

"They were handy and they're fully trained soldiers, sir. It's just they don't normally carry . . . we've taken up position inside the retaining wall."

"Civil war is the last thing we—"

"Sir, there's more. Valera preempted *Holoworld* and *Newsnet* for a six o'clock announcement. The other nets will no doubt follow—"

"No!"

"I agree, but how will you stop him?"

"Where are you now?"

"Branstead's office." He flushed. "Don't take offense. Valera's people have him in custody, and his puter had links to everyone from—"

"Get me McFrey from *Holoworld*."

"The president? I'll try." His stubby fingers stabbed at keys.

We got a machine, then a stubborn puter, then a secretary. By the time we worked our way up to McFrey's chief aide, I was fuming. I leaned into the simulscreen, my voice shaking. "Put her on this very moment. This instant!"

The aide's face disappeared. A few seconds later, Belinda McFrey, the world's most powerful netizen, looked down on me from the screen. She said coolly, "You rang, Mr. Sec— ah, Seafort?"

"Valera gets no bandwidth."

"That's not for you to say."

"But it is. Under martial law—"

"Which the Senate has repealed."

"Valera is engaged in treason. I won't allow him access—"

"You don't control the nets." Her tone was smug. "Don't even try."

"As Secretary-General—"

"You may not still be SecGen. That's debatable."

Perhaps it was only that she interrupted my every sentence. Perhaps it was her smug superiority. Whatever the cause, I snapped. "Donner, flash this call to *Newsnet*, live feed. In fact, transmit worldwide. Flank."

"Just a moment." Clicks. A buzz, and silence. "Done."

"Belinda McFrey has insisted on giving aid and comfort to those who would overthrow the ordained Government of Lord God. Now do I—"

"I did not."

"—Nicholas Seafort, sole executive of His Government and plenipotentiary of the Patriarchs of His Reunified Church while martial law remains in effect—"

"You take on a lot, Seafort."

My eyes blazed. "—declare Belinda McFrey, former president of *Holoworld*, excommunicate of His Church and His people. We do, on behalf of Lord God Himself, turn from her aspect, reject her perfidy, and banish her from our midst!"

Her face was pale. "Now, look. You can't just—"

"*GET THEE GONE, CREATURE OF SATAN!*" With a slash of the hand, I cut her off my screen. "I do warn and adjure every citizen that to consort or do business with a person excommunicate is a capital offense, and merits excommunication of the offender."

I glared at the screen and at the world. "Let all media take notice: Cisno Valera shall not be heard while he stands in opposition to Lord God. Trifle not with perdition!"

I snapped off the screen, sat trembling. What I had done was arguably legal. The authority granted under martial law was breathtakingly broad. I represented His Government in its every aspect, including that normally exercised by the Patriarchs.

Nonetheless, what I had done was a travesty. No, an obscenity. I had defied the Patriarchs outright, spurned and insulted them to their faces. Didn't I deserve excommunication far more than the frightened woman whose soul now teetered on the edge of damnation? Was I not already excommunicate, in His eyes, if not in the view of the cowardly Patriarchs? If I were to declare any traitor excommunicate, why choose a mediaman whose sole offense was to allow Valera a voice? Why not villainous Admiral Hoi, or Simovich, down in Lunapolis? Was not their treason far more overt than hers?

No time for disgust. "Comm Room, connect me with the chief of staff's office in the Rotunda." I waited. "Donner? Evacuate your troops. No, you heard me. Why? Because they're not the enemy. I'll fire on Lunapolis if I must. And on Earthport. But not on ground forces, however misguided. Oh? Perhaps you didn't understand: that was an order."

I bore out his protests. He was a brave man, and stubborn.

When at last he acquiesced I said, "You yourself may stay, if you care to give me a hand. Key into the outdoor public address system. Hurry, please. And aim your caller's vidlens out the window. I want to see the troops I'm talking to. Feed picture and sound live, to whatever nets will run it."

We had more time than I'd supposed; it was a full half hour before the first patrols of the Thirteenth Armored Cavalry moved through the undefended gate. They held their laser rifles at the ready, moved cautiously, eyes searching the many windows above.

I took a deep breath. These moments might be my last chance to brace my falling Government.

"Soldiers of the Thirteenth!" Far below, my voice boomed over the Rotunda speakers. "I am the Secretary-General. Go no farther. By entering the U.N. compound, you war on God!"

Three or four joeys exchanged nervous glances.

"General Ibiera and General Taubeck are relieved of command. Go no farther, I say. You there! Sergeant, with your hand on the gate!" The man stopped as if struck. "As you value your soul, fall back! Through the gate, this instant!"

Uneasy, he took a few steps back.

"I have ordered General Donner's troops to stand down. We will not shoot you this day. We will not defend the Rotunda with bullets or beams. We will defend it with the righteous wrath of Lord God."

For a moment, all was still.

"The world watches your every move. Let the vengeance of humankind strike dead the first man to befoul these precincts. Shoot any officer who orders you through those gates. It is treason, and abominable in His eyes. Shoot any officer who bids you fire on your fellow troops within the compound.

"Soldiers of the United Nations, go to your homes. This revolt, this treason, is not of your making. It will collapse of its own weight. You need not die, or kill, for traitors' greed.

"This is Secretary-General Nicholas Seafort, wishing you the blessing of Lord God."

I keyed off my caller, held my breath.

At the gates, no one moved.

"You vile son of a bitch!" Admiral Hoi was livid. "Lieutenant Tse was my nephew. You goddamn murderer!"

"They were armed rebels boarding a U.N. warship."

Arlene had summoned me to the bridge for Hoi's call. I was tired, disheveled, and cross.

"You're the—" He bit it off. "How can I send the boy home to my sister? He looks like . . . in two hours I open fire!" Our truce would be done.

I said, "We've passengers aboard."

"That didn't bother you before."

"Let me off-load them."

"No. I won't let you anywhere near the Station."

I glanced at Arlene. "Why not?"

"You're too devious, and besides . . ." He grimaced. "Too many of my officers know only your public image. They trust you. I won't risk subversion."

Impasse.

"Mr. Hoi, surrender now and I'll spare your life."

"Goofjuice. I have the upper hand. Two hours." The screen went dark.

I keyed the caller. "Engine Room, flank speed. Pilot, all power to the thrusters. Get us to Fusion safety. Lieutenant Sanders!"

Arlene jumped. "Yes, sir? I wish you wouldn't do that."

"Sorry. Fusion coordinates for Titan. Have Mr. Pyle run calculations as well." On my ships, Fusion coordinates were checked and rechecked. "Baron, you too."

Two hours, before we'd need their coordinates. I yearned

to pace, but even in light gravity, I dared not move. When Dr. Ghenili saw me again, he would not be pleased.

I'd told Jeff Thorne to make a very special call. I rolled my chair from one bulkhead to another, waiting for the response to come through. If I didn't hear back within two hours, my plan would be stillborn.

Anthony Pyle bent to his calculations, tongue between his lips. I smiled. Once, when I was a youngster, I'd been made to do the same.

This wasn't my watch; I was free to leave the bridge. But I was too keyed up to sleep. Besides, I'd have to be back when we Fused. No Captain would dream of letting subordinate officers Fuse on their own. If something went wrong, he'd be the one who had to explain.

Of course, if something went wrong, there'd be little to explain. The ship was unlikely to be found.

"Thorne to *Galactic*."

Thank Lord God. Once we were Fused, he'd have been unable to reach us.

"He agreed, sir. But he said to tell you a personal invitation would have been more polite." Thorne's tone was disapproving.

I rolled my eyes. "That's like him. Pay no attention. Now, as to the rest?"

"In hand. A few hours. Best of luck, sir."

"And to you."

Thorne had been circumspect. I approved. It was unlikely anyone was listening in to secure Naval frequencies, but one never knew.

Fifteen minutes later, I fed Fusion coordinates to our puter. "Bridge to Engine Room, prepare to Fuse."

"Prepare to Fuse, aye aye." A moment's pause. "Engine Room ready for Fuse, sir."

I ran my finger down the screen. The fusion drive kicked in. The stars shifted red, then blue. As the drive reached full strength they slowly faded to black. We were Fused, hurtling past normal space at supraluminous velocity. Our external sensors were blind. *Galactic* was dependent entirely on her own resources, as was any Fused ship.

We'd be no more than a few hours. Hardly enough time to settle to sleep. At her console, Arlene yawned conspicuously, twice. She must be exhausted. We'd none of us caught up on our rest.

She yawned again.

"That's quite enough, Lieutenant." I glowered. "If you want me to go to bed, say so."

"I'd like you to go to bed, Captain."

Well, I'd asked for it. "Hmpff. Send a med tech to our cabin, to help me out of the chair." I rolled off.

When I'd first captained *Hibernia*, I'd been awed at the size of the Captain's quarters compared to the wardroom I'd known. Compared even to *Hibernia*, the Captain of *Galactic* slept in awesome luxury. The compartment was easily twice the size of our passenger cabins, which themselves were lavish. My cabin was fitted out in magnificent splendor. Wasteful. An outrage. Nonetheless, the head was a marvel of design and comfort, and the bed . . .

I'd first seen the cabin a few hours earlier, when it still held Stanger's gear. I'd summoned the purser, brusquely ordered him to remove it. I needed no reminders of the man I'd murdered. No, executed. It was one death for which I felt no regret.

The med tech left me lying on my bunk, spine throbbing, waiting for a new dose of pain blocker to take effect.

Still, I felt a strange sense of peace. My confrontation with Bishop Saythor had been so calamitous, so absolute, that I had nothing left to rue. Having rejected the God I loved, I was alone, in the forever of the universe.

Yet, that freed me for the present. I could nourish Philip, cherish my beloved Arlene, succor Mikhael for what little time was left before I sank into the fires. And, for the moment, I had my ship.

I'd been raised to Lord God, and duty.

Now there was only duty.

I lay staring at the overhead. There was no possible way I'd sleep, not with my pain and my anguish.

I slept.

Some hours later we Defused. Two hundred twelve thousand miles outside Titan's orbit, amazingly close for one jump. Fusion drives were inaccurate by about one percent of the distance traveled. I made a quick recalculation, and a corrective jump. We emerged so close that *Melbourne* registered immediately in the sensors.

Alexi's old ship had left Earthport before the coup. An interstellar vessel performed many roles. One of them, unfortunately, was to serve as tourist transport. The cruise to the Jovian satellites, for example, was famous. An intrasystem Fuse made the voyage a tolerable length, and the public approval gained by occasional tourist jaunts helped support the Navy.

The Titan cruise was another such waste of resources. Alexi had been wise to arrange his leave to coincide with the journey. The ship would be filled with a gaggle of politicians, celebrities, mediamen, and the like. No fit company for an honest sailor.

I had no idea where Captain Fenner's loyalties lay, but Alexi had spoken approvingly of him. It would have to suffice. In any event, I doubted he'd try to flee. Moored at Titan's Orbiting Station, he was too close to Saturn's satellite to Fuse, and in any event *Galactic* bristled with laser cannon.

I had Lieutenant Garrow summon *Melbourne*'s Captain aboard to receive dispatches from Admiralty. I rolled my chair back and forth, to the middies' growing annoyance, waiting to learn if he'd comply. Certainly Fenner knew my visit to Titan was no routine matter; ships were spread so thin that it was rare one encountered another outside home port.

To my vast relief, his gig soon appeared in our simulscreens. Not long after, he was piped aboard.

Josh Fenner was a rather short joey, with a grave mien. We reviewed my orders from Admiralty, that gave me authority over his ship. "Very well, sir. What can I do for you?"

"I need to, ah, borrow *Melbourne*."

"You do." His eyes bored into mine.

"For a few days, no more. Anton Bourse is aboard, is he not?"

He gaped. Even such an eccentric as I wouldn't disrupt the schedules of two great liners merely to meet a holostar. Even if he was the world's premier entertainer. "You want to meet him?"

"No. I want him dead."

Almost two days to wait. It nearly dissolved what was left of my sanity. I roamed the ship in my motorized chair, or at least those parts of it I could reach. I had the midships and aft gravitrons turned low for my visits, but the improvised controls were erratic at best; sudden gravitational surges left me breathless and gasping with pain.

Chief McAndrews supervised repair of the corridor hatches; the circuitry was complicated and difficult, especially as to the bridge overrides.

I joined the passengers for the evening meal. They were immensely relieved that some form of routine had been reestablished, even if the Captain they'd known was a bloody mutilated corpse, and his replacement gaunt and silent.

Mikhael languished in sickbay. I visited every few hours, even when I should have been stretched in my bed, warding off the effects of exhaustion.

His eyes were red, his body sore. His spirit, deflated.

"Would you like to visit the bridge?" In other days, joeykids had been awed by its splendor.

He shook his head. "Not really."

I said brightly, "How about *Melbourne*'s bridge? Alexi would have wanted you to see it."

"I did, before his last cruise. I don't want to think about it."

"It?"

"Him." He turned away, tucked his pillow under his head, left me contemplating the curve of his back.

"Son . . ."

"I'm nobody's son." His tone was sullen.

"You're angry I couldn't save you from Karen?"

"When I try to be brave I wet my pants or get beaten to a pulp. It's not fair. I can't be like you. Nobody can."

"Don't ever try," I said through clenched teeth, "to be like me. You don't want to be that."

Something in my tone caused him to peer over his shoulder, and slowly, reluctantly turn. "Pa?"

I nodded, not quite able to speak.

"What is it? What's changed in you?"

"Nothing." I couldn't tell him I'd defied the Deity, and been broken. But "nothing" wasn't the truth. "I don't have much left in life, Mikhael. I'd truly like you to be my joeykid."

He lay listless, from time to time sniffling. Then, "Pa, am I glitched? Do I need rebalancing?"

"No, son, you're a teener. You need love, and a bit of aging."

By now I could at least recognize my lieutenants, and was forming an impression of their abilities. Arlene, in our precious hours of privacy, broke tradition to discuss her observations with me. It was one of the few perks of the Captain's wife.

On a long cruise an officer in her position would be

lonely. No crewman would trust her. Whether or not she revealed their confidences, they would assume she had. But for now it didn't matter; we were only briefly posted to *Galactic*. When this was over, if I lived, I'd seek some quiet corner for retirement. A place with low gravity. Lunapolis, perhaps. They were building new warrens there, with comfortable quarters.

"Nick . . ." We snuggled in bed. I'd tried lovemaking, but my spine wouldn't allow it. The movement was too much.

"Yes, hon?"

"That child . . . promise me we'll have it."

"After all we've been through?"

"You changed your mind?" A tinge of sadness.

"No." I hoped it was truth. "I'm . . . lost inside, hon. How could I raise—"

Her palm covered my mouth. "Don't think about it. Trust your instincts. You were as troubled then as now, and look at P.T."

"Yes, look at him." Grief-stricken, morose. Lethargic. And articulate as always, so the cause of his sorrow came easily to his lips. If I could add his misery to mine, gladly would I have done so.

"He'll survive." Her pity was less than I expected. "Wounds heal. He'll find another boy, or girl."

"A girl this time, I hope."

She giggled. "So do I." Then, "Promise."

"I swear by Lord—" I couldn't do that. "I promise by everything I hold dear, we will make another child."

"Thank you, love." Drowsily, we drifted in space.

"You're bloody right it's canceled! It brings him up to ten." I flung my holovid across the console. "Who told you to issue my cadet demerits?"

"I'm first middy." Edwin Speke's face was tense. "Anselm's been moping about the corridors. You should have seen how sloppily he came to attention when I—"

"Who told you to put him at attention? Mind your own affairs."

"If that's the way you want it, sir."

I sat fuming. I'd assigned Tad no duties. I wasn't even sure he was a member of the ship's company. His darkness of the soul had enveloped him like a shroud. I'd have to spend time with him. Or better yet, put him with someone who could set an example. I tottered on the edge of despair.

Yes, a cadet was subject to midshipmen's orders, and Anselm should have been more responsive. But he wasn't a member of *Galactic*'s wardroom, and Speke needn't have noticed him.

It was chance, pure seniority, that made a first middy. As Jeff Thorne had known when I was a boy, no leader could ask a willingness, a spirit, he himself couldn't provide as example.

Later, I visited P.T. in the cabin they'd assigned him, struggled out of my chair in the light gravity, gave him a fierce hug. "I love you, son. Remember that always."

"Fath?" He searched my face. "You make it sound a farewell."

"It is. I have to go."

"Where?"

I told him.

When I was done, he stirred. "I'll—"

"No." I spoke softly, but with a finality that brooked no argument, as in his youth. "Not this time. Perhaps I'll be back. With Lord God's—" I bit back the obscenity. "Perhaps."

Below, in the engine room, Chief McAndrews looked morose. "The corridor hatches will seal, but the bridge overrides—the wiring's fused, somewhere in the bulkheads. We'll find it, sooner or later." He scowled. "Make that later."

"Keep at it." I glanced up to his panels. "And the gravitrons?"

"Directly wired." He glowered at the mess I'd made of his

circuits. "It'll give me something to do on the way to Constantine. In the meantime . . ." The grudging hint of a smile. "Hope you don't mind a drop to zero gee now and then."

"I'll survive." I'd do more than that; only light gravity made my injury tolerable. "But the passengers . . ."

"I know, sir." Groundsiders were notorious for their ineptitude in anything less than Terran gees.

I was wheeling myself back to the bridge. As I rounded the corridor, voices ahead.

" . . . thrash you myself, do you hear?" Derek Carr.

"The Captain canceled—"

"I don't care what Mr. Seafort said. His every move is agony, he's hanging on by a thread, and I won't have a whiny cadet adding to his worries!"

I would turn my chair, go around. A long way, but . . .

"I wasn't—"

"Stand at attention, Anselm! Did I release you?"

"No, sir!"

"By God, that does it! Now what, you're crying? What in *hell* is the matter with you?"

"I don't know." The boy's voice was tormented. "Cashier me. Beach me. Let me go home."

I braced myself for Derek's explosion. It never came. His tone was reflective. "I felt that way once. I was just your age. Like you, too old to be a cadet."

No response.

"I begged to be cashiered. I whined, just like you. I had snot running from my nose, just like you. Not on your sleeve, damn it!" His voice softened. "Use this."

"Thank you, sir." A whisper. "What happened?"

"He took me into the corridor. He let me cry, and—I don't know how, but he sent me back to do my duty, and I was glad to. For him." A pause. "Is this by any chance about Bevin?"

"Yessir."

"Ahh. Did I ever tell you about my friend Sandy Wilsky?

A young middy on *Hibernia*. Come along, we'll find a softie. He was killed, on airlock watch I should have been standing. I blamed myself, of course. As you do."

"I prayed for it to be Danil!"

"God doesn't hear such prayers. He just understands. Don't cry again, I didn't mean . . . well, perhaps I did. Come along, joey. A part of me was grateful it was Sandy had the airlock, and for months I felt such contempt for myself . . ."

The voices faded.

Thank You, Lord God. For doing what I could not.

A tenuous peace held at the Rotunda. U.N.A.F. made no effort to enter the gates. Neither did they withdraw. The six o'clock hour came and went, with no broadcast by Valera.

From what we could gather from transmissions, both factions had paused, awaiting my capture or death, or the unlikely possibility that I'd oust Hoi and Simovich. The Assembly had supported my enviro package and was generally assumed to be with me; the Senate was firmly in opposition. It didn't matter; I'd dissolved both bodies.

U.N.A.F. Command remained neutral, with only a few isolated units committing themselves. One such patrol had captured Jerence, and still held him.

All depended on timing. I called Arlene, Derek, and Captain Fenner together for one last conference. Again, they assured me all was arranged.

I set the caller to shipwide frequency. "By order of Admiral Seafort, Lieutenant Arlene Sanders is granted the temporary rank of Captain."

Fenner returned to *Melbourne*.

We Fused.

"The cadet asks to speak to you, sir." Midshipman Speke was exceedingly stiff and formal.

Escorted to the bridge, Anselm waited to be released.

Then, "I'm sorry, sir. I'll try to do better." He shifted. "That's all I had—that's all, sir."

"Thank you. Dismissed." As he turned to go, I blurted, "Danil's death was my fault, not yours. Attacking *Galactic* was a suicide mission. I shouldn't have allowed—"

"Pardon, sir. But that's what we're for. Cadets and middies, I mean. We're military. We accept the risk."

"Did Danil?"

He gulped. "Not of outright murder. He was terrified."

"So were you."

"Yes." His eyes met mine. "Yes, I was."

"I couldn't imagine otherwise. Could I ask you a favor, one which no commander may require of an officer?"

"What, sir?"

"Would you pray for him with me?"

"Oh." His eyes filled. "Oh, yes. I'd like that."

"Tonight, then. I'll call you to my quarters."

I watched him go. Something in his stride resembled the assured young middy I'd first met.

"They're bringing him out now, Ned. The casket is wrapped in poly, to protect it in handling. Level 7 portholes are lined with spectators. Few have dry eyes."

The death of Anton Bourse shocked the public. It was perhaps the only event that could drive the attempted coup from the front pages. *Melbourne*'s Captain, in a universally applauded gesture of respect, had suspended his cruise to return the beloved holostar's body to Earthport Station for transshipment and burial.

Even for *Melbourne*, Admiral Hoi would have been suspicious, had she proposed to dock at a bay. But Captain Fenner hove to alongside, in full view of the Station, and well within the range of her laser defense.

"The effects of decompression are not for the squeamish. The casket will remain closed. Burial is slated in California for Wednesday."

Restless, I flipped my suit radio from one frequency to another: news zines, Earthport Traffic Control, even distant Lunapolis.

Mediamen and their holocams lined Earthport Station's portholes as the joey who'd made millions weep was brought out of *Melbourne*'s vacuum hold and floated into her launch. A sealed coffin, due to the tragic decompression accident that claimed him.

"Tomorrow, a special shuttle will carry Bourse ground-side, to his many admirers."

The launch sailed slowly into an Earthport bay, his grieving retinue aboard. Squads of armed sailors were vigilant, even now fearing a ruse. But only a handful of Bourse's young staff passed through the airlock. Many were in shock.

Melbourne would resume her itinerary, two days late. Two dozen of her passengers disembarked, and were ferried across to the Station. Perhaps they'd booked the cruise only to mingle with Bourse. Their places would be taken by others.

"Permission to disengage capture latches." Captain Fenner, from his launch.

"Bay is cleared and decompressed. Disengage when ready, Melbourne.*"*

"—famous for his portrayal of William, last king of—"

The launch released its hold on the Station, sailed back to *Melbourne.*

"—departure control, bearing 090, 64, 282, repeat—"

A tremendous crash. I groaned.

A distant voice. "Are you all right, sir?"

Scraping sounds. A wrench. Light.

"Help him with his helmet."

"Aye aye, sir."

"Careful, his spine is injured." Sergeant Gregori frowned at his anxious cadet. Together, gently, they lifted me from the coffin, set me in a wheeled chair. Laboriously, we stripped off the rest of my suit.

"Where are we?"

"Level 4 overflow accommodations, sir." A crowded sparse gray cabin, one of several we'd been assigned.

"They didn't put you in a hotel?"

Sergeant Gregori looked pious as he stripped off his civilian shirt. "We insisted on staying with our idol's body. The Hilton refused."

"How many are we?" I knew the answer, but needed reassurance.

"Seven sergeants, two middies, eighteen cadets." With a grunt of satisfaction, Gregori donned his Academy blues.

"The laser pistols?"

"Passed through in Bourse's gear, sir."

I eyed him. "I've owed you an apology a long while, Sarge. Since the Booker incident."

He held up a hand. "We were all rather upset, Mr. Sec-Gen."

I nodded acknowledgment. "The rest of it?"

"No word yet."

As expected. But I fretted nonetheless. If Jeff Thorne's arrangements fell through, I'd have loosed a bloody fiasco.

Our intricate plans had left my nerves in shreds; every phase had to fall into place just so. But it was the only way I could see to free both Earthport and Lunapolis.

Our sleight of hand with *Melbourne* was one part of it. Admiral Hoi would assume I remained on *Galactic*; no one on the Station knew I'd transferred to *Melbourne* at Titan.

Jeff Thorne had flown to Devon, bearing Hazen's orders to send all Academy's drill sergeants and three hundred advanced cadets aloft to Academy's Farside Base. To make sure, the Commandant said, that they weren't caught up in civil war.

I couldn't risk interception of Hazen's orders from Farside; I could trust only Thorne to deliver them.

The enthusiastic cadets, along with half a dozen midshipmen, were bused to London Shuttleport, their duffels neat-packed, uniforms crisp, faces scrubbed. We were aware that Earthport Station's new masters vigilantly watched incoming shuttles from Earth, lest I smuggle troops aloft. But Academy craft always bypassed the Station, sailed directly to Farside.

In the silent, airless night the cadets left their shuttles and clambered across the dust to Farside's waiting locks. Within the Academy base, Hazen addressed them on my behalf. He asked those who'd scored best in riflery, athletics, and hand-to-hand combat to volunteer for a dangerous mission.

I'd been most explicit in my orders in this regard. Once more, I would use cadets beyond their years. But this time, I'd tell truth. Our heroes would die undeceived.

They'd volunteered, to a man. But only a few were chosen for Earthport Station; an Academy shuttle lifted them aloft once more, where they'd waited for *Melbourne* to Defuse from Titan. Then they'd swung across to her waiting lock on a cable, to save the time of the two vessels mating. We had to Fuse again, and quickly, before the starship emerged from the far side of the moon to reveal our presence to Admiral Hoi or Lunapolis.

We Fused back to Titan and confirmed to Arlene, Captain of *Galactic* in my absence, that we'd taken on our small expeditionary force. Were Titan's scientific station more spacious, I'd have off-loaded *Melbourne*'s passengers, willing or no, so as not to put them at risk. I'd had no choice but to involve them in my schemes.

Melbourne had Fused once again, to Earthport, with the sad news of Anton Bourse's demise.

We'd concluded that while *Melbourne* might off-load to Earthport a few of my middies and cadets disguised as Bourse's staff, if more than a handful disembarked, Admiral Hoi's suspicions would be raised, and we'd risk Captain Fenner's passengers to no avail.

Fenner had taken personal charge of his comm room, to make sure no unauthorized messages were sent. In actuality, none of *Melbourne*'s passengers were allowed onto Earthport, save our small fighting force.

Anton Bourse roamed *Melbourne*'s corridors, his discomfiture soothed by the thought of untold millions in free publicity awaiting him. Meanwhile the starship cruised to Fusion safety. Shortly, it would Fuse to Titan once again, and continue its cruise.

I'd used Arlene as well. I could entrust *Galactic* to no one else; at all costs the vast, magnificent starship must not fall again into the rebels' hands. Derek was trustworthy, but until days past he'd never been more than a middy. Arlene, on the other hand, had served with distinction as a lieutenant. But who was I to thrust such grim responsibility on her? When I apologized, she kissed me on the nose.

At Earthport it was now fourteen hundred hours. We would strike at nineteen hundred, to coordinate with Farside's remaining cadets, who had their own mission.

Here on Earthport, our goals were Naval Headquarters, where the Station's laser defense control was located, and the civilian administrator's complex.

Eleven emergency corridor hatches were between our quarters and laser defense control. Sergeant Gregori assured me each cadet knew his target. I called up a Station map on my holovid, insisted that each youngster show me his assigned hatch.

"You have the bars?"

"Yes, sir." Midshipman Speke, his cheeks flushed. He pointed to a stack in the closet. "We're to take them as we leave."

"If someone tries to stop you?"

"No warning. We shoot." His eyes were solemn. "Sir, you can count on me. I swear it." He'd come a long way, this lad who'd rolled his eyes with impatience, and so infuriated Alexi.

I smiled. "Who's in charge of my transport?"

"Until we seize a cart, I am." Gregori.

"Try not to throw me out."

He eyed the chair with distaste. "You won't wait here?"

"Of course not. Getting me there is half our goal."

I sweated out each minute, checking my laser pistol over and again, making sure I had ample recharges in my pouch. I slipped on my helmet, for its radionics. I keyed my stunner on and off.

If necessary, we'd try to take Naval HQ by force, but I had lingering hopes that my presence might persuade some of the rebels to lay down their arms. Hoi had admitted to the same fears, and I couldn't see a reason for him to lie. Unless, of course, he'd meant to lure me to the Station, but he wasn't so devious as then to refuse me entry. Was he?

Seventeen hundred hours. "Any news?"

Gregori looked at me strangely. "No, sir."

I flushed. We'd have no news, unless of a catastrophe.

"UNS Galactic *to Earthport Naval Base."* Arlene, relayed from my suit radio. *"We're returning to Station. Hold your fire."* At this moment she'd be some two hours' cruise from Earthport, minimum Fusion safety.

It was a long while before the reply came. "This is Captain Landon, speaking for Admiral Hoi. Do not, repeat, do not approach the Station."

"Sir, I intend to off-load our passengers."

Eighteen hundred hours.

"Earthport Traffic Control to Galactic. *Take up station at coordinates 320, 31, 108 until further—"*

"I must disembark my passengers." Arlene's tone was cool. *"I will proceed to within one-third kilometer, opposite bays four through six."*

No response.

Eighteen thirty. A handful of Academy sergeants in civilian dress strolled out for a walk. I had Gregori help me into my cumbersome thrustersuit. If we had to retreat from the Station, I'd be less of a burden already suited.

At eighteen fifty, Edwin Speke handed out alloy bars.

Awaiting their send-off, cadets fidgeted, tapping bars against the deck, checking their pistols, shifting from foot to foot. It gave us opportunity to reprimand them sharply, and reduce our own unbearable tension.

Eighteen fifty-five. "Go!"

With the energy of youth the cadets crowded through the hatch, raced off to secure the corridors.

"Lunapolis squad to Seafort." A voice I knew well.

"Hang on, sir." Gregori spun my chair, whipped me through the hatch. He pounded down the corridor. An Academy sergeant took up position at each side.

I keyed my suit caller. "Go ahead, Tolliver." We'd finally decided on ordinary public comm channels, on the grounds that they were the least likely for a military force to use, and therefore the least likely to be watched. In *Melbourne*, I'd had my suit modified to receive them.

"They're cycling through, sir. Lieutenant LeBow has charge of the lock. No casualties as yet."

As yet. My lips tightened.

Jeff Thorne had summoned my old aide Edgar Tolliver from his Lunapolis vacation. Shortly before zero hour, Tolliver had wandered to the Lunapolis airlock from which the crowds emerged to see the light show in the crater.

On his own, he'd overpowered the bored watchmen, who carried not even a stunner. At once, cadets had begun pouring in, fresh from debarkation from the Academy shuttles that had landed just past the crater, not far from where we ourselves had been picked up, on our own flight from Ghenili's clinic to Academy.

Eighteen fifty-eight. In our Earthport corridor, an alarm clanged. Perhaps a midshipman had been spotted blocking a hatch. Perhaps some alert joey in the administrator's office noticed a stampeding herd of cadets on his screen.

We passed a hatch. The cadet guard fell in alongside, his laser drawn. I snarled, "Set the safety!" A stumble and he'd blow us out of the Station.

Nineteen hundred. The corridor hatch ahead slid out of its pocket, slammed toward closure, stopped with a jolt at the bar. Nearby a cadet danced with dread. "Hurry! Hurry, sir!"

"Hold tight, Mr. Seaf—" Gregori flew at and over the blocking bar. For a moment I was airborne. We hit the deck with a thump. My spine exploded, but I gripped the armrests as if my life depended on them. Perhaps it did.

The next hatch, and the next. A corps of cadets panted to keep pace. It must be Gregori who led Devon's morning runs.

"UNS Galactic *to Earthport Naval Base. Approaching on course 320, 31—"*

"You are targeted, *Galactic.* Seafort, begin braking immediately, or we'll—"

"Sir, Captain Seafort is not aboard."

Galactic's role was ambiguous. Her presence, and the power of her lasers, added a factor to the situation that wouldn't be entirely to Earthport's liking. She might have to rescue us, she might simply be held in reserve. In any event, if I'd ordered Arlene to remain at Titan, I wasn't sure she'd have obeyed. I assumed Hoi wouldn't allow Arlene to offload passengers, but her reminders that they were aboard might stay him from firing his lasers, if she engaged in no overtly hostile acts.

Nineteen oh three. Ahead, the hatch to Naval HQ, blocked open. Outside, three guards, spread-eagled on the deck. Sergeant Gregori looked grim.

"Of course, Seafort's aboard. Abandon course before I—"

"Lunapolis to Seafort. Our joeys are halfway to the Naval base. No alarm yet. Don't know why."

"Straight through!" I pounded the chair. "Hurry." I whipped off my helmet.

"Where to?"

"Admiral Hoi's office. Second corridor. Third hatch, or fourth." Just past the corridor to the Naval shuttle bays.

He raced me through the hatch. "No prob—"

A withering blast of fire. Sergeant Gregori coughed, fell away. My chair careened forward on its own. A cadet threw up his arms, spewed thick gobbets of blood from a smoking cavern in his chest.

I screamed, "I'm Seafort! Hoi wants to see me!" I spun the wheels, avoiding a looming bulkhead. "Hold your fire!"

A face darted out from behind a hatch, ducked back. "Kill the son of a—"

Sergeant Smith's tone was low and urgent. "Get Seafort out!"

"No, Sarge!" I spoke loudly, so all could hear. "Admiral Hoi will see me." Carefully I rolled my chair clear of the protective fire of my cadets. "Will he not?"

A laser pistol appeared, aimed at my chest. For a moment it was touch and go. Then a pair of very nervous sailors dashed out, hauled my chair into the seclusion of their inner corridor. I slipped on my helmet. "Seafort to Lunapolis squad: proceed as planned. Seafort to Earthport squad: hold your positions. I'll be in touch. *Galactic*, hold your fire."

Pistols aimed, safeties off, the Lunapolis seamen wheeled me into Hoi's inner office, the one in which we'd once met. A huge simulscreen dominated his far bulkhead. Lights gleamed. Perhaps they were from *Galactic*, fast approaching the Station. There were few other ships in the vicinity, except local transports and vessels in the repair bays.

Admiral Hoi rose from behind his desk, haggard, drawn, eyes like coals. "I'll take that." He checked the laser's safety, pointed it at my forehead. "Anything to say before I execute you?"

"Yes. Out, you two." My tone was peremptory, and to my astonishment, the sailors started to obey. Hoi drew in his breath with a hiss. They hesitated. Grimacing, he motioned to the hatch. They fled.

"Hoi, Simovich here. The bastards are in my warrens."

Hoi ignored the speaker. "Try anything and I'll kill you instantly." He regarded me. "Why did you come?"

"To take your surrender."

"Why would I do that?"

I took in his unshaven face, the sunken eyes, the sneer in his tone. And suddenly I knew. I would tell truth. But given his agitation, it would likely result in my death.

"Because," I said, "you want to."

"Goofjuice."

I leaned forward. "Because you know what you've done is wrong."

"Ah, the great moralist." His pistol didn't waver. "I thought you'd have better cards."

"Because you know mutiny is never the answer."

"So you burst into my office, killing my joeys."

"Because you know revolution is an affront to Lord God."

"You're hardly one to tell me—"

"Because you hate what you've done."

"I've done nothing that—"

"And what it's made you become."

"STOP THAT!" A hint of anguish. He sat on the edge of the desk, aimed the pistol with both hands. "For God's sake, Seafort."

"Yes. For His sake." My gaze was steady, never leaving his.

"Mr. Seafort, we're at the Lunapolis Naval warrens. They've set up defenses. Heavy fighting."

"Who in hell"—his eyes narrowed—"are you to lecture me? You murdered my nephew. You burst his eyeballs! You boiled his blood so it burst through his skin! Did you give decompression warning, Seafort? Did you?"

"No." We all made our beds. Now I lay in mine.

"You vile creature."

"Hoi, are you in control? They'll take my laser cannon in a few minutes. Answer!"

His eyes locked on mine, he groped for his caller. "Hoi here."

"I need you to blow six of my warrens, surrounding the Navy wing."

"Simovich, I've got Seafort."

"Where?"

"In my office. A laser sighted between his eyes."

A sigh of relief. *"Thank Lord God. I'll get out word. His life for their surrender."*

"It won't work." I looked apologetic. "Their orders were quite specific."

"There's a complication, Andre. *Galactic*'s back."

"What's her intent?"

"It's not clear. Seafort will tell me."

"Actually, I won't. I've a laser in my pouch. Push too hard and I'll reach for it."

"I'll kill you."

"Precisely. You'll have no communication with *Galactic*, and no means to surrender."

Hoi frowned into the caller. "Simovich, tell your men we have Seafort. I'll get back to you." Hoi set down the caller. "Now, as to the capitulation of your forces—"

"Your forces. You'll surrender."

"Why?"

"For the sake of your soul."

"Don't trouble yourself about my soul."

I looked unflinching into the black emptiness of his eyes. "If I don't," I said, "who will?"

From his innermost depths, a strangled sob. Then, "Good-bye, Seafort."

I gazed into his eyes.

He fired.

White fire parted my hair. Behind me, over my head, the bulkhead crackled. I sat like a stone.

"Do you *want* to die?"

"Perhaps I must, to end this." I hadn't answered him, but he didn't seem to notice.

"It made perfect sense," he said. "The way they laid it out. You're a traitor, of course."

"Yes." To Lord God, and to His vicar on Earth.

He spoke as if to overcome an objection. "In the ultimate sense, you are. Truly. Our survival depends on colonial imports. To secure them, a strong Navy is vital. And now, when it counts, you withdraw your support. We had to stop you."

"Not by threatening your people."

"Mine?"

"Ours. The laser cannons aimed at Earth are an abomination we never should have allowed. We'll put an end to them." I stirred. "It's time, Admiral. Hand me the pistol, and call your sentries."

His tone was reflective. "It wouldn't be for you."

"No." My voice was soft. "For you."

"Show me Captain Seafort alive and well, or I'll blow the Station apart." Arlene, in a tone that brooked no argument. In the screen, *Galactic* loomed ever larger. Her rear thrusters flickered out. In a moment she would begin to brake, from the bow thrusters.

"May I?"

Wearily, he nodded.

I slipped on my helmet. "Captain Sanders, I'm unhurt. Stand by for orders."

"But—"

"Captain."

"Aye aye, sir." Her smoldering voice promised a reckoning.

"Hoi, why are you letting him transmit? Does he have the Station?"

The Admiral's pistol wavered. Stolidly, I watched the screen.

"Not yet."

"These goddamn lunatics . . ." Simovich's voice broke.

"He sent cadets! He's making my joeys shoot children! I can't hold, unless you blast out their warrens." Abruptly, his voice took on a chilling resolution. *"I'm taking out* Galactic.*"*

Hoi lunged for the caller. "Wait, we'll negotiate a—"

"Mr. Sarnaur, banks five through seven. Full fire!"

"NO!" I tried to lunge from my seat, fell back gasping.

Light travels from the surface of the moon to Earthport Station in three seconds, no more.

It was a lifetime.

"Hoi, stop him!"

The invisible beam caught *Galactic* to starboard, well aft of the disks in which crew and passengers dwelt. The hull glowed and melted. If that were all . . . if the relentless laser beam flickered out . . .

"Simovich, hold your fire!"

From *Galactic's* innards, a flare. Fire spewed, was instantly extinguished by vacuum.

"What did he—" Hoi.

"Oh, God, no." I swallowed. "Propellant. He hit tank storage."

Galactic, like any vessel, was driven by thrusters. In smaller ships, the propellant was warmed in a central tank, then pumped to thrusters as needed. *Galactic,* because she was so much larger, had several such tanks. A major one was in the aft cargo hold.

Powered by tens of thousands of pounds of igniting propellant, *Galactic's* stern began to swing to port.

To compensate, Arlene fired port thrusters. The maneuver swung *Galactic* full on to Earthport. Propellant spewed from her forward thrusters as well; she was trying to stem her hurtling approach to the Station.

Her port thrusters began making headway against the relentless blast of fire from her starboard breach. Her course steadied.

The beam from Simovich's Lunapolis lasers flicked anew.

A small section of the intricately curved alloy of *Galactic*'s Fusion tube melted. The starship was too close to Earth to Fuse safely, but in desperation, Captains had been known to take the gamble. Some got away with it. Now, Arlene wouldn't have the chance.

"Shut down your lasers, Simovich! Cease fire or I'll bomb you myself!" Hoi's voice was wild. "Turn them off!" He stared at his simulscreen. *Galactic* grew larger. And larger.

Hoi stood frozen, like a rabbit in onrushing headlights. The starship grew inexorably. He shook himself, leaped for the caller. "Christ, she'll hit! Lasers, fire at will! Break her up!" Instantly, as if they'd been waiting for his order, tracking beams locked on the approaching behemoth.

I lunged my chair to Hoi's desk, tore the caller from his hand. "BELAY THAT! HOLD FIRE!"

Agonizing seconds passed, under the pitiless play of the laser beams. *Galactic*'s bow portside thruster burst into flame, sputtered out. The vessel could no longer brake.

The tracking beams faded.

Coolly, Arlene shut down her port thrusters, fired starboard thrusters at full power to slew the unstoppable ship away from the Station.

Alarm bells shrieked. *"Decompression alert. All Station personnel abandon Levels 4 through 6!"*

Galactic's bow swung ponderously away from the Station's vast disks. The great starship loomed huge in Admiral Hoi's simulscreen. Paralyzed, I could only watch, desperate for a reprieve from the laws of physics.

"Captain Seafort, Edgar Tolliver reporting. They—I mean, *we* have the Lunapolis laser cannons. Simovich is—"

"Station's corridor hatches to shut in thirty seconds!"

"Come on, Arlene!"

Galactic filled the screen.

"Please please please please." Hoi's voice was a dull monotone. "Please."

Full emergency power to the thrusters, Arlene. Burn them out if there's need. *Turn.* The bow is clear. The blast of fire from the wounded stern will swing her, sooner or—

Galactic struck.

In desperate, terrible slow motion, she scraped along the unyielding mass of the Station, opening jagged rents in her starboard side beginning a hundred meters from her bow. As her inertia dragged her past the Station the gash spread aft, into the ship's Level 1 disk. Into Level 2. I groaned. Level 3.

"Earthport Level 5, sections three through six decompressed! Relief personnel report to emergency stations!"

A great gout of flame spewed from *Galactic*'s forward hold. I clasped shut my helmet, automatically ran my hands down my suit seals.

"What have we done?" Hoi's voice was tormented. "Seafort, what have we done?"

The great starship scraped clear, momentum still rushing her onward. In a slow-motion spin, she drifted slowly past the Station's holocam, into the dark night.

"First Officer Reyins aboard UNS New Orleans. We're heavily damaged and decompressed at Earthport bay six. I'm trapped on the bridge, can anyone help?"

I was on my feet, bearing my own weight and that of the heavy thrustersuit. How I'd gotten there I had no idea. Sweat poured off my frame.

"Now hear this." Hoi's voice was hoarse. "I return Earthport Station and all its facilities to Admiralty and to Secretary-General Seafort's government. Cease all resistance."

Grasping my canes I lurched to the hatch.

"Seafort." The Admiral's eyes were anguished. "You were right. I surrender." His right hand offered a ragged salute. His left raised the pistol to his temple.

Steaming blood splattered my suit, the side of my helmet. I staggered through the hatch.

Walking with canes wasn't so bad, if one ignored the

white-hot lightning, the vicious stab, the blunt fork all slowly sawing me in half.

"Mr. Seafort, are you all—"

"Out of my way!" I swung past the startled Midshipman Speke. If I locked my knees just so, I could swing past the upright position, launch into the new step without pause. And each one took me closer to the shuttle bays.

Twenty meters. Fifteen.

"*UNS* Galactic *to all vessels and Earthport Station, Mayday.*" Arlene's voice was calm. "*Request immediate assistance from all boats to evacuate passengers and crew.*" Galactic had four launches. Each could hold thirty-six. And two gigs. Eight each.

"Sir, let me get the chair—"

"Damn the chair to hell." I'd never use it again. First I'd die. Ten meters.

Beyond the shuttle bay lock, the bay's giant outer hatches were open to the night. I caught a glimpse of Earth, huge and splendid against a black velvet cloth. I stabbed the panel, lurched into the lock.

Midshipman Speke, unsuited, could only watch. "Where are you going?"

"To my ship!" The launch bay hatch slid shut. In moments that lasted eons, the lock cycled.

Safe in their pressure suits, half a dozen service personnel stared from the open bay hatch as the blazing liner sailed past.

Two hours of air in my tanks. Legs stiffened, I leaned against a bulkhead, stowed my canes. We were in vacuum, at near Terran gees. That meant I'd need nearly full power, until I was free of the Station's gravitrons.

I keyed my thrusters, launched myself.

"*Galactic,* we are mining vessel Anaconda III moored at Earthport. We're sending our launch. Stand by."

I'd miscalculated; I was too low. I keyed more lift, but I

was late. As I sailed out the hatch my foot caught a sailor's helmet. I wondered if I shattered it.

The problem wasn't in my overtaking *Galactic*; she'd made a mighty effort to brake her momentum. The problem was matching velocities, as she slowly rotated.

"Galactic *advising we've lost most of our thrusters. Will attempt to stabilize spin—*"

Her Level 2 launch bay was open. Suited figures milled about the bay. Braking, I drifted into the bay, waiting for the kick of the gravitrons to pull me down.

Nothing. Cursing, I reversed my lifters, touched the propulsion. Not too hard; my legs couldn't stand much of a jar.

"*All passengers, don your suits. This is no drill. Chief, can you stabilize the gravitrons?*"

Passengers would be nearly helpless in zero gee. An officer—I couldn't recognize the face behind the fogged helmet—had one arm wrapped around the shuttle's hatch stanchion. With his free hand he swung one flailing passenger after another into the hatch.

I keyed my thrusters, floated toward the airlock that separated the shuttle bay from the Level 2 corridor. As I ducked inside, the lock hatch slid closed. Leaning against the bulkhead to support myself, I waited impatiently for the lock to cycle. Finally the inner hatch opened. A horde of suited figures swarmed in from the corridor. They knocked me to the deck. Men and women clawed for handholds. Someone trod on my arm, pinning me. I prayed my helmet wouldn't crack.

The corridor hatch slid closed; the lock cycled. The frantic mob tumbled out into the launch bay, leaving me dazed, but breathing. My suit was unpunctured. I slapped closed the hatch, pulled my stunner from its pouch. Once again I cycled.

A dozen figures launched themselves at the lock, flailing at anything in sight.

"All passengers should now be suited. We're in imminent danger of decompression. If you need help—"

A stunner would work through a suit, if pressed hard to the torso. Apparently the milling joeys knew that, even in their panic, and managed to avoid me. One frantic woman, however, clawed past me with desperate haste.

"You can't go through—"

"Out of the way!" Her elbow caught my helmet, snapped back my head. For a moment I thought my neck was broken. I jabbed her with the stunner. She went limp. I pushed her from the lock.

She'd been unsuited.

"You there, break open the next suit rack!" Derek Carr, stunner in hand, held back a frenzied throng. A sailor fumbled at the panel.

"I've got it. Stand away." Tad Anselm's hair and uniform were awry, as if he'd been in a fight.

I gripped his arm. "Get suited."

"Aye aye, sir. As soon as—"

"You, before the rest."

"Aye aye, sir." He opened the rack, grabbed a full-size suit.

This section of the corridor was aired. Regs absolutely prohibited use of thrustersuits in an aired environment. I thought of fumbling with my canes. Bloody hell. I glanced behind to make sure no one would be caught in my exhaust, lifted toward the next section, and the ladder.

The corridor hatch was sealed shut. Midshipman Anthony Pyle stood guard. "You can't—oh, it's you, Captain." A clumsy salute, to his helmet. "Vacuum on the other side, sir. I can't open for you, else this section will decompress."

"Get me to the bridge."

"A few minutes ago the west ladder was still open. I don't know." His eyes were troubled. "We're losing sections, sir. The heat melts—"

I was already gone. I fired my thrusters at full power, skimming over the heads of milling passengers and crew.

The west ladder was four sections away. None of the intervening hatches were shut. I sailed through, tilted myself to soar up the stairs.

"Slow down!" Panting, Derek pulled himself from one handhold to the next. His blue uniform was plastered to his wiry frame.

I snarled, "I told you to get suited."

"You told Anselm. Where are you off to?"

"Is Arlene all right?"

"Issuing orders from the bridge, a few moments ago."

I grabbed his wrist, let my thrusters push us along. "Mikhael?"

"On the first lifeboat, with the children. Crying but unhurt. I checked his suit tanks myself."

"Thank you."

"He's one scared joey. I'm going to kill whoever fired on us."

"That ass Simovich, down in Lunapolis."

"Chief Engineer, water's gone on Level 5 and I need it NOW!" Arlene's tone was grim. *"The fire's out of control. I can't put it out by decompressing sections where passengers—"*

Derek said simply, "I'll call challenge." Dueling was legal, though frowned upon. Though, while Admiral Simovich held an active commission, he couldn't be . . . I thrust down the thought. It wasn't time for reprisals.

"Fath!" P.T. launched himself from a handhold. "Mom's on the bridge. She won't leave. *Galactic's* breaking up."

I snagged him, drew him close. "Get yourself suited!"

"The problem is our oxygen stores and hydrazine propellant. The hold's on fire, and so is launch bay one. The internal bulkheads aren't as strong as the hull, so—"

"PUT ON A PRESSURE SUIT!" I shook him like a puppy.

"—they collapse, and the fire spreads. We can't de-air until—"

"Where's a suit rack?" I peered.

Derek said, "Just past the corridor hatch. Back in a moment." He swung along the handholds with an agility that belied his years.

P.T.'s fingers picked at his tunic. "Fath, only vacuum will quench the fire, and vacuum will kill passengers. Mom's got the engine room joeys working with hoses but—"

Derek swam back, a suit over his arm.

Again, I shook him. "Son, put on your suit!"

"When Mom does, but she won't listen. Fath, we're losing the ship. She won't let me on the bridge to—"

Derek raised an eyebrow. I nodded. He touched Philip's ribs with the tip of his stunner. Philip's back arched. His eyes rolled up and he went slack.

Together, Derek and I manhandled him into the suit. I checked and rechecked the seals, made sure the tanks were full. I gestured to the rack. "Now you, old friend."

"That was the last one." He shrugged. "There's more below. Let's get him to a lifeboat."

"How many are launched?"

"Two I know of. Probably three by now." Out of four. Thank Lord God *Galactic* foundered near Earthport, and not in the vast emptiness of interstellar space. Groundsiders sometimes asked why starships carried so few launches to serve as lifeboats. The answer was obvious: the ship itself was our lifeboat. If she failed, what mercy was in off-loading passengers and crew to ill-equipped launches, light-years from rescue?

Between us, we guided Philip's limp form down the ladder, in the direction of the launch bay.

"Purser Doorn, call the bridge! All purser's staff to Level 5, section eight. We've almost two hundred passengers trapped without suits in section nine." Arlene's voice was hoarse. *"Empty the section seven and eight racks and stand*

by. I'm sending the master-at-arms to blow the hatch to nine."

Two suited sailors stopped us. "Fire in section seven, sir, just beyond the bay!"

"The corridor hatch?"

"Holding."

"The lifeboat?"

"Launched, sir, but I hear there's another docking." Earthport would send any boat it had, regardless of hostilities.

Clasping a handhold, Derek grunted as he pulled on the leg of P.T.'s suit. "I'm not sorry."

"What?"

"That I came. I want you to know that."

"I am." It sounded too gruff. "If any harm comes to you, what of the Hope Nation Government?"

He snorted. "They'll manage. My grandson's been praying I'll step aside. He needs a bit of seasoning, but . . . here, I've got him." He steered Philip toward the bay airlock. "When we were boys, you wouldn't let me follow you to *Challenger.* All these years I've wondered what would have become of us. You've given me a chance to retrieve my youth, and . . ."

"Yes?"

"I'm grateful. Haul him through the lock. I'll suit up."

Fewer passengers obstructed our path than when I'd arrived. Letting my thrusters do the work, I wrapped an arm around Philip's limp form, maneuvered toward the launch bay lock.

"Master-at-arms, have you reached Level 5?" Arlene would be beside herself, pacing the bridge, piecing together scattered reports of disaster.

The airlock hatch was closed. I hammered on the panel. The hatch slid open. I hauled P.T. inside. A wide-eyed passenger grappled her way in, hauling another figure behind. A middle-aged man, heaving for breath within his helmet. His face was purple.

The lock cycled. I snapped, "He's hyperventilating. Turn down his mix."

"Radwin, you hear him? Turn it down!"

The outer hatch opened.

The launch bay was empty, its hatch gaping. Scores of suited passengers milled about.

"Oh, God! Oh, Christ!" The woman's voice was shrill.

I growled, "Don't blaspheme." It was automatic.

From the Level 2 corridor we'd left, a hollow boom. The vibration coursed through my boots, jarred my spine.

I said, "There are lifepods—" They, too, were gone from their rack. "You don't need a boat."

"Are you glitched? We can't stay here, the ship is—"

"Launch yourselves. Key your emergency beacon. Let the Station find you."

"Easy for you to say, in a thrustersuit. If they don't . . ." She shuddered. They would drift helpless. It was every sailor's nightmare.

"They'll find you. Every vessel in orbit will be looking."

"I can't!" She dragged her companion to the hatch. "Try another lock. There's got to be a boat—"

"This is my son, and I'm sending him." I keyed Philip's emergency transmitter, pressed my helmet to his, in what would have to pass for an embrace. "Go with God." I looked to the others. "If you stay together . . ."

"No!" She fled into the hatch.

"How?" An older man, whose limbs trembled.

"Use your utility ropes. Grasp each other. Here!" I hauled another figure close. "Tie yourselves together, like this. With all your beacons sounding as one, there's no way they'll miss you!" First a few, then more and more frightened passengers joined our subdued conga line. I keyed my suit mike. *"A ship's officer to bay two, flank!"* If they had someone to lead them . . .

The last of my passengers clutched at me as I tied him to

the others. His eyes were wild. *"Pray for us sinners in the hour of our—"*

I made sure Philip's own rope was secure. "Step out. You'll float, just as you're doing here. It's the same zero gee. Hurry, joeys are behind you."

The lock cycled. A figure stumbled through. "Midshipman Aaron report—Jesus, what are you doing?"

"Two demerits. Mind your tongue. Tie yourself to the last of them. Be quick."

"Aye aye, sir." He brushed soot from his helmet. "There's fire in the corridor."

"Out the hatch! Aaron, transmit every five minutes on emergency channels. Tell them you have—count helmets, and tell them. They'll come for you. Keep your joeys calm."

"Aye aye, sir. What about you?"

"I have a thrustersuit. Kick off hard. Try to pull them clear of the ship." None of their suits were powered. If a gout of flame reached out . . . Lord God forbid.

Please, Sir. Philip is innocent of my sins. Send me to my punishment, if it saves my son. Please. Please.

Please. I pushed Philip's limp form after the others.

My child, my brave boy, drifted unconscious into everlasting night. Would he be cold? Perhaps he'd need a blanket, as I'd given my son Nate, when I pushed his casket out of . . . I swallowed.

"Seafort, this is Cisno Valera. You've been impeached by the Senate. Give me one good reason I shouldn't take the Rotunda."

I keyed my mike. "Hang yourself, Valera. Save us the trouble."

I turned to the corridor airlock. The hatch was open. I bent forward, tapped my thrusters, sailed into the lock. I jabbed the panel. The lock cycled. The inner corridor hatch refused to budge. Cursing, I reached for the spanner in its emergency panel. Making sure the airlock hatch behind me was properly sealed, I manually spun open the hatch.

In the corridor, the overhead panels were scorched and blackened. A fine mist pervaded the air. Sprinklers don't work as intended in zero gee.

"Anyone here?" No bodies, thank heaven. I jetted toward the far hatch, sealed now.

In the suiting room, something moved. I slowed, reversed course.

Amid the empty racks Derek sat on a bench, half-suited, an annoyed look on his face. His lips were stained with blood.

I pulled myself down, hooked a leg around the bench. "What—"

"I think my ribs are stove." His voice was steady enough. "The blast hurled me into the bulkhead. I was bending . . ." He tried to shrug, grimaced in pain.

I finished clasping his suit. "Where's your helmet?"

Derek pointed to a shattered visor. "Some joey borrowed it. Left his."

"The bastard."

"I wasn't in condition to object." His tone was wry.

I looked about; the racks were empty. "There's more suits in the next section. Or a passenger cabin; someone will have left one behind. Come."

"I'll wait."

"No." Gently, I put my arms around him. "I prefer your company." A gout of flame had blackened the corridor before the hatch slammed shut. Lord God knew what lay beyond the section hatch. Vacuum, or perhaps the fires of Hell.

Keying my suit, I lifted him from the bench. Even in zero gee, the stress made him wince.

The first cabin we came to was locked. So was the second. Desperate, I pulled free my laser and blasted the lock. Inside, a swirl of belongings, but no suit.

I tried a third, nearer to section seven. "There's got to be—" I backed into the corridor.

From the corridor hatch, a crackling.

Oh, Lord God.

I dived into the cabin.

Arlene was tense in the speakers. *"Level 2 section seven hatch failing! Passenger alert, section in flames!"*

A gout of fire roiled past the open hatch. A blast of heat. I slapped the cabin hatch panel, knowing it was no use; I'd lasered the lock. Derek clung weakly to my neck.

"Hang on, it's—" Abruptly, the flames receded. "There, you see?"

"That was close." Derek's face was gray with pain.

From the far end of the corridor, a popping sound.

I blanched.

A rush of air.

"NO!"

Perhaps it was the defective launch bay hatch. Perhaps it was the hatch to five.

The cabin erupted in a cyclone.

Derek's arm tightened around my neck.

Our eyes met. In mine, horror. In his, resignation.

Section six decompressed.

Derek's eyes never left mine. His bloody lips formed the words, "Not sorry." I launched myself at the section five hatch.

The hatch was sealed. I slammed the panel. My spine contorted in agony. I slammed it again.

Nothing.

Derek stiffened, kicked. His hand scrabbled at my shoulder. Teeth clenched, I forced myself to watch the unbearable.

The friend in my arms grew still. But not before I saw what eyes were not meant to witness.

I hate You, Lord God.

From the depths of my twisted soul, I hate You.

22

Wearily, I launched myself back to the launch bay air-lock.

It was the launch bay hatch. The blast of fire had over-stressed the damaged seal. Setting down my precious burden I wrenched the useless hatch out of the way.

The bay was empty, deserted. Emergency lights pulsed in the gloom.

Breath rasping in my helmet, I bent forward, launched myself at the gaping outer hatch.

From without, the ship seemed solid and indestructible, until one perused her more closely. A great rent in the cargo hold still spewed fire. Most of Levels 2 through 4 were ablaze, except those sections in vacuum.

I checked my tanks. Half an hour. It would suffice.

The hatch to the Level 1 launch bay was sealed. With a puff of propellant I drifted to the service hatch, jabbed at the lock panel. I cycled through.

Pandemonium.

"Purser Doorn, report! Damn it, has Doorn abandoned ship? Anyone see him?" Arlene drew breath. *"Now hear this. Any sailors left on Level 3 or 4, report to the suiting party on Level 5. The fire's nearing section nine, we've got to get the remaining passengers suited and out—"*

At least a hundred figures clung to the packed launch. Some joeys were suited, some not.

Half were sailors.

I set my suit mike to shipwide frequency. "Passengers only, on the launch!" I drew my stunner and, after an instant's reflection, my laser. "All crew off!"

Not a soul moved. If anything, they struggled more desperately to gain access.

There was no pilot.

"You! Name and rank!"

"Prong yourself, ya frazzin—"

I lunged with my stunner, caught him in the torso. He folded. Someone lunged at my arm; I twisted the barrel, stunned my attacker insensate. "Get those two off! You, name and rank!"

He was barely more than a child. "Armando Flores, sir! Seaman first class." His eyes were wide.

"Off the launch. Give me a hand!"

For a moment he clung to his stanchion. Then, reluctantly, he kicked free.

Someone edged behind me. I whirled, menacing him with the stunner. Her. A woman, unsuited, mouth working in panic.

"Get away, joeygirl!"

She launched a vicious kick, forgetting she was in zero gee. Windmilling, she drifted off the deck, helpless.

"All sailors off!" I brandished my laser. "I'll count to three. One . . . two . . ."

Half a dozen sailors lunged to the hatch. Twice as many clung to seats, to stanchions, to the hull. I'd have to do it.

Gritting my teeth, I fired.

A blast of flame and sparks. A figure jerked from a seat, floated twitching.

Screams. Curses.

Every sailor in the launch kicked toward the hatch. In a moment there were none but passengers aboard.

Ten in suits, thirty without. And I had seventeen unsuited sailors. "You, with suits! Take them off. You'll be safe in the launch."

No one moved.

"I'll count to three. One . . . . two . . ."

"Wait!" A woman tore at her clamps. "You bastard!"

"Be quick!"

In minutes ten sailors outside the launch eagerly donned suits. I motioned to the unsuited passengers. "Crowd into the launch. It's only for a few minutes; the air will last. Now, you sailors without suits."

The launch was packed beyond capacity.

"Anyone rated to pilot?"

A hand shot up, went down again. Armando Flores. Hesitantly, "Lieutenant Garrow is signing me off next week, sir."

It would do. "Get in; you'll drive. Take her out gently, do you hear? Drift free of the ship. The Station will guide you." I slapped shut the hatch.

"*Chief McAndrews to bridge; the fire's almost on us. We're retreating to the emergency engine room airlock. Power may not hold—*"

"What about us?" A suited sailor.

"Tie yourselves together. Launch yourselves toward the Station. Use your emergency beacons."

"*Evacuate Level 5, sections three and four! Midshipman Pyle, report by caller!*" Arlene sounded haggard.

"What if they don't work? What if—"

"If you prefer, stay here and die." I kicked off to the corridor airlock.

The Level 1 corridor was deserted. Emergency lights glowed gray in cold dim silence. No sign of fire.

"*Lieutenant Mains, is there a frazzing lifeboat in bay three or not? These damned sensors—*"

My suit readout flashed yellow; I was low on thrust. Best

save what I had. I hauled out my canes, propelled myself from bulkhead to deck to bulkhead.

As I neared the section hatch, it slid open. Hardly believing my fortune, I drifted through. It slammed shut behind.

I was in section four, wherein lay the bridge.

I propelled myself toward the corridor bend. Ahead, a thud vibrated the bulkheads. Another. Light flickered rhythmically.

"Station, we need every launch you can muster at Level 5 launch bay. Attention rescue vehicles: we've two hundred passengers and no—"

I swam onward.

A hatch slid open. Inside, Arlene hung on to a console, awkward in her cumbersome suit. *"McAndrews, are you there? Don't abandon the power grid!"* She keyed her caller. *"Bay three!"* She stabbed at the console. *"Someone in the comm room, respond to bridge!"*

The hatch slammed shut.

I gaped. The bridge was a fortress; nothing short of a demolition team could force it.

Abruptly the hatch opened.

"Arlene!" Through my suit radio, our words went shipwide; I didn't care.

"Watch the hatch, Nicky, the damn puter's glitched. Must be the heat. Fire in section four below."

"Get out! Abandon ship!"

"Passengers are trapped on five!"

The hatch slammed shut, immediately opened again.

"You can't help them!"

A slim figure kicked along the handholds. Cadet Anselm. "Sir, what should I do next, the—"

The hatch shut.

I asked him, "Any lifepods left?"

"I don't think so."

The hatch slid open. Arlene said quickly, "If McAndrews feeds us power, we have the lift, I have corridor hatches. The goddamn purser jumped ship; I have middies and sailors helping joeys into suits. We rounded up a hundred fifty suits, there's still—"

"Hon, we're out of time!"

"I can save them, Nicky. Five minutes." She slammed the console. "Goddamn readouts!" She keyed her caller. "Burris, round up more suits for Level 5, section eight! Pyle, how many? . . . Sixteen, Burris!"

Alarms flashed. No doubt they screamed as well, but in vacuum we couldn't hear them. Arlene's thick-gloved fingers jabbed the console. The warning lights faded. Seconds later they flashed anew. The hatch slammed closed.

The deck under my feet lurched.

The hatch opened. "Arlene, right now!"

"Damn. All right." She thumbed the caller. "Away all boats! Middies, leave off your search and—"

The lights dimmed. Controlled by the crazed puter, the alloy-reinforced hatch began to drum open and shut with breathtaking speed.

"How the hell do I get out?" If the hatch caught her, it would crush her to pulp.

"Block it! A console chair!"

Or your cane, you idiot.

I lunged across the corridor.

The hatch shut, its frenzied flapping stilled.

I waited in a frenzy, to jam my cane into the opening.

WHOOMP!

The deck buckled. I shot into the air. Into the vacuum.

Anselm hauled me down.

The hatch slammed open.

Arlene's suit smoldered. Deck plates caromed off the bulkhead. A spinning fragment of plate slashed a jagged tear in her suit. The console burst into flame, instantly quenched. Tongues of fire licked greedily through the broken deck.

A last puff of air, from her suit.

The hatch slammed shut, and open.

Arlene whipped off her useless helmet, shot me a look of longing and regret so fierce my heart turned to ash.

The hatch slammed closed.

I lunged toward the bridge.

A hand hauled me back.

"Don't touch me! I'm Captain!"

"No, sir. She is."

A staggering blast. The bulkhead bulged. The hatch burst from its panel. The bridge was a white river of fire.

"Abandon ship, sir! NOW!" Someone tugged at my suit. *"NOW!"*

I broke free. "Arlene!"

"No! You can't!" Somehow, Anselm barred my way.

I yanked free my laser, aimed at his head. *"MOVE!"*

The boy recoiled. I brushed past, dived to the volcano of the bridge.

From behind, arms enveloped me, knocked the laser from my grasp.

Fighting, crying, screaming, I was dragged backward along the shattered corridor.

In my helmet, a cacophony of terror.

"Abandoning *Galactic*'s engine room, send assistance! We're five holding on to a pod—"

"Help me! Help me! Someone help—"

"—Level 5 lock and it won't open! Can anyone hear! I'm trapped in—"

"—on fire and we're burning, Christ we're burning up the heat hurts—"

Level 2. I had no recollection of the journey.

The ladder to three.

"Wait! Let me get Derek!"

No response, just the relentless pull on my suit. Dully, I struggled to break free. My legs wouldn't cooperate.

"Two minutes' air left. Is my beacon working? I can see the Station. The readout's flashing red, why don't you ans—"

"—*Machinist's Mate Vinson in the gig. How do I steer this thing? Where the fuck are we?*"

"*The Lord is my shepherd; I shall not want. He maketh me to lie down in—*"

An airlock. Its hatch wouldn't respond.

A corridor drifted past. My breath rasped in my foggy helmet.

"*Anaconda's launch unloading at the Station. We'll be back as soon as—*"

Galactic's lights flickered.

A corridor hatch, hanging crazily from one socket. The cadet pulled us through. "Almost there, sir."

"*Christ I'm lost. I'm spinning, everything's a blur!*"

"Let me go! I'll break you. I'll cashier you. I'll—"

"*Mama!*"

"Almost there." His voice was soothing.

A gaping hole in the hull. Anselm disappeared.

Free at last, I tried desperately to orient myself. Which way to the bridge?

"*Yea, though I walk through the valley of the shadow of death—*"

Where were my canes?

"*No more air and I—*"

The relentless cadet kicked his way from a passenger cabin, with a blanket. He draped it over the ragged gash in the hull. "Careful, sir. Don't touch where it's sharp."

Derek, old friend. Arlene, my love. I won't leave you. I promise. I swea—

"Now, sir!" He pushed me to the hole. Into the night. I flailed in unexpected terror, but his fingers were firm on my wrist. In a moment he slipped through after.

"*—for thou art with me; thy rod and thy staff—*"

"*Galactic*, Earthport Control. Say again your condition. We are sending every possible—"

"Sir."

We drifted from the stricken ship.

"Sir!"

My voice came from far, far away. "What is it, Anselm?"

"Key your beacon. Have you any propellant?"

"Some."

"I know you're in shock. Can you aim your thrusters?"

"—goodness and mercy shall follow me all the days of my life: and I will dwell in the house—"

"Yes." My voice was weary.

"—of the Lord—" Very softly, *"forever."*

My tank gauge blinked a warning. I sighed with regret. Ten minutes: enough to reach Earthport. Even oblivion was denied me.

I gathered the boy to my chest. He wrapped himself around me, hugging tight, his helmet in the crook of my shoulder. I sighted on the distant Station, keyed my rear thruster.

Silent, lost in our separate miseries, we watched the stricken ship diminish. From time to time a detonation wracked her bowels; a flare of light, that slowly faded.

She was so great an undertaking, so proud a vessel. So many hopes had ridden in her. So many lives.

Abruptly her lights flickered, and vanished.

Together, as one, Anselm and I sailed toward the Station.

A tremendous explosion, aft of the disks. Tongues of fire licked the night. *Galactic's* hull crumpled. Spewing a gout of propellant, the aft third of the great ship broke away. It spiraled toward the blue sea of Earth.

Absently, I stroked the boy's shoulder. "It's all right, lad." One of us wept. I wasn't sure which.

Reluctantly, wearily, I turned my eyes to Earthport Station.

Epilogue

An honor to meet you, sir."

I acknowledged what was meant as a compliment. "So you'll be off to Constantine. What's your specialty?"

"Crop engineering. Now that Earth's doubled its agricultural imports . . ." A quick smile, at her husband. "Fallon is an A.I. psych. He'll be monitoring puters for psychoses." She shifted. "Well, I don't want to take up your time."

"A pleasure to meet you." It was almost true. I grasped my canes, worked my way to my feet.

In Lunapolis, Dr. Ghenili's eyes had been reproachful. "Severe damage. I tried to warn you."

"What's my prognosis?" I'd endured two lengthy operations, to repair the trauma I'd caused. A month, flat on my back in a rigid body cast. A ceiling I'd come to know all too well.

"You're incredibly fortunate. You'll walk, after a fashion."

"With canes?"

"At first. Perhaps, with enough therapy . . ." He left the hope unstated. "But the matter of gravity . . ."

"The gravitron chamber hurt like hell."

"And that was only ten minutes. You'll never stand full

Terran gees again. Oh, perhaps lying on your back, loaded with painkillers, but . . ."

"I understand."

"It's feasible, in an emergency. But once you went groundside, you'd have to remain, in unending misery. Your ganglia can't tolerate another liftoff."

I'd be permanently grounded. "How much gravity can I take?"

"When the inflammation's subsided, I'd guess half a Terran gee. Perhaps a touch more. Let the pain be your guide."

"It hurts even now. Will it ever stop?" Not that I deserved relief.

"The truth? I'm not sure. I think the pain will lessen considerably. If it isn't tolerable, we increase the pain blockers. There's a good chance that in time . . ."

Did the man ever finish a sentence?

"I'm sorry, Mr. Seafort. You brought it on yourself."

"Aye, I did that." By my thrashing about, aboard Galactic. *By my willful disregard of His will.*

"Ari Bin Yuffef."

"You're Israeli?"

"Palestinian." His voice dripped with contempt.

"You're seventeen. Where are your parents?"

"My father's at prayer."

"You've had schooling?"

"Some. It's not mandatory."

"I'm aware. Have a pleasant voyage."

With a disdainful toss of his head, the boy stalked off. Nineteen months to Constantine. Perhaps he'd learn—or be taught—manners.

An Admiralty Board of Inquiry had convened to assign blame for the loss of Galactic, *with eleven hundred passengers and crew. As Anselm had reminded me in extremis, Ar-*

lene, not I, had been acting as Captain when the ship foundered.

Perhaps it was that Admiralty now consisted only of those members who'd flown to Farside in response to my summons. Or perhaps there was blame enough, without besmirching the name of my wife. Arlene had merely followed orders in returning her ship to Earthport. She'd fired no weapons, even when fired upon. Admiral Hoi was held responsible, and particularly Admiral Simovich.

For eleven days Boris Simovich had held out in the depths of his innermost warrens, while U.N.A.F. troops and Navy cadets had waited patiently outside. Only after the food ran out did he emerge, shrunken and fearful, to submit to arrest.

His trial lasted three days. No political arguments were allowed, or heard. It was not at my behest that he was sentenced to hang at Lunapolis, where he'd been captured and tried. Hanging at one-sixth gee is a drawn-out affair. I was told he kicked and struggled for many minutes. A prisoner of Dr. Ghenili's clinic, I did not attend. But General Donner, newly appointed Secretary of the U.N.A.F., did.

I turned to the attentive middy. "Why did you put in for *Olympiad*, Mr. Speke?"

"Same reason as *Galactic*." Perhaps he realized how curt he sounded; abruptly his tone became more congenial. "They're sister ships, sir. It's the same cruise."

"But Captain Stanger chose you personally. Without him . . ."

"It will be different, yes, sir." He blushed. "I know you've thought ill of me. That day we met . . ."

I nodded. His impatience had irritated even Alexi.

"And my speech can be, ah, extravagant." When Jared had tricked him out of his weapon, he'd responded with a torrent of foul language.

"If you were a cadet . . ."

"Yes, sir. Mr. Stanger warned me about my temper. Once"—he blushed furiously—"he had me caned."

"On the other hand," I said, "you performed admirably when we retook *Galactic*. Well, no doubt the first middy will keep an eye on you." Speke wouldn't be senior, this cruise. The middies had been chosen with great care.

From my clinic bed I'd worked overtime signing decrees, to embed our enviro policies before relinquishing martial powers.

Starting in three years, time enough to enter into contracts with the colonies, Earth would forgo virtually all harvest of its seas. It was hoped that a five-year fishing moratorium would allow the myriads of ocean dwellers to reestablish themselves. Virtually the entire resources of the Navy were consigned to ship home substitute protein. Much of it was soy-based, though on Pampas and Rolleo, beef was a prime export.

The sudden increase in demand would be a heavy economic strain; we'd be a far poorer system when we were done. Perhaps power would shift permanently to the colonies. I doubted it. Earth's resources were simply too stupendous, her resilience a matter of legend.

At the same time, we would end once and for all the indiscriminate pouring of waste into the seas. Numerous new sewage facilities were planned. Their construction would be given highest priority, along with air scrubbers for every manufactory on Earth, without exception.

A colossal undertaking? Of course. Expensive? That was hardly the word. The trick was to spread the contracts among so many industries, so many powerful corporations, that every one of them would avidly resist any lessening of our commitment. Branstead had taught me well, and Robbie Boland.

*　　　*　　　*

Jerence Branstead emerged from imprisonment shaken but unharmed. The rebel U.N.A.F. unit that seized him had twice threatened him with summary execution.

Cisno Valera had disappeared entirely. He'd last been seen on the outskirts of the U.N. compound, where he'd been encamped with his troops ever since my broadcast. Some thought that as his U.N.A.F. units melted away he'd gone underground to foment new rebellion, others that he'd been shot by some joey loyal to the government.

It mattered little; he'd become a joke, a figure of derision, for his vacillation. The streets surrounding the U.N. compound had once been held by the Easters and the Fdears, two of the more formidable transpop tribes. Perhaps he'd wandered too far from camp, and met a rough justice. In some quarters I was still known as the trannie SecGen.

Even while the remains of Galactic spun slowly into the wisps of Earth's outer atmosphere, the finishing touches were being put on Olympiad, her much vaunted sister ship. There'd been some hasty restructuring of cargo bays, to further separate—and reinforce—storage of hydrazine and bottled oxy.

A horrid waste of resources, Olympiad, but she was so far along in construction it was far less expensive to complete her than to abandon her. Scandalously opulent, even more so than Galactic, she held thirty-four hundred passengers, a crew of almost nine hundred. A city, more than a ship.

Galactic's seven hundred surviving passengers, and much of her crew, had been transferred to the gleaming new starship.

It was too late to eliminate separate dining halls and the more spacious cabins, but my intervention caused swift upgrading of the lower dining hall, to match the decor of the upper. And cabins were assigned by the number of occupants, not by social ranking. Those who didn't like it could wait a few years for another ship.

By the time I emerged from Ghenili's clinic, trying not to wobble while walking on one cane, Olympiad's loading was well under way.

Not many passengers refused boarding. In part, that was because *Galactic's* tragic loss wasn't deemed a design flaw. All Naval ships had laser shields, but none were designed to stand up to the massive laser cannon of Earthport or Lunapolis, the searing weapons that ravaged the streets of Lower New York in the Transpop Rebellion.

Built to break up asteroids thrown at Earth by the fish long years past, they no longer served legitimate need. I took advantage of my military and moral authority to dismantle them entirely. Marauding fish were less of a danger than was some General or Admiral facing too great a temptation. Earth must never again be held hostage.

There is a mood in public affairs that by some mystery becomes pervasive. In the case of the rebellion, it was to put the matter behind us as quickly and quietly as possible. Reluctantly, I acquiesced. The terrorists, including all of the Eco Action League, were hanged. So were five former members of Admiralty. In most other cases I allowed clemency.

However, I was determined not to lie or evade the truth, especially as to my own responsibility. At the repeated entreaties of my chief of staff, I declined media demands for interviews. Jerence Branstead knew I wouldn't speak so lightly of politicians' misfeasance as public opinion would wish.

Nonetheless, those stories that leaked out tended to glorify my role. They ignored my stupidity in sacrificing the head of Hope Nation's Government, to no purpose. And my callous use of cadets, mere children, to bear the brunt of our fighting. The fact that many of them emerged as heroes was no excuse; there were those who died before their time.

The media knew nothing of how I brutally rejected Danil

Bevin's plea for life, when I might have surrendered to Stanger and perhaps talked him out of his treason. Or how I hesitated that fatal moment that killed Arlene. Had I thought to thrust my cane in the hatch a second earlier . . .

In all this, the Patriarchs were ominously silent.

To my infinite surprise, the Roman Catholic Bishop of Rome visited Lunapolis, and heard my confession according to his ancient Rite. After, he blessed me, and failed to rebuke my overt renunciation of Lord God. Bishop Saythor, he said, was impetuous, and my admonishment that my coin belonged to Caesar bore truth. The Church was no more than man's attempt to understand Lord God, he told me, and I shouldn't lay her failings at His doorstep. He kissed my dampened cheeks before he left.

Nonetheless, the Patriarchs must have found my presence as uncomfortable as I did theirs. Saythor had a number of choices: to renounce me, to ignore me, or to embrace my views. None were palatable; perhaps that was why they urged Admiralty to offer me a remarkable alternative to my Lunapolis retirement.

"You wanted to see me, sir?"

"Come in."

At my insistence, Charlie Witrek wore an officer's blues, though Admiralty had placed him permanently on the disabled list.

He peered myopically across the bridge. "Ah." He faced me, saluted stiffly.

They hadn't done a bad job with his features, though it was disconcerting to see him with brown eyes instead of blue.

"As you were." He relaxed; I regarded him gravely. "I'm so glad you came aloft." I'd written two long letters, finally prevailing on him to join *Olympiad*'s cruise.

"Thank you, sir." His face relaxed into a familiar smile.

"You've settled in your cabin?"

"Yes, sir." A pause. "It's a bit awkward. Not," he added hurriedly, "that I'm complaining."

"What's the problem?"

"It's just . . . I dress like a middy, but don't sleep in the wardroom. I call you 'sir,' as I should, but have no duties because I'm not on the active list and never will be. It's . . . strange. I'm sure I'll get used to it." A bright smile. He ran his fingers through his hair, tugged the knot on his tie.

"Yes, I've been thinking about that." I leaned back. "I doubt this will work out."

A momentary alarm. "Sir?"

"Admiralty, in its wisdom, has declared you disabled. You couldn't possibly return to active duty."

"No, sir."

"Unless you were so ordered."

He frowned. "I don't . . . are you toying with me?"

"Why, yes, I am." I savored the moment. "Charlie, when we set sail, I am the absolute authority aboard ship."

"Of course."

"As soon as we cast off, I'll recall you to active duty. I want you in the wardroom."

"Sir, I can't stand a watch. I don't see well enough to monitor the instru—"

"We have eleven middies; I don't need watchstanders. But some of them are quite young; you'll be a good influence. And I need you elsewhere."

He blinked. "Why?"

"Look at this behemoth." I waved past the bulkhead, to the entirety of the ship. "We've three thousand passengers, Charlie. Three thousand! And more crew than—*Olympiad* is more city than ship, and I have to keep it running smoothly. From day one there'll be complaints, demands, delegations, disputes . . ."

His lips twitched. "Like the Rotunda."

"Only worse, because there's no escape. I'll need help managing." I'd thought it makework, when I'd dreamed up his assignment, but now I wasn't so sure. "You know my style, and how I operate; you're the ideal candidate. Help me." My voice grew soft. "Please."

"I'd give anything to . . . but, sir, are you doing this out of pity?"

"No." I realized it was true. "I need officers I trust absolutely."

A subtle tension seeped out of his frame. "Aye aye, sir. I'll report to the first middy. Who is he?"

"You, Charlie." I'd arranged it most carefully. The other middies already knew, and were under orders to say nothing until I'd told Witrek.

A look of wonder, that dissolved into joy. "You mean it? Really?"

"Yes."

"Lord God bless you." He couldn't contain himself, did a little dance on the bridge decking. "Nothing could thank you enough!"

"Keep an eye on Speke, by the way. He needs steadying."

"Aye aye, sir." He shook his head, still dazed. After a moment he dabbed at his eyes. "Look!" He laughed aloud. "Look what I can do!"

Why did I accept Olympiad?

I don't know.

It was time I ceased to be SecGen. After martial law, the populace needed someone more . . . well, more clement. From a brooding retirement I would dominate the Senate's deliberations, the Assembly's every vote, whether I wanted to or not. If I stayed in home system, I couldn't avoid the media forever, and sooner or later I'd be asked a question that forced me to reveal my opinion of the cowards who populated our government.

And where could I go? Certainly not home.

I had no home. My Washington compound had been bombed out of existence. Cardiff was a fetid nightmare. I fervently hoped Philip would have his wish, to end his days there. Besides, I couldn't go home to Earth again. I'd live in torment, unable to lift off to gentler climes.

Arlene had said it first, though it was the stuff of my dreams. The only contented days of my life had been on the bridge of a starship. Derek understood; that's what had drawn him to his death. Of the same mind, Arlene had resumed her uniform without a moment's hesitation, served happily, and sacrificed herself to save hundreds.

Even now, I dreamed of my lost youth. The physical exuberance, the unmitigated joy of being. The joy of a life unspoiled. But Arlene was dead, forever lost. My life would not, could not, ever hold joy. I felt empty within, scoured clean of passions. It brought a curious freedom.

I couldn't return to my youth, but some small part, I would reclaim.

"Sir, capture latches ready to disengage." Pilot Van Peer. To my astonishment, he'd survived the destruction of Academy's launch by the simple expedient of jettisoning himself the instant Stanger's first laser struck. He'd clung, in his thrustersuit, to *Galactic*'s hull until he judged it safe to set out for the Station. He liked chess, I recalled, as did I. Perhaps, during the long silent watches . . .

"Very well." I keyed the caller. "Departure Control, *Olympiad* ready for breakaway."

"Proceed, *Olympiad*. Vector one five nine from Station. Godspeed."

"Pilot, take her out, and set course for Fusion safety."

My resignation as Secretary-General was transmitted to the Assembly, and would be effective the moment *Olympiad* Fused.

"Sir, Mr. and Mrs. Catharta and their children." Midshipman Rafael Delgado, sixteen, dapper and assured. Brilliant in nav and math, his file said. We'd see.

"Very well." I swiveled.

"A pleasure to meet you, Captain." Hector Catharta held out a callused hand.

I took it. We chatted awhile, about his work as hydronicist and agrobiologist. His wife was a lovely woman, a poet. Their four children were unformed as yet, and squirmy. I was glad when they left the bridge, though I couldn't fault their manners.

"Pa!" Mikhael Tamarov burst through the hatch, Cadet Anselm a step behind. "The lounge has Arcvid!"

"Wonderful." My tone was sour. I ignored his breach of protocol; I'd opened the bridge to passengers this day. As for the cadet, he was off duty, and I would allow him almost anything. Except alcohol.

"It has a dual console!" Mikhael's shirt was damp from exertion. A stylish new tunic, one of several I'd selected for him, in the expensive Earthport shopping concourse. I smiled; we'd have ample time to encourage grooming. He exulted, "Tad plays too!"

"Very well. An hour of Arcvid for every hour of calisthenics."

A squawk. "That's not fair!"

"Such is life." If I didn't impose such a rule, he'd soon become a glaze-eyed, finger-clenched Arcvid addict.

"You can't do that!" His eyes blazed.

I said nothing. After a time he fidgeted. "I take it back, Pa."

Still, I waited.

He wilted. "Sir, please. I apologize. An hour for an hour."

I tousled his hair, gave him a casual hug despite the undisguised curiosity of the lieutenant and Pilot on watch.

Mikhael had mounted an impressive campaign. An alarming number of costly vidcalls to Moira, in Kiev with her daughter. Tearful pleas, to me. Promises of good behavior. At last, he'd secured our mutual consent.

I was, frankly, glad to have him share my huge and luxurious cabin. He was a promise unkept, a debt unpaid, and, to boot, he was becoming a rather likable joey. A touch too casual about bathing, too quick with his temper, but . . . each day, Alexi's likeness was more pronounced. Several evenings, I'd made him sit and memorize a verse of the Old Testament, while I sipped at steaming tea. I wasn't sure why. Did we all become our fathers, in the end?

In any event, Mikhael didn't seem to mind. And his constant questions to Tad Anselm about a cadet's life . . . Well, if it came to that, ship's stores included a set of grays.

And Anselm could use a companion, in the months I'd make him wait before I restored him to middy. Whatever Derek had said to him, in the intimacy of their private talk, his soul seemed refreshed. He went about his duties with renewed determination, yet, despite all, I caught an occasional wistful look, a silent plea for acknowledgment and praise that for once in my life I wasn't loath to give.

Perhaps I had mellowed.

Perhaps age had made me softheaded.

The next passenger entered, escorted as always by a middy. "Hello, sir."

"Edgar?" I shot up from my seat.

"Interesting place." He looked about, made a show of examining the consoles. "They call it a bridge?"

"Tolliver, what in hell—what in the dev—" I gave up. "What are you doing here?"

"You ruined one vacation." His tone was acerbic. "I'm not entitled to another?"

"Vacation? Nineteen months of—"

"I'm retired. My children are grown. What else should I—"

"Nonsense! Goofjuice!"

"All right, I knew you were aboard. I admit I rather enjoyed your brief summons to duty, at Lunapolis. And I thought in a quiet watch we could talk over old times."

"Passengers aren't allowed to visit the bridge."

"Odd, then, that I'm standing on it. And surely even Captain Seafort is occasionally off watch."

I glowered. "Who put you up to this?"

"Up to?" His eyes widened in innocent protest. "You suppose I'm not capable of—"

"Edgar . . ." A warning in my tone.

"I gather I'm supposed to quake. I remind you I'm a civilian. Only Naval officers quiver in their boots."

I rolled my eyes. His goading knew no bounds; it would be a hellish voyage. "Who did this to me? Donner? Jeff Thorne?"

"*For* you. Both of them."

"You gave up a normal life to—"

"Why, Captain, isn't your company tantamount to normal life?"

I glared.

Imperturbable, he met my gaze.

"Only as lieutenant," I finally growled, quelling a contentment I would never admit. "A ship has but one Captain."

"Hmm. You assume I'll jump to reenlist. Now, if you add my seniority as Captain to my years as lieutenant—"

"You'll be senior lieutenant. I know, I can read length of service pins." I'd make it up to Lieutenant Cather, one way or another.

"At least I'd have charge of the barrel. I'll be able to shield the middies from the worst of your tantrums."

"Tolliver!"

"Yes, sir?" He raised his eyebrows. After a moment, "I suppose, if you insist, you'd better swear me in."

A few moments later he left, accompanying Lieutenant Cather to orchestrate a hasty rearrangement of Level 1 cabins. I sat bemused, while we thrust toward Fusion safety.

All was well belowdecks; I'd insisted on Chief McAndrews in the engine room, and no other. Perhaps, somewhere, I'd find a tobaccoing apparatus such as his father had ignited in my distant past, and teach him the odd habit.

The ship's many passengers would, from time to time, have to abide an abrupt reduction of gravity, as I made my inspections. And those who preferred full Terran gees could dine on Level 5. I'd had the forward gravitron set to one-third Terran. At my orders, Chief McAndrews would raise it an imperceptible fraction each day. Nineteen months to Constantine, nineteen months back. Eleven hundred fifty days; I had time for patience. Perhaps, just perhaps, Dr. Ghenili's prognosis might be thwarted.

So. I stirred in my luxurious leather chair.

Does life come full circle? No, not really. But once in a while, if one is truly blessed . . .

My smile faded. I was hardly that. Lord, I meant every word I said about hating You. I still do. You took Arlene and Derek, in a manner most contemptible. Don't tell me You couldn't have prevented it; I know better. I can't forgive that, and never will.

I know, having renounced You and Your Church, I'm not supposed to talk to You. Do I even believe in You? Perhaps not. I promised I'd never speak to You again. I certainly don't expect You to answer. I don't even expect You to listen; I know I'm utterly damned. But as You no doubt know, I'm too old to change my ways. So, I find myself talking to You, now and then, with wary, reluctant respect. It's all right. You don't have to listen. I'll just talk.

"We're approaching Fusion safety, sir." The Pilot.

"Kristen, Fusion coordinates for Constantine, please."

"Aye aye, sir." The puter's response was prompt. She flashed the figures onto the simulscreen.

"Mr. Van Peer? You too, Rafael." Obediently, the Pilot and the duty midshipman ran their duplicate calculations.

"Figures agree, sir, to six decimals."

"Very well. Feed them to the puter."

"Coordinates received and understood, Captain." Kristen's tone was cheerful.

"Thank you." I thumbed the caller. "Engine Room, prepare to Fuse."

"Prepare to Fuse, aye aye."

I gazed with longing at Earth, receding in the screens.

Philip had visited, three days before launch.

He was more somber now, but with a hint of undiminished pain in his eyes. I'd embraced him, kissed him gently on both cheeks. "I'm so sorry," I told him for the tenth time. "I could have saved her."

"No. You forget I attended every session of the Board of Inquiry. I have their report on download."

"If I'd only—"

"Fath, Mom wasn't yours to save. She died doing what she thought right."

"And Jared—"

"Don't. *Please!*" He waved off my unspoken thought. "I'm not over that. I can't—" A deep breath. "Sorry. I get emotional. But don't imagine for a minute I think it was your fault." He took a few breaths for calm. "You got the package?"

"It's in cold storage." A most carefully packed, sealed container from the Fairfield Fertility Clinic, containing what remained of Arlene on this earth. Dr. Janson would soon perform the implant into the young, healthy, extremely well paid woman in a cabin on Level 5, who'd contracted to be host mother.

I'd made a vow, one I'd keep. We would make a child, Arlene and I. I hadn't yet chosen the sex, but I suspected we'd have a girl. She'd carry on for her mother. And in some small foolish way, I might atone. When she matured I might be past seventy, but, so what? I examined my newly unwrinkled face in the mirror. Damned if enzyme treatments didn't actually *work*. And for the first time in years, my knee didn't ache.

Still, hon, I'll miss you so. Now and forever.

"We're ready for Fuse, sir."

"In a moment."

In my cabin, Philip had smiled. "I have another gift. Open it when I've gone groundside." He handed me a small box, rather heavy.

"Thank you, son. You're sure you won't come along?"

"I've work to do." His eyes turned serious. "Andrus Bevin has been distracted, since Danil . . ." He made a face. "And with your new legislation, we're overwhelmed. You have no idea, Fath, what started out as your edict . . . enviro restoration's well and truly caught public imagination. New ideas keep popping up . . . Bernili has a plan for reseeding the ozone, one that will actually work. And the solar shield—even ski-lift stocks are rising! You did it, Fath. You remade the Earth."

"You'll do it. I only ordered it."

His tone was sad. "The man who saved the oceans, the air, the fields . . ." He stood, thrust hands in pockets, and said with anguish, "I'll show you holos, but it won't be the same. Why can't you be allowed to see it?"

"I don't deserve to."

"*Thou shalt see the land before thee; but thou shalt not go thither unto the land which I give the children of Israel.*" His eyes glistened.

"Oh, son, I'm not Moses."

"Aren't you?" He pulled me into a fierce hug. "Good-bye, Fath. Come home safely."

Now, three days later, on the bridge, I unwrapped Philip's present.

"Oh, no." I turned anguished eyes to Midshipman Speke. "Not this."

"What, sir?"

Father's old, worn Bible. The one from which I'd learned my lessons, at our rickety Cardiff table. In the corner, the teapot hissed gently. Father watched with dour approval.

Where on Earth did P.T. find it? I'd given it, with all Father's things, to Annie, when I left her in Cardiff. She'd since died. Philip must have traced Eddie Boss, her husband, and retrieved it from him. I wondered if Eddie had known it would go to me.

I slipped open the Book, glanced at a passage.

Whom shall I fear? The Lord is the strength of my life; of whom shall I be afraid?

Hah. We'll have to talk about that, You and I.

In the meantime, there was my ship. My boy Mikhael, and Tad. My daughter to be. My long exile, in a city in space.

And duty.

"Engine Room, are you ready?"

"Engine Room standing by."

A last, long, wistful look at Earth. I slid my finger down the screen.

"Fuse!"